BLOOD FEVER

Blood Fever

LAURIE BELL

Laurie Bell

First published by Laurie Bell in 2023
Copyright © Laurie Bell 2023
www.solothefirst.wordpress.com

Blood Fever
ISBN: 978-0-6455747-3-9
Cover design by Pat Naoum, Red Tally Studios
Publishing services by Mark Furness, Liquorice Light
Publishing

ABOUT LAURIE BELL

Blood Fever is Laurie Bell's seventh novel

Laurie Bell lives in Victoria, Australia with her partner who she adores. As a sci-fi and fantasy aficionado, she maintains an active blog of science fiction, fantasy, and flash fiction pieces (found at www.solothefirst.wordpress.com). She has had several short stories published in the *Antipodean SF* e-magazine on www.antisf.com and in *Etherea* magazine. And of course she has many new books on the go.

For Gerry

ABOUT *BLOOD FEVER*

Mich Janelle is a disgraced Hunter who wants to find out who set her up for murder.

Zeth Wen made the worst mistake of his life, and now a space cruiser full of children are dead.

Rel Charley was a child of alien occupation and is now a man facing prejudice at every turn.

When the PIs are forced to team up to solve the gruesome murder of a mid-level tech smuggler, no one is happy. But as the clues piece together and the bodies pile up, the three must work together if they are to prevent a shocking conspiracy to kill millions.

As Zeth and Rel face their demons to prevent a bloodbath, Mich must wrestle with a voice that has lived inside her mind since she was locked away, one that whispers ... kill them all ...

An electrifying sci-fi thriller from the author of *White Fire, Boss From Hell,* and *The Stones of Power* series.

Chapter 1

"This stop is D4 Prime. Passengers for D4 Prime, please disembark in an orderly fashion. This line will now run express to the central planets. On behalf of TS Cruisers, I would like to take this opportunity to apologize for any delay in your journey. Thank you for traveling with us today."

Mich Janelle bit back a groan at the timestamp on her comm unit. D4 Prime's travel hub time was currently half ten. She was late—really late. The sweat beneath her armpits and her hot, tacky skin raised her ire. Lack of sleep lowered her tolerance. To everything. It put her in quite the feral mood. Not a great mental state for a job interview.

Fleetingly, she thought about rescheduling. TS Cruisers were notorious for running over their posted arrival times. Her hopefully soon-to-be boss would understand. She needed this job. It was the only interview she'd been able to secure. If she didn't get it ... she shook the dark thought away. She'd get it. She had to.

Grabbing her bag from the overhead bin, she hustled for the exit. D4 Prime wasn't a big world and she'd arrived at an awkward hour. With luck, she'd get through security quickly. Lack of funds meant she'd have to walk, adding further to her delay.

Moving rapidly down the kinked jetbridge, she eyed the rips and worn edges with unease. It allowed dull sunlight into the gloomy interior. D4 Prime had been hit hard in the

initial bombardments and it seemed the local planetary offi-
cials hadn't started drip-feeding the rebuild money into this
sector yet. Hardly surprising. In the aftermath of the war, most
worlds had prioritized government spaces and medical hubs.
Mich stepped over a particularly nasty gash in the bendable
smart plastic and headed into the travel hub beyond, pushing
past the stragglers, her temper simmering.

When her position in the security check line didn't move
for twenty minutes, she was ready to boil over. She felt every
tick of passing time as a pounding beat counting down to her
empty future.

At last, she arrived at the stained counter, held out her
wrist for her identification chip to be scanned and glared at
the green-suited security official. He eyed the projected hologram of her face then tilted his long nose up as he made a
show of carefully examining her actual features. She mashed
her lips together to prevent complaints about his time-wasting
and forced a smile.

"And your purpose for traveling here today?" His wrinkled
face scrunched as his gaze tracked the Red Alert line on her
ID profile.

Mich knew what it said. She gritted her teeth. "Job interview."

"Uh-huh. And your permission to travel?"

"Is right there on my hologram, as you can see."

He sneered. Leaning closer turned his gray skin shiny under
the harsh overhead light. "We don't want troublemakers here."

She bit back the response she wished she could give and
forced out, "Yes sir." Time ticked away in the back of her mind.

"The name and location of your interview?"

She sighed. "Daeh's Private Investigators Agency. The interview is for a detective role with the owner, Steven Daeh. And
I'm very late."

The security officer grinned, exposing sharp teeth. "Good luck with that. You have a temporary visitor pass. You don't get the job, you depart D4 Prime within three days. Understood?"

"Understood."

He gave her another long, searching look that was probably supposed to be intimidating before waving her along. Mich ran past milling passengers and burst out of the hub into the weak natural light of D4 Prime's distant twin suns.

"You need a ride?"

Mich glanced at the local woman sitting inside her hovering taxi. Her gray skin appeared almost silver under the gloom of the vehicle's interior, and her white hair held an oily sheen. Not a flattering light for anyone. Not that the sunlight outside was any better. D4 Prime was a world that never saw darkness and it showed in the depressed facial expressions, gray-tinted skin and heavily shadowed eyes of its native inhabitants.

Unable to afford the fee, Mich shook her head at the driver. Instead, she raised her eyes in search of a street sign. She spotted one, obscured by holographic graffiti. *Hell's spawn.*

She called up her comm unit's holomap and plotted a course, feeling more time ticking away. She turned left and moved off at a fast trot.

*

Mich wriggled in her seat and did everything she could not to tap her feet against the worn carpet. Grinding her teeth together, she straightened her back and glared at Steven Daeh's sallow assistant. He had introduced himself as Sveen and was deliberately moving things around on his desk to avoid looking at her. She assumed he knew. It seemed everyone had heard. Rumors flew faster than interstellar spaceships, and the gossip and innuendo that surrounded her downfall seemed to be whispered wherever she turned.

All she needed was a job. That was the first step to clearing her name. The only step she had.

Her knee bounced in place, betraying her nerves. She stilled it with a grunt, pressing her hand hard into her thigh. He'd sign her. He had to. There was no other result she could accept. She needed the money—yesterday.

Glancing again at the closed door leading to the chief detective's office, she wondered what was taking Daeh so long. Sitting here gave her too much time to think. Sara McCroy, her assigned psychiatrist, had picked up on her restlessness and had made a point of analyzing it during Mich's second assessment. An interrogation couched as analysis. Four long hours of torture, and Mich should know—she'd been tortured by professionals.

Focusing her gaze on Sveen, Mich watched him touch each of the figurines leaning against his terminal screen. Clearly a nervous habit. There were eight. The one at the end was rare, if she wasn't mistaken. Mich searched her mind for the figurine's name.

"Are you in pain?"

Sara McCroy's voice interrupted. Mich's memories flashed involuntarily back to her assessment, sitting in that plain beige office. McCroy's obvious attempts to get inside her head had been laughable, but she'd endured them. She hadn't had a choice.

McCroy, a dark-skinned woman with an ample figure, had stared unblinkingly at her and Mich had felt the harsh judgment down to her core. She'd faked scratching an itch on her back to hide her need to squirm. *Stop staring.*

"No." Her intention had been to keep all of her responses to McCroy's questions short.

"You seem uncomfortable."

"It's been a long day." She'd stretched out in her seat to appear relaxed and stared at the empty drinking glass on

McCroy's desk. Fingerprints were smudged all over the glass, turning it smokey, and crimson lipstick stained the rim. Her breath had caught as she'd eyed the smudge of color. *Not the same; it's not the same.*

"Mich?"

"What?" She'd glanced back to find McCroy's crimson lips pursed. The woman blinked slowly. "I asked if your other assessments went well?"

"Oh sure, yeah. They were fine."

"Were they?"

"Yes."

"If I don't clear you, Hunter Prime Marke will not allow you back."

"He got me out."

"He did. You're his responsibility. That doesn't mean you are not an ongoing risk."

"Then why get me out?"

"You'll have to ask him."

Mich remembered straightening in her chair as the dig had hit home. Her eyes had shifted back to the glass. "Yes. I'm fine. Ready to get my life back."

"Are you?"

I have to be.

Pushing the memories of her exit therapy session on the day she left The Clinic out of her mind, she glanced at the chief detective's closed office door and sighed. Sara McCroy had been doing her job. Perhaps that was why it had been so hard, watching her dangling the bait, hoping Mich would bite. She'd been aware of McCroy's probing, felt her twisting fingers searching Mich's brain, but Mich had kept her out, humming softly. There was no way McCroy was getting inside to see how fractured her mind had become. What made McCroy think she could sit in judgment over Mich, making decisions that would affect every part of her life? Stuck in her little office all day, asking questions she already knew the answers to. McCroy couldn't possibly understand.

A tune drifted into Mich's periphery. She pushed it back. *Not now.*

She caught Sveen staring at her leg and followed his gaze down. It was twitching. *Damn it.* In an explosion of movement Mich jumped to her feet.

"Ma'am, he is not ready for you yet." Sveen's voice sounded harried. *What did he have to be stressed about?*

She stared him down. A light sheen broke out across his gray-toned face. He swiped a finger beneath his long nose and sniffed, breaking eye contact. "Please sit, I ... I'll try again." He tapped his screen harder than required. A flush painted his cheeks. Mich sighed and looked down, examining her hands.

The door to the chief detective's office opened with a sharp tug, revealing a tall blue-suited, gray-skinned figure. Mich couldn't hide her flinch at the sudden movement.

Steven Daeh scrutinized her for a long moment. She couldn't read his expression and that worried her. Inside her mind, she screamed, but she held his gaze. He wouldn't know her mental state unless she exposed it. Eventually, he gestured for her to enter. He didn't step aside, so she was forced to brush against him as she passed through the doorway. Her hand touched his jacket and her recoil was dramatic. She cringed at the reaction. *Another failure.* She was too close to the edge and she was slipping.

Inhaling sharply, she ended up with a mouthful of his cologne—something peppery. At least it wasn't cinnamon. Still, she held her breath until she was clear of his scent. That damned tune was back dancing in the corners of her mind again.

"Mich Janelle?"

She eyed the man seated at the desk. *When had he sat down?* "Sir?"

"You are here about the job?"

She forced herself to breathe deeply, expanding her stomach and counting to eight before exhaling equally slowly. Hopefully her face was not as red as the heat blooming in it suggested. "Yes."

His gaze searched her face for every minute movement, assessing her reactions and drawing his own conclusions. Her skin itched. "You used to work for the central government as a Hunter?"

"Yes."

"Hunters are well trained."

"Yes."

"Why do you want to work here, of all places?"

That feeling of being prey was back. "You know my story."

"I want to hear it from you."

She narrowed her eyes, assessing him in return. Steven Daeh's agency had a good reputation for getting the job done. Daeh himself was reportedly harsh but fair, and also an ex-Hunter. That would either work in her favor or severely against her. "I was a Hunter and now I'm not. I didn't do what they said I did."

"So why not go back?"

"They threw me under."

He studied her. "Tell me about Temok Marke."

Mich clenched her jaw. She couldn't help it. Determined, she forced her fingers to relax and worked her jaw open. "My ex-boss."

"He got you out of The Clinic."

"Yes."

"Why?"

She couldn't answer that.

She didn't know the answer to that.

It was the one answer she desperately wanted. She'd lost everything. Her job, her dream, her home. All of it. And even after she got out, she'd still lost everything.

"I have a copy of your file."

Hell's spawn. She didn't speak, but her stomach sank. *He knows.* She clenched her fists and waited for his rejection.

Daeh sat unmoving, his face emotionless as he recounted her Hunter stats. "You were good. But out there, doubt will kill you quicker than a blade. Do you think you're up to it?"

She didn't respond.

"Your reflexes can be retaught. It's your mental assessment I'm concerned about."

Damn McCroy. Gripping the armrests of her chair, Mich leaned forward and hissed, "How can Sara McCroy make a judgment on that? She's an office rat. She has no idea what it takes to be out there. I did nothing wrong." Mich's pulse was in orbit. She could feel it pounding like a hammer in her neck, fast and growing faster.

Daeh pressed his hands into the surface of his desk—a sign of frustration? Staring into his face, she spied the muscle of his right eye twitching. "How can I be sure?" he said.

The last thread on her frayed nerves snapped. "So I'm damned by my history? I was framed. But my word is clearly not enough. How can I prove I'm no longer 'crazy' when I *never* was? I need a job. I do good work. I'm fast and I don't complain—much—and I'll do whatever spawning job you have on the books that no one wants. You know my training. You've done it yourself—yes, I looked you up too. It's what I do. I can do this."

"Once a Hunter."

"You of all people know Hunters are not unbreakable, un-touchable or omnipotent. They are not always good. Or right." She clawed at the armrests on her chair. The urge to run ex-ploded inside her; she wanted to storm out, shouting, "Take the job and shove it out an airlock." She might be unbalanced —crazy even—but she wasn't useless. She could still work.

His eyebrows drew together. She was getting all sorts of facial tics and couldn't read them. Was she reaching him or not? He had been a top-notch Hunter. One of the best. A stickler for the rules and cool as a k-cit in a crisis. Nothing could break his focus. If she wasn't so angry, she'd be shocked he was showing her anything at all. The mask of Steven Daeh was Hunter canon. A legend, no one broke his mask of indifference. She had no idea what it meant that she had.

"You need a new detective or not?" she asked him.

"I'm inclined to give you a shot." He paused, during which time her heart sank again. "You will be on a Watch and Report case, and you will be required to check in every day. Keep this with you at all times." He held out a tracking disk.

She jumped to her feet and slammed her hands down on his desk. "That's barely better than a desk job." The tracker meant she didn't have any personal freedom. Was that typical of probation here, or was it just her? How could she look into her own case if she was on that tight of a leash?

He steepled his fingers, his face a mask once more. "It's your only option. If you won't accept that, then you're not hired."

She'd take it, of course. It was a start, one she desperately needed. As long as she was out there, she could look into Tripness—*kill them all.*

The jerk of her head nearly exposed her thoughts.

Her real mission was to discover the identity of the man who had destroyed her life. This way, it would take longer. She wouldn't get the same resources as a detective on a fully active case. Maybe, with a few successful cases under her belt, he'd give her more freedom, and better access.

Daeh spoke, seemingly reading her mind. "I'll require a psychological assessment completed every half year."

"No."

"No?"

"I was set up. Someone within the Hunters did this to me. I'm not incapable of doing my job. I am not unstable." She'd keep repeating it until she was blue from lack of oxygen. It was the truth.

"You're paranoid and you doubt yourself. It's not a good combination." And there it was—he didn't believe her either.

A flicker of doubt danced through her mind, like a shadow projected on a wall. Was he right? Could she trust her own fractured thoughts? She'd hoped this man—this ex-Hunter—might help her. Obviously not.

For now, she'd play the game. Drop the accusations, be a good little low-level detective and bide her time. She'd get the proof herself and expose the traitor to get her justice—and her revenge.

Sitting back down, she said sullenly, "No tests."

"Then you will remain on Watch and Report cases. I have an agency to run, Janelle. I won't put my company's reputation at risk. Do you understand me?"

"Fine."

But when she asked for the mission details, he hesitated. Holding onto the tablet he pulled from his desk, he stared at her intently before he handed it over. She skimmed through the report silently. There was an image captured from what was probably a street camera of a man with long cherry-red hair that covered his face and blended into his head, arms and any other part of his body not covered by his clothes. She couldn't make out much of his features other than the thin lips and bulbous nose. A man from the settlement on Shol— the planet's low temperatures had forced that particular hairy mutation, it made sholans instantly recognizable.

"His name is Yetti," Daeh said.

"Aptly named," she said drily.

Daeh's nose twitched. "You know your One Earth history?"

"Only old fairytales."

"Well, it's not relevant to the case. Yetti is a tech smuggler currently living on Ketal Seven."

An outer spiral world well out from the central planetary systems. Mich realized with a silent sigh that she'd have a long flight ahead of her. She'd have to rent a ship or book passage on another TS Cruisers line. Hopefully Daeh would give her an advance on her first pay chip.

"Find Yetti and report back on who he works for. I want the name of his contacts and anyone he meets with on a regular basis."

"And then what?"

"That's it."

Sounded boring. Still, it would get her far away from her old Hunter circles, the only positive she could see from working this case. Watch and Report. *What a nightmare.*

Raising the tablet level with her eyes, she winked on her personal eye port and synched to the agency-issued device. Yetti's file saved to her private storage bank. A flash of light indicated the transfer was complete. She handed the tablet back to Daeh.

"They didn't take your chip?"

"They deactivated it."

He nodded. "You've had it scanned for malicious software?"

Containing her snort, she nodded. "First thing I did when I got it back on."

"Then welcome to the team, Janelle, and good luck."

She forced the request through gritted teeth. "I'll need an advance on my pay."

He pointed to her wrist. "Sveen will organize a company identification hologram for you. It includes an expense account. Keep all your tokens. You'll need to justify every spend."

She sighed. More tracking. *Just great.*

"Be careful out there."

How dangerous could a surveillance mission be? Standing, she nodded, exited the office and headed straight for Sveen's desk.

At least she was back to work. Her stomach flipped at the unfairness of it all. *Don't show any weakness.* Bile rose up in the back of her throat. She swallowed it away and told Sveen that Daeh had ordered she get the identification hologram.

She tapped her foot as she waited. Actually, this was perfect. She'd have plenty of time to research Tripness now, the failed case that had ended in her arrest—*kill them all.*

The case had started on Planet Five, one of the six central planets that made up the political core of the spiral. Ketal Seven's distance from Planet Five would cause an irritating delay, but she'd be able to get basic information from the company's servers. Surveilling Yetti would give her time, and time was all she needed.

Finding the connection between Tripness—*kill them all*—and the Hunters would be her launching point. Even if it took dissecting the lives of every one of Tripness's five hundred employees, she would find the link. And when she found it, she would kill them all.

Chapter 2

The departure terminal seethed with passengers making their way off-world. It forced Zeth to separate from his partner, Rel, in order to search for the target.

Zeth raised a hand to scratch his unkempt beard. Wading through the crowd was a mission in itself. Manic laughter, children squealing and the mixed scents of a dozen different restaurants created a barely contained sense of chaos. A red-headed boy in a green pullover hurtled into Zeth's legs, bringing an unusually violent curse to his lips as the kid's bag smashed into his junk. The little bugger looked up, blue eyes widening and mouth falling open, exposing his crooked teeth, the front incisor missing.

The boy pointed to Zeth's chest. "Are you a cop?"

Eagle-eyed scamp! Zeth tugged his ratty jacket closed over his shoulder holster and the glint of the gun there. "No."

When he and Rel discovered The Spiral Guardians deadline had been pushed up, they'd taken off for the hub, leaving no time to change out of their disguises.

Six months they'd watched the gang, and The Spiral Guardians were finally making their move. Zeth trusted Rel's intel. He trusted Rel. They couldn't fail now.

Raising his head as the kid darted away, Zeth eyed the surging crowd. Travelers with trolleys and hovering baggage carriers blocked every door and walkway. In the cacophony of noise and light, it was next to impossible for Zeth to maintain his

usual focus. There was a constant bombardment of announce-
ments that flooded the air, flashing in the space above their
heads in neon-lit holograms. Calls to inform the weary and the
excited of changed arrival and departure times, and advertise-
ments that ranged from Ketal Seven's stone fruit plantation
fruit hamper specials to Tripness's *'No questions asked, no job
too big or small'* courier services to a sale on pure, crystalized
water.

Zeth tapped his earpiece to call his partner, but the resing
thing popped useless static into his ear. The travel hub's communication systems had to be generating a blocking signal.
Damn old tech—always created issues synching to the new
stuff. It was like hunting through a labyrinth blind, and now
deaf. His lack of control over the situation made Zeth twitchy.

Where the hell was Rel? His partner had a gift for technology. The only thing that could have prevented Rel from hacking the hub's communication signal already would be …

He must have eyes on the target.

With a sliding movement, Zeth weaved his way through a
group of gathered school children. High-pitched voices quickly
surrounded him. Directly in front of Zeth, two black girls with
emerald tresses squealed and clutched at another girl who
jumped up and down, enormous grins splitting their faces
wide open.

By the One! Zeth winced at the volume of the next squeal.
The rapid chatter died away as he tried to wriggle past.

"Ew!"

"Rank."

The girls giggled.

Without turning, Zeth scowled. His gaze shifted sideways,
catching sight of their smirking faces and, beyond them, the
narrowed gaze and furrowed brow of their teacher. As though
she'd heard Zeth's unspoken thoughts, the school marm
clutched her tablet to her crimson coat and stared him down.

Zeth turned away only to find he was completely surrounded. *What a nightmare.*

*

"You cannot let this go on, my dear boy." Her honeyed voice flowed softly into his ear, wrapping around his confused thoughts and twisting them into a focused point of pain.

"I can't?"

"Of course you cannot. Speak to the ketallian; his work is good—exactly what you need."

"Yes. What I need. What you need, right?" He waited, desperate for her answer. She would tell him what to do. She would help him; she had promised.

"Dear boy. It is what she would have wanted. Justice and peace all in one. It will be perfect."

"Yes." He sighed deeply. She was right. He stroked the brooch's surface, etched with her pretty face. She looked so beautiful and full of life.

"You will do it?"

"Yes." His fingers caressed the face again and the voice in his ear sighed happily.

"Good boy."

*

Willing the school marm to take command of her unruly charges, Zeth silently cursed again. He would never find his partner in all of this madness. As he twisted, he caught a whiff of his own eye-watering body odor before another high-pitched scream pierced his ears. Straightening his shoulders, he found himself face-to-face with the furious teacher.

"Get away from the children."

"Madam, I—"

"The TS Cruisers Express to the central planets boarding gate has been altered. Now boarding from gate eight. All passengers, please proceed to gate eight, your transport will be departing in fifteen minutes."

Pushing greasy strands of mud-colored hair out of his eyes, Zeth read the nearby gate number—seventy-six—and cursed as a wave of people sprinted for the new gate. They jostled him from one foot to the other as they shoved past.

A man with a fat, shiny face stepped right into Zeth's path. "Hey, watch it!"

"Sorry, mate." Zeth raised his hands, though he was pretty certain the larger man was at fault.

The man bared yellow teeth and shuffled around Zeth, growling at the three girls who'd commented on Zeth's stench. Zeth eyed the angry man carefully, fingers flexing next to his belt, prepared to act if the big guy did something untoward.

The man growled again, before circling the girls, hitching his backpack higher over his shoulder and lumbering away.

Zeth's surge of adrenalin dissipated. Again he wondered where his wayward partner had gone. He flicked his comm to life and froze as something sharp jabbed into his spine.

"Move!" a deep-throated voice muttered right into his ear. A shove between his shoulder blades forced him forward.

Curse the One.

Zeth didn't so much as twitch. "Relax, mate. I'm—"

"Quiet," the voice hissed. "Move."

Zeth had been made. Somehow the target had targeted him instead. *How?* He felt a steady pressure build against his spine. If he allowed himself to be prodded into the crowd, he'd be unable to act against his attacker without endangering nearby travelers. Digging in his heels, Zeth became a rock. If this guy wanted him to move, he'd have to up his game. The object in Zeth's back pressed harder but didn't penetrate his jacket. Not a knife then. Zeth twisted. The man turned with him, keeping his face hidden. The object didn't move from the center of his back.

Glancing at the civilians around them, Zeth judged he had sufficient clearance and made his move. He stepped hard on his attacker's instep, ramming his elbow into the man's ribs. His attacker grunted. Zeth spun and jammed a fist into the man's neck.

The attacker, a weedy pale figure, coughed hard. His hands flew to his neck, clawing at his throat as if he could somehow pry his smashed larynx apart. He doubled over.

A woman screamed. Someone shouted, "Get back!"

Zeth ignored them. With sharp, economical movements, he grabbed a fistful of hair and wrenched his attacker up. The man gaped like a grounded fish. Zeth launched his fist into the man's gut and he retched, eyes bugging. Long scratch marks marred the pale skin of his arms. He dropped what appeared to be a stylus.

A junkie?

Zeth slid his foot behind the man's leg, grabbed a fistful of shirt and tripped him to the ground. Zeth followed him down, falling to a knee. The attacker stopped moving as Zeth's weight pinned him down.

With one hand Zeth rifled through the man's pockets. He removed three wallets, eight charge cards and four identity chips. Zeth's heart dropped. This guy was not a member of The Spiral Guardians—he was just some random mugger.

"Raise your hands!"

Zeth glanced up and into the barrel of a hub cop's gun. Moving slowly, Zeth held his wrist out. A hologram of his private investigator identification sprang to life, casting a blue tint over his hand. The hub cop's weapon didn't move. Zeth released the mugger's shirt and spread his hands wide, keeping his right wrist exposed, but not rising out of his crouch. He willed the cop to see past his hobo appearance. "Officer, I'm a private investigator on a time-critical case. I need you to let me go." The cop's scanner flashed and beeped affirmative, confirming the hologram was legit.

"So you can attack more innocent travelers? You steal that hologram, son?"

Zeth peered down at his own frayed, threadbare shirt, oil-stained trousers and filthy skin. He understood the skepticism; he just didn't have time to deal with it.

He gestured to the mugger's bounty. "Not innocent. Besides, he attacked first."

The hub cop's tightly drawn brows relaxed.

Zeth rose to his feet. "You can handle this?"

The cop's lip curled. "I think I can."

Turning in a circle, Zeth eyed the crowd that had gathered to watch the drama unfold. Arms were outstretched in his direction, holding up recording devices or comm units. The travelers who had been waiting at gate seventy-six were gone.

"Oh hell." The hub cop's alarmed mutter snapped Zeth's head back, hunting for the next drama.

A heavy-browed man with close-set eyes and an unkempt beard that rivaled Zeth's sprinted toward them. The officer raised his gun before Zeth pressed down on the barrel. "My partner," Zeth said as Rel skidded to a halt.

"Got it! Got a shot of the target," Rel shouted.

Zeth held out his hand, ignoring the twitching cop. Hard as it was to see under the mass of hair, Zeth was sure Rel's eyes narrowed when the cop's gun rose again. Zeth shook his head minutely.

Rel's gaze fell to the unmoving mugger on the floor. Zeth shook his head again. Rel shrugged and held out a wrinkled piece of shiny plastic. One look at the 3D flash image caused Zeth to swear brutally.

"What?"

"I just saw him. He's heading to gate eight." With Rel at his heels, Zeth moved like a bot-racer. Lungs bursting and thighs screaming, he ran as fast as he could along the concourse.

Thoughts of the three girls and the boy in the green sweater spurred him on.

I had him! He was right in front of me.

Rel came up alongside Zeth as he turned down the docking corridor. Gate eight was at the end, but sealed doors barred their way. The waiting area was devoid of people and eerily silent.

Panting, Zeth paced the length of the window, searching in every direction for the departed cruiser. Rel grabbed his shoulder and pointed up. Zeth followed his partner's hand until he spotted the fat-bellied cruiser clawing its way to escape velocity.

"Damn the One!"

Rel turned, his face grim. "Maybe he didn't board?"

Zeth spun again, hunting for a hub assistant this time. "We have to call them. Get them to turn the cruiser back."

Rel pressed his comm unit to his ear.

A blinding flash of yellow and white light flared above them, lighting the night sky.

Beneath his bushy beard, Rel's face lost all color. "Res it!"

Zeth's heart lurched. Running to the window he stared up, his hand slapping at the reinforced glass. "No, no, no!"

"Zeth ..."

He couldn't look away. The flash of light had faded into a spray of small black objects hurtling toward the ground below. An ear-splitting *whoop-whoop* tore through the empty boarding area.

Zeth's voice was soft. "I had him. He was right in front of me." He'd had the terrorist in his sights. How could he not have seen the evil in those crazed eyes? *Those children ...*

"Dresh! I didn't get his image fast enough. I'm sorry, Zeth."

"He was right there ... I didn't see ..." Zeth's chest hollowed out. His stomach jerked and he swallowed back bile.

Rel's eyes closed and he swore again. Zeth crossed his right hand over his body, uttering a soft prayer to the One, begging Her to look out for the children unjustly sent Her way. He also asked for his own forgiveness. She would be the only one who could grant it.

Chapter 3

Mich squished her body, twisting in a futile search for a more comfortable position. Surveillance was one of the most uncomfortable jobs in existence, made worse by the fact that she'd chosen to do it. She now had a fully formed hatred of tiny hovercars, rivaling her intense dislike of the rain, squalls, sleet, torrential downpours and showers that dominated the local weather forecasts. Ketal Seven's gray sky filled her days and her nightmares. It was a pleasant change from their usual content. She tugged her jacket tighter around her chest and slumped lower in her seat. Even with her jacket layered over a hooded sweatshirt and jeans, she was freezing.

For weeks now, she'd followed Yetti on his daily jaunts to cafes, the Ketallian Third University and his favorite bar— not at all ironically called The Dive. She'd watched him escort numerous women out of the bar to his rundown motel room, and out again the following morning. She'd caught short naps when she could, recording while she slept so she didn't miss anything, and had hacked and cloned Yetti's comms in an effort to gather intel.

Not that there was anything to miss.

She noted down his meetings with clients, anyone he did business with and any random strangers he came into contact with. There was nothing notable, and Mich was bored.

Surveillance was often boring, it was true, but by now, she was thoroughly bored of being bored. She'd already tried to hack Tripness's company site—*kill them all*— and the screen had frozen before the staff page could even appear. The altranet signal here was appalling.

Was this really what she'd escaped The Clinic to do with her life? Temok Marke's face flashed into her mind, his thin lips pressed tightly together after informing her she was out of the Hunters. Eyes cold, angry at her or at himself that she'd failed her reassessments. Even now, her hands trembled thinking about that moment.

She stretched her arms forward. The sore muscles in her shoulder and neck twinged with discomfort. In her lap was her updated surveillance report. She figured if she had to be bored, she might as well be bored and get her paperwork done.

Mich scrolled back through the tablet's file. Her eyes caught on her initial description of Ketal Seven. *Trell is the 228th island of the 3163 located in the southern hemisphere. Ketal Seven is a planet of islands linked by great bridges that cross the planet's surface like a child's game of pick-up sticks. It rains thirty-eight out of every thirty-nine days, and everyone who lives here is miserable.* A fact she could attest to. *Skein City is the capital of Trell and Yetti's home away from home.*

And her description of Yetti. *Yetti Tilscki. Typical middle-aged male sholan.* It must be bitterly cold on Shol to have caused such a mutation in the human settlers. *Red hair with gray at the temples covers his face, neck and hands.* She assumed the excessive hair covered the rest of him just as thoroughly. Fortunately, his neutral-toned clothing saved her eyes from *that* unwanted sight.

She flicked over to the descriptions of the people she'd observed him meet with regularly. Also the working women he'd met with only once. She'd not seen him spend time with a woman on the regular. The working women seemed happy enough to go with Yetti, though she didn't understand it herself. The few times she'd got within spitting distance of him, his stale odor and the wafting stench of his well-worn clothing had quickly forced her away. Not a bad technique to avoid anyone hanging around who might pay attention to his business.

Mich stared up at the third level of the budget motel Yetti was staying in. The Skein City Gem was the worst kind of dump. Yetti had an internal room hidden away deep inside the blocky square building with no outside windows. The only reason you didn't have outside windows was because you were paranoid someone was out to get you—or someone actually was out to get you. Mich was the only one watching Yetti, so paranoid it was.

There was no way to see into Yetti's room, but she could see the entrance and the outside stairs. She'd know if he left.

The presence of the two women Yetti had brought home with him tonight implied he wouldn't be going out again. Emitting a sigh, Mich pressed back into the insufficiently padded seat cushion and twisted her body to the right, stretching her left leg out to full extension before doing the same on the left side with her right foot. She scrolled back through her compiled client notes:

#1. Sal "Tiny" Mekaim. Suspected member of The Rebel Killers (TRK). A local and rather violent tech gang. Extensive criminal record. Attached.*

Description: Mid to late thirties. Ketallian native. Five foot nine inches. Pink-hued eyes. Slim build. Tattoo of ketallian bird of prey across back of the neck. Battenhold death mask tattoo on left upper arm. Shaved head.

[Note: Explosives expert. Beta personality. Potentially attempting a coup? Further investigation required.]

Date of meeting: Ketallian Mid Day.

Time of meeting: Ketallian 6:17 rotation.

Location of meeting: Island Mac Four. Cafe Sevens.

Items requested: Unknown.

Items delivered: Island Mac Four. Storage warehouse unit H45. Unidentified tech. Two crates of water (sighted and labeled).

Follow-up meeting: Next K-End Day.

*See appendix eight.

#2. Sinn Faber. Suspected leader of Trell faction of The Spiral Guardians.

Description: Late fifties. Ketallian native. Six foot eight inches. Deep-set pink eyes. Right eye squint. Large belly. Limp—suspected bad right ankle. Shoulder-length graying hair tied back in a low ponytail.

Date of meeting: K-Second Day.

Time of meeting: K-14:05 rotation.

Location of meeting: Island Trell. Behind bar The Dive.

Items requested: "Seven of special six", "three of special fifteen" and one barrel of salt water.

[Note: Need to break this code.]

Items delivered: Tech? Six crates (unknown). One crate (sighted). [Note: Appears to be random parts for Freer Five spaceship. Is this translation of special six?] One barrel of water (sighted and labeled). Three crates (contents unknown). [Note: Special fifteen?] One crate of plumbing tubes (sighted and labeled).

Follow-up meeting: Next week. Date to be confirmed.

#3. Woman One

Description: Early thirties. Ketallian native. Five foot two inches. Curvaceous. Brown hair streaked with purple.

Date of meeting: K- Fourth Day.

Time of meeting: K-18:00 rotation.

Location of meeting: Island Trell. Picked up from the bar The Dive. Traveled directly to Yetti's motel, The Skein City Gem, room 308. Female ketallian departed alone the following morning at K-6:20 rotation.

Items requested: None.
Items received: None.
Follow-up meeting: None.

#4. Woman Two.
Description: Late thirties. Ketallian native. Six foot one inch.
Pink-hued eyes. Busty. Blond shoulder-length straight hair. Nice
smile.
Date of meeting: K-Fifth Day.
Time of meeting: K-18:00 rotation.
Location of meeting: Island Trell. Picked up from the bar The
Dive. Traveled directly to Yetti's motel The Skein City Gem, room
308. Female ketallian departed alone the following morning at
K-6:35 rotation.
Items requested: None.
Items received: None.
Follow-up meeting: None.

#5. Kata Bel. Suspected tech dealer.
Description: Early twenties. Ketallian native. Five foot seven
inches. Thick build. Pink-hued eyes. Tattoo of the One on left
side of the face.
Date of meeting: K-End Day.
Time of meeting: K-10th rotation.
Location of meeting: Island Siple. Third warehouse under
Bridge T-168, pylon four.
Items requested: Unknown.
Items received: One barrel of water (sighted and labeled). One
small* crate [Note: Handled with extreme care by both Yetti and
Kata]. Two large* crates.
Follow-up meeting: None.
*See Appendix fourteen for crate size.

#6. Peal Fivam. Barman at The Dive.

Description: Mid-twenties. Ketallian native. Five foot nine inches. Slender build. No visible body art. Short cropped black hair.

Date of meeting: K-End Day.

Time of meeting: K-15:08 rotation.

Location of meeting: Island Trell. Bar: The Dive.

Items requested: Booze. Top shelf.*

Items received: Water (sighted and labeled). Unidentified liquid in bottles stacked eight by six in six crates. [Note: Booze, presumably.]

Follow-up meeting: Next K-Mid Day.

*See breakdown Appendix sixteen.

She added a new entry for this evening:

#7. Woman Three and Four.

Description: W3: Early twenties. Ketallian native. Six foot. Straight long blond hair (length to mid back). W4: Early twenties. Ketallian native. Five foot seven inches. Short cropped brunette hair, shaved to skull on left side, one tress tinted pink.

Date of meeting: K-First Day.

Time of meeting: K-18:00 rotation.

Location of meeting: Island Trell. Picked up from the bar The Dive. Traveled directly to Yetti's motel, The Skein City Gem, room 308. Female ketallians departed together the following morning at K-6:56 rotation.

Items requested: None.

Items received: None.

Follow-up meeting: None.

Mich sighed again, breathing fog onto the plasti-glass of the windscreen. Her comm link buzzed as it received the same message Yetti just received.

[Incoming message]: Need delivery. Urgent. Pay triple. Planet Battenhold. Two days. Will confirm location shortly. Confirm. Di.

[Outgoing message]: Confirmed.

No information on what was to be delivered, but to get to Battenhold in two days, Yetti would need to depart tomorrow evening at the latest. Which meant Mich had another budget trip in her immediate future. Just what she needed.

She leaned forward and rolled her shoulders one at a time. This mission would be endless if Yetti didn't give her something flash-crete soon. She'd started investigating Yetti's clients to keep her boredom from sending her mind back to the endless nothingness of The Clinic. She hummed softly as she flicked back through her notes to find her entry on "Di". She added the new delivery instruction:

Charlmehn Di

Description: Mid-to-late sixties. Presumed ketallian native. [Note: Only seen at a distance. Need to get closer for specifics. Possibly heavy-set though that could be the clothing choice. Possibly light or gray hair. Possible eyeglasses. Not Yetti's usual client type. Looks more like a university lecturer. What is his deal? Worth investigating further.]

Date of meeting: K-First Day.

Time of meeting: K-11:31 rotation.

Location of meeting: Island Trell. Ketallian Third University Bar: The Snapdragon.

Items requested: Unknown.

Items received: Unknown.

Follow-up meeting: Unknown.

Mich deleted the word *Unknown* beside the follow-up meeting line and entered *K-Third Day (Planet Battenhold. Exact Battenhold location to be confirmed)*. She'd have to book passage on the same ship out as Yetti to keep him in her sights. Hopefully, he'd call the travel hub in the morning and give her a heads up on the departure time. She had a jump bag already packed and had pre-paid her room. She could drop everything and follow. Again. Not one of the off-world trips Yetti had taken so far had gained her any new insight into the identity of his boss.

The cloned comm activated again, a call this time. Mich flicked on the speaker and hit record.

"I'm busy," Yetti snarled.

"Five of the special four. Twelve days."

"I'm busy." Yetti's voice was clipped. Annoyed, but not angry. Mich made out female laughter in the background of the call. Yetti groaned.

"Take the order, man."

"Fine. Five of four in twelve. Got it. Don't call again tonight. I'm off-world tomorrow afternoon. Should be back in six days."

"Got it. Thanks, man."

The call ended. Mich leaned her head back against the car seat. A six-day trip. Terrific.

Rubbing at the tension knotting her neck muscles, she huffed out another long sigh. Watching Yetti was such a waste of her time. She was getting nowhere and her lack of progress was devouring what was left of her sense of calm.

A tap on her side window startled her upright. She hadn't sensed anyone approaching. Mich brushed a hand over her hidden pistol and wound down her window at the smiling woman.

"Excuse me, love. Would you sign my petition?"

Mich bit back a snarl. "For what?"

Salmon-colored eyes blinked at the venom in Mich's voice. Damp white curls sat flat against the woman's head. "The infrastructure rebuild bureau's being shut down. My daughter lost her job. It's a disgrace."

Mich didn't need this. "Madam, the war end—"

"It's all crumbling, falling apart—"

"I'm not from here," Mich snapped, gesturing for her to move along. The ketallian glared but left Mich alone, walking off down the street. No doubt searching for more strangers to harass. Mich wound up the window.

While the petitioner was annoying, she wasn't wrong. Ketal Seven was the perfect example of the galaxy's inability to blend new, post-war tech with the more prevalent pre-war technology. Aging vehicle fleets and a lack of properly trained maintenance staff were evidenced in the almost daily accidents Mich had seen since arriving in Skein City. She'd also observed crumbling roads, heard whistling wind widen cracks in building façades and witnessed multiple vehicle pileups when air traffic lights failed in short succession.

The further she ventured from the gleaming travel hub, the less advanced technology became, and the faster old machinery appeared to deteriorate. It wasn't only the vehicles that had become dangerous over time; old technology was everywhere, from the infrastructure to the schools and the medical centers. All of Skein City relied on pre-war technology—and it was all falling apart.

Ketal Seven was by no means alone with this problem. D4 Prime and Janing were just as bad—most mid to outer spiral planets had suffered from severe tech shortages since the end of the war.

Mich glanced up toward Yetti's room and scrunched low in her seat again, crossing her arms over her chest. She ignored the rumble in her stomach and settled in for a long night.

Chapter 4

Rel crouched beside the water-stained crate that stank like the takeout sharmish noodles he'd eaten last week. He pinched his nose closed and tried not to breathe. Keeping his fidgeting silent was a losing battle. Zeth better hurry his ass back before the smell seeped into his coat. Rel liked this coat.

Taking a shallow breath, he peered around the edge of the crate. Light from Billings' three moons lit the ground enough to see the shopfront was deliberately cast in shadow, wide awnings and super long plastic shutters. It gave all the appearance that nobody was home. He held his gun steady, though his fingers were freezing. Huffing out a breath sent a curl of fog into his face and the split second of warmth made his nose drip. With his free hand still clenching his nostrils closed, he sniffed quietly.

At a shuffle of clothing and the scrape of a boot against flash-crete he snapped his head over his shoulder, his finger pressed to his gun's trigger guard. A flash of teeth and a whispered "hey" confirmed it was his partner.

"Hey," Rel replied, his voice equally soft. Zeth's dark hair, beard and black coat blended into the night and once he hunkered down and stopped moving, he seemed to disappear. Rel should be used to it. Zeth's stillness was legendary. Because of the semi-darkness surrounding them, he couldn't quite see his partner's red-rimmed eyes, but he knew they were focused wholly on him. That one uttered "hey" was thick and claggy and contained all his partner's still unshed emotion.

"By the One, is that—"

"Sharmish? Smells like it."

"I am never ordering that again. I'm over this weather too." Zeth didn't twitch so Rel had no way of knowing if his partner felt the cold as he did. Rel blew on his fingers, clenching and unclenching his hands to keep the blood flowing. "I've called the locals. We have ten minutes at best before they arrive."

Res the locals. "Ten?"

"Yep." Zeth pulled his gun from the holster under his arm in one slick move, checking it was fully charged. He pulled a second gun from his boot and checked that too. Rel was not surprised at Zeth's need to act. The guilt of getting so close and not stopping the terrorist was eating him alive. Rel felt that same itch, but he worried that Zeth's desperation stemmed from a need to prove himself rather than a need to close the case. Rel's grim smile was lost in the shadows. If Zeth felt he had to atone, then Rel would run beside him into hell, and do everything he could to pull his partner out with him on the other side.

Rel's own weapon was an extension of his body and beneath his coat, his second holster held his other piece. He wouldn't need it. He closed his free hand in a fist around the shoulder strap of the small bag he carried. A little ball of warmth sat low in his belly at the thought of finally getting to test his home-made grenades. Much to Zeth's disgust, he lovingly referred to them as his "puppies".

"We'd better get moving."

Zeth rose and disappeared into the darkness.

Grabbing his bag, Rel withdrew one of the puppies. The casing was icy-cold. It would warm up quick enough. He pressed a button on the side and tucked the globe under the rank crate. Rising to a crouch, he darted around the wooden side to make further deposits as he made his way toward the rear door of the spiritual shop that was a façade for the local faction of The Spiral Guardians they'd been tracking.

In his ear, Zeth's signal popped loudly. Rel tapped his earpiece, sending back confirmation he was ready. His internal countdown was near completion. As he always did before a mission, he sent a quick prayer to Melita, picturing her sweet smile and the crinkle of skin around her eyes. The scent of honey filled his nose. "Love ya, babe." He barely gave breath to the words. His chest gave a familiar jolt at the memory. Tradition served, he focused on the doorway.

Heat blossomed against his back as the roar of synchronized destruction echoed around him. Shrapnel and pieces of wood hurtled through the air. Before they even hit the ground, Rel kicked in the door of the shop and started shooting.

*

The firefight was short. In the aftermath, Zeth surveyed the bodies at his feet and felt no absolution. In his mind, he pictured a little green pullover, heard the shrill giggle and girlish cheers, saw unpainted nails clutching a tablet against a background of red.

In the distance, Rel attempted to placate the local authorities, his voice tight with forced calm in the face of shouted abuse. Zeth lowered his gaze to the body in front of a table covered with wires and tubes. Open mouth and wide eyes— shock frozen on the dead man's face. The hole drilled into his forehead seeped blood. Around Zeth lay the ruins of the terrorist cell, but, if anything, the gaping hole in his chest grew wider.

Raised voices drew his head up. Rel was standing toe-to-toe with a black-armored man, and it seemed Rel's notoriously thin patience had worn out.

"—and you didn't wait."

"We deemed it pertinent to enter immediately," Rel retorted, employing an oft-quoted line. Zeth had given him a list years ago of lines to use on local law and legal professionals.

The armored man's face was red, his tiny eyes narrowing further as he threw his hand around in a wide arch. "Pertinent? Where is your evidence?"

Zeth released a slow breath. "Chief, what's the problem here?" he asked, stepping up to rescue Rel.

"You rogues didn't wait for us and this entire faction is dead."

Scowling, Zeth pointed to the table of implied death. "That's the evidence." He could hear his partner counting under his breath and rested a hand on Rel's arm in support of his battle to hold his temper. The muscles under his fingertips bunched tighter. Zeth stepped forward, drawing the police chief's attention and giving his partner time to calm down. The chief growled and gestured at the table impotently.

Voices and footsteps echoed around the room as black-armored figures searched the shop's storage room and kitchenette. Two women cataloged the tools littering the shop floor while a man in a light green jumpsuit examined the body hanging upside down off the ladder that lay against the back wall. The officer by the door watched Rel and the chief with unabashed interest, eyes shadowed.

"What connects The Spiral Guardians to the hub explosion? Nothing here indicates these assholes masterminded that action." The chief pressed forward, getting up into Zeth's face.

"They are a gang known for explosives. They *have* explosives. They're connected," Zeth insisted, feeling heat rise under his collar. His body tensed. "These are just kids' party decorations, right?" The bucket of metal shards looked ominous all on its own. Paired with the spray bottles and the jug of clear liquid, it was clear these men had been planning something big.

"We can't ask them now, can we?" the chief shouted.

Zeth fought to keep his breathing regular. "We've had them under observation for—"

"Where's your link? Evidence? Proof? I see nothing here to tell me *what* they were planning. What I do see is the premature slaughter of potential suspects by private investigators who have *no authority* here."

Zeth felt Rel yank on his shoulder as he surged forward. All he could see were bright, innocent, happy faces. Zeth grabbed the officer by the throat and growled, "We know."

Rel pulled him back. Zeth stumbled, catching his balance and shot a glare at his partner. Rel's face remained unusually passive.

"We've been gathering evidence on these guys for *years*," the chief spat. "This was not an isolated cell. I want the old man, not this small fry."

"The old man?"

"The boss. The head of The Spiral Guardians. What? You didn't know that from your six-month-long investigation? Cucking transients!" The chief's voice had drawn the attention of the other officers in the room. They watched the exchange with barely disguised interest. One in particular drew Zeth's gaze. Sneering at private investigators was one thing; the poisonous contempt aimed at Rel was another.

Zeth's vision narrowed.

"Come on," Rel urged.

Straightening his back, he shrugged Rel's arm off and eyeballed the racist officer. "And what's your problem?" The man tore his glare from Rel, startling back at Zeth's sudden proximity.

"Back off, buddy."

Zeth stared him down until the man looked away. Zeth spun back and advanced on the chief, his blood boiling. "Where were *you* when that carrier exploded?"

The chief held his stare but remained silent. It was all the acknowledgment Zeth was going to get, and it sucked the air from his lungs. "At least we stopped the next attack." Zeth spun on his heel and strode toward the door.

"What about the attack after that?"

Rel grabbed Zeth's arm again, pulling hard. He said something, but it went unheard in the roar of white noise that filled Zeth's ears. He swung around, fury driving him back to the chief. Rel was in front of him in an instant, pushing him back and turning him toward the door.

Zeth stormed from the shop, the door shuddering closed behind him. Zeth doubled over, fingers digging into his hips as he sucked in the icy air outside. Rel squatted in front of Zeth's feet and stared out over the cityscape spread below them. They were too far from the city center to hear the beeping horns of the slow-moving hovercars, but he could see long lines of headlights snaking through the sky, circling tall shadowy buildings in the distance.

Swiping an arm over his brow, Zeth fought to locate his calm. He had to control his emotions and find his still place. It was the only way to focus. He couldn't recall a time he'd ever felt so angry.

"We did what was needed," Rel told him, staring straight ahead.

An ache, like a stone, sat in his gut. He stabbed at it, hearing children laugh, but the hurt didn't shift. "I need a drink."

Chapter 5

"All passengers for the Trayeska Line, please change cruisers here at Pou. This line has been altered to stop at all planets. I repeat, this is a Battenhold Line cruiser, stopping all planets to Battenhold. On behalf of TS Cruisers, we thank you for traveling with us and hope you have a safe and pleasant journey."

The occupants of the cruiser's third compartment groaned their frustration and shuffled uncomfortably within their seats, searching for bearable positions from which to endure the coming take-off.

So much for a nice quiet space hop. Mich sighed and adjusted her earpiece to re-establish the orchestral music she'd been listening to before the pilot had become so chatty. Focusing on the soaring notes blocked the incessant tune that continued to play in the back of her mind. It brought a temporary peace.

Fiddling with her communication unit, she contemplated logging onto the free altranet signal to continue her social media stalking of Tripness—*kill them all.* Ultimately, she decided against it. The free access was not secure enough for what she wanted to do. She did keep the feeds open, though, mindlessly flicking through them, as if absorbed in what she was staring at.

Mich's compartment teemed with pink-eyed natives from Ketal Seven and the more hirsute travelers from Shol. The other passengers were mostly greenish-toned people from Dressand, plus three blanket-wrapped sleeping men from Utcher. Just looking at them brought a chill to Mich's skin. She tugged her jacket tighter and buried her fingers under her armpits. Though she sat in the aisle seat of the center walkway, she could just make out the travel hub's bright lights and flashing holograms through the small port windows.

Her stomach rumbled. She eyed the pre-prepared plastic containers TS Cruisers provided upon boarding and quickly decided against opening one. Liquid seeped from the packaging onto the service trays, giving each box a slimy appearance, and the stench wafting up had her suppressing the urge to retch. They were lucky to get food at all. TS Cruisers was a budget service for a reason. Passengers around her ate ravenously. Food pieces flew through the air as the sholans talked among themselves with great passion. Sauce dripped into bushy beards and splattered the carriage with every wild gesture. A piece of partially chewed fruit landed on Mich's armrest. She flicked it away, her lip curling.

She'd always believed the origin story *One Planet* was a myth, regardless of the numerous religious nuts who believed otherwise. Studying her fellow travelers out of the corner of her eye, she winced at the raucous laughter and random excessive gestures. It was a struggle to believe she could be distantly related to any of these people, let alone that they all originated from a single planet eons ago.

She glanced over the four occupied seats on either side and over the twelve rows that made up the carriage. Her slight frame was squished uncomfortably between her armrests. She ran her fingers along the raised bump of the private investigator identification chip inserted under the skin of her right wrist, right next to her personal identification chip. It had hurt like hell going in.

Yetti sat two rows in front of her. The urge to confront him was growing stronger with every second she spent in the cold, cramped compartment.

She dropped the volume on her earpiece to focus on Yetti's conversation with the man beside him. Closing her eyes, she feigned sleep and shifted her head so his words became clearer.

"I said to him, your wife was dying. The trial didn't kill her. He refused to listen. What the hell, I took the contract anyway. I've got a soft heart."

Yetti's fondness for telling stories was slowly driving her mad. This current story was in its sixth iteration since boarding alone.

A loud screech announced the cruiser's take-off, and she dropped her comm to her lap, losing her breath as she slammed back into her seat when the gravless system failed for the third time since their departure from Ketal Seven. Groans and grunts filled the compartment as the passengers around her struggled to adjust to the extra pressure.

Her training held her in good stead, and she adjusted quicker than the others, her vision clearing just as the bag above Yetti's head broke free from its securing straps. It tumbled to the center aisle walkway, along with several others, and slid over the stain-covered laminate toward the back of the compartment as the angle of their ascent increased.

Mich thrust her foot out, her body moving sluggishly against the growing pressure, and stopped the bag. Releasing her security belt, she dragged it close to her feet and pulled a thin metal strip from her jacket pocket. Twisting the lock-picking strip inside the bag's lock, she activated the magnetic disrupter. She forced her head to either side and glanced at the passengers around her. Many displayed gritted teeth and squinted eyes. No one was looking in her direction.

The ringing in her ears grew louder as the cruiser reached escape altitude, so she couldn't pinpoint the exact moment the latch clicked open. She rifled through the balled-up clothing, praying they had been laundered recently. A slim cylinder the length of her finger located beneath a stained toilet bag caught her eye. She slipped the cylinder into her sleeve, re-latched the lock and pushed the bag away. Now freed of its position against her leg, the bag slid the remaining distance to the back of the compartment.

"We apologize for any inconvenience caused to passengers from the loss of our gravity-less system. We assure you the loss is momentary and ask all passengers to remain seated for the duration of take-off." An electric squeal ended the announcement.

Within minutes, the cruiser leveled out and the gravless system reengaged with a *thunk*. Mich sagged into her seat as the pressure on her chest lessened. The compartment lights flickered, raising apprehension among the passengers. She looked up, alarmed, but the lights stayed on.

Gods damned old tech and old infrastructure.

"Well. That was very unpleasant," Yetti complained. He climbed to his feet, clutching the nearest seatback to steady himself. "Was that my bag?"

Mich withdrew her earpiece and tapped it violently, turning her face away as Yetti stumbled past. Replacing her perfectly functional earpiece, she watched Yetti retrieve his bag. He checked the locks and swayed back along the aisle, clutching the seatbacks to pull himself forward, his footing unsteady.

Contemplating a stroll to the relievers in the next compartment to spy on him from a different angle, she smiled as Yetti, after throwing his bag back up into the overhead rack, passed his seat and continued on to the end of the carriage. She'd give him a few minutes before following.

Curiosity ate at her to examine the cylinder now residing up her sleeve, but she'd have to wait until she was alone. Raising her arms in a long stretch, she let the cylinder slide to her shoulder and, with a strategic scratch, dropped it into the pocket lining her jacket.

"Cramped, isn't it?" a voice said into her ear.

She looked up to find a bearded face mere inches away. Rancid breath swept across her cheek. She swallowed and drew back from the salt-and-pepper-haired sholan. Regarding him with a wary eye, she said, "Yes, though not as bad as some."

"Not as good as others," he replied, huffing again into her face.

She nodded, an effort on her part, considering. Over his shoulder, she could see the blackness of space and tiny pin-pricks of light through the port windows. She concentrated on the view to settle her stomach.

A *thwack* and a sharp grunt from the front of the compart-ment had Mich and her new friend on their feet, along with many of the passengers around them. A dark blood-colored sholan with a scraggly beard snarled and grabbed at the shirt of a thin man in a black coat, lifting him high up off the ground. The sholan beside Mich growled, the sound reverberating low in his chest. Pocketing her comm unit, she brushed her fingers across her company-issued weapon before returning her grip to the seat in front. She couldn't give herself away, not when Yetti could return at any moment. Her skin crawled with every impact of a fist or a knee. The violence of the sudden attack was shocking. She smelt cinnamon and craned her neck, head swiveling as she hunted for the source before the fighting recaptured her attention.

Once, she wouldn't have been bothered by such a fight— might have even enjoyed it. But after The Clinic, she was dis-concertingly aware of her vulnerability. All she could see was their huge size, large fists and muscles. Her breathing grew short, and her palms dampened.

"They won't kill each other, will they?" The tremble in her voice now was not all false.

The sholan beside her growled again. It took her a moment to understand it wasn't a growl, but a laugh. "Young fools.

Trying to prove who is stronger. Ignore them; the fight will be over soon enough."

But within minutes, it grew, drawing nearby passengers into the fray. She shot a glance at her seat companion. "Are you sure?"

He bared his teeth. "Maybe."

Feeling threatened, even though she was several rows back from the battle, she inched from her seat. Her heart thumped an anxious rhythm. The man in the black coat clipped Rusty-Red over the ear and slammed a meaty arm into his chest. He grabbed hold of Rusty's shirt again and flipped him over his shoulder. The whole carriage shuddered with the impact of Rusty's head against the compartment's wall. Mich eyed the bloody smear his face left behind. Rusty didn't move, and so the battle ended. The gathered spectators swarmed the victor, slapping his back in monstrous congratulations.

Mich waited until the loser groaned and twitched before she dropped into her chair. Her hands were shaking. A cruiser full of sholan. What else should she have expected?

A hairy hand touched her arm. She glanced at it, fighting hard not to flinch.

"Did I not say it would be over soon?" The man grinned, his eyes staring deeply into hers. "I am Befa."

She nodded and pulled her arm away casually.

Befa leaned closer. "You are young to be traveling alone."

This much attention was too much—she had to extricate herself now. Staying in character, she shrugged. "Not that young."

He squinted, examining her face. "Huh, no. Not young. Still, it is a long trip." He tried to touch her again and she nearly climbed out of her seat. Befa leaned back, his shaggy eyebrows meeting in the middle of his forehead from the strength of his scowl.

"Bathroom," she offered to excuse her abrupt move. It occurred to her then that Yetti had been gone too long. "Excuse me," she muttered.

Befa leaned back.

Mich approached the corridor leading to the relievers. Peering around, she was disturbed by the distinct lack of people. Every other time she'd gotten up, she'd run into long lines. A whisper-light shiver crossed the back of her neck and she paused. The corridor was empty. Shaking off her uneasy feeling, she moved to the end of the short passageway, targeting the door with the engaged light. She bashed against it with a fist. "Hey, anyone in there? I need to go."

No response. She pressed her ear to the door and held her breath, listening for signs of life. Nothing. Her stomach curled.

The strip of metal she'd used on Yetti's bag made a reappearance and the reliever door's lock succumbed to swift manipulation.

Fingering the dented, second-hand pistol nestled at her back, she edged the door open. Something squelched as she stepped into the dark cubicle. The light snapped on, revealing the squelch came from her boot landing in a pool of blood. Now free, it ran past her in rivulets through the open doorway. She swallowed at the sight of the body that had, only minutes before, been the living, breathing, irritating Yetti.

Skin crawling, she pressed her weapon back into her waistband and peeled her fingers from the grip—*kill them all*—with great reluctance. No odor emanated from the cubicle other than the usual bathroom smells. She stepped carefully over the blood to get a closer look. With two fingers, she moved Yetti's head gently to the side.

Hell's spawn. She drew back, sickened by what was left of Yetti's face.

After a moment's hesitation, and making sure to avoid looking into the sunken crater that was once his face, she ran her hands over his clothing, searching for a clue as to who killed him. What had Yetti done to meet such a fate? Suddenly afraid Yetti's killer might have seen her, she rose quickly and turned around. Was the killer hiding nearby, watching her, waiting for his chance?

There was only silence. Her heart pounded. Finding a body in a locked, empty room brought back nightmares still too close to the surface. It was happening again. This was another set-up. Her back was suddenly against the wall and she had no idea how she'd gotten across the hall. Her body cried out for escape. When nothing happened, she forced her feet to return to the body and examined the reliever door from the inside. No damage. She checked the outside handle. Faint scratches against the metal latch told her that at some point, the door had been forced open, and not by her. But if it had been yesterday or last week, she couldn't tell.

She considered the possibilities. As far as she was aware, no one had left her compartment after Yetti. However, the fight had distracted her for several minutes. She could have missed someone leaving. And there was one other compartment with easy access to the same reliever block, so anyone there could have made their way here without her knowledge.

There was also the possibility the culprit was not a *who* but a *what*. It wasn't unheard of for parasites to possess a living host and kill them when grown large enough to survive on their own. She searched the floor for residue. There was no sign of a slime trail or any other such indicator. Besides, the amount of blood pooled beneath the body implied most of Yetti had been intact before the injury.

Covering her mouth again, she leaned down to check the sholan's head wound. The edges were scorched, not eaten, and the remaining skin and brain looked almost cooked. So, not a parasite. Not a wound from a laser weapon, either. Feeling a little light-headed from her shallow breathing, she turned her head, distancing her stomach from the view by focusing on the door.

Someone on board the cruiser had killed Yetti. Mich stared back over her shoulder at the empty corridor. The cruiser's lights flickered again and this time, they went out. She drew her weapon and held her breath until they came back on. Heart in her throat, she lowered her free hand from her chest.

"Are you not well?" a male voice asked from the corridor behind her.

Mich spun around, her pistol held steady pointed at her seat companion. He stumbled back, spied the lifeless form behind her and growled. She didn't mistake it for laughter this time. Straightening his shoulders, the sounds—both angry and fearful—grew louder.

Hell's spawn, not again. Mich tucked her weapon out of sight and spoke quickly.

"I found him like this." She held up her wrist and activated the chip bump exposing her hologram to his view. "I'm a private investigator. Name's Mich Janelle. I suggest you stay out of this, sir."

Befa stared at her wrist. He had no way of judging if she was telling the truth.

"I would appreciate you returning to your seat," she told him.

He acknowledged the request with a nod and backed away down the corridor, scrutinizing her carefully over his shoulder with every step.

She sighed, relief weakening her knees as she contemplated the body at her feet. "I guess you won't be leading me to your boss after all."

Mich exited the cubicle and shut the door. She slammed her gun butt into the handle to break it, tugging hard to ensure the door wouldn't open. That should prevent the crime scene from being disturbed until the cruiser reached the next station point. She had to uncover Yetti's murderer before they landed. But how?

A locked-room murder. Mich felt sick to her stomach. The thought of quitting skittered across her consciousness but she already knew two things stopped her. One, she wanted her life back, and that included the respect and confidence she'd once had. Two, she wanted the man who had set her up.

The compartment lights went off. A bloody knife and dead eyes appeared out of the darkness. She gasped. The lights snapped back on, exposing the empty corridor around her. "Hell's spawn!" *Just a memory. It's not real.*

She scrubbed her hands down her trousers, wiping away the remembered blood. This incident would halt her investigation into Tripness—*kill them all.* Her personal mission would have to wait until after Yetti's killer was captured and she was cleared from suspicion.

She returned to a compartment a great deal quieter than the one she had left, though it was not as hostile as she'd expected. The two sholans who had been fighting now sat together. When they caught her eye, they flinched and turned away. She examined the room. Every sholan actively avoided her gaze. Befa's entire body leaned as far away from her as his seat allowed.

Mich removed her bag from the overhead locker and dropped into her seat with a thud. The communication she sent was brief.

Yetti dead en route to Battenhold. Will arrive on Bendal within two standard hours.

—Janelle

Chapter 6

Rel still felt cold. A bone-deep block of ice nestled in his stomach, freezing his blood and sending continuous shivers through his body. Zeth squinted, swaying to music only he could hear and mouthed at his empty beer glass. It appeared he hadn't noticed the lack of liquid inside. Gone was his usual rigid posture and calculating gaze. Every now and then, he broke out singing.

"Despro." Slouching lower in his seat, Rel worried this case might have finally broken his friend. The pain he desperately tried to hide was clear in his partner's eyes. Signaling the barman for a top-up, Rel knew he should stop—he should be the sensible one and look after his friend, given his soused state—but he couldn't bring himself to put down the resing glass.

Rel needed the fire in his throat and the heat it brought to warm his belly. A full-body shudder shook his frame. The curse he'd heard many times spew from his father's mouth felt dirty in his own. Another gulp from his glass did little to wash the filth from his tongue.

Zeth collapsed into the chair opposite, still croaking his bawdy love song.

"Will ya shut ya trap!"

"Sing it with me, Rel." Zeth jerked the beer glass toward the stage where he'd been making a fool of himself. Only one head-bobbing halfwit was clapping. The rest of the bar's patrons didn't move, buried in their own regrets and time-travel wishes.

Beer sloshed dangerously close to the lip of the fresh beer glass Zeth had somehow got his hands on. "Rel, Rel, come on, get up and sing with me."

"Give it a rest." Rel leaned his chin into the hand braced on the sticky table and tore his gaze from his own empty glass to stare at his friend. Zeth was slightly fuzzy. Rel blinked, and then blinked again, but Zeth didn't return to focus. Yeah. He'd possibly had enough. He was still cold though.

Raising a hand, Rel gestured to the barman for another re-fill. "Ya hungry?"

Zeth's beard was damp with beer and spittle from singing. Long greasy hair fell past his shoulders, looking flat and sad, sticking to his forehead and cheeks like a creeper vine. Their case—at last over—had been long and draining. Undercover as two homeless beggars, they'd sat watching that Spiral Guardians terrorist cell for months, observing the comings and goings of members and tracking the shipments of weapons.

Yesterday's break had led to the disaster at the travel hub. Zeth blamed himself, but really it was Rel's fault. He'd taken too resing long to find footage of the driver. They'd known something was planned, but the operative swap at the last minute had surprised them. Johnstone, the bomber, was a new face and by the time Rel got his picture ... it had been too late. The hub's communication systems had also screwed with their earbuds. Rel should have expected it and had a backup in place—it's not like it was the first time old tech had fritzed the newer stuff. Rel had thought they'd have more time.

A beer burp brought bile up his throat. His father's curse filled his head once more as he swallowed. One hundred and sixteen passengers. Rel scrubbed his dry eyes and sniffed.

A loud screech sent his gaze flying to Zeth as his partner slid his chair over the floor. He thumped Rel on the arm. "Hey, hey! We should get pizza!" Zeth's eyes were unnaturally shiny.

Rel shrugged the sweaty arm off. "Yeah, bud. Let's do that." He pushed to his feet, wavering for a moment before he pulled Zeth up beside him. Zeth grabbed Rel's arm for balance and they stood there, frozen, until Rel chanced walking. He stayed upright, which was a miracle, though his head swam like his brain was in zero-g.

Zeth was another story, hitting the floor in an ungainly tangle of limbs.

Rel stared at him for a long moment then threw back his head, belly-shaking laughter exploding from deep within.

Zeth peered up at him and blinked stupidly, which made Rel laugh harder. And it felt great. "Come on, pal," he grunted, pulling Zeth to his feet.

"Hey, you're one of 'em, aren't ya?"

Tension tightened every muscle at the slurred words. Rel let out a deep sigh and turned to face the speaker, a pudgy man with the flushed face of inebriation. He was standing in front of two other men—obviously friends, given the number of empty glasses littering their table. The man who spoke pointed straight at Rel. His drinking buddies snickered, pushing at their friend's shoulder, egging him on.

Zeth staggered as he turned around and raised his finger to point back. Rel slapped it down. "Don't."

"No, no, Rel, that jerk just—"

"Let it go," Rel said, playing the voice of reason. Unusual for him. He slung Zeth's arm over his shoulder and turned his back on the drunk.

"You're draal, aren't ya?" the jerk called. Heads lifted or turned as eyes widened in Rel's direction.

Rel was drunk, yes, but not so incapacitated that the guy was going to get under his skin.

"Hey, freak! I'm talkin' to ya."

Then again, Rel was pretty resing drunk.

He staggered around, pulling Zeth, who cheered softly in his ear. The yeasty stench of stale beer and pickled avian eggs assaulted his nose. Rel slapped a hand against Zeth's face to turn his head away and glared at the Jerk.

"Are ya?" The Jerk demanded again.

The bar grew silent. Rel waited.

"You, mate, are out of line," Zeth announced suddenly, stumbling forward. He slipped from Rel's grasp and fell against a nearby pillar, clutching at it as if it were the mast of a sailing ship. "He's only half-draal. Can't *you* see that?" His hand flung out. "I feel like you need some manners."

Jerk's friends stepped forward, Big Chin in a sky-blue shirt on the right and Tiny Ears in a white shirt with armpit stains on the left. Four men at another table also climbed to their feet. Rel let a smile creep across his face. He broadened his stance and clenched his fists.

About resing time.

The seven men charged. Zeth let out a wild cry and waded into the stampede. Rel let his anger loose and started throwing punches. A blow to his cheek shook him hard. He saw stars but ducked the next fist and sidestepped the man Zeth threw in his direction. He let the dead weight hit the floor at his feet. Rel took a knee to the stomach and gasped, air exploding out of him in full force. He retaliated with a right hook, dropping Tiny Ears, and sucking in a harsh shuddery breath before lashing out with an elbow to the Jerk's nose. It cracked with a satisfying thwack. The Jerk screamed. Rel pummeled him with another round of punches.

A piercing whistle split the fight. Rel froze mid-punch and straightened, panting hard. The brawling group was quickly surrounded by the bar's security, who were either clones or brothers. As one, they flexed their giant muscles. "Dresh!"

Rel crashed to the pavement outside. A groan slid from his mouth. His chest hurt, his wrist ached and his elbow didn't bear thinking about. A throbbing pain suggested his nose was broken. When he touched it, it didn't have that squishy feeling he'd felt so many times before, so probably not broken, but close.

"Rel?"

"Yeah." Rolling his body, Rel flopped onto his back and stared up at the night sky. Thousands of stars twinkled back at him, as though amused by his predicament. The cold night air settled into his limbs and made a home.

What would it be like, he wondered, to not be different. The harassment never went away. There was nothing good inside his skin. Zeth would argue the point if he knew the direction of Rel's thoughts. The warmth in his chest generated from his friend's total acceptance was enough to thaw the ice around his heart. Without Melita to heat his blood, he didn't see much point in fighting the truth. He *was* a freak. Behind him, the dark façade of the bar did nothing to dim the moon's glow. Turning his head, he spied Zeth's elbow. Rel batted at it with his hand and received a pained moan in response. Lifting his head as high as he dared, Rel peered around but couldn't see their attackers anywhere. They must have been thrown out on the other side of the bar.

"Rel?"

"What?"

"I'm cold." Zeth's voice held a whiny quality that grated on Rel's ears.

Frost clouds billowed from Rel's mouth as a huff escaped him, followed by another.

"What's so funny?"

"Thinking of ya tomorrow morning. Always bitching at me for starting bar brawls—ya fault this time, pal."

Zeth let out a chuckle that ended in a moan. "By the One, my leg hurts."

"Knee?"

"Same one. Yeah."

A thump came from somewhere near Rel's head along with the rustle of clothing. Rel cracked his eyes open, wondering when he'd closed them, and stared at his partner. Zeth rolled onto his front and pushed up with his arms, one leg outstretched to avoid pressure on his bad knee. He froze when a high-pitched beeping started from Rel's left thigh pocket. Rel slapped at his leg until the beeping stopped.

"Who's that?"

"I dunno." Rel lay there for another minute, listening to Zeth flop about.

Quit ya whining. Look after ya friend. Who he was wasn't going to change. Making sure Zeth got through this emotional hell was what he *could* do. Uttering a heartfelt groan, Rel sat up. Head spinning, he swiped away the frost forming on his beard and staggered to his feet. His stomach immediately rebelled. He managed a few steps before he doubled over and vomited.

Weaving on unsteady legs, he moved away from the sour stench and helped Zeth stand. Slinging his friend's arm over his shoulder, they limped like a three-legged canine down the dark street and away from the bar.

Their hotel was only a block away, but they were gasping when they stumbled into the lobby. The concierge gave their appearance a horrified stare, so Rel brandished their room keycard to forestall the argument and dragged Zeth to the elevators.

"Hey, hey, what was the call?" Zeth asked, leaning loose-limbed against the side of the elevator car.

"What?"

"Your comm? Who was it?"

Rel shrugged. *Res it. I'm gonna feel like crap tomorrow.*

Zeth straightened before toppling sideways, landing against Rel. His hand flapped at Rel's pocket.

"Gedoff."

"Who was it?"

Rolling his eyes set his head pounding again. Rel pulled the blasted communication unit from his pocket, and swore.

"What?"

"Screen's cracked."

Zeth burst into laughter. Rel ignored him and squinted at the message, distorted by the cracks in the supposedly unbreakable glass. It took an age for his vision to clear. The elevator gave a soft ping and the doors sprang open. Rel didn't move. "Res it to hell!"

"Hey?" Zeth asked, clinging to the open elevator door to stay upright.

"We've been called in."

Chapter 7

Mich hung her head and slumped further down on the bench. The stark corridor was empty in either direction. Not a single plant, picture or shelf with ornaments distracted her bored gaze, and no one walked past to bother her with empty platitudes. Just as well. She wasn't in the mood for inane chit-chat. The rented weighted anklets chafed.

Bendal's lower gravity, the same low gravity that gave the locals their long limbs and loose gaits, had her feeling frumpy and short by comparison. The additional weight required on her belt and ankles slowed her down, which didn't help her current mood. The lower gravity led to a colder surface temperature too, and she tugged her jacket closer around her body. *It's bloody freezing.*

Her search of the cruiser had turned up no further leads on Yetti's killer. Throughout the final leg of the aborted journey, she'd remained on edge, breathlessly waiting for a blaster shot or explosive bullet to strike her down. The constant fear put her back into the terror of her past: harsh voices demanding her acquiescence, fighting the feeling of phantom hands gripping her arms. In order to focus, she spent her time searching the cruiser from end to end, interviewing every passenger and the cruiser's crew, finding peace in the familiarity of procedure. Dead bodies and murder investigations had never bothered her before. Hell's spawn, it was what she was best at—or, it had been.

She stared at her hands. The tremble was still there. The realization sat like a heavy element in her chest. When she'd insisted to Daeh she was ready to work, she'd honestly thought she was. Her reaction to Yetti's death, however, was something she'd never experienced before.

Why am I still doing this? She exhaled every bit of air in her lungs and waited, empty, her eyes closed. What did the life of one minor tech smuggler matter in the grand scheme of things? It didn't. How he died didn't matter either. She inhaled, slow and steady.

The bendalian authorities had been thorough but slow. She'd sat through all of the insinuations and assumptions she could stomach regarding her presence on the cruiser and Yetti's suspiciously timed death, breathlessly anticipating her arrest. So much so that she'd been shocked when the officers finished their interrogation and let her go. As she'd fled the stuffy office, they'd suggested—more like commanded—she stick around while they questioned the remaining passengers.

Mich ignored the suggestion, and now waited outside the office of the medic performing the examination of Yetti's body.

After the two-day cruiser journey, now would have been the ideal time to catch up on her thwarted rest. After all, there was little she could do until the autopsy was complete. A vision of what had been left of Yetti's face appeared again in her mind. Her eyes popped open and she stared at the wall opposite. Sleep was not an option.

She could try the local databases for any companies affiliated with Tripness—*kill them all.* If she took advantage of Yetti's death, she could get herself reassigned to a case on one of the central planets. From there, she would have much better access to the company's servers.

"Mich Janelle? Please come in."

Damn it, she must be tired if a mere medic could sneak up on her. She looked up to find a skeletal figure in a white coat standing before her. White, not blue. She waited for the shivers, for her skin to start crawling, for the overwhelming desire to hide to swamp her, but nothing happened.

Huh. Well, that's a good sign.

She climbed to her feet. The medic stood at least two hands taller than her. His flat bendalian ears were pressed close to his skull, nose slits vibrating as he breathed.

Time to get this case wrapped up. Find out how Yetti died and pinpoint who on the cruiser could have done it.

"I am Healer Bicet. You are here about the body?"

"I need to know what killed him."

"Blood loss," he answered, walking toward the desk.

She followed him slowly, her gaze darting around the room as her skin tightened. Half the room was partitioned off with a plastic sheet and the medic's desk was positioned a few feet in front of it. She eyed the door. Four paces to freedom.

Healer Bicet folded his long-limbed body into his chair and rolled closer to his desk. Clasping his hands together, he placed them down on the completely bare surface. Mich pulled her jacket tight against the chilly air and sat, nearly leaping back off at the touch of the icy seat. *Damn, that's cold.* She hoped the chill was designed to suit the bendalian's preferred comfort level and not because the partitioned room also functioned as his operating theater. She kept her gaze on the healer, though her back itched with the desire to check behind the curtain and ensure no one was hiding back there.

"What caused the blood loss?"

The medic grinned, exposing only yellowed gums. "Mich Janelle, you have brought me a fascinating case. One I very much want further details on, from a strictly scientific point of view, of course. Now, I understand you were once a Hunter?"

How does everyone know that? She cautiously nodded.

"Then you should be familiar with most available weaponry. Even so, I doubt this is something you will have encountered before. The blood loss in the sholan was caused by a reaction to the distilled essence from an Enferrie flower."

"Enferrie flower?"

"A special breed found on few outer spiral planets. The flower has many useful properties and there are currently several studies on the flower's use as a pain reliever under review. I've recently spoken to the Head of Research at Calcryon, in fact, in regard to their drug trials."

"Why?" Mich queried, curious. Bicet's interest was highly suspicious. He just happened to know about this flower?

"My doctoral thesis was written on the Enferrie flower. I am rather an expert."

If he does say so himself. They hadn't asked him to participate in the studies, had they? Perhaps his interest was more a product of being rejected as an expert?

Bicet continued. "Thus I can assure you, at full strength the drug can cause a fatal reaction."

"It's a poison?"

"It can be. How the poison was injected into the sholan, I am still unsure. But once the poison entered his body, it remained dormant for two standard days, and then *bam!*" Mich jumped as the medic's fist hit the table, hard. "The Enferrie chemical reacted with the host's blood and caused a catastrophic and highly explosive end."

Mich pictured Yetti's face and the crater that had reformed it. Disturbed, she stirred in her seat. "Nasty." So it *was* an assassination. Yetti had been targeted two days prior, meaning the killer had not been on the cruiser at all. She rubbed her palms across her thighs and stared at the door as she ran Yetti's movements back in her mind.

On the day in question, the sholan spent almost the entire day locked away in his motel room. He'd emerged twice, once to pick up supplies and then again that evening to find women for entertainment. Both times, the crowds outside had been thick. He could have been poisoned at any time. This was no straight-up murder.

Okay, now she was interested.

Why had Yetti been killed? Had his death been the result of a business disagreement or a personal vendetta? Yetti's contacts might have discovered he was being followed and murdered him before he could be arrested.

Healer Bicet coughed lightly. Mich forced her gaze to his face as his gestures grew more excited. "Mich Janelle, it is no easy matter to get hold of such a poison. It is a forbidden export item."

This information narrowed her search considerably. No tricked bookie or sore employee was behind this kind of an attack. It had to be someone with the means to get hold of such a poison, and the motive to kill with it. She'd have to return to Skein City on Ketal Seven to investigate further—but did she want to? With Yetti's death, her case was now officially closed. All she had to do was finalize her report, hand it back and wait for reassignment. Besides, she needed to focus on what was more important—her own investigation into Tripness—*kill them all.* She'd have to let Yetti's death go.

Still, she had to ask, "What exactly is your interest in this poison, healer? You seem far too enthused for pure scientific curiosity and your paper was published years ago, wasn't it?"

"I confess, I do have a personal interest in your case. As I said, my initial doctoral paper was on the Enferrie flower. To write a follow-up would certainly aid in future aspirations."

"Aspirations? You're looking into it in the interest of your own career?"

"I believe we can assist each other, investigator."

Mich bit back her snort. "Are there obvious symptoms related to this poison?" she asked instead, thinking about what she would write in her final report. "What are the signs someone has been poisoned?"

The bendalian pursed his lips. "The Enferrie flower's poison is quite unique. It affects different species in different ways —different symptoms, you understand—and is therefore extremely difficult to diagnose. You can see why it is a favorite among the more nefarious class. So in the case of a sholan—an explosive chemical reaction. In another species, there would be different symptoms, such as excessive bleeding or organ failure."

"Nasty," she said again.

"Indeed. As I said, it is a rather fascinating flower."

"I can see why it would make an interesting study."

"You will keep in touch, inspector? If anything comes up around this poison, or if I can further assist you, please do not hesitate to call me."

"If any other bodies turn up, you mean?"

He stood, smiled and accompanied her to the door. "Did you want to take the body with you?"

She stared him down. "No. Someone from his family may come forward to claim it after his death is announced." She paused. "If they do ..."

"I will contact you immediately."

Thanking him for his time, she made her way toward the medic center's exit, her mind unable to let go of the image of Yetti's dead face. He had been killed by an extremely rare and more than likely insanely expensive poison. But why?

Reaching into her pocket, she removed the thin cylinder she'd stolen from his bag. Flipping it over in her fingers, she examined its smooth surface for any mark. Nothing. Was this thing somehow connected to Yetti's death?

Once, she would have demanded full investigation rights to the case, determined to get to the bottom of the mystery. Now, she'd hand it all over to Daeh, along with her report, and let someone else solve it.

Slipping the cylinder back into her pocket, she caught the stink of her shirt. Her plans for the morning crystalized quickly. She wanted a bath, then she had to book passage to D4 Prime.

*

"Do you have an appointment?" Sveen's nasal tone grated on Mich's nerves. It had been a long, tedious trip with many stops, bad food and loud children. Mich was not in the mood to be gregarious.

She yanked the annoying tendril of hair that kept falling over her face behind her ear. Aware her surly attitude wouldn't convince Daeh's assistant to help her, she couldn't stop herself from clarifying. "My name is Investigator Mich Janelle and an appointment with the chief is what I'm trying to get."

Sveen sat high in his chair and stared down his nose at her. His shirt was impeccably pressed and it rubbed her all wrong. She glanced at her own wrinkled and probably smelly shirt. She'd come straight from the hub after yet another massive flight delay, not wanting to waste any further time by getting changed. Perhaps she should have.

Sveen's lips quivered. If he smirked at her, she'd jump over his desk and throttle him. She forced a smile onto her face and breathed slowly out through her nose.

"Oh dear. I'm afraid I can't help you. Mr. Daeh is not taking walk-ins this afternoon. You should have called first."

"I did. You wouldn't put me through to him or set up an appointment."

"Well, I am sorry. Mr. Daeh has no time available today. I can slot you in sometime on—"

Mich slammed her hands on his neat pile of color-coded files. "Tell him I'm here and I'm not leaving."

*

"Good morning, sir." The cheerful hello came from an equally cheerful young man walking past his van at a brisk pace. A little black dog yapped around his heels with excited energy.

"Good morning," the older man responded in kind. His hat was pulled low over his brow and he peered furtively over his shoulder through gold-rimmed spectacles, watching until the young man and his animal moved out of sight. When they disappeared, he lifted a box the size of a small suitcase from the back of the van with his weight distorter. The little device was scratched and bent where he had dropped it but it still hummed softly in his hand. The box shifted on its own and floated gently toward his waiting hands. He placed it with care onto his empty trolley.

He scratched at his stubbled jaw and peered into the distance again, checking that no one was in sight before he aimed the distorter at the next box. Gloved fingers closed over the label covering half of the word *Glassware*. Arranging the second box on top of the first, he lined up the edges with meticulous care.

Chapter 8

When the door opened, Mich stormed inside and halted in front of Daeh's desk.

"I expected you earlier," he told her, walking around to resume his seat.

Doing her best to calm down, she stared at the picture frame on the wall behind her boss's head. The holograph print was of a legendary city from the One Planet story. Earth—the supposed place from which all life came. The city this print depicted was called New York. Glass towers rose high into a sky empty of ships and space-capable aircraft. *What a load of rubbish.* Earth was nothing more than a fairytale; nevertheless, it was a pretty picture. It suited the room well, catching the afternoon light that streamed in from the large bay window over her right shoulder.

Daeh gestured toward the empty seat in front of his desk.

"I had a little trouble with your staff," she complained, dragging the single chair to the side of the room in a childish attempt to upend the intimidating power game Daeh was trying to play.

It didn't work. He loomed over her even sitting down. She felt uneasy under his steady gaze. "Whom you have now aptly terrified."

She did her best to appear relaxed. "I try."

"You're tired." His eyes flicked over her face. She couldn't meet his stare for long. Her gaze drifted again to the city print on the wall.

"I am. It was a mostly boring assignment, up until the end." She went through her report describing Yetti's movements—who he spoke to and where he went—and concluded with the discovery of his body in the cruiser's toilet.

"The killer was not on board?"

"All the passengers were investigated and subsequently released. I included the bendalian security team's findings at the end of my report."

"And your search?"

"I found no sign of the killer. It was a messy crime scene. Blood spatter obscured any evidence of what weapon was used to inject the poison. The medic who examined the body—Healer Bicet—believes Yetti was poisoned two days prior to his death on the cruiser."

"So you found nothing?"

Mich pulled the metal cylinder from her pocket.

Daeh took it from her and held it up to examine it in the sunlight.

Leaning forward, she said, "I've not seen anything like it."

"Nor have I." He rolled the cylinder over in his hands and ran his fingers along its length. "Interesting." He placed it on the desk. "I concur with your assessment. There is more going on here that requires further investigation."

She stared at a deep scratch in the surface of the tsktsk wood desk edge. The minor imperfection in the orange hardwood bothered her in a way she didn't understand.

Now Daeh would reassign her. What would it be this time? With any luck, it would be somewhere drier. The best-case scenario would be a mission on one of the central planets.

Daeh said nothing. She glanced up to find him staring at her. He did not blink.

"I've submitted my report for the follow-up investigation. Will I get a break or are you planning to assign me another Watch and Report case immediately?" Part of her hoped he'd say she could take a few days. She wanted to locate a small apartment with a secure altranet server. Tired as she was, her fingers itched to start hacking.

"You don't want to look into Yetti's death?"

She straightened, her voice pitching half an octave higher. "Yetti's murder? You put me on light duties. Are you rescinding that order?"

"No, your status hasn't changed."

"Then it doesn't matter if I want the case."

Daeh didn't twitch. "Do you?"

She took a moment to think about it. Staring at her hands where they rested in her lap, she picked at a hangnail on her little finger. If she took what she thought he was offering, it would be a real chance to turn back the clock. To become what she was before ...

She slammed her mind down on the memory but a fragment crept in.

With cautious steps, she moved inside, eyes darting in every direction to examine the scene. The bedroom was a mess of sheets and blankets. Pillows strewn across the carpet as though scattered in the throes of passion. Two empty drinking glasses resided on the bedside table. The body on the bed stared sightlessly at the ceiling.

The dead man was alone, but there was a second glass on the bedside table. Someone else was here, or had been. She could smell cinnamon in the air—like a cake recently dusted.

She crept in on silent feet, her weapon gripped in both hands as she searched for intruders. The apartment was empty. Releasing a deep breath, she lowered her arms and inched closer to the empty drinking glasses. One was stained with lipstick. She leaned down until her face was close enough to the glass to breathe on it. That was her lipstick color. The natural hue she favored was hard to find, given many beings preferred bright, gaudy colors.

Mich spun, heart thrumming, and took in the scene. Hairs on the pillow beside the body. Her hair. Before she could imagine who was setting her up or why, a sharp sting pierced her neck. She slapped at her skin, pulling away a sharp needle.

The drug worked fast, freezing her body and sending her to her knees. She could see movement in the doorway. A man she didn't recognize was watching her silently—he held a small dart gun in his hand. She collapsed face-first into the carpet.

Her eyes snapped open on Daeh's face. He gave no indication he'd noticed her lapse. He stared at her with those mysterious eyes, but kept his face passive. There had to be a catch. Yes, she wanted her life back. Yes, she wanted a career unhampered by a requirement to work on light duties. Could it be that fate was getting involved? She didn't give much credence to fate and karma, or the idea of an ultimate purpose. Her life was her own—her mistakes too. But taking the case would mean suspending her own investigation. Like hitting reset on her life again. Could she handle that?

Daeh waited patiently.

Taking Yetti's case didn't have to mean completely halting her personal investigation. It wouldn't be easy, but if she managed her time well and set up a base with a strong secure connection, she could continue. It would be slower; that was all. The delay might even work in her favor. The Hunter who'd betrayed her would let their guard down as time passed. And then she would strike.

Daeh straightened, sensing her decision had been made.

"Yes. I want the case."

"Good. I'm assigning you to work with Rel Charley and Zeth Wen."

Anger was a fist in the center of her chest. She jumped off her chair, unable to sit still while her career was thrown around like a digi-ball. Pressing down on his desk with her hands, she demanded through clenched teeth, "Don't you think I can handle it alone?"

He didn't answer.

"You don't trust me."

Without breaking their eye lock, Daeh pressed a finger to his terminal, activating the dormant screen.

"Sir?" Sveen's voice floated up from the device.

"Send in Team Five."

So he'd decided on this course of action before she'd even entered his office. Her chest ached. *Why let me believe I had a choice?* With the threat of babysitters watching her every move, her plans went up in smoke. Tears prickled but she willed them back and stared at her hands. They were pressed so hard into the desk, her fingers were white. *Just quit.* Then she'd have all the time in the world to investigate Tripness—*kill them all*—and her imprisonment. But if she did that, she'd lose all of the resources and access that even her light duty status as a detective allowed her.

The room descended into a long silence until the door sprang open and two exceedingly hairy men sauntered in. Through thick beards and long, unkempt hair, they appeared relatively human. The texture of the hair was wrong for them to be from Shol. One might have been part draal, though it was hard to tell. With all of the whiskers, the two men could have passed for twins.

"New case?" asked the one on the left. He was the taller of the two, and wore a navy-blue shirt with black trousers. A trail of detritus from muddy boots followed him in through the doorway. He held his body tightly, as if a spring was coiled in the center of his spine, forcing his body upright. Mich caught his gaze. He stared at her for a moment and then looked away. No challenge there.

The man on the right put her on edge immediately. Dressed all in black, he stared at her blatantly, maintaining eye contact when she glared back. "Howdy, chief," he said, stopping in the center of the room.

Neither man had a detectable accent. If the shorter man *was* part draal, he hid it well. Boots blocked any sight of a foot claw and under all the hair, Mich couldn't tell if his neck was ridged. She let it go. It didn't matter what he was; all that mattered was that she had to work with him. She cringed from the blast of body odor that slammed into her as they moved closer.

"Gentlemen, sit down," Daeh said. His gaze didn't leave Mich's face. The men dragged chairs from the wall over Daeh's polished floor. Several words were muttered between the pair, something about a drinking binge or a bar fight. Mich couldn't make it out. They talked in half sentences and mumbled innuendo. She was surprised Daeh let them get away with such disrespectful behavior, but he said nothing to silence them.

"Who's the kid?" the shorter man asked as he sprawled in his chair.

She glared at him. It was only her need to remain professional that prevented her from dropping her head into her hands and screaming.

When Daeh remained silent, the men took the opportunity to study her. She felt their eyes crawl over her body and held herself still under their inspection, refusing to squirm or shudder, though it was a near thing.

The taller man eventually addressed Daeh. "Sorry about the appearance, sir. We didn't have time to clean up."

"Sveen said ta come right in," the other added.

Daeh leaned forward. "You have a new case. Mich Janelle will be working with you."

"Chief, we don't work with rookies." The shorter man eyed his partner and the two men grinned at each other.

Mich wanted to shove her gun under this man's nose and demonstrate her qualifications. She also wanted to flip them off and walk out. She did neither. Instead, she tuned out of the conversation entirely and replayed Yetti's last days in her mind. If she was to be forced to work the case with these men, she needed somewhere to start. Ketal Seven was the planet Yetti had been on when poisoned. Perhaps the bar he'd visited the night before he left for Battenhold? Those women he'd brought home should be questioned.

After a while, she became aware Daeh was staring at her again. The thumping headache brought on by too little sleep was growing worse, tightening her jaw and bringing a twist to her belly that suggested it was turning into a migraine. Sleeping in a bed was starting to reach romantic fantasy heights. *Why doesn't he say something?*

"Mich Janelle, I'd like you to meet Zeth Wen and Rel Charley."

"Rookies prefer rules. We don't have time for that, chief. You'd be better off assigning her to another team," said the one Daeh identified as Zeth Wen, the taller man who sat so eerily still.

"Yeah, quick on ya feet, that's how we work. Seat-of-the-pants stuff, ya got ta move fast around us," Charley added snidely, somehow sprawling lower in his seat.

"Hell's spawn." Mich broke her silence at last. She skewered the two men with a glare. "Even a rookie wouldn't have trouble targeting all of those clichés."

"Janelle," Daeh warned.

"Well, well, she has a voice." Charley straightened in his chair. His eyes narrowed in her direction. She felt his gaze run over her again.

Daeh ignored them. "Janelle has the information that you need. I suggest you go clean up. She can brief you later."

Wen rose to his feet with such economy of movement, it was like he sat one minute and stood the next, with barely a breath in between. He was stretching a hand toward Mich to shake when Daeh's words registered. "She's got the brief?"

Charley laughed and scrubbed a hand over his face. "Not a rookie then."

Daeh shook his head. "Gentlemen, Janelle is an ex-Hunter."

At that, the two men shot each other a look full of eyebrow movements. "Hunter Michele Janelle?" Wen queried.

Her reputation had preceded her once again. Stomach roiling, she rose to face them and raised an eyebrow of her own, waiting for the question to be asked. She willed her hands not to tremble. The men shared another glance then smiled broadly.

"We'll prep the ship," Wen said. "We're at docking point three. Our ship is called *Lazydragon*. Give us time to clean up, then come on over. Where are we headed?"

"Ketal Seven." Mich took Wen's hand and, at the greasy feeling, just as quickly dropped it.

Wen rubbed his grubby fingers against his thigh. "Sorry." He grinned. With a brief nod to Daeh, the two men left the room.

The minute the door closed, Mich exploded. "You have got to be kidding me!" She stomped toward the door.

"Behave, Janelle."

Mich paused, her hand on the doorknob, and peered at him over her shoulder. She smiled sweetly, but said nothing.

This was going to be an unmitigated disaster. All of her personal plans were now in complete disarray. The thought of babysitters watching her every move brought a flush to her face.

"They're good investigators. I'd like them to stay that way."

Mich squinted at her new boss. Why did he assume she'd be the one to cause trouble? If he was implying what happened to her at The Clinic made her dangerous, why assign her to an established team?

He gave her the smallest hint of a smile. *He's winding me up? Seriously?* She scowled and pushed the door open with both hands.

His next words stopped her. "I wish you would tell me what happened."

A woman's voice whispered seductively in the back of her mind. *"Our little secret."* Mich had thought that voice had been banished from her subconscious. Apparently, it was only lying in wait, ready to ambush her when her guard was down.

"I can't." She slammed the door shut behind her. At least, she tried to slam it. To her consternation, the door had been fitted with pressure pads. It closed at a reduced speed with a soft click. Sucking in a deep breath, she stood just outside, trying to calm her racing thoughts. If she was going to work with these unknown men, then she needed more information. And she knew exactly where to get it.

Chapter 9

Mich dropped the nail-sized drive onto the bed and glanced around the sterile suite with a practiced eye. She'd stayed in a lot of hotel rooms once upon a time; she recognized the layout and knew what made a room more comfortable. Window on the south side, queen bed, altranet access including the movie and serial database and, most importantly, a giant bath. She needed a few hours to herself. In silence. Alone. So she'd rented a room for half a day. Initially, she'd planned on taking a nap, where she could sleep without having to look over her shoulder. Fallout from The Clinic heightened her need for security. Shortly she'd be on a ship, enclosed in a small unescapable space with two unknown men. This would be her last chance for a solid safe sleep. Now that she was here, however, a long hot relaxing bath was in order. Grabbing a cleaner's steam bag from behind the door, she shoved her jacket inside and sealed the catch to activate the cycle.

The call to Beth had been a lot more productive than she'd anticipated. Unlike when she'd asked for information on Tripness—*kill them all*. That had been frustratingly unproductive. Mich might not be a Hunter anymore, but her contacts were still willing to deal for cash, and Beth had access to file servers all across the spiral. She'd pulled both Zeth Wen and Rel Charley's investigator files, and for a reasonable price too.

Slumping onto the bed, Mich debated delaying her bath to read the information on the files. The files won. She snatched up the drive and inserted it into the small port at the base of her neck. The data displayed directly onto the small screen a whisker beneath her cornea. She scanned past the men's case files and went straight to their histories.

Zeth Wen—a single man reared by three men on Shallshall. She could find no explanation for his adoption, only that his home life had been happy until he lost one of his parents in the war. That loss was the reason he gave in his entrance exam for entering the Shallshall spaceflight academy. With decent scores in all subjects, he had every appearance of an affable man with strengths in leadership and solo pursuits. Her eyes widened. His pilot scores were off the chart. Hers had been good, sure, but his were unbelievable. It was at the academy, she read on, that he'd become inseparable friends with Rel Charley, who was indeed part draal. She was curious to know how Rel had managed acceptance into the academy, and skipped to his file. There was no indication he'd been given special consideration, but it was the only way he could've got in, given his heritage.

Blinking, she paused the data feed. She'd been taught in school that the draal originated from another galaxy and had traveled here with the sole intention of invasion. Mich didn't really remember the attacks, only the long periods of time spent in the shelters with her grandmother on Janing. Her skin crawled at the memory of the old woman's constant disapproval. Mich rolled onto her side and stared at the wall. The children of the draal were one of the unfortunate byproducts of the occupation. Hated and persecuted on many worlds, very few half-children were ever granted access to, or given training for, governmental positions. The prejudice against the invaders still affected the judgment of many in power. She wondered what was so special about Rel that he'd been one of the lucky ones. His file didn't say. It made her curious.

Mich jumped to her feet to fetch a glass of water. She drained it and returned to lying back on the mattress. She winked to reactive the file and continued reading.

Rel Charley's file tag recorded he'd been widowed three years ago. There were also multiple discipline reports for alcohol abuse and fighting on school grounds, ending in both Zeth Wen and Rel Charley being booted from the academy.

Well, that's concerning.

She flipped to Rel's scores. Specialized weapons and disposals subjects, and high marks in all. A volatile marksman. Great.

The two men had been hired by Daeh and mostly sent to investigate cases on the outer spiral. She assumed that was due to Rel's heritage rather than their specialized skillsets. On paper, Charley and Wen's working methods sounded insane. Their cases were bloody and, by their own accounts, frequently resolved with fatal consequences. Her eyes narrowed. Were these men nothing more than adrenalin junkies who created their own action when they became bored?

Regardless, the men's lack of adherence to the various planetary rules and regulations should work in her favor. All she had to do was convince them to work separately then slip off on her own. Under no circumstances could she let these men know she was secretly investigating Tripness—*kill them all*—and its connection to her personal circumstances.

A light touch to her cornea deactivated her port. Sliding to the edge of the bed, she grabbed her toiletry bag. Now that she knew what to expect, it was time to clean up and go brief her—hopefully temporary—partners.

Chapter 10

"So, who do you think she is?"

"Janelle? An ex-Hunter."

Zeth rolled his eyes. Rel was in one of his surly, post-drunk moods. Now that they were sober, they knew they had to clean up before their passenger arrived. On their own, how they looked, and smelled, didn't matter so much. Mich Janelle might not appreciate their post-mission bachelor lifestyle or lingering smell.

Ducking his lathered face out of the prison cell-sized bathroom cubicle, he checked Rel hadn't decided on a little morning-after drinkie to take the edge off his hangover. Rel glanced up from the terminal, his face twisted in confusion. Zeth saw there was nothing to worry about. Already showered and shaved, Rel was a man Zeth hadn't seen in months. His hair was cut short and jelled into sharp spikes away from his face. "Trying to impress?"

Rel flipped him off.

Chuckling, Zeth returned to the mirror, but froze mid-turn. He poked his head out of the bathroom again. "What in the One is that?"

Rel fingered the sliver of trimmed hair running in a line from his lower lip to his chin. "Like it?"

"No. It looks like you spilled hanglehair sauce on your face. Get rid of it."

"Nah, I like it."

Zeth returned to the bathroom, shaking his head. Rel had done many, many stupid things in his time, but this one was right up there.

As he shaved, more and more of Zeth's old self emerged to stare back at him from the mirror. It was a relief to see he hadn't changed all that much, other than a few more lines. Wild-eyed innocent faces filled his vision. Zeth banished the memory quickly. He didn't know when he'd get over what had happened. Deep inside, he didn't think he should.

Flicking the tap, he cupped his hands beneath the spray to splash recycled water over his face. The cold liquid washed away the cream, but not the stomach-churning guilt. He turned away from the mirror, unable to look at his own face anymore.

Scrubbing his head with a towel, he ran a comb through the knots and pulled his thin, dark hair into a tail behind his head. Though he'd cut its matted lengths, he'd decided to keep it long enough to fall to his shoulders.

Rel had closed the terminal and was sitting at the rikki board, throwing a silver game piece between his hands. Mouth wide, Rel threw back his head and burst out laughing when he caught sight of Zeth. Zeth ignored him and headed for the cockpit. Rel followed, still chuckling. "Ponytail?"

Zeth glared. "That bit of dirt on your face washes off, right?"

His partner shrugged. "Trying it out." He collapsed into the copilot's chair. Together, they ran through the pre-heat sequence, checked their readings and responses, and made sure all systems were operating smoothly. Rel shut everything down again as Zeth moved into the seat behind the pilot's chair to check on navigation.

"So. Janelle?"

"Ya've heard what I have. Think any of it's true?" Rel slouched back in his chair and kicked it around in a lazy circle.

Zeth stared at his partner as he thought about it. To be honest, he didn't know what to think of the woman. Gossip told several different stories; the only consistent detail was that Janelle had risen too far, too fast. Some said she'd killed a client. Some said she'd killed an informant. The only thing they all agreed on was that she was unstable. There was even a rumor that suggested she'd been set up, but conspiracies lay everywhere. Who could tell what story was true? Steven Daeh trusted her enough to give her a shot, and there was no way she'd be authorized to work as an investigator if she had a criminal record. Zeth turned his gaze to the ceiling. "Daeh wouldn't have her working a case if she wasn't up to it."

Rel stopped the slow spin of his chair by planting both feet firmly on the ground. "Yet we've been assigned ta work with her. Res it, there's more going on here than we've been told, Zeth. They say she's crazy."

"They say *we're* crazy."

His partner smirked.

"It'll be two days travel to Ketal Seven. Wonder what we'll be doing there." From the way Daeh talked, Zeth assumed she was in charge, and he didn't like it, especially given her checkered past.

"We'll find out when our new friend gets here. Where is she anyway?" Rel started his chair spinning again. With the scent of a new case in his nose, Rel was never able to sit still.

Zeth knew his friend's energy would burn itself out shortly. Until Janelle arrived with the brief, he'd have to put up with his partner's impatience. "You know women."

Rel shrugged, though his eyes dimmed. Zeth was instantly sorry. Of course, Rel knew women better than Zeth—he'd been married, after all.

Rel appeared to allow the momentary melancholy to slide off. "Need any pointers?"

Zeth smirked. "I'm good." He could handle women, though he preferred men romantically. Mich Janelle would likely prove a different species altogether. The gleam in her eye put him on edge.

"Ex-Hunter. Moody." Rel raised his eyebrows. "Wonder if she's talkative?"

Zeth squinted at his partner as the hairs rose on the back of his neck. Rel liked to test new people, treat them the way his first impression told him would be the most irritating. Zeth usually enjoyed watching Rel's head games blow up in his face, however, spending the next two days in the confined space of the *Lazydragon* would be stressful enough without Rel doing his level best to wind the woman up. He knew there was no point warning his partner off his appointed task, and Zeth figured if Rel was going to do it anyway, watching her reaction might give him an insight into her operating style. If she was a danger to herself or to them, it would be better to find out now rather than in the middle of a firefight.

"She was quiet in front of Daeh." Zeth touched only the controls needed to tell the computer to find their quickest jump zone.

Rel eyed him. "Her rep has me twitchy."

"Agreed. Something's not right there. Do you think she—?"

The display in front of Zeth beeped as the calculations completed. It beeped again as a loud clang sounded from the main hatch.

"Well, well. Sooner than expected. Let the games begin," Rel said with a grin.

*

Mich dumped her duffle bag and backpack at her feet before turning a wide circle to examine her surroundings. She missed her own sleek Swish series Runner with a fierce ache. When she'd been arrested, it had been sold on her behalf. Not that the extra money had helped her case.

Lazydragon was a ship of oddities. From outside, it looked like a newish, overweight yacht, with no visible weaponry and inside, it looked like they'd built it by hand with the rejected pieces from a tech scrap yard. And she still couldn't see any weaponry.

Door seals hung loose or were missing in places, overhead lights were cracked or just not working, and the visual screens scattered throughout the main room were clunky, old-style 2-D monitors jammed in place with exposed wiring and mismatched connectors. Her eyes found every shadow. The room was filled to bursting with old, stained and sagging furniture, yet there was a comfort here that surprised her.

She directed her gaze at the man watching her. Well, at least one of the men cleaned up nicely. Funny, but with all the hair and dirt before, she hadn't taken much notice of Wen's eyes. She'd be hard pressed to miss them now. His shallshall cheekbones were muted in this light, but his eyes were glorious. They reminded her of the sea, deep blue becoming green as his head moved into the shadow cast by the bulkhead above, the only part of his body that moved.

His stillness grated on her nerves. *What's he hiding?*

"Where's your partner?" she asked. The sofa appeared sturdy enough, but there was a faint odor she couldn't identify emanating from the leather that put her off sitting down.

"Cockpit. We planned to leave the minute you arrived."

Mich picked up her bags.

"Your bunk's that way," Wen said, pointing toward a corridor over her left shoulder. "The end one. Dump your stuff then come on up." He strode away, tilting his head to avoid a wire dangling from the cockpit doorway.

The room he'd directed her to was barely wide enough for the single bed but, much to her surprise, it looked clean. Mich dumped her bag and headed for the cockpit. Halfway there, *Lazydragon's* engines roared to life beneath her feet. The vibration rose up her legs and settled into her stomach. The pitch was low—smooth—not like the old decrepit engine she'd expected. Curious as to what else she didn't know about the ship and its owners, she stepped inside the cockpit and a soft gasp she couldn't stifle fell from her lips. Row after row of new, high-tech and mostly illegal equipment gleamed from every corner. It was beauty in tech form, and she fell instantly in love, wanting to caress every panel, gush over the sleek lines ... and was that a control board for C-casing missiles? Oh. She could swoon.

There were too many monitors set up to account for a ship's standard flight equipment. Convinced there was more to this ship than appearance let on, she wondered what other surprises were stored within its frame.

"Strap in."

Mich blinked at the second man's sudden appearance. Had Rel Charley been watching her reaction all this time? Her skin itched at the thought.

The broad-shouldered man pushed Mich aside and dropped into the copilot's chair. His hair was cut short, emphasizing the raised ridge of muscle on his neck. Her gaze dropped immediately to his feet. Sans boots, the rear claw captured her attention. Now she could see the draal in him. His face was cleaned up, though he'd left a bit of hair on his chin. The seat behind Wen was empty and Mich sat, peering into the monitor beside her chair. It showed a view of the bay below and the docking tech seated at a console to the right, tapping commands into his board. Two techs emerged from beneath *Lazydragon,* dragging the disconnected supply link behind them. Wen swept his fingers across the touch panel, kicking the engines to midline, and grasped the control stick lightly. It looked like he was waiting for their clearance codes to be processed.

Charley twisted around to stare at Mich with clear, amber-colored eyes. "Still heading ta Ketal Seven?" The intensity of his gaze was unsettling.

She nodded.

"So, what's the case?" he asked, his fingers drifting over the hair on his chin.

With a deft touch on the stick, Wen lifted *Lazydragon*'s nose and directed the ship along their assigned clearance corridor. The pilot's body tightened when Mich didn't immediately respond to his partner, but he didn't glance back. The three investigators were pushed deep into their seats as he initiated the superdrive to pick up speed. They approached the planetary barrier quickly and, with a loud pop in their ears, entered space.

The pressure keeping Mich pinned to her seatback eased, and her body relaxed. Her emotions tightened, though, as her thoughts darted from the next few days enclosed in this ship to their upcoming mission. Step one—brief the two men. Together, they would need to devise a plan to track back Yetti's movements and discover who he'd spoken to and where he'd been on the day he was poisoned. Then she had to figure out a way to escape their attention and start her own, private mission.

A yawn took her by surprise. Then again, maybe sleep should be step one.

Rising, she slipped into the gap between the men and glanced at the navigation screen. Numbers scrolled rapidly down the display. "Once we're in altraspace, I'll let you know why we're heading to Ketal Seven. Right now, I need sleep." Mich released another jaw-splitting yawn as she edged out of the door.

Behind her, Charley muttered, "Interesting woman."

Mich smirked to herself and shook her head—he had no idea.

Chapter 11

Mich gazed at the bedframe of the bunk, but all she saw were stars, countless stars, stars that stretched into long, thin lines invading the ship and invading her. Lightspeed measured in the time it took her eyes to imagine a star to the time the star shot past.

A memory hit her like a punch to the gut.

Stars were projected onto the ceiling at night, like the swaying shapes could soothe them into sleep. Screams traversed the superficially soundproofed walls of her room. The door of her cell rattled. It clacked open; her head snapped up.

Releasing a gust of breath, Mich blinked rapidly and focused on the mattress above her head. She blocked out the sounds in her mind by humming. Meditation usually calmed her tortured mind, but with the surfacing of the unwanted memories, her thoughts now spiraled.

A bald man, small and dumpy, waddled in, carrying a silver tray. Without so much as a glance, he removed a syringe from the tray and pierced her arm with it. She flinched, desperate to protest. He gripped the back of her head with one hand and brought a plastic cup to her mouth. She coughed at the foul stench and tried to pull away, but her arms were stuck fast, her head held tight in his unyielding grip. Her submission was a bitter reality.

She coughed, gagging at the memory. Healer Travnell. She would never forget his voice, or the look in his eyes when he spoke to her. His fingers were a phantom vice on her cold skin.

Now was not the time to get sucked down into her past. She had Wen and Charley to keep an eye on. If she screwed up this time, her life wouldn't be the only one at risk. Taskly haunted her dreams, and rightly so: she'd failed him. She couldn't have two more lives on her conscience.

She dragged her tired body from beneath the bunk and snatched up her jacket, dragging it on. Some of the fine chocolate strands had come loose from her braid and hung around her face. Annoyed, she pushed them back behind her ears and strode from the room.

"These men are dangerous," a voice in her ear whispered. *"You must watch yourself around them. They will betray you."*

Mich spun, checking the corridor around her ... she was alone. She shook her head but the voice was already gone. A headache prickled her temples. *Not now.* She'd thought she was getting better.

Sucking in a deep breath, she let it go slowly and counted to ten. When she was projecting a facsimile of Calm Mich, she stepped out into *Lazydragon*'s main living quarters.

Rel Charley hunched over a squat table that looked designed for rikki. At Mich's entrance, he examined her body with a long lingering look. "D'ya have anything else in ya wardrobe? That jacket should be scrapped."

Mich raised her arm and eyed the hide covering it. It was fine. Sure, the leather was a little worn in patches, scorch marks were burned across the front near the buttons and there were stitches right across the back where she'd had that close encounter with a bandit's blade ...

She dropped her arm and pinned Charley with a glare. "You've got a bit of something there," she said, rubbing her fingers across her own chin.

A burst of laughter drew her attention to the doorway. Wen leaned against the wall, his body as still as a statue. Only his eyes and his eyebrows showed his good humor. "I said something similar. You hungry?"

She nodded and followed him into the smallest kitchenette she'd ever seen. One bench, no wider than her backpack, with a countertop stove. Several blackened pots hung overhead, securely fastened into place with thick fabric straps and giant pegs. The cupboard door built into the counter was open, exposing the mismatched dishes also locked in place by faded black securing straps. Staring suspiciously at the concoction steaming in the large pot on the stove, Mich could only hope the meal was edible. It certainly smelled interesting. Wen expertly ladled some of the mixture into a bowl and pressed it into her hands. He nodded toward the ship's main living room area.

"So," he said, sitting beside Charley on the couch, "what's the case?" Charley attacked his meal like a man who had not seen food for days, not even glancing up for her response.

Mich sat cross-legged on the floor and stirred the soup, grimacing as lumps of green and gray vegetables bobbed to the surface. Barely dipping her spoon, she sipped at the liquid. The tang of lime and spices exploded on her tongue, warming her mouth and throat. *Oh, that's nice.*

As she ate, she explained her earlier mission to watch Yetti and track his contacts then described his murder, the weapon used to kill him, and the mysterious object she'd found in his belongings.

"Enferrie flower? Never heard of it." Wen lowered his bowl to the floor beside his chair and straightened. "Sounds like a great hunting tool."

Charley raised a brow. "What's the point in hitting an animal with that thing? Two days gives it enough time ta come after ya, and if it explodes, how d'ya get a trophy?" He shook his head. "Nothing wrong with a stunner."

"A stunner didn't work against the ptarri fish on Tella Minor. I remember the swollen jaw you carried back, and no ptarri." Wen's mouth twitched.

Charley pointed at him. "It worked on Shesja."

Wen snorted. "Shesja was mean and a racist. He deserved to be in pain."

The argument sounded like one the men had often. Mich tapped her spoon against her bowl to regain their attention. The hollow ding drew her gaze down. *Empty?* It was a good thing she'd finished the entire bowl, though, because talking about the effects of the poison quickly killed her appetite. As she spoke, she noticed Charley put his own bowl on the floor. It seemed hers wasn't the only appetite lost.

"As I said, it's not pretty," she concluded, reaching into her pocket. She withdrew the cylinder and placed it onto the table with care.

Charley picked it up, examined it and passed it to his partner. "It's a piece of metal."

"A heavy piece of metal," Wen added.

"A long, heavy piece of metal," Charley concluded, sprawling back in his chair. His hand tapped on his knee.

"Well, I'm sure glad I have you two experts here to help." Mich rolled her eyes. If they were always like this, she'd worry more about killing them herself than getting them killed.

Wen's eyes narrowed. She'd observed that other than for a few large gestures, when Wen focused, his whole body became still. Charley was the complete opposite. He didn't seem able to sit without twitching, not even for a moment. His feet tapped, he scratched, his leg bounced. There was always a part of him moving.

"So, we're supposed to find out what this is?" Wen asked. At Charley's raised brow, he amended. "What this long, heavy piece of metal is? And hope that whatever it is will lead us to Yetti's killer?" Leaning forward, he put the cylinder on the table. His brows knit together as his mouth twitched in one corner. "That's pretty flimsy."

"What else have we got?" Mich crossed her arms over her chest and clenched her fingers into the leather of her jacket. Why bother asking for her opinion if they were just going to disregard it?

"What makes ya so sure this resing thing"—Charley pointed to the cylinder—"has anything ta do with it? Why d'ya think the sholan was killed for any other reason than someone objecting ta the way his breath stank?"

She stood and snatched the cylinder from the table. "I know."

"Yeah, but what makes ya so sure—?"

Wen clipped Charley over the back of the head, the movement so fast and unexpected, Mich reared back at the shock of it. "She's sure." He pitched his voice low so that it only carried to his partner. *Does he really think I can't hear him?* "And Daeh trusts her, so we trust her." Louder, he said, "We need a plan."

"I thought you said you don't like plans?"

They both frowned, the identical expressions of suspicion and confusion telling her that she'd said the wrong thing.

"What, ya just expect us ta land on Ketal Seven and find the killer? Where are we supposed ta start?" Charley asked.

"The Dive. It's the bar Yetti frequented."

Charley's eyes lit up. His file mentioned a fondness for alcohol. She should insist Wen take the bar. "There's also the storage bay where he kept his more illegal tech items. The ones that wouldn't fit into his hotel room."

"Ya go ta the bay, I'll take the bar," Charley immediately suggested.

Wen eyeballed him and waited. Charley met his stare. Mich watched them negotiate silently and opened her mouth to inform them she would be checking both locations herself when she hesitated. If she let the men investigate the places Yetti had been, she could stay on board *Lazydragon* alone. Surely their altranet set-up would get her into Tripness's server—*kill them all.* Yes, this was perfect.

She twitched her hand until Wen looked at her. "You can both take the bar and the bay. I have some files to hack into once we land. Of course, if you two don't want to split up, I can handle the bar."

Wen shook his head. The slight movement expressed his thoughts clearly. "No, we'll be fine."

Mich caught Charley's smirk and suppressed one of her own. With any luck, she'd find a way to keep them busy for the entire investigation.

Wen glanced at his timepiece and stifled a yawn. "I suggest we get some sleep."

"Ya go, I'll watch the screens." Charley picked up his bowl, grabbed Wen's empty dish and the one Mich still held, and sauntered to the kitchenette.

Mich stood as well. She wouldn't argue the need for sleep. The headache she'd been fighting to keep at bay all afternoon now thudded heavily behind her eyes, and the urge to lie down was getting the best of her.

Wen disappeared as Mich headed toward the bunkroom. Charley called her name with a soft voice, stopping her just outside the door.

"It's small, but we call it home. If ya lonely, ya can always join me." He leaned on the doorframe and wiggled his eyebrows. Mich flinched, immediately scolding herself for displaying such an obvious tell. He'd been assigned by Daeh to watch her, and would no doubt report her behavior back to their boss. She wasn't supposed to be afraid of anything. Observing Wen and Charley's interaction reminded her of better times, when she hadn't understood how fragile her sense of security was. *Fake it!*

She held Charley's gaze and snorted loudly. The look in his eyes told her he'd noticed the delay between his question and her response. Turning her back on him, she slunk away to her quarters.

*

Searing pain tore Rel from the arms of his beautiful wife and awakened him with a start. He'd fallen asleep on watch. *Dresh.* He grabbed at the cramp in his calf and stifled a yelp at the pain radiating from the area. Pulling his leg off the panel he'd squashed it against, he forced the muscle to stretch. When that didn't work, he struggled to his feet and hobbled around the cockpit, groaning loudly.

Zeth burst through the doorway. "What is it?" he demanded. Rel just looked at him. Zeth stared for a moment longer before sliding into the copilot's chair, covering his mouth with his hand.

"It's not resing funny," Rel growled. The cramped muscles suddenly relaxed and the pain eased, but he continued to hobble around, afraid it would reoccur.

The woman raced into the cockpit, her weapon gripped tightly in her hand. Trousers zipped but not buttoned, wrinkled shirt and creases on her cheek indicated how quickly she'd launched out of bed. Her lips tightened as she observed the room. Rel's hand—the one rubbing his calf, rose to his waist. His finger-sized throwing knife was hidden in his belt, which was still attached to the trousers pooled on the floor. Zeth, a frozen figure beside him, waited for her move. She stared at them for a long moment, huffed, spun on her heel and left.

"Nice ta see she has a caring side," Rel grumbled, dropping his hand.

Zeth rested his fist on the console in front of him, his body still angled to eye the door. Rel flopped into the pilot's chair and resumed rubbing his aching leg.

"You're just pissed she caught you in your shorts, buddy. I'll stay here. You go and get some sleep."

Rel glanced down at his current state of undress. All he wore were his purple monsters on green satin boxers. "Hey, I was comfortable." With a glance at the doorway he added, "She was ready for a fight. Who was she gonna shoot?"

Zeth nodded his head once. "Saw that."

"Hard ta miss. She's on edge."

"Well, to be fair, it's not a pleasant case."

"Still ..."

Rel pulled his pants on, clapped a hand on his friend's shoulder and headed for the living area.

Janelle sat at the rikki board, sipping some foul concoction. He hadn't pegged her for the herbal tea type. He knew for a fact they had none on board—she must have brought it with her.

What's next? Resing colored throw pillows on the sofa?

She didn't raise her head or acknowledge his presence, but every muscle in her body was wound tighter than a ship's conductor coil. Rel gritted his teeth and squinted at her. She was looking at the bit of metal from the dead sholan's bag, rolling it between the fingers of one hand.

"Keep staring and I'll pop them out," she said.

So she was aware of him. Rel kept staring.

The woman raised her eyes and skewered him with a look that would have convinced a smarter man to back down. Rel dropped into the seat beside her. Somehow her body tensed even further. He figured, any second now, she was going to explode. He didn't like what his instincts were telling him, but he couldn't just come out and ask.

She held out the metal piece. "What do you think?"

He stood up, moving slowly to keep from spooking her. Keeping his body loose, he wandered to the other side of the room, all of ten paces, and wished the room was wider. The altranet console would make a good leaning post. When he glanced back, she was watching him, her face expressionless.

Rel shook his head. "No idea what it is."

"I know it's important. It's got to be." She slammed the cylinder down onto the table, scattering game pieces everywhere.

"Oh man, Zeth's not gonna be happy with ya. He'd finally caught me in a Mix Lot. Won't happen again, let me tell ya and ..." She didn't react to his amusement. In fact, she didn't peer up at him at all, her gaze was fixed on the table, where the long, heavy piece of metal had broken into pieces.

Chapter 12

The most recognizable item among the pieces was a data drive. Mich glanced at the oddly shaped pieces of plastic scattered around it. She had no idea what they were.

Charley took one look at the pieces and began to fit them together. Eyes focused, brows drawn together, lips pursed. His movements were sure and confident, so Mich watched in silence as he worked. Within seconds, she found herself staring at a tiny dart with an empty rear canister.

"You've seen one of these before, I take it?" She held out her hand for the thing. The plastic was cold—not held by Charley long enough to pick up his body heat. It was barely heavier than a quarter piece of peeled orange stone fruit.

"Yeah, it's called a spike. It can only be inserted inta a specific made-ta-order finger pistol. The individual pieces can't be scanned. It's a one-shot dart that dissolves after use. No evidence left behind. It's the perfect weapon ta smuggle inta restricted areas." Charley moved to a pile of clothing thrown haphazardly in the corner and returned to the couch with a small leather holster. From it, he withdrew a clear plastic pistol the length of his finger. He inserted the spike. The dart fit perfectly. His face was somber. "The specs aren't available through the usual channels. Ya need ta build it from scratch. I've never seen another one. The spike is usually designed like this one, but it can be modified by a good tech ta fire a mini canister explosive."

Mich recalled his weapons scores from his file: he knew what he was talking about. "So it's a dart? Probably designed to be loaded full of Enferrie poison, I'm guessing. Killed with the very weapon he was smuggling? Hell's spawn." Mich rubbed her eyes and thought back. She'd spent days watching Yetti and was well aware of the tech smuggling and his occasional foray into minor level drug-dealing. There had been no indication he was moving weapons. *Had there?* She would have to go back through her notes and re-examine the evidence to be sure. Sweat broke out across her neck. This was the connection she'd been looking for. Had Yetti smuggled spikes and vials of this Enferrie poison in for someone to use and been killed to prove it worked? Or were they cleaning up now that Yetti was no longer necessary to their plans?

After a moment, Charley stirred. "I'll tell Zeth." He disappeared into the cockpit before Mich could remind him about the data drive.

Unwilling to link the unknown drive into her personal port, she crossed to the nearest console, connected it and waited.

*

Zeth took the gun from his partner, popped the seal and removed the dart. "A spike, huh? A lazy sholan carrying a spike but not the weapon that fires it? For who?" Nothing in the case brief indicated Yetti was a murderer or assisted in murders, but this kind of highly restricted weapon was not being used for display. Someone was planning to murder someone. But who and when? And why? "What's going on here, mate?"

Rel shrugged, but his gaze was drawn in and he was wearing his pondering face. "Janelle didn't know."

"I'm thinking it might not be a good idea to split up when we check the sholan's haunts. Yetti had his hands on a rare weapon. That he was murdered by the same weapon raises a lot of questions." The woman had been quick to suggest they split up to investigate the different locations. Zeth now wanted them to stay together simply because she wanted them divided. He hadn't argued the point at the time because it was one thing not to trust her; it was another thing entirely to *tell* her they didn't trust her.

On the other side of the cockpit, Rel waved a hand to get his attention. "Well?"

Zeth rose. "Was this it? The only thing in the cylinder?"

"Yeah, and the data drive." Rel swore and sprang to his feet.

"What data drive?"

Rel raced out through the door. Zeth ran after him.

When they reached the central room, they found Janelle staring blankly at the drive in her hand. Zeth stepped forward, concerned he'd spook her if he moved too fast, and took the drive from her hand. Janelle made her way to the couch, where she sat and resumed her frozen state.

Zeth and Rel leaned over the console.

*

"My guess is that Yetti was used for delivery to the location on the chip, which is clearly in code. I don't think he knew what he was carrying," she said softly, rubbing at her neck. That chip detailed the amount of the poison ordered. That much was not used for one murder; it was enough for hundreds. "We don't have the poison. Presumably it's already been delivered."

"If the data on the chip is accurate," Wen said.

"What we can read of it. No reason to presume it's not," Mich pointed out. "The cylinder was hidden in his bag. With Yetti dead, whoever killed him has no idea we know what we know. Why was he still carrying the weapon? Did he order one for himself, or did he just not get the chance to deliver it? Would he really have been killed before completing the order?"

"Depends on who killed him, doesn't it?" Charley said.

"And we don't have that information," Mich said. "He clearly knew about the poison. The chip was clear about that."

"If he was shipping spikes, he knew exactly what it was going ta be used for. Might've been planning ta use it himself and someone got the drop on him first?" Charley mused.

"I didn't find a finger pistol on him," she reminded him. Mich tapped her hand against the sofa arm while she thought back. "I followed him for days. Admittedly, that isn't enough time to get a read on a man, but I don't think he shipped the poison to use it himself. Delivering it to someone, maybe."

"Delivering the spikes and the poison makes him a killer. Six spikes, that data drive says. He had only one in his bag, so who has the other five? At the very least, he's an accessory," Charley argued. He sat slouched in one of the armchairs, his legs splayed wide. His arms were crossed over his chest and his feet tapped the ground. Mich stared at them, willing them to stop.

"He had to have known what they were." Wen clenched an empty glass tightly in one hand. "Maybe he knew you were following him and concealed what he was really doing?"

"If he made me, it would have been easy to shake me. He sure as hell wouldn't have let me get that close to his belongings." There was no chance Yetti had spotted her. She might be rusty, but she knew how to follow a person.

"So we split up. Find out where the spikes were being delivered and who ordered them," Wen decided. He stretched for the nearly empty bottle on the bench.

"Won't find 'em," Charley said, retrieving his glass and waving it in the air. "Whoever's taking delivery will know by now it ain't coming. They'll have gone off the grid. I think he already delivered it."

"And what's this one then—a spare?" Mich asked.

"Maybe he wanted a trophy?" Wen refilled his partner's glass before tipping the last shot into his own.

Mich eyed Charley's rapidly disappearing drink. Wen didn't seem concerned. She tried to relax, but being cooped up in the enclosed spaceship with two drunk men filled her with unease. Her gun was in her bunkroom with the rest of her belongings. Her fingers twitched, wishing for the familiar weight to be in her hand. "Yetti's death was announced by the local authorities just before I left Bendal. If the buyer didn't kill Yetti, then Charley's right—they'll have gone to ground. We won't find them."

Wen tilted his glass. "So the question is: who hired Yetti?"

"And who killed him?" Charley finished, staring mournfully at his now empty glass.

"Yetti had several meetings with a member of The Spiral Guardians."

"Fans of explosives," Charley immediately said. "We had a run-in with a faction of The Spiral Guardians recently."

"Oh, how'd that end up?" Mich queried. The tightening of the skin around both of their eyes gave her the answer. *Not well.*

"There was also a member of TRK," Mich told them.

Wen sat back. "Really? So, two gangs known for a free and enthusiastic willingness to murder."

"Big bangs, yes. Poison, though? Could be a woman," Charley suggested.

Mich pursed her lips. "Yetti did enjoy the company of several ladies—of a professional kind."

"Any of 'em look good for this?"

"They seemed happy enough when they left. We'd need to speak to them to be sure. His preference came from The Dive. There's an adjoining brothel." She hummed. "The last communication I intercepted said Yetti was traveling to Battenhold to meet a man named Charlmehn Di," she offered. "Delivering something. Which is why we were on the cruiser when he died."

"What do ya have on Di?"

"Nothing much. My initial search found a simple man, recently widowed." She cringed inwardly at her word choice. Charley was a widower. Hopefully he wouldn't react badly to the reference. She continued quickly. "No red flags. Works in marketing and public relations; all low-level stuff. I didn't get into a detailed history because Yetti was headed out, and the cruiser he booked had crappy interplanetary connectivity." She hadn't been following Yetti long enough to gauge his relationships properly. "I don't think it's him."

They sat in silence.

"So, the plan stands?" Wen asked. "We split up and track Yetti's last movements? We need to find out who his boss is, and who placed the order."

"Wonder if whoever ordered the spikes received their full shipment?" Charley mused. "Could be angry they were missing one. Took it out on Yetti?"

Mich raised a hand half-heartedly. "If Yetti was not the specific target, that rules out the prostitutes. So, who *is* the intended target? And why ship so much of the poison? It's more than what's needed for six spikes." She hummed. "Regardless of Yetti's involvement, he was smuggling rare weapons and way too much poison. What was his client planning to do with it all? I doubt it's for recreational use."

They each took a moment to digest that. Mich finished her drink and cradled the empty glass in her hands.

"Not sure we should split up," Wen said, breaking the silence. Mich was glad to see that rather than fetch another bottle, he placed his glass on the ground behind his chair leg.

That data on the chip disconcerted her and she knew her own case had to take a backseat. No matter how her ego screamed at her to take care of herself first, she'd become a Hunter to help people. Though she was no longer a Hunter, it was who she had been, before The Clinic. If she wanted her life back, she had to remember that. Shipping this poison in such quantities was not something done on a whim. More people were going to die, and it was her duty to stop that. "I agree."

Wen's eyebrows rose into his hairline. "You've changed your mind?"

"No one else knows about the cylinder. It was excluded from the official announcement and I didn't tell anyone about it except Daeh, after I returned to D4 Prime."

"You said Yetti was a tech smuggler. He procured and shipped items from one location to another?" Wen confirmed.

"Yes. He was the kind of guy who'd get you what you want when you want it," she confirmed. Leaning forward, she clasped her hands together. "Mostly old technology—ship parts and the like. He spent a lot of time at the local university too."

Wen placed his empty glass on the table. "What were Yetti's weaknesses?"

She thought back. "He liked to drink, liked women and the occasional card game. Typical guy, you know?" She caught the blank look the two men shot each other. "Tell me I'm wrong?"

They each raised an eyebrow and shrugged. Mich replayed the data they'd just read back in her mind, searching for clues. "The drive contained the requisition and delivery records for six spikes. That's potentially the size of a small case, right? For six cylinders? I never saw a case like that in Yetti's possession." She stood and paced to the wall. Yetti hadn't carried anything other than his duffle bag stuffed with clothes. But what about his pockets? Could the spikes have fit? No, it wasn't possible. She'd searched his body.

"Who was he getting them for?" Wen mused.

"TRK or The Spiral Guardians," Charley suggested, his eyes locked onto Mich's.

She threw her hands up. "I don't know." Dropping her arms, she stared at the wall above his head, letting her thoughts wind back to Yetti's appearance on the cruiser. He hadn't looked sick.

"What did Yetti do during the time ya followed him? Maybe there's a clue there."

"He mostly traveled from his motel to The Dive and back again. He hit the back alleys a lot, and the Skein City travel hub. I noted down all the staff and customers he appeared friendly with. They're in my surveillance report." Charley's leg tapped a beat on the floor. The unfamiliarity of the tune irritated her, and she didn't know why. "We'll need to backtrack Yetti's movements and talk to his clients." She pursed her lips. "What's your link uptime like through altraspace?"

"Not bad. Might run a bit slow if it's a large download, but for general search access, it's pretty good."

"Log me in. I didn't have time to run a detailed search algorithm on Tiny, Faber, Di or the women at the brothel before Yetti boarded the cruiser. I'll hack their communication histories. See if anything pops."

"We'll have to split up. Travel to Battenhold and Ketal Seven." At the strength of Wen's voice, Mich looked up. His expression made it clear he didn't like that idea. Even though it would mean getting out on her own she shook her head. "We need to know who Yetti was shipping the poison to. He didn't take it to Battenhold. Didn't take the other spikes either. The client must be on Ketal Seven."

"That eliminates Di."

Charley's eyes narrowed. His voice was low when he said, "The killer knows Yetti is dead. If he's got both the poison and the spikes, all we're gonna find when we land are a lot of bodies."

Chapter 13

Mich directed Wen to land on Trell. Naturally, they arrived in the middle of a thunderstorm.

"You said the trip would be the easy part," Wen yelled. *Lazydragon* lurched and jerked from the hand-sized hail pummeling the shields as they hit the lower atmosphere. The ship's outside lighting barely made a dent in the dark cloud cover, meaning visibility was non-existent.

Mich sucked in a breath, her body slamming sideways in her seat. Her security straps bit deep into her shoulders as the displays below Wen's fingertips flickered and fuzzed. He was flying blind. She wanted to close her eyes, but pride kept them open.

"The trip was. I never said anything about the landing." She gripped the panel in front of her in a failed attempt to keep from being shaken to pieces. She'd be covered in bruises by the time they made it to ground—if they made it to ground.

"You couldn't have mentioned the lightning?"

She grimaced. She'd forgotten the lightning. After all, the last time she'd traveled here, it had been via TS Cruisers and she'd been so paralyzed by the loss of gravity, she hadn't paid much attention to the lightning. Each strike was powerful enough to freeze sensor equipment and, of course, *Lazydragon* was hit the moment they crossed the shield barrier.

Every panel and light in the cockpit blinked out, plunging them into darkness. Mich's mouth flew open. Her heart seemed to stop beating. Everything in her body took on a lightness that told her the gravless system had failed too. In the darkness, she heard the crazed screams of The Clinic's patients. *"Breathe deeply, my dear."* The sound of the woman's voice drove a spike of fear into Mich's heart, jumpstarting it and sending it racing inside her chest.

Intense concentration on the battering rain against the forward shield drowned out the voice. Rain which she'd thought was loud before became deafening without the shields in place to muffle the roar. The ship was battered by the extreme weather and without her straps, she would have been thrown onto the ceiling with back-breaking speed. The turbulence they'd experienced earlier was nothing more than a gentle breeze compared to the violent back and forth that hit them now.

Forcing herself to breathe, Mich fought back tears and held on.

Lazydragon fell.

*

Rel dove under the console, curses flying as he worked to restore power.

Zeth fought the inactive controls, praying for the sensation of pressure against his fingertips. There was no response. His stomach was somewhere around his ears as gravity took hold.

Backups! Where the hell are the backups? With one hand, he found the switch. He swiped it. Nothing happened. The second, third and fourth time were useless too.

Rel pushed out from under the console and dragged his body forward, grunting as he gripped and forced off wall panel holds. He disappeared into the blackness behind them.

Another lightning flash brought momentary, blinding illumination, impairing Zeth's vision further. In that instant, the controls jerked against his hands as power was restored. Zeth let out a yell of triumph and dragged the controls up. *Lazydragon* would not become the hungry planet's meal today.

Rel ran back in and dove under the console again.

Zeth blinked to dislodge the dark splotches scarring his vision. He couldn't see the displays beneath his fingertips, flying by memory and instinct alone. Rel rebooted the ship's sensors, possibly by kicking anything he could reach.

"Pleasure Yacht *Lazydragon* AFG, stick to your current course. We anticipate a break in the storm in five."

Giant spotlights cut through the dense cloud, the powerful beams penetrating the heavy rain to guide the incapacitated ship to land. Every time they shone into *Lazydragon*'s front screen, Zeth was blinded anew.

The cockpit's lights came up again. Rel shouted in glee as screens full of unintelligible data flashed twice before snapping back on. Zeth glanced down at the information on wind direction, water density, angles of descent and their current speed and cut that speed instantly. Adjusting their course, he directed *Lazydragon* toward the Skein City's travel hub.

There was the barest bump as the ship landed. Rel was up and out of his seat the moment they touched ground. "I'll tie her down," he shouted and disappeared. Zeth switched the roaring engines over to their cooling cycle. It was always the strangest thing—the trip through space was silent, yet the engine's roar, even as it slowed, was painfully loud. After a moment, a distinctive ticking could be heard, marking the end of the cycle. Over it, the sound of the cascading rain grew louder.

Zeth peeled his stiff fingers from the control column. Beads of sweat rolled down his neck and pooled in the small of his back. "What a trip," he muttered.

Music drew his gaze to the woman seated behind him. Mich was humming—her eyes closed, her face serene. "Hey, we're here."

Her eyes snapped open.

"You didn't happen to bring a raincover, did you?" he asked, pointing at the water blurring their view.

She groaned and stood.

Woman has no fear. Maybe she really is crazy ...

*

Feeling eyes upon her as she stepped from the cockpit, Mich focused on Charley's face. He stood in the open hatchway, water pouring from his hair and jacket. He shook himself like an animal, but his steady glare didn't leave her face. Did he blame her for their rough landing? A bitter wind swept around his frame and into the ship. She shivered. "Something's flashing in ya kit. Saw it when I grabbed my coat."

Hurrying to her room, she snatched the communication unit from the top of her bag before the reality of their almost-crash suddenly hit home. She doubled over, gasping, head dizzy as her shivers intensified. Throwing her comm onto her bunk, she dragged a thick pullover out of her pack and pulled it on. Slumping down on the mattress, she hung her head between her knees.

Breathe, just breathe. Wen was certainly a talented pilot, she had to give him that. The way he'd held on and waited for power to be restored and just trusted that Charley would get it back was truly impressive. There had been no waver in either of their voices, just clipped responses and happy shouts when the power came back on. Her stomach churned and she moaned. She couldn't hide in here for long. *Pull it together!*

Closing her eyes, she breathed deeply as the familiar voice in her head ordered. Music danced at her periphery. Becoming conscious of it, she snapped her eyes open. She would not show her belly to these men. Staring at her hands, she willed them to stop shaking, breathing slow and steady.

After a minute, the tremble stopped. Clenching her hands into fists, she stood, reaching back across the bed. She tapped the device on and recalled the message waiting in storage, squinting at the name. Healer Bicet? *What does he want?* A hologram burst into the air above the device.

"Investigator Janelle." The pale bendalian medic squinted into the viewer. "You asked to be informed when the sholan's body was claimed? Thirteen hours after security announced his death, I was visited by two men, asking to view the body. They destroyed what was left of it. A scarred shizernet and a sholan with a pronounced limp. Injury to left knee—perhaps recently dislocated. Both men escaped detention. I'm afraid they didn't leave their names. I am intrigued, and I think you should be. Please call me if you have any questions, or if I can help you in any way." The message ended as abruptly as it began.

Bicet clearly wanted his name attached to this to raise his profile, but it sounded like he'd be attentive to any questions. Worth keeping the good doctor on call.

So, Yetti's body had been destroyed. *They're cleaning up. We're running out of time.*

"Mich? You coming?" Wen called from the inner hatch.

She stared at the empty doorway. That Wen felt okay using her first name implied a familiarity she hadn't encouraged. These men were her colleagues at best. Not friends. She intended to keep them that way. Her gun lay on the bed. Black with a sleek grip designed for a smaller hand, the barrel was as long as her finger, and painted with a red stripe. She pulled the clip from her portable charger with a hand that no longer shook and slammed it home. Fully armed, she slid the weapon into her waistband and searched her bag for her holster. If she was going to do this, it would be better to do it visibly armed.

*

The storage bay was dank, dark and there was an odor she couldn't identify floating like a rotten cloud above the cracked flash-crete. She gagged as they walked through it, and had the awful feeling her clothing would carry the stench for days.

Water stains from the leaking roof coated every wall, and flash-crete panels were crumbling or just plain missing everywhere she looked. It was easy to pinpoint the parts of the bay that were pre-war era; many of the loadbearing walls were still scarred with damage from large-scale, ship-based weaponry. *Why would Yetti store the spikes here?* She wasn't exactly sure why anyone would store anything here.

She was still fuming that Charley went to the bar. The two men had actually flipped a rikki card for it. Mich had been the prize for the loser. She'd argued it but the decision had been made. Wen trusted that his partner had control. Mich didn't. Her opinion didn't matter. Wen clearly had control issues. He hadn't let her come here alone. Or was that trust issues? Well, the feeling was mutual.

"Great place," Wen said. She felt his glance in her direction. As they walked, he mumbled more complaints into her ear. "I am suddenly fighting the urge to store something in here long-term. Food, maybe?"

Was he trying to make up for the blatant mistrust earlier, or for treating her like a booby prize? She had no intention of accepting his apology, as weak as it was, and continued to ignore him.

Entering the central building forced her gaze to the storage towers soaring overhead. It felt like the cracked and broken windows were glaring down at her, judging her and finding her wanting. Her skin prickled as she imagined hidden eyes, observing their every step. It was the same feeling she'd had after her release from The Clinic, the one she carried with her even now. Of course, Wen was watching her behavior too; she knew this would be her first true test. She had to prove she was capable—that she could still do her job. She straightened her shoulders. *Time to get to work.*

She headed straight for the reception desk, Wen trailing along behind her. She could practically taste his reluctance to let her lead.

It was freezing in the drafty bay and the longer they were outside, the more she felt the chill. Pulling her sleeves down over her hands, Charley's snarky comment from earlier came back to her, about her jacket being the only thing she owned. He wasn't far off the mark. Everything she'd owned had been stripped from her when she'd been committed. Right now, the jacket's familiar weight kept the rain from drenching her pull-over, and blocked out most of the bitter cold. They needed to move this inside fast, before they froze.

She pressed her wrist to the plasti-glass in front of the lone security guard who appeared at the door. The glass magnified the hologram that shot up out of her chip. She announced, "Investigators Janelle and Wen. We need information and you're going to give it to us."

The security guard blinked at them in confusion. His eyes darted from Mich to Wen and back again. "Investigators?" The guard's uniform was rumpled, like he'd recently been asleep. "There hasn't ... ha-hasn't been any trouble here. I-I-I don't understand why you—"

"It's not necessary for you to understand. We need a list of storage clients and their bay numbers."

The guard gaped at the hologram and wiped his palms against his trousers. He was nervous. *Good.* She leaned forward. "Excuse me, Mister ..."

"Themarican."

"Mr. Themarican, if you could get me those lists ..." The guard twisted from side to side, as though trying to find some-one. Mich followed his gaze. She stood alone in front of the desk. Wen had disappeared. For a moment, she steamed that he'd just up and left her. Then she figured it was good. She could handle this without his presence. A familiar peace fell over her. *I've got this.* Breathing deeply, she gestured toward a door she hoped led to an office.

"I can't get you what you want," Themarican complained.

Mich opened the door. "Try."

Chapter 14

Peering cautiously around the end of the corridor, Zeth listened. He'd heard the metallic whine of a charging weapon come from this direction, but the hallway ahead was empty. Instinct told him something here was connected to this case. A known tech smuggler using an anonymous storage bay? Come on, that raised so many red flags. He doubted this facility was wholly legit.

When sneaking away from Mich Janelle, he'd initially planned to search for a terminal to hack or an office to toss to discover what was truly going on in this storage facility. Raised voices had caught his attention and he'd swung this way instead.

At the end of the corridor, he found a section of room-sized units. He inched toward the door of the third unit down after a frustrated yell sounded from inside.

"Hojipis Telroy! What are you doing?" A hunched-over blue-gray-skinned being with a shiny bald spot shook his head at another man, who could have been his twin, only younger and with lighter hair. The man, presumably Telroy, kicked an empty container off his foot where it had clearly become stuck. It crashed into the wall and bounced back, a long dent now marring its side. "I told you not to touch anything!" A third man stepped into the doorway, his broad hunched back blocking Zeth's view of the rest of the unit.

Telnaks? What are telnaks doing on Ketal Seven? The distinctive slumped shoulders and deformed spine ridge that identified the men's planet of origin was clear even under the navy-blue coveralls they wore.

"Ah, shut up, Da. Just because you're the oldest doesn't make you the boss. The old man wants his order. Six crates of the good stuff. Six. We delivered six. Yet only five went off. Yetti cheated us and the old man."

The telnak blocking Zeth's view moved away, exposing a man dressed in a guard's uniform tied to the chair. Da raised his pistol and waved it in the guard's face.

The guard struggled against his bonds. At his feet was a small case easily large enough to hold six vials of poison. Or six spikes. Zeth held still.

Six? The number caught his attention. As did Yetti's name. *Enter now or wait?* His stomach clenched with the excitement of breaking this mission wide open, though his nerves tingled. Waiting would put the guard at risk, but that case looked promising. His gun was steady as his fingers flexed over the grip. *Wait to hear more.*

Decision made, he settled back on his haunches. Da continued. "I don't want to kill you, but I need to know where Yetti's stock is. There should be a sixth crate of Joy. The old man ordered six. I won't be cheated. The old man comes calling, I won't be the one to blame. You hear me? Where's the crate?"

Joy? That's what The Spiral Guardians called their explosives.

"Something was kept in here." Da gestured to the carry case at his feet. "Other than that. Which I will be taking as payment."

The guard shook his head. Bloody spittle trailed from a missing front tooth. Any words he might have uttered disappeared under a barrage of grunts and whistles. Raising his pistol, Da shot. Blood splattered across the unit's walls as the guard's body slumped heavily in the chair.

One, no! Zeth's mouth opened, his body coiled, ready to jump. He'd made the wrong call—again. He gritted his teeth hard enough to send a spike of pain up the side of his face. One hand dropped to brace his crouch, which had become unsteady. He swallowed hard against the nausea swelling in his throat.

Yes, he could burst in there and arrest them, and a voice that sounded suspiciously like Rel's urged, *"Take the case now. If it holds the vials, then it's mission solved."*

Surprisingly, a voice that sounded a little like Mich Janelle countered that argument. *"It's too late to help the guard now. Focus on the mission. Follow them. They'll lead you to the old man."*

Zeth's logical mind told him Mich was right. He'd wait it out and follow the telnaks back to their base. He settled back, eyes narrowing as he committed their appearances to memory.

"Dead men don't tell us what we need to know, Da," the third telnak muttered. He hovered behind the smaller man, his hands flexing as his gaze swung from Da to the guard and back again.

"He wasn't gonna tell us anything, Parra. He didn't know nothing."

"You sure?" Telroy asked.

Da bent to pick up the sealed case. "This is probably worth something to someone. Let's go."

Zeth ducked back and scampered along the line of units until he reached the corner. Behind him, the telnaks exited the unit.

Waiting a few moments, Zeth went after them.

*

"Play it through again, slowly." Rel pointed to the images frozen on the display screens covering most of the wall. One showed the split-vision of two camera angles from inside The Dive. The second showed both sides of the street outside. Four cameras, four angles—it'd have to be enough.

He'd arrived at The Dive an hour earlier, shoving his holo-gram identifier under the nose of the bar's supervisor, a long-bearded dwarf, and demanded access to the surveillance footage. After a beat, the dwarf capitulated and brought him to the security room above the bar. Rel's mouth was dry, prod-ding him to head downstairs. He fought the urge and ordered the footage from a week ago, rolling back until he located Yetti's exit on the day he must have been shot. He watched the sholan stumble as the tape reversed. Dresh, he recognized the signs: Yetti was drunk, almost blindingly so. He played the footage forward, examining the women standing with Yetti. One was blond, one was brunette and both were dressed in tight clothing that exposed a lot of skin. They clutched Yetti's furry shoulders and struggled to hold him upright as he me-andered through the bar. A waitress in a little black dress stood in the far corner serving a drink to a slumped-over woman. As Rel watched, another sholan—one with long silver-streaked hair—rose from a table in the back and exited after Yetti, limp-ing badly. *Interesting. Yetti's being followed.*

Rotating his finger in the air, he waited for the dwarf to replay the recording. Slouching in the chair, Rel observed the moment Yetti's grainy image—sober—entered the bar all the way through to his drunken exit. The tech thief, in mud-splattered trousers and a black jacket, sat at a table close to the counter and appeared happy to talk to anyone who would listen. The worst sort of barfly.

Fifteen minutes in, Rel watched the silver-haired limping sholan dressed in khakis and a tall humanoid in a flower print monstrosity of a shirt enter the bar. They made their way to a table in the back, with a clear line of sight to where Yetti sat drinking.

The waitress reappeared, moving through the bar handing out drinks and retrieving empty glasses. She touched many of the patrons as she passed, and was spoken to by all. Evidently, she was well-known to all of The Dive's regulars.

A cleaner bot moved too close to a table at the rear and, with a flash of light, toppled backward. The two men were armed and not afraid to use their weapons, it seemed. *Res it— who are these guys?*

Rel skimmed forward through the next few hours of footage, ordering the dwarf to stop the tape just as Yetti rose and tripped before weaving his way toward the back room.

He focused in on the gray-haired sholan at the rear table. He was speaking into his hand. A little further into the footage, a tall shizernet with a large scar across his eye entered the bar and walked directly to the table, kicking the cleaner bot away as he approached. Though he couldn't make out the man's thick, scaled skin from the camera's blurred image, it flared under the bar's fluorescent lighting, a clear sign of his race. The waitress darted forward to drag the bot behind the counter. The dwarf who was now sitting beside Rel appeared on the screen and helped the waitress move the bot away.

The dwarf mumbled mournfully, "T'was a good bot, that one. Barely required maintenance and never dropped a bottle."

On the screen, Yetti stumbled into view, each arm wrapped around a woman.

Rel gestured for the dwarf to pause the footage. *What does that resing shizernet have in his hand?* He requested to play the tape forward. The shizernet raised his hand. "Go back." Yetti and the women wavered past and the shizernet brought his hand up. Yetti faltered.

The image was too grainy. Rel turned to the dwarf. "I need this vision." Maybe he could clear it up using *Lazydragon*'s specialist equipment.

Rel took over and replayed the footage one more time, clicking through frame by frame. He held his breath as he leaned close to the screen.

One thing was clear enough: Yetti lurched *after* the shizernet's hand rose.

Dresh! I need a drink.

*

Mich's foot tapped rapidly as she waited for Themarican to locate the correct keycard. He sorted through his large ring of cards with meticulous care. She wanted to rip the ring from his hand and find it herself. Or pull out her gun, shove it up his nostrils and demand answers. What she really wanted to know was where the hell Wen had disappeared to. Instead, she waited with increasing impatience for the guard to find the damned keycard.

"I'm not supposed to do this," he grumbled worriedly. All right, she got it, he wasn't happy, and her presence was putting him further on edge. That his first assumption was that she'd resort to lethal force told her a lot about the usual clientele. Being polite and understanding might work faster. She backed up a few steps to give the man breathing room.

Themarican found the keycard and swiped open the office door.

Forcing a smile, she asked in a soft voice, "I am sorry for the trouble, but can you access the system files for me?"

He frowned, tugging on the door sharply when it jammed against the swollen wooden frame. "I can switch the damned machine on for you, but I don't know how to work it."

She nodded. You couldn't expect the holo-badge to get you everything.

Not a paper, disk, folder, comm unit or quill was to be seen inside the empty office. Peachy-cream walls mirrored the ceiling and the floor. Even the console and chair were the same pale color. Themarican thumbed on the terminal. It was the only item on the desk. At least there was a terminal.

"Can I go?" he asked, scratching his chest. He peered toward the door.

Assuming he had to return to duty or catch up on his sleep or do whatever it was he did on his shift, she was surprised when he added, "I need to check on my partner."

Her face grew cold as all heat fled her body. "There's someone else here?"

Themarican nodded. Maybe Wen had gone in search of the other guard? *But how did he know there was a second man?* While she pondered her temporary partner's absence, Themarican took the opportunity to leave.

The terminal beeped, drawing her attention to the screen. Mich decided to find the guard after she retrieved the unit number, it was the reason they were here after all. A flashing dialogue box asked for a ten-character password.

There was nothing in the room to give her a clue to what it might be. She had little to go on to help her hack the program, knowing she couldn't just enter random numbers or letters; the system undoubtedly had a security check in place, where the wrong attempt would shut it down.

Searching the desk's double set of drawers, she found nothing. She'd never come across a completely paperless office before. The entire client list must be kept on this computer, and it didn't appear backups were kept on the premises.

On a whim, she reached under the desk and ran her fingers along the edge. With a gasp, she snatched her fingers back and stuck the middle one in her mouth. Pulling it out, she examined it closely. A faint angry red line crossed the pad. As it bled, she reached back under the desk and tugged the assaulting piece of paper from its hiding spot. *Well, wouldn't you know it; a manager with a bad memory.*

She entered the mix of letters and numbers and the storage database unfolded before her eyes. Within seconds, she found Yetti's details. A folder on the desktop rewarded her search with the master code to all of the bay's security grills. She closed the file as Themarican stumbled back in, his face a sickly pallor.

"Don't concern yourself. I've found what I came for," she told him, hoping to forestall any complaints.

"My partner's been shot."

Mich jumped to her feet. "What? Is he still alive?" Themarican shook his head. "Where is he?" She prayed Wen had nothing to do with this. It would be a lot harder to get answers from a dead man.

Themarican pointed vaguely back the way he'd come.

"Show me," she demanded.

Chapter 15

By the time the guard pointed his wavering finger at the right door, Mich's heart was racing. The storage unit belonged to Yetti. This couldn't be a coincidence.

The space inside was empty, save for a squished box and the body of a man dressed in the same security uniform Themarican wore. The back of his head was blown clean away. Mich glanced at it once, then fixed her eyes firmly on the far wall. She twisted back to look at Themarican. "What was kept in this room?"

The guard shook his head. He'd grown paler during the run to the bay. There was now a perceptible quiver in his shoulders. "Who would ... why ...?"

She had no words for the man. A patch of brighter white near the dead guard's chair pointed to something being stored in here for a long time. The patch was a rectangle, about the length of her forearm. "What was his name?"

"Who? I don't know who killed him." Themarican's voice trembled. "Where's your partner? How do I know he didn't do this?"

"Your friend's name?" Mich pointed to the body. "My partner didn't shoot your colleague." She forced herself to look at the wound. "This was done by a 1.75mm laser pistol or higher. Wen carries a 0.55." The blood spatter triggered another flash of memory. *Blood dripped from a knife over her fingers and soaked into the bedding. The body on the bed stared up at her blankly.* Mich turned her face to the wall while her head cleared, blinking rapidly to dispel the image. Blood seemed to trigger her memories, and now was not the time to become distracted.

"His name is—was—Ketrau, Marcino Ketrau."

She nodded. "I'm sorry for your loss, sir. I suggest you call in the local authorities."

With a shaking nod, Themarican stumbled from the room. As soon as he was gone, Mich sagged against the wall. To avoid her gaze falling on the body again, she closed her eyes. *Two bodies in less than a week.* There was no detectable smell; blood shone where it pooled around Ketrau, and still dripped slowly from the man's body. He hadn't been dead long. Back in the storage bay office she hadn't heard a thing. The murderer might still be on the premises. Close by. Watching her.

She opened her eyes on the ankles of the slumped figure, telling herself she should get up and search the building for the shooter. She needed to find her missing partner and locate the security footage from the bay's entrance.

She didn't move.

Whatever Yetti had kept in here must have been important. Why kill the guard in such a brutal manner otherwise? Ketrau would've carried the master key to all the bays, just as Themarican did. "What did you keep in here?" she murmured.

"A carry case."

The answer came from the doorway. She didn't jump or otherwise show her surprise, though it was a near thing. Her reaction no doubt disappointed Wen. She circled her head in his direction. "What carry case?" Her question was quickly followed by another. "What happened to you?"

Wen glanced down at his torn, sopping wet clothing. His vest was gone, and his shirt was sliced open at the shoulder, where a bloody scratch showed beneath. He limped into the bay and stopped beside the dead guard. Crossing his hand over his chest, he closed his eyes and muttered a brief prayer. After a moment of silence, he opened his eyes and hobbled toward Mich, shifting his body to lean against the wall. Once he stopped moving he was like a statue. No fidgeting or twitching. No part of him moved.

She wanted to shake him for not telling her where he was going. She didn't move either.

"If you were wondering what used to be stored in here"— Wen pointed to the patch of white floor—"It was a carry case. Before you ask, I don't know what was in it." He looked at the dead man. "I saw the guys who killed him. Three telnaks. I followed them toward an orange stone fruit plantation east of here. It's not far."

"Telnaks? What are telnaks doing on Ketal Seven?" She shook her head. That wasn't important. "Where'd they go then?"

He glanced away. "I also lost them at the orange stone fruit plantation."

Mich's stomach twisted sharply. "I don't remember seeing telnaks with Yetti." If Yetti had stored the spikes or the poison here, then the missing telnaks had it now.

"They supplied Yetti with several crates of explosives. They think Yetti cheated them. They took the case."

"Don't move!" A shout through the open doorway had Wen drawing his pistol and turning on the figures standing there. Mich's head snapped up as her hand dropped to her gun.

Four men stormed into the unit. Dressed in the cerulean uniforms of the Skein City Security force, three of the four men wore a single bar on their right bicep. Their weapons swung toward Wen, becoming their immediate threat. Mich raised a hand toward the Coordinator, the one with the senior stripes. "Relax, we're the good guys. I'm Mich Janelle; the guy with the pistol is Zeth Wen. We're private investigators with the Daeh Agency. We're the ones who found the body."

Instead of lowering their weapons, the officers swung them at her. *Well that's promising.* She waited silently. Wen remained still, his weapon held steady. For a long moment, no one moved.

The Coordinator's eyes narrowed and he stretched out a hand. "Identification?"

Mich inched her fingers toward her wrist. She made sure to keep her movements slow and her hands visible as she activated her chip's hologram.

Beside her, Wen flashed his own hologram. One of the junior officers approached and scanned each wrist for confirmation. The stalemate between the officers and the investigators continued as the Coordinator examined the holograms carefully. "Clearance number?"

Wincing inwardly, Mich realized she should have told Wen that Daeh had not given her a full clearance number. Now was not the time to explain why not. "Go ahead," she said.

Wen's brows drew together and he stared at her intently as he rattled off his code. The same junior officer entered the information into his scanner, and there was another long, tense pause until the device emitted a high-pitched affirmation. The officers relaxed and holstered their weapons. Wen waited a moment longer before he put his away in one slick movement.

Both investigators were escorted from the unit and told to wait while the officers sealed the scene. Mich acknowledged the order with a soft groan. Wen buzzed Charley's comm. Charley didn't answer. Once they were alone and before Wen could speak, Mich said, "After we've given our statements, we need to check out that plantation and find that carry case."

"I'll go. You keep the meeting with Rel. He'll expect one of us, and I'm the only one who saw the telnaks."

She didn't agree with the plan to split up—a telnak was a telnak, after all, and three of them together wouldn't be hard to find—but Charley was not answering his comm. One of them had to go get him. Staying together at this point was a bad move. "I don't like the idea of you going in without backup."

He snorted. "From what I understand, you used to do it all the time."

"Yes, but I always worked solo. You're *used* to backup."

He gave her a long look.

Sighing, she said, "Keep a communications buzz open. After I've collected Charley, we'll follow you."

"Good luck convincing him to leave the bar. If he's dug in, you won't get him out easily."

She knew she should have raised her concerns with Wen that morning when he let Charley investigate The Dive. She'd been right not to trust the man. Now she had to drag a drunk man twice her weight out of a bar. *Great.*

*

Separated from Wen as soon as they entered the security center, Mich was put into a small interview room. When the door shut behind her with a solid *thunk*, her neck began to itch. They'd better not keep her here long. She worked on slowing her breathing, not wanting to let on just how badly the size of the room bothered her. No matter how determined her will, her breathing sped up. She pinched hard at the inside of her wrist. Pain radiated to her hand. Closing her eyes, she focused on the sting to drive the music in her mind back into the darkness.

Her eyes snapped open when the door creaked. A woman, younger than Mich, stood in the doorway. She was thinly built with straight black hair scraped tight into a ponytail. Her uniform was perfectly tailored with nary a wrinkle. The badge on her left breast named her Welks. She looked too young to be running Mich's interrogation, but maybe that was because Mich felt so old and tired.

"Your name?" Welks's voice was hard and cold, and her heels made a sharp clacking sound as she strode inside. She sat down, keeping her back impossibly straight, and stared Mich directly in the eyes.

"You've already seen my holo and the clearance code my partner gave checked out. Are you really going to play this game?" Mich groaned inwardly when the woman didn't blink.

"Your name?" she repeated. Her voice implied she could do this all day.

Yeah, well, we'll see about that. "Michele Janelle."

"Why are you on Ketal Seven, Janelle?"

"Working a case." Mich stilled her fingers. The other woman would be examining Mich's body language for clues. She knew her shoulders were a tense line and her muscles were clenched too tight, betraying her discomfort at her situation. Well, that was obvious. She wasn't happy.

"What case?"

Mich bared her teeth in a grin and forced her body to relax, slouching back in her chair. *Make her think you don't care how long you're kept here.* "That's confidential."

"How long have you been on Ketal Seven?"

"That's confidential, too." Welks could look it up by checking the Skein City's travel hub logs, of course. Which, if she was any kind of decent investigator, she'd have already done.

The woman didn't flinch under Mich's stare. "How long do you intend to stay on Ketal Seven?"

"I'm afraid that's confidential." *How long to drive this woman completely crazy?* Mich guessed a few hours, then made a bet with herself that she could make it sooner.

"Janelle, you are not being helpful." Welks's eyes narrowed. *First slip.* "I am merely trying to establish ..."

"That's confidential too."

"What is?" Welks blew out a breath and put her hands on the table. *Second slip.*

Mich mirrored her actions, leaning forward to press her fingers to the polished surface of the interrogation table.

"Whatever your next question is going to be. And the one after that, and the one after that."

Welks clenched her hands, her lips thinned. "Janelle ..."

"I am not authorized to provide you with the details. What's your security chief's name?" She hid her smile as the woman's eyes widened.

"My chief's name does not concern—"

"It does if I'm to inform my boss how you're wasting my time instead of assisting me and my team."

Welks's face flushed. "Janelle, I think we both can guess what my chief will think about wasting your time. I can sit here all day and ask you these questions."

That's it. Try and get control back. The threat didn't bother Mich, though the thought of being trapped in this room all day ate at her projected calm. She pushed the uncomfortable feeling deep inside her mind. Private investigators were not liked by local planetary police forces—their lack of authority and the fact that their very presence tended to end in violence meant they were not usually happy coworkers.

Welks would keep her here if she thought it would cause Mich trouble. Mich could have argued. Could demand they work together, that lives were at stake, but she had no real evidence—not yet. All she was, was annoyed. She kept her breathing steady. *Don't show it.*

"Why were you at the Keepstation?"

She'd been wondering when Welks's questions would get to the storage bay. Suppressing another smirk, she replied, "I'm afraid that's confidential."

"Janelle!" Welks snapped, her nostrils flaring.

"Yes, officer?"

"Did you murder Marcino Ketrau?"

"No."

The woman straightened, as if sensing a breakthrough. *Poor thing.* "A direct answer?"

"Officer Welks, while I cannot give you information about my current case, I can confirm neither myself nor my partner shot Marcino Ketrau." It was a struggle not to roll her eyes at the desperation pouring off the woman. Welks had finally got an answer, and she wanted more.

"So, Ketrau was just an innocent bystander?"

"Yes."

"Did you see who shot Ketrau?"

"No." Well, it was the truth. *She* hadn't seen who shot Ketrau, and Welks hadn't asked about Wen.

"Why was Marcino Ketrau murdered?"

"I don't know."

"What was kept in the storage bay Marcino Ketrau was murdered in?"

"I don't know." To be fair, she wasn't trying to be annoying now ... well, not entirely. If the officer had asked if the storage unit had something to do with Mich's investigation, she would have told her yes, it did. Welks just hadn't asked the right question.

"Tell me about your partner."

What does that have to do with anything? "He's not my partner."

Welks's head tilted to the side as she examined Mich's response. She rose up out of her seat and leaned forward over the table, staring intently. "A moment ago, you said otherwise."

Mich sighed inwardly. How did she explain this without raising even more questions? "Technically, he is my partner. Temporarily. Zeth Wen already has a partner. I was asked to assist them on this case only."

"Who is this other partner? Is he here in Skein City?"

"His name is Rel Charley and he is currently investigating another location."

"Which is where?"

"I'm afraid that's confidential." Mich almost let her grin escape at the woman's exasperated expression.

Welks sank back into her chair. "What do you think of Zeth Wen?"

"What?" Mich's surprise at the question must have shown on her face. The woman pressed, as if scenting blood.

"Do you trust Wen? You've already said he was in the storage unit before you got there. How can you be so sure he didn't kill Ketrau?"

Well, that was an interesting question. She didn't know him, not really. She was being forced to work with him and his partner, but that did not mean she trusted him. To trust, she needed evidence and that would only come with time. She didn't plan on working with either man that long. "What reason would Wen have to kill Ketrau?"

"Are you planning to be of any help at all?" Mich could see little beads forming around the edges of the poor woman's hairline. "Let's go back to the start, shall we?"

Mich didn't hold back her frustrated sigh. As promised, she was going to be here all day at this rate.

Chapter 16

Rel was up to his elbows in trouble. Not an unusual state for him really. Two bodies lay unconscious at his feet. Luckily, in a place like this, folk didn't usually make much of a fuss over things like that.

The three men across the room seemed to have a problem with it, though. The one on the right, the one who'd started this mess, was a tall, skinny ketallian. Tiny eyes narrowed, making them even smaller. He looked like a walking broom. Rel chuckled at that image. The man stepped forward only to have his companions pull him back. If the front man was a broom, then that made the men behind him the dustpan and the trashcan.

"Pick 'em up and res off," Rel told them. He grinned wildly when his words emerged with barely a hint of alcoholic slur. The men glared, their hands hovering near their belted weapons.

Rel didn't blink.

At last, their hands fell open and they inched forward to pick up their fallen friends.

Once the door closed behind them, Rel allowed his shoulders to drop. He tugged his jacket tighter around his body; the chill was back. The warmth that filled him during a fight never lasted long these days. In his head, he heard the names again. The icy feeling he was so familiar with flowed over his skin.

"You're not here to drink and fight," Zeth's voice reminded him. His partner's advice often played on repeat in the back of his mind. *"You have a job to do."* But as he gazed into the empty bottle, he recognized it for the lost cause it was. The most important question at this point was whether or not to buy another drink, and that was decided for him when a fresh bottle appeared at his elbow. He raised his head, the dismissal dying in his throat as he ogled the woman standing at his side.

Tight around her chest, the charcoal dress flowed like water over her hips. Long, dark hair caressed her shoulders and floated around her elfin face, inviting touch. It was the waitress he'd seen in the surveillance footage. She was far prettier than the video had suggested. She watched Rel through pink eyes highlighted with shimmering turquoise and pushed the fresh bottle, glistening with moisture, closer to his fingers.

He wrapped his hand around the beer and slugged half of the contents. The yeasty smell lingered in his nostrils. "Thanks." The woman sat and quirked him a smile. Rel asked her name.

In response, she pointed to her pretty mouth and shook her head. Her hands danced as she signed something.

Heat drifted up over his face. "Don't understand."

From a pocket, she pulled a data pad and a scratch pen. He figured the basic tech would work well enough in a place like this. It wasn't like she'd be called upon to talk much. She bit her lip and scribbled quickly, *Can't talk.* Beneath it, she added: *How did those men offend you?*

Rel lowered his voice. "Why can't ya talk?"

Avoiding the question! accused the pad in reply.

"Ya don't want ta know," he told her, handing the pad back.

Now that he had the chance to examine her closely, he realized her made-up face had deceived him. The genuine lack of fine lines around her eyes and mouth suggested she was younger than he'd first thought. What was a woman like her doing in a place like this? He estimated she was the same height as Mich Janelle, but unlike the investigator, this woman didn't have the strength or ability to protect herself. She smiled, ducking her head as if embarrassed by his scrutiny and let out a tiny silent chuckle. That's when he spotted the unnatural shadow inside her mouth.

Resing hell! He reeled back in horror as realization dawned. The woman's tongue was gone.

She sobered quickly, watching his reaction warily, staring up into his eyes. Tongue-pulling was only done on criminal children or slaves. He wanted to know who had done this to her and why, but held back. She wasn't looking for sympathy or a handout, touching his fist with gentle fingers. There was something genuine in her face when she looked at him. Something innocent and sad, something understanding. It reminded him of another time and another woman. One he missed with every aching beat of his heart. To his surprise, he found himself telling her about the disagreement and why it had escalated. The stolen seat which led to a push, the push to a shove and then name-calling had begun—"chammy" and "drizerd" were the ones he'd finally lost his temper over. The group wanted a fight, and Rel had happily obliged.

The names made you angry?

He handed the pad back. "Well, I'm not happy about 'em." He'd heard versions of the names all his life. His earliest memories involved being kicked around the backstreets of Heolden City by the schoolyard bullies, of the bruises and ruined clothing, of the recognition that he was different. It wasn't until he was older that he'd understood the hatred for him was misplaced hatred for his father, the general of the draal Eighth Fleet and leader of the forces that had occupied Heolden City, the capital of Rel's home world, Keltar Prime. When Keltar Prime was liberated at the end of the war, Rel had been left behind with the other half-draal children, and he'd never been allowed to forget his heritage. Even now, eighteen years after the occupation, the abuse suffered by occupation children was rife.

Of course, Melita hadn't cared about any of that. Memories of her loving smile swept over him and he cursed again for her loss. Shaking the melancholy thoughts from his head, he refocused on the waitress. She held out her pad again for him to read.

Why were you upset?

He shrugged, slamming his heart shut, and swallowed another mouthful of beer. Enough of this. The young woman continued to write, her hand moving rapidly. His head was buzzing, whether from the lights, the noise and the alcohol or from her, he couldn't determine. Had she drugged him? He was drawn to her—not just to her looks, though she was pretty enough. He wanted to know her story. To see her as she had seen him. Guilt cramped his stomach. How could he think about this young woman this way? Melita was his one true love. His only love. He rubbed a hand against his chest.

The waitress looked at him quizzically. His blood heated and his face flushed with shame. *Would Melita understand?* It had been so long since he'd felt a gentle touch. He found he wanted to prolong their conversation, as one-sided as it was.

She tapped the pad and he glanced down. *Why did they anger you? They were words, names. Ultimately, they mean nothing.*

Rel opened his mouth, but the waitress held a finger to his lips and pointed back to the pad, swiping up to move the page.

Your anger is misplaced if the words themselves caused such pain.

"It's who I am," he told her, staring at the pad for so long, she tightened her grip on his hand. His silence sat like a block in his throat. He'd only spoken about this to Zeth and, of course, Melita. He didn't know this woman—maybe that was why he felt like opening up? Her judgment wouldn't matter, and he had no plans to see her again.

He didn't meet her eyes as he spoke, focusing his gaze onto the brown glass of the bottle he'd just drained. His voice was only a whisper as he told her of his draal father. He noticed her flinch—a familiar reaction. Zeth had reacted the same way when Rel first confirmed his parentage, but unlike anyone else Rel had ever met, Zeth had told him to get over it, and stoically took the punches Rel had subsequently thrown. Zeth had thrown a few of his own back, accusing him of hitting like a three-legged pantac.

Zeth understood Rel like few ever had. As a result, Rel would do anything for the man.

Another squeeze brought him back to the bar. The woman had written more. *It's hard to be different.*

Suddenly uncomfortable with the certainty he'd told her way too much, he handed the pad back and clambered un-steadily to his feet. The waitress grabbed his arm, her mouth moving angrily when he tried to pull away.

I can help you, if you'll let me.

"What d'ya mean?"

I watch things. Two bottles appeared on the table as her words disappeared from the pad. *You're searching for something. I can help you find it.*

Rel looked at her with renewed interest. A woman like her would have great value in a place like this. Unable to speak, some men would think she also didn't understand. And with the loss of one sense, her others would be stronger. Her body language skills proved that already. His instant attraction led to him opening up to her in a way he would never have done normally. Was she playing with him? He ran their conversation back through his fuzzy mind. He'd said nothing confidential, but he was suddenly aware of the danger he was in. Warily, he asked again, "What d'ya mean?"

Who are you looking for?

Res it. How had she figured out he was searching for someone? He hadn't activated his hologram. He lowered his voice, feeling exposed. "D'ya remember everyone who comes through here?"

She took a sip of her drink, her throat fighting hard to swallow down the thick liquid as she wrote one word: *Everyone?*

"A week and a bit ago, a large red-haired man from Shol. Left with two women. D'ya remember him?"

Her eyes narrowed as her face took on a faraway look. *Talks a lot? His name is Yetti?*

"That's him." Rel leaned closer.

Yes, we all know him.

"What else d'ya remember?"

He was sweaty.

His eyes widened. "Sweaty?"

Like he was nervous. He kept checking over his shoulder and such.

"Scared?"

She shrugged. *Yes and no.*

Ambiguous to say the least. The woman's eyes suddenly darted to every corner of the bar. She wrote quickly. *Put your arm around me and stand up. Act drunk. We have to go.*

Curiosity had him doing as she requested. He stumbled to his feet and dropped an arm around her waist. Slurring his words with a raised voice, he said, "Let's go then, sweetheart." Holding onto the woman, Rel's hand soaked up her warmth. It spread along his fingers, up his arm and burrowed into his chest. His face heated again and his next stumble was not entirely faked. *Be careful, Rel.*

He let the waitress lead him to a room at the rear of the bar. There, he found an exit behind several stacked storage crates. As they moved into the shadows, there was a yell behind him and the sound of pistol fire. The yell became a scream, and the front room erupted in chaos. Rel pulled the waitress to a halt and glanced back. The woman caught his indecision. She tugged on his hand lightly, pulling him into a doorway where there was a stairwell, leading down into the darkness.

Hesitating, he glanced back. *How had she known the room would erupt like that?* He turned to stare past her into the pitch-black doorway. Her hand clenched around his fingers— her palm almost scalding his skin. Behind him came the unmistakable slap of fists against skin. A glass shattered and wood cracked. Rel nodded.

Fingering the weapon at his waistband, he quickly followed the waitress into the tunnel's gaping maw.

Chapter 17

All light disappeared. *Resing hell.* The heady scent of the waitress' flowery perfume danced around Rel in the darkness. The warmth of her hand was his anchor. She seemed to know exactly where she was going, and led him further into the dark. Rel had trusted her so far this evening, he figured he might as well trust her to get him to the other end safely, though he kept his hand on his weapon the whole way.

And plowed into her when she suddenly stopped. Faded light trickled in through wall cracks, highlighting the outline of a door. The woman opened it and tugged him inside.

"And who do we have here?" a high-pitched voice squealed in delight. Two clammy hands pulled Rel from his voiceless companion straight into bright light.

Rel's vision blurred as he threw his arms up to shield his face. He blinked rapidly, head dizzy from the light and the smell of ... flowers? When his vision cleared, he found the voice originated from an older, heavier-set woman dressed head-to-toe in purple. Looking over her head, he was confronted with a room full of lavender lamps and lilac furniture. The chairs looked soft, with pillows and over-stuffed cushions galore. Hallways branched off in multiple directions and he could make out a number of doors spaced evenly along each corridor. *Despro take it!* The waitress had brought him into the bar's adjoining brothel.

Now he wished he had drawn his weapon; he might have to shoot his way out.

The madam ogled him in delight and squealed again, running her fingers along his arms. "What a man, what a man." As suddenly as she'd grabbed him, she let him go and spun around with a flourish, "Carma, darling, wherever did you find him?" The waitress, Carma, grunted and pointed toward the ceiling.

The woman grinned at Rel. "My name is Sima. Welcome to my House. Come in, dear boy. No need to be nervous, no one here will bite ... well, unless you ask them to, darling. Now, do you want to view a list, or do you want them to come out one by one?"

"I ain't ..."

Sima pushed him into an over-padded armchair situated close to the fireplace. It was so close to the flames, he was honestly shocked the material hadn't ignited.

Carma clutched the woman's flabby arm and pointed to her own chest.

"Darling, he doesn't want you," Sima scolded, gently lifting the waitress's hand away.

"Yeah, I do," Rel said, dragging himself from the hot, confining chair.

Sima's brows arched high, but Rel stared her down and waited. "Into disability, are you? Very well." Sima sniffed and reached into the drawer beside her chair. She removed a yellow swipe card and pointed to the timepiece above her head. "Payment is forty per half rotation."

Carma latched onto Rel's wrist and led him down the nearest corridor. Unlocking the third door, she gestured inside and glared back down the corridor at Sima. The madam watched her with suspicious eyes.

The moment the door closed, Rel pointed. "Yourra trick? I said I needed help, but not that way. I can get a woman on my own, ya know." He knew he sounded petulant when he reiterated, "Really."

With a grunt, Carma pushed him onto the nearby bed. He grabbed her waist to stop her, but she pushed him back aggressively. Just as he relaxed into the feel of her soft body pressed tight to his, she pushed out of his grip and removed her data pad from a hidden pocket.

This is only in case Sima walks in. We have to talk and this is the only private place I know.

Rel read her words and flopped onto his back. Now that he'd held her, he could only think of her as a warm, full-bodied woman. She smirked at him and Melita's face flashed into his mind. "Go ahead," he said, keeping his voice low. He wasn't sure how thin the walls might be. In his head, he could hear Melita laughing her ass off at him.

Carma climbed off his legs—much to his disappointment—and lay down at his side. She held the data pad above his face and angled the screen. *Yetti was here last week.*

He could tell her Yetti was dead, but held back; better to find out what she knew first. The woman rested the pad on her knee to write, while her other hand rubbed her throat unconsciously. He focused on her lips as she mouthed her words. Leaning into her side, he watched them appear on the screen.

Yetti tells the same story every time he comes in. He buys a lot of shem-milk and talks to anyone who will listen. He gets one of Sima's women for the night, sometimes two, but he always takes them back to his place. He never stays here.

"What kind of party-worker goes with a sholan?" Rel asked. Shem-milk was extremely intoxicating, and the men from Shol were not exactly known for their gentleness. He was surprised the tricks went with Yetti at all.

Carma shrugged. *He pays well.*

Rel wanted to ask how she knew that, but figured he wouldn't like the answer. She watched him intently, as if waiting for that very question. When he didn't voice it, she gazed at him curiously.

The women never stay long.

He didn't find that strange at all, and said so.

Carma shook her head. *Not with Yetti, with Sima. The women come back from Yetti's apartment the next morning, but a few days later, they disappear.*

Dragging his body off the bed, Rel paced to the wall. That didn't sound good.

She tossed him the data pad. *Last week, there was a storm, worse than usual, and it brought a lot of nasty characters into the bar. There were two men waiting for Yetti; a man with a white scar across his eye, scaly skin and sharp nails. The other man had yellow eyes. I've never seen them before and they've not been back since. They sat at a table with another sholan. They watched Yetti all night.*

That confirmed what he'd seen on the surveillance footage. The waitress was pretty observant. Again she reminded him of Melita. So resing smart, yet determined to hide it. This woman was more than this place. So why did she stay? He thought of her missing tongue. Perhaps she had no choice. He handed the pad back. "Did these men ask about Yetti specifically?"

She shook her head, writing quickly. *I don't think he knew they were there.*

"Why d'ya notice them?"

Her shudder answered the question. *They scared me. They killed a cleaner bot when he moved too close to their table, and he was only doing his job. I didn't like the way they watched Yetti. I was afraid for Sophie and Terri—the two who went with him that night.*

"The women okay?" Rel sat down on the bed with his back to the mute woman.

She held out the pad. *They are the only ones to leave with Yetti and still be working for Sima.*

"Well, that's odd," he said. "Can I talk to them?"

The data pad fell to Rel's lap as Carma leaned over his shoulder and pressed her lips to his neck. He read her demand as she snaked her hands under his arms, stroking his chest lightly.

"Not the payment I had in mind," he said. She pulled him close and lay back on the bed. He kissed Carma passionately and rolled to pin her beneath him.

He hoped Melita would forgive him.

*

Zeth stretched to relieve the tension headache gathering at the base of his neck. No doubt Rel was drinking himself into a coma while Zeth was stuck in the rear tray of a crop carrier, squished between some foul-smelling orange balls of fruit and the unrelenting steel floor. He couldn't shake his lingering annoyance at his interrogation by the local authorities. They'd hit him with question after question about how he'd found the security guard's body and the telnaks he'd accused of doing the actual murder. The locals didn't want to believe him. He saw it in the stubborn officer's eyes and in the flash of his teeth. Still, they'd let him go, though they were probably tracking him somehow. Zeth hadn't spotted any eyes following him, but he could feel them. Even through the walls of this carrier. He wondered if Janelle had got out yet or if she was still being questioned.

Orange dust choked him every time the vehicle hit a thicker pocket of air, sending dust bouncing up off the tray and into his face. There was a canopy over his head, so at least he was out of the rain. A small comfort.

Grousing to himself, he cursed Mich for making the choice to go after Rel seem the less appealing option, driving Zeth to choose the opposite. Res his ego; he should have gone after Rel. Zeth spent the next half standard inside the sickly sweet-smelling metal tray. With a jerk hard enough to throw him into the wall, again, the hovertruck juddered to a stop. Hobbling out, Zeth thanked the driver through gritted teeth. It was a tremendous acting job, he thought, as the carrier rumbled away, spitting a muddy gravel shower at him in farewell.

He rubbed his bruised rear and surveyed the sodden road. Rain beat down on his skin, turning the orange dust into a wet paste as he eyed the large wall surrounding the plantation. Fortunately, the carrier left him just outside the gated entrance. He peered through the bars at the growing produce. Each orange-tipped stalk towered over his head by a few feet. In the distance, Zeth could just make out three flat-topped sheds at the other end. He hesitated; the crop might appear passive but from his earlier encounter, he knew how dangerous those stalks truly were. The edge of each umbrella-sized leaf was razor-sharp. His chest still stung where he'd been slashed during his earlier aborted run. If he went in via the main gate, he'd have to announce his presence and give his identification. He didn't want to give the telnaks any chance to escape. He winced at the memory of the dead guard's vacant gaze. He owed the man retribution. Failure to track the telnaks was not an option. Besides, if they had the poison this was his chance to stop them before more people were killed. *Sneak in it is.*

Every time the wind blew, Zeth was forced to duck and weave to avoid the jagged edges brushing his face. He didn't always dodge fast enough. The blade-edged leaves sliced at his skin with eye-watering intensity. The incessant rain lightened to a drizzle, and in the sudden quiet, a familiar sound reached his ears, a soft buzz pulsing gently against the exposed skin of his face and neck.

Someone was flying over the field.

Zeth crouched. Sharp leaves whipped dangerously overhead as the vibration increased. He gripped the closest stalk and held his breath as the carrier crossing the field stopped directly above him.

Zeth stayed low, an immobile figure beneath the leaves gyrating in a frenzy under the down-blast of the pulse engine. The vehicle gave a mechanical groan and shuddered before it continued off across the field. With the scent of wet dirt in his nostrils, Zeth crawled through the mud, alert to any sound of the carrier's return. The telnaks better be at the end of this resing nightmare. If he'd gone through all of this to find they'd already left, he'd be pissed.

*

Three men waited inside the small office with growing impatience. The large gray sholan with tiny eyes swiped his hands over the interface to the large wall board, trying to find the game. Stupid machine wasn't registering his request.

"How long?" The demand was hissed from the scaly man in the corner.

The third man turned sharp yellow eyes on his partner and watched his clawed fingers flex. "Soon."

The sholan, fed up with his lack of progress, flung the small panel interface across the room, letting out a loud growl as it shattered on impact. "Why are we here? Where is he?"

As the words left his mouth the door opened, nearly hitting him in the back. The human they'd been waiting for walked in, followed by a graying blond-headed, pink-eyed man. The three figures straightened. The old man stared at the damaged device on the floor. His eyes narrowed behind small gold-rimmed spectacles.

He approached the yellow-eyed man and stared him straight in the eye. "Is it done?"

The yellow-eyed man nodded, overriding the urge to step away. "The three are on their last breaths as ordered. I retrieved the spikes."

"And my missing crate?"

"Gone. But Yetti paid for his betrayal."

The old man turned to his ketallian companion. "I want them packaged. Then remove every trace." The ketallian acknowledged the order and left the room. The old man waited until the door closed before he addressed the yellow-eyed man. "Clean it all."

The yellow-eyed man grinned. "Consider it done."

Chapter 18

Mich read through the file for the third time in as many minutes. The information didn't change, but she reread it with the vague hope it might anyway. She had to get after Charley and follow Wen to the plantation, but figured the two men could handle themselves a while longer while she dealt with the file's contents.

After her long interrogation, she'd returned to *Lazydragon* tired and in need of a shower, fearing the key and codes the men gave her wouldn't work. She was pleasantly surprised to find she had no trouble gaining access. The moment she stepped into the entry hall, a flashing light from the wall monitor caught her eye. From Daeh and addressed to Janelle, the file she downloaded was a three-dimensional clip; surveillance footage of the inside of a laboratory: twenty-two seconds of an empty lab. The notes included in the file reported the lab was a level-three containment laboratory located on Senth Prime. *Level three?* That was high for a university. Daeh did not say what the lab contained.

The quality of the recording was impressive. Using *Lazydragon*'s holographic equipment, she was able to remove the layers in the image to move closer. Enough that she could make out the labels on the empty bottles in the sink. A flash was all the warning she received before the image disappeared.

Hell's demons! Reviewing the recording frame by frame, she discovered the flash originated from a box on the bench.

Enlarging the three-dimensional image to fill the ship around her, she stepped inside the room and sliced closer to the box to examine the source of the explosion. The label stamped onto the exterior read *Glassware—handle with care.*

A document file in the same message reported the resulting explosion killed three lab assistants and damaged two nearby buildings. The autopsy report on the bodies made for a difficult read: the explosion had been severe enough to melt bone.

She ran through the rest of the file. There were four more surveillance videos, and four more explosions. The location and timestamp of each video showed the explosions occurred simultaneously on the five different planets. Each explosion originated from a box labeled "glassware". A signature. *But whose?*

A sixth box failed to detonate. The report she read speculated the contents were saved due to the poor quality of the explosives. Delivery had been traced to a distribution warehouse owned by the East End Postal Service on Senth Prime. Black-and-white video footage from the inside showed a man in a large hat and coat removing boxes from inside a white van. The van was found abandoned nearby, and two sets of fingerprints had been discovered inside.

One set was unknown; the other belonged to Yetti.

Closing the file, Mich stared into the distance. Battenhold was one of the targeted planets. She recalled Charlmehn Di wanted Yetti to meet him on Battenhold. Coincidence? Only she didn't believe in coincidences. Why had Yetti been summoned to meet Di on Battenhold? There had been six spikes and now six boxes—five explosions that should have been six. Perhaps the bomber planned to branch out into bioterrorism? Di was nothing more than a marketing man. There was no link. This had to be the work of The Spiral Guardians. Mich needed evidence and so far she had nothing flash-crete.

She took the opportunity *Lazydragon*'s access and codes gave her to log onto Tripness's company server—*kill them all*. It took a few minutes to hack the staff access portal via the company's altranet page—a simple matter of picking a name from the caption below the staff congratulations photo. Using the name, she manipulated the company ident comm-mail address, found on the contact page, and cycled through her list of standard passwords until *Confirmed* sprang up in green.

From there, she searched for share-drive access. Pressing hard on her right pupil, she activated her eyeport. Rifling through the drawers next to her knee uncovered a handful of data drives and a pair of socks. She rapidly pulled her hand back when she realized the socks had been worn.

"Hell's spawn," she spat, glaring at them.

Holding one of the fingernail-sized drives close to her eyeport, she waited for her remote connection to make contact. Deleting what was on the drive, she blinked through her personal files until she located her snifferbot. Copying it to the drive, she then inserted the device into *Lazydragon*'s terminal and uploaded her bot to Tripness's server—*kill them all*. The sniffer was programmed to root out keywords and code alterations, and would take several days. Her original case against Tripness—*kill them all*—had been to investigate the tainted shipments of medical supplies sent to Yeshele. If she could find evidence the delivery codes had been changed, she could track the changes back, hopefully leading to the culprit who'd made them, and perhaps expose the identity of the mastermind who put her in The Clinic.

Mich glanced at her timepiece and swore again. Fifteen minutes later, she entered The Dive.

The entry door slammed off the wall and swung drunkenly back and forth on damaged hinges. Silence stretched across the bar as the inebriated crowd took in her appearance and her holstered pistol.

"Can I help you?" a voice whispered from the darkness.

Mich remained still until her eyes adjusted to the darkened interior then glanced at the figure at her side. The little man rose only to her waist, his black beard brushing across the liquid-soaked floorboards. He gestured with one gnarled hand. "If t'would please you, come inside as the chill air attempts to sneak its way past. T'would be unfortunate for another customer to raise a complaint."

She acknowledged the request with a nod and stepped inside, shaking off the pearled rain spotting her jacket. She followed the little man down the beer-stained stairway. The main bar was three times the size of *Lazydragon*'s main living space. Tables and chairs lay scattered around the edges of the bar, almost obscuring the steps leading to the second level. Drink bots darted conspicuously to and from the counter, which ran the length of one wall.

"Had some trouble?" she enquired, watching two of the cleaner bots stack several damaged chairs and a broken table into a pile.

"We are likely to experience trouble most hours," the dwarf replied. The twinkle in his eye spoke more of what had happened than his words implied. "We may be a university bar, but drinkers come in all ages."

She gambled. "Tall man, short hair on his face, spiky hair on his head, part draal. Can you tell me where he is?"

"Ahh." The dwarf nodded. "Yes and no."

She waited.

The dwarf remained silent.

Mich waited longer.

"Back room," he relented with a twitch. She tilted her head again in thanks.

"Looking to forget the world?" a husky voice breathlessly whispered into her ear as she stepped onto the floor.

Shaky scarred hands and dead eyes were all Mich needed to see to snap, "Yes, but not with you." She twisted her wrist and activated her investigator's hologram. It wasn't a Hunter's badge, but it got the message across. The addict's eyes widened and she disappeared into the crowd. Mich released a shaky breath. She'd taken more than enough world-escaping drugs to last her a lifetime—none of them by choice. She couldn't understand why someone would want to lose their faculties on purpose.

As she crossed the room, she had the crawling sensation of eyes, dozens of eyes, burning into her back. Glaring, she targeted as many of the hostile stares as she could, and when it became obvious she wasn't there for any of them, conversation, stilted as it was, quietly resumed.

When the ambient noise climbed high enough to cover the sound of her entry, she opened the rear door into the corridor beyond. It took only moments to find the hall and the door down into the bar's brothel. Mich gaped, outraged, as she stepped into the travesty of fashion entryway. *Purple?* Pleasure houses, such as the one she'd walked into, focused more on the workers than the décor, but hell, this room was a fluffy pillow nightmare. The heavy floral scent assaulted her and, fighting a cough, she turned and startled as, out of the nightmare a plump figure rose, her outfit blending so perfectly into the lace and fluff that Mich had the fleeting impression of a cushion rising to greet her.

"I'm looking for a man," Mich said, and immediately winced at the way that sounded.

The lace-and-fluff woman nodded sagely. "Aren't we all, darling. What sort of man?"

"A customer." Mich flashed her wrist holo, but the gesture didn't create the impression she'd hoped for.

"Well, darling, we have plenty of those. You'll have to be more specific. My name is Sima. Welcome to my House." Sima sat and rested her hands lightly on the padded arms of the chair. As Mich described Charley, the woman glared down her nose and heaved a breath that was more of a sigh. Leaning to her right to check the open book at her side, she pointed to the corridor on her left. "Third door. He pays before you take him. Send Carma back, please. And no blood, if you can help it," Sima said smoothly, turning her gaze back to Mich. "Darling, are you sure you don't want me to organize someone for you?" She ran her hands across her ample chest. "It'd help you relax, and you do appear in desperate need of a relaxing experience."

Mich stifled the shudder that ran through her. *No.*

"Darling, I have pretty women with ample bosoms, boys with muscular chests. A dreynak with three arms and ... other things." She lowered her voice to a conspiratorial whisper. "I even have a shadowkeeper. I'm sure we can find something to meet your needs."

Mich's head came up. Shadowkeepers were well known for their knowledge of body-melding, mind-blowing experiences. They were also highly illegal. She paused before smirking. "I can't work out if you're trying to bribe me or distract me."

Sima let out a great sigh. "Go and play with your contact, but remember, I have a clean service here, if you—"

"I get the idea." It took Mich a minute to find the right door and, with a loud knock, she slammed it open. Inside, she found Charley exactly as she expected to find him.

"Thanks for the warning," he muttered, locking eyes with her. A whore, kneeling at his feet, stopped her ministrations and peered up at Mich curiously.

Mich dismissed her immediately. "Sima wants you."

The whore wrote something down on ancient-looking data pad, handed it to Charley and darted past Mich with a glare.

"How much did you pay for her?" Mich demanded when the whore was gone. The look Charley shot her was surprising in its intensity, his anger contrasting so severely with the immense comic consequence of literally being caught with his pants down.

Remaining seated, he dragged them on, glaring at Mich until she raised her hands. "What?"

"You interrupted because ...?"

The stare-down continued until Mich remembered why she was there. "A file came in. We have more evidence linking Yetti to terrorist activities. A bomber claimed responsibility for several explosions on several planets, each one taking out half a city block. We need to find Yetti's boss ASAP. Did you get anything on Yetti, or did you not bother? How long did it take to find that whore—?"

"Contact."

"—when we need ... what?" She stopped as his words registered.

He gestured toward the door. "She's my contact. She was giving me information."

"She was certainly giving you something."

Charley's glare became a grin. "So she was."

Mich almost snorted; inwardly, she laughed. It had been so long since she'd felt amused she wasn't entirely sure what to do with it. It made her uncomfortable. To solve her problem, she said, "Wen hasn't reported in. I can't raise his comm."

Charley jumped to his feet. "I thought he was with ya?"

"We were forced to split up."

"Where'd he go? Ya should've stayed with him! That's the rule: stay with ya partner." Charley found his shoes hidden beneath the comforter on the floor; his shirt was tangled in the sheets behind him. Tugging them on, he gestured for her to continue.

She wanted to point out his hypocrisy. He'd left Wen with Mich and managed to have a rather diverting afternoon. That was hardly staying with your partner. Instead, she recounted their adventure in the storage bay, including the dead security guard, the missing carry case and her subsequent interrogation at the hands of the local security force.

"He went after 'em alone?"

"You could've stopped him?" This bickering wasn't getting them after Wen any faster.

He must have reached the same conclusion, because he closed his mouth and nodded. "Fine. But the woman comes with us."

"The prostitute? Have you lost your brain?"

"Waitress, actually. Carma has information about Yetti."

Mich paused. The pros and cons of letting the waitress tag along swam through her mind. On the one hand, she could get hurt; on the other, she might have valuable information they could use to track Yetti's movements more precisely. Glaring at Charley's face, her shoulders dropped. It didn't appear he was giving her a choice. "Fine."

As he haggled with Sima in the front room, Mich moved to stand beside the waitress. Carma watched Charley and Sima's excessive hand gestures with wide eyes. Mich leaned in and whispered, "If you want to help, find us at the travel hub." Carma made eye contact and tilted her head. After a moment she nodded and darted down one of the corridors.

On the way back to the bar, Charley pulled Mich to a stop. "What about Carma?"

"I told her if she had information for you, we'd be at the hub. Her choice."

"Res it." Charley spun on one foot. "Ya shoulda told her she *had* ta come with us. No, we shoulda dragged her out of there. How will she get outta that hellhole without me?"

Mich chuckled. "Some hellhole. Apart from the color, it's better furnished than your ship. She'll come. She wants to." That much was evident.

"Wait." He yanked Mich to an abrupt stop just before the exit. "If they figure out I'm an investigator, she'll suffer backlash."

"Why do you care? I'm sure the drunks won't even notice us." At his pleading look, she threw up a hand. "Fine."

Conversation came to a standstill when they emerged from the back room. Holding Charley's arm tightly and tugging him forward, Mich gave all the appearance that she'd found the man she was looking for. Unwilling to correct their view, she dragged him roughly across the floor. He scuffed his feet and groaned pitifully.

"You make him real comfy in whatever alley you leave him in," one drunken voice called out. Raspy chuckles followed them to the door.

"Find what you need?" The dwarf appeared at her side so suddenly, Mich had her pistol out of its holster before she realized who was addressing her.

"And more," she said and hauled Charley from the bar.

Chapter 19

When Zeth convinced the carrier driver to drop him at the plantation, he'd been warned there was only one way to the warehouses at the other end; official invitation from the owners and a personal escort through three checkpoints. With a few extra coins, the driver told Zeth of another way across the field—unofficially.

He had not, however, mentioned the harvesters.

Zeth stood in the middle of the field, squinting against the sunlight shining off eight approaching harvesting machines. The hairs rose all over his body as reality set in. The harvesters were stretched in a direct line between where he stood and the factories ahead. Stacked two deep to ensure they didn't miss a single piece of ripened fruit, they appeared as large metal beasts moving on serrated wheels larger than his torso and strong enough to grind him into the dirt.

They created an impenetrable wall of metal limbs slowly slashing their way toward him. The top arm pulled bulbous orange heads off stalks, while the lower arm reached out to scoop the fallen fruit into its container-like belly.

There was no way through. He glanced back only to find a second row of harvesters. *No way through and no way back.*

Careful of the razor-sharp leaves surrounding him, he moved sideways, hoping to clear the row before they reached him. He swiped a hand over the sweat beading his upper lip. He was moving too slow. Every glance back showed the machines gaining on him and the line of harvesters was tightening, the machines on either end traveling a fraction faster, forming a semi-circle, locking him in. *Res res res!* His heartrate spiked as he stopped dead.

One harvester growled and grumbled loudly, its bellows rolling over the field like thunder as it rotated away from the line. The machine might have been full or maybe it was damaged, but as it trundled away, it left a gap. It was small, but it was a gap.

Zeth checked his position. This was going to hurt.

Keeping his head low and his neck covered by his arms, he ran into hell.

By the One!

Sharp stings from the dangerous leaves peppered his chest and arms. A stalk swung wildly at his face. He threw himself to the ground, rolled and came up without lost momentum as a metallic arm swiped sideways, decapitating the stalks right in front of him. He swayed out of its reach and ducked the next swipe. Breath caught in his throat, he twisted sideways and kept moving. Always moving. *Don't stop.* He had no time; he had to get past and he wasn't going to make it.

A machine on his left ground noisily to a halt. Its giant arms stopped swiping and, creaking loudly, folded inward. Zeth was running before he had time to change his mind. Heart thundering, panting hard, he pushed his tired muscles faster. His vision narrowed until all he could see was the smooth metal side of the monster growing steadily larger before him.

The harvester turned as he reached its enormous wheels. Grabbing at the metal protrusions, he hauled himself up the machine's side and climbed under the retracting arms. Swinging precariously, he reached the opening of the machine's full storage container. Zeth grabbed for the edge as the pit expanded beneath him.

He fell, landing hard among the fruit. The hatch above his head slid sideways, sealing the container shut with a loud clang. The silence inside was shocking. His legs still trembled from his exertions and, swiping a hand over his face, he scrubbed away the sweat covering his skin. Gasping raggedly, he drew mouthfuls of the sweet, fruity air into his lungs.

The machine picked up speed, sending fruit and Zeth bouncing around inside the compartment.

After today, he suspected he'd never eat orange stone fruit again.

*

"Got everything?" Mich asked, exasperation pouring from her voice.

"That depends; we don't resing know what we're walking into," Charley snarled back.

Wen had not reported in by the time Mich and Charley reached the *Lazydragon,* and it made Charley snap like a Janing muck gator. Surely he trusted his partner more than this? They couldn't possibly do every investigation glued to each other's side. His anger, no doubt misplaced worry, confused Mich. She watched him carefully, uncertain of his triggers, as he read the files from Daeh. His head hung low, brows drawn tightly together as he pondered the information. She drummed her fingers against the sofa arm. *Make a decision already!* He'd initially demanded they wait for the waitress. He'd since changed his mind, insisting they go after Wen immediately. His back and forth was driving her crazy. He refused to leave either mission to Mich, and her annoyance from his lack of faith was starting to spread like an allergic reaction.

Charley's hovering and his arguments for and against were sending her blood pressure into the atmosphere. Her hearing became more acute as every sound magnified—the rustle of his clothing, the quick breath he took before speaking, the wet chewing sound he made as he second-guessed his decisions.

"Would you sit down!" she spat, unable to take any more of his dithering.

"What?" His head rose sharply.

She couldn't stay here. "I'll be up front, keeping an eye out for your friend." She could feel his eyes on her as she stormed away but had no intention of explaining her irritation. What did he think she would do if she went after Wen alone?

Her body still brimming with rage, she stomped into the cockpit and released a long breath, letting it hiss out from between her teeth as she sagged into the pilot's chair. Glancing at the door, she wished she could lock it. Charley was worried for his friend—she got that. *So why am I angry?* Scratching hard at her neck, she stared blankly at the ship's controls. The feeling that she ought to be out doing *something* niggled, leaving her unable to sit still.

Twisting to the terminal on her left, she switched it on. The altranet connection bar flashed at the top of the screen. She could log into the Tripness server—*kill them all*—and watch over her snifferbot's progress until Charley made a decision he could stick to.

Then again ... she shot a glance at the door. If he came in and saw what she was doing, he'd report it to Daeh. Besides, her bot wouldn't be finished with its search yet. Best to leave it alone for now.

Movement caught in the corner of her eye drew her gaze to the hub floor. "Your friend's here," she called loudly.

Charley let the waitress on board. Mich continued to keep watch. Something bothered her, itching at her skin. *"Don't trust them,"* the voice in her head whispered. She knew if she spun around, there would be no one else in the cockpit.

Rel Charley wanted to trust Carma. Mich wondered why.

She'd never trusted anyone on sight. Hell's spawn, she didn't even trust people she'd known for years. An image of her parents flashed into her mind, but she slammed down on those thoughts like dropping a detonation shield. There were the so-called friends she'd made at school, the ones who'd barely hesitated to knock her down in their rush to rise above her. And then, The Clinic. Mich had survived on her own for so long now, she didn't know how to trust anyone. The second you let people in or believed they'd be there for you, they let you down. She'd paid the price for trusting in people, left rotting in The Clinic for over a year. Her knee bounced rapidly as memories ambushed her. She tugged her jacket tighter around her chest, but try as she might, she couldn't stop the memory from unwinding.

Her cell dropped to minus temperatures at night in winter. The Gathering Room was worse. Located in the center of the secure building, the high ceilings and tiny windows made the cold somehow greater, sending chills through every patient. Thin, clinic-issued pajamas didn't help. Colored pictures spray-painted onto every wall were a mockery of the freedom just beyond the energy shield.

The imagined scent of cinnamon filled her nostrils until she choked on it. The bony nurse with the narrow green eyes took one look at Mich and fetched a wheelchair, helping her into it without fuss.

"Shall we go for a walk, dear girl?" Cold hands pressed down upon her shoulders before Mich was pushed from the room. They moved down the corridor at a rapid clip while Mich struggled to breathe. Above her, the nurse hummed a tune Mich had never heard before and she focused on the sound. This allowed her to regain some control over her mind and soon, she was breathing easier.

When they reached the large glass door in the foyer, her breathing deteriorated again. She focused on the glass. Her reflection was distorted, a pale and malformed demon dancing back at her with a wicked grin.

"It is okay, my dear. You are quite safe with me. I have per-mission to take you outside to see the gardens. They are truly lovely this time of year. It will be such a treat for you."

Mich broke the memory's spell by jumping to her feet. She paced the small cockpit, feeling the walls creeping in. Her skin was clammy, and she swiped at her upper lip with her hand. She pictured Wen and Charley as she first met them; wary, cautious, their shared looks and raised brows. They were as suspicious of her as she was of them. Hell's demons, Charley had shadowed her every move, watching intently from the hidden corners of the ship, and he'd manipulated their argu-ments to ensure he would go to the bar alone while his partner followed Mich to the storage bay like a chaperone.

Charley had made it clear he didn't think much of her. He didn't even trust her to go after Wen alone. Daeh had assigned her to their team. He wouldn't have done that if she was able to work alone.

The voice in her head spoke again *"Watch them carefully. They will betray you."*

She pinched her arm sharply and stifled a yelp. A blossom of red welled up under the sensitive skin. The voice became her own once more.

Feeling twitchy, she leaned over the console to reactivate the outside alert and dragged her tired body from the chair.

Just because Rel Charley and Zeth Wen were investigators didn't mean she could trust them. If the past two years had taught her anything, it was that she couldn't trust anyone.

Chapter 20

With a clang and an even louder bang, the harvester slammed sideways and the storage compartment's lid slid open. Fruit, along with a battered man, fell out onto a rapidly moving conveyor belt.

Zeth dragged himself up and over the belt's security rail just in time to avoid being squashed flat beneath the giant mallet. Sucking in an unsteady breath, he climbed to his feet. The scent of sweet juice hung heavy in the air, almost suffocating in its intensity. Everywhere he looked, traveling belts sorted fruit off in different directions.

He fingered his weapon but didn't draw it. *Where did the telnaks go?* This was where they'd been heading when he'd lost them. The three warehouses were the only buildings for miles around—they had to be here somewhere.

The warehouse was the size of a decent ship dock; he could have parked *Lazydragon* eight times end to end inside it, or landed one decent-sized battleship right in the center with room to spare. Warmth on his skin brought his gaze to the warehouse roof. Tiles were broken in random places, wooden beams exposed in others. Through one large hole, he could see patches of blue sky. Sunlight dappled the warehouse floor, lighting the way to a metal staircase against the far wall. *Of course it stops raining now.*

Sneaking under the belt, he made his way to the stairs and climbed up three at a time. He found an unlocked door at the top, inched it open and disappeared inside.

*

Carma was scribbling on her data pad when Mich returned to the central living space. "It better be important information she's got," Mich grumbled, considering the woman seated on the end of the couch. The clothing Carma had changed into looked like something straight out of a circus tent—or a bad porno. Mich swallowed her snide remark and watched Rel take the pad gently from the waitress's hands.

"Her statement is here."

"She can't just tell us?" Written confessions were never as good as a spoken report.

The woman directed her gaze away as Charley said, "She can't." At Mich's quizzical look, he continued. "She's had her tongue pulled."

Mich jerked back. Tongue-pulling was an awful crime. For a moment, Mich felt sorry for the poor creature, then her gaze hardened. Just because the woman had been treated badly in the past didn't mean she could be trusted now.

Carma raised a second pad and shook it.

Mich snatched it from her hands. *Do you want the information or not?* The words were sterile without the accompaniment of tone. Nonetheless, Mich felt the woman's anger radiating from them.

She would take the information, of course, but she would double-check it. "Do you have anything else you want to add?" she snapped. Charley glared at her. Heat rose up along Mich's neck at the acknowledgment of the aggressiveness of her tone. Why should she feel guilty?

Carma made a complicated gesture with her hands. Mich shot a look to Charley. "I can't read sign," he admitted softly.

Mich shook her head, anger still bubbling beneath the surface of her skin. Her voice was sharp as she told him, "Neither can I."

The waitress sighed heavily and gestured to the pad. When it was back in her hands, she wrote *Yetti smelled good.*

"Yeah, he did." Mich focused on Charley. "We've got to get after Wen." Turning to Carma, she said, "Thank you for your assistance. If we require anything else—"

"We're taking her with us." Charley's look dared Mich to argue.

"What?" Positive she'd misheard, she waited for clarification.

Charley simply stared at her.

Mich curled her top lip in response. He'd been compromised —couldn't he see that?

"We ain't leaving her here!" he exploded.

She flicked her gaze to the watching woman.

I'm coming!

Faced with two identical glares, Mich threw up her hands. "Fine." Holding up the pad, she said, "I'll read this in my quarters. Take us to the plantation."

Lying on her bunk, Mich read over Carma's statement. The woman was exceptionally detailed, describing the scarred shizernet and the yellow-eyed man carefully. Hadn't Healer Bicet mentioned a man from Shizer—a scarred man?—who sounded like the same one Carma had seen following Yetti.

Several passages struck her as requiring further investigation. One in particular appeared to have greater meaning than Carma had initially ascribed to it. Mich sat up, alert, scanning the page again, this time searching for the elusive thought she'd had upon her first reading.

When the gray-haired sholan arrived, he kicked the cleaner bot away from the table. I was told to move it and had just grabbed the broken server-arm when I heard him ask the shizernet, "Is it done?"

The shizernet said, "I tagged one." I noticed the yellow-eyed man staring at me, so I had to move away.

I served Yetti another shem-milk. It was his third, and when he finished he asked if he could to go through to Sima's to talk to Terri. Sima likes his coin, so I sent him back.

There was a large bald man sitting at the bar talking loudly into his comm unit. He said, "A telnak?" I only listened because I've never seen a telnak before and I wondered if the man was going to describe what they look like. I saw the sholan sit up and stare at the bald man, like he'd heard the man say something interesting. The bald man said "Thirty? Thirty is ridiculous."

The sholan leaned forward and even the shizernet was watching him carefully. The bald man said something about the orange stone fruit plantation. I didn't understand what he was talking about, but the sholan laughed loudly when he heard it and the three men shared a strange look.

Yetti came out with Terri and Sophie then, and I was surprised because Sophie doesn't usually double. They were holding onto his arms like they had to help him walk. I thought that was weird because, yes, he'd had a few shem-milks, but I've seen Yetti drink way more than that and walk away perfectly fine.

After Yetti left, the three men disappeared.

Wen told Mich three telnaks had killed the security guard at the storage bay, and now Carma had referenced telnaks. So they were linked to this case? They needed to find these telnaks as soon as possible.

Mich left her quarters to search for the woman. "Tell me more about the bald man." She held out the pad for Charley to read the section she'd marked. Carma shook her head, looking confused.

Charley considered the pad. "A telnak?"

"Yeah." Mich leaned toward the woman. "In your notes, you said there was a bald man at the bar talking loudly into his comm unit?"

Carma angled the screen so Mich could read her words as she wrote them. *Yes, I remember. He ordered a Qinoa.*

Mich snorted. A Qinoa was a woman's drink.

Carma grinned but kept writing. *He said a telnak organized the meeting at the orange stone fruit plantation.*

"Is that what he said exactly?" Mich demanded, moving closer to the woman.

She raised an eyebrow and wriggled back, away from Mich.

Charley sat down on Carma's other side. "My partner, Zeth, is at the orange stone fruit plantation. Anything ya can tell us might help when we go looking for him. Where were they meeting?" He took Carma's hand gently, drawing her gaze to his face. "Think hard. Have they met him before? Do they know what he looks like? What did he say *exactly*?"

Chapter 21

Zeth stepped into the empty office. Along the rear wall was an elongated window that overlooked the warehouse below, with a desk and chair positioned to observe the factory floor. A door on the opposite side of the room revealed a corridor. Zeth peered each way. Which direction should he choose?

The lack of laborers disturbed him. Surely this packing plant wasn't completely automated? The buildings looked fairly run-down, but each sorting machine, conveyor belt and harvester ran with the smooth efficiency that indicated maintenance was conducted regularly, so where was everyone?

If the telnaks weren't here, he might be on a wild belinga chase and not know it. Zeth had spent a week hunting a belinga once, a few years back. Rel had been beside himself with laughter when he found out. Zeth still refused to believe the knee-high jumping marsupial with glittery horns was just a fairytale.

He chose to go left. He swiped open the first door he found, discovered it was an empty office and moved swiftly to the next room. Dirty dishes confirmed someone was here somewhere. He had a fleeting suspicion he might have lost the three men. If they had the Enferrie spikes, then they were potential terrorists and dangerous. His stomach clenched hard enough to bring a grunt to his lips. He would not let another terrorist escape his grasp.

From up ahead came the murmur of voices. Creeping closer, he pressed his ear to the door, making out an argument beyond. Voices rose and fell in sharp waves. He drew a knife from his boot and jammed it behind the sensor casing. There was a spark as the sensor died. Shoving his knife into the track stopped the door sliding open. He pried it open just a crack, hoping the slight movement wouldn't be observed by those inside.

"It's too volatile. I don't want it going off before it's time."

"I told you it's the best stuff on the market." The telnak's voice was instantly recognizable; the other man was unfamiliar.

The ping of his knife blade snapping sounded horrendously loud, and the door Zeth held jerked away from his hands.

Da, dressed in the same navy coveralls he'd worn earlier, stared at Zeth in surprise. Beside him stood a large, bald human in a well-fitted gray suit. His hand was outstretched in Da's direction, revealing a silver interlacing circle cufflink. The three men gaped at one another silently.

Then, all at once, they moved.

Zeth pushed forward, slamming his shoulder into the surging telnak. The quick movement toppled Da into the unknown man, knocking them both to the floor, groaning loudly.

Drawing his weapon, Zeth held a finger to his lips, his heart thudding crazily at the sudden confrontation. "Shh," he whispered and pressed the barrel of his gun to the telnak's nose. Distract and confuse, it was the quickest way to break up a fight. Da's bulbous eyes expanded then slid cross-eyed as he stared up the barrel. Zeth gestured for the two men to get up, and growled when they didn't immediately move.

The bald man pushed Da off his legs and climbed to his feet. Squinty blue eyes examined Zeth carefully. "This is no way to negotiate," he said, his voice too high for a man of such size.

Da got up and raised his hands. "Jarrick, he's not one of mine. I don't know who this man is. Wait ..." Da twisted to face

Zeth. "This is a set-up. You never planned to give me the coin. You were going to steal it from me all along." Da threw himself head-first at Jarrick, punching and kicking like a wild animal.

Jarrick fell back with a startled cry.

For a few beats, Zeth watched the two men fight, wincing as Da fought dirty—with the street smarts of short sharp jabs and well-placed knees and elbows. Jarrick's arms flailed. He had no form, slapping and thwacking away with abandon. They didn't seem to remember he was even in the room. Bemused, he raised his weapon and fired into the ceiling.

The two men froze.

"Are you done?" Zeth asked. Jarrick scampered backward as Zeth pointed his weapon at the telnak. "Where's the case?"

Da shook his head. "What case?"

The rear door slammed open, barely missing Jarrick. "You will need to speak with my brother. Mr. Jarrick—" Parra stepped into the room, followed by ...

What the hell?

Behind the telnak, in walked Rel. He locked eyes with Zeth, waggling his eyebrows. He was dressed in a gaudy suit that looked a size too large for his frame. Mich Janelle, wearing a pretty dress, trod quietly behind. Though her eyes were cast down, Zeth could see tension tightening her frame.

"Parra, what is this?"

The short telnak moved to his brother's side. "Da, this man said his name is Jarrick. He gave the correct codes."

Rel gestured dramatically, "What the hell is this? Ya said this was a private buy." He pointed at Zeth with a sneer. "Are ya cheating on me?"

Zeth pointed his own weapon at Rel. Inwardly, he smiled, pleased his partner was here. Rel hadn't identified Zeth, so it was clear he was posing as a stranger. This was not the first time a scenario like this had played itself out between the two men on a case. Zeth waited, happy for Rel to take the lead.

"Grab him," Da snarled.

After a brief struggle, Zeth was pushed to his knees, his own weapon pressed tightly to the back of his head. He remained calm, knowing Rel had his back. He reviewed the location of the men in the room with the barest flicker of his eyes. The telnaks stood arguing quietly in one corner. Jarrick—presumably the real Jarrick—was beside the door, alternating between clasping the back of his head and rubbing at the large bruise blossoming over his chin. Mich waited against the wall, examining her nails as if she was not at all interested in or bothered by the men with all their guns. Rel stood behind Zeth, holding Zeth's pistol. He tapped Zeth's back with the barrel three times.

Zeth closed his eyes. Rel was pulling a Buyer Beware con. He suppressed a groan; he hated this scam.

In the corner, the telnaks' argument grew louder. "Da, they have the correct codes."

Da slapped his brother hard over the head and pointed to the bald man. "So does he." Da gestured at Zeth. "And *he* is trying to steal it."

Rel interrupted. "I don't have time to stand around here debating this. I want the case."

"As do I," the suit said.

"They can't both be Jarrick." Parra ducked to avoid a second head slap.

"Really?" Da snapped. The two telnaks raised identical pistols, one pointed at Rel, the other at the suit. "Show me your ID."

Rel shrugged. "Jarrick is, of course, not my real name, and I won't share my real identity with the likes of ya. I have the money ya asked for. Give me the case. Kill these two for all I care."

The bald man drew himself up to his full height and carefully slipped two fingers into his jacket pocket. Zeth tensed, holding his breath as everyone watched the man silently. When he raised his hand, he held an identification chip between his fingers.

Rel sighed. "Well, res it."

Zeth hit the floor as the room erupted in gunfire.

When the shooting ceased, Mich Janelle stood in the center of the room, Rel beside her. They were the only two left standing. Jarrick and the two telnaks stared blankly up at the ceiling as black blood formed growing pools around their bodies. *Where in the One did she pull a weapon from?*

"So, hopefully ya know where this damned case is?" Rel asked.

Using his partner's help to pull himself up off the floor, Zeth's stomach curled. "You're not gonna like my answer."

"You've been here how long and you don't know where it is?" Mich dropped to her knees over Da's body and quickly searched his pockets.

A burst of heat rose up Zeth's neck and he changed the subject. "Bar fight?" he queried, pointing to the bruises on Rel's cheekbone.

"Not important. My contact, Carma, overheard a conversation about this place and a telnak. Janelle connected the dots. Carma gave us enough info ta set up the Buyer Beware. Knew ya'd figure it out."

Mich stood. "There's nothing on them. The case has to be here somewhere." Directing her gaze toward Zeth, she asked, "Where's the other telnak? You said there were three?"

"No idea."

Rel pointed to Mich. "Split up and clear the building."

She shot him a dry look and disappeared through the open doorway without another word. Rel didn't move. When Zeth looked back, Rel cocked an eyebrow. "Ya look like ya've been run over by a harvester."

The two men raised their weapons and moved toward the door Da and Jarrick had walked in through earlier. Rel counted down from three. On one, he kicked the door open. Zeth swept forward, covering the room beyond.

It was empty.

*

Finally alone, Mich stalked the empty passageway, swiping over each door sensor as she passed. Every one was locked. She would return later to force them all open.

In the silence, her mind drifted. Wen had looked like he'd been attacked by someone wielding a sword, and she wondered what had truly happened to him. Her thoughts moved from his appearance to the man himself. What would he make of Charley's new friend? Would he let his partner keep her? Mich didn't like the idea of the woman waiting for them on *Lazy-dragon* alone. Who left an unknown source unsupervised on their ship? Carma's watching eyes and silence grated on Mich's nerves in a way she didn't fully understand, but she did know that the woman made her decidedly uneasy.

A loud thump drew her attention to one of the doors she'd just tried. Holding her breath, she leaned in and could just make out a soft groan beyond the door.

As she prepared to shoot the sensor, there was a loud pop and a sucking noise. Mich froze. The moans stopped. A flutter in her stomach rolled right up through her body at the cessation of the sound. She grabbed her comm unit.

"Yeah-lo," Charley drawled.

"Found something."

"Be right there, wait for—"

She cancelled the link. Pressing up against the door, she called, "Hunt—"

Damn it, she wasn't a Hunter anymore. "—hey, you in there. Open the door."

Usually when she made a demand at a door, the response was the sound of running feet. Now, there was only silence. A glance over her shoulder showed no sign of the other two investigators and she heard nothing more through the wall.

She opened fire on the lock, and the door slid open.

Mich gagged at the sight, stumbling back until she hit the corridor wall. Taking rapid, shallow breaths, she slammed her eyes shut and didn't open them again until she heard the two investigators approaching.

"Told ya ta wait for us," Charley snarled, ducking into the room.

A moment later, Wen dropped to the floor beside Mich. "It's a mess in there."

"Yeah." She stared at the wall. At the sound of Charley's voice, she turned her head to look him in the eye.

"The same as Yetti?" He held a black-stained carry case.

"No—not quite. It affects each species differently."

"Lotta blood."

"Yeah," she said, turning her gaze back to the wall.

Both men were silent. The remaining telnak's body had partially dissolved. His head and hands were intact, but not much else. Mich could still see the black blood in her mind.

"Gonna have to call this in," Wen said. He didn't move any closer, for which Mich was thankful. She swung her gaze from the wall and pinned him with eyes that felt like they were on fire. "The case?"

Charley opened it. "Res it!"

Mich leaned forward to peer inside.

The case was empty.

Chapter 22

"What do you mean, empty?" Steven Daeh glared through the screen as if he could drag the answer out of Mich with just his eyes. Those gray orbs sent the hairs on the back of her neck quivering.

She shrugged, knowing she had no answer her boss would find acceptable. In truth, she was lost as to what it all meant. This investigation had been a fiasco from the get-go and right now, she had no idea what her next move should be. She sat stiffly in the front seat of *Lazydragon*'s cockpit, looking up at the communication screen. Wen sat beside her with Charley occasionally leaning between them to interject.

The sound of water pounding the ship's roof told everyone it was raining again. Another violent storm. Mich watched, amused, as Charley and Wen were forced to raise their voices in order to talk over the noise and each other.

Charley rested one hand on his partner's shoulder as he pressed forward to emphasize a point. Wen didn't seem bothered by it. As the shorter man moved closer, Mich pulled back, uncomfortable with his physical encroachment, even with a good six inches of space between them. She forced herself to sit straighter, her throat tightening at the impression of Charley's body against her back.

And then there was Carma. Mich figured Charley would want to continue where they'd left off as soon as he could, but she hadn't seen him touch the woman at all. Was she wrong about his attraction to her? *If so, then why is she still here?* Carma had given them all the information she had. She now sat in the living area, reading a tablet, and was the infuriating reason they were all jammed into the small cockpit to make their report.

Charley had warned his partner about their *guest* on their way back to the ship and Wen hadn't seemed at all surprised his partner had brought home a stray. If it happened that regularly, where did all the women go? *Lazydragon* had the appearances of a bachelor transport, so romantic partners didn't stay for long. Mich wondered if Carma had any idea how temporary her presence here might be. Maybe Charley kept a harem somewhere, and when the current case was over, he dropped them off and continued on his merry way. Mich snorted at the image, receiving identical raised eyebrows from the men beside her. She waved them away with a muttered, "Sorry."

Daeh stared at her through squinted eyes. "Janelle, are you well?"

"I'm fine." When the silence grew too long, the humor from her thoughts was smothered by a rush of anger. "I'm just annoyed we don't have any answers yet."

Daeh's eyes softened. "You saw the body?"

She nodded.

"Any idea where the telnak was when he was infected?"

"The body is being assessed now. I'm not confident in the local man. I'd like to request the healer who examined Yetti on Bendal to assist. He knew exactly what to look for. He's a bit self-focused but he'll do a good job of it. I think he'll be on the first ship here if it helps him get a paper out of it. In the meantime, we track the telnaks' movements back through their connection to Yetti."

"The telnaks were shipping explosives. Had a deal with 'the old man'," Wen said.

"The old man?" Charley repeated, sitting up straight.

Mich tilted her head. "Charley?"

Daeh nodded. "The leader of The Spiral Guardians is referred to as 'the old man'."

"The Spiral Guardians do love their explosives. That file ya sent. Six bombs," Charley mused.

"But not poison. That's your priority here. You need to find how and when the telnaks were hit and by who," Daeh said. He eyeballed Mich again. "Headache?"

"I'm fine," she grumbled, turning away from her boss's suspicious stare. She didn't want the men beside her to know how fragile she was feeling. It was bad enough Daeh—*their boss*—was asking about her health right in front of them. She sensed Charley staring at her now, and knew he was wondering what was wrong with her. She focused on the screen. "I'm fine," she repeated. "I'm sick and tired of staring at bloody, disintegrating or blown-up corpses. Why wouldn't I have a headache? We need to catch whoever is doing this. The carry case was empty. We haven't found the spikes."

"Go on," Daeh said with a nod. He leaned back in his chair and steepled his fingers.

Wen opened his mouth, but Daeh held up his hand. "Janelle, talk it through. I want your thoughts on this."

Mich slumped further down in her chair and nodded. She closed her eyes. Releasing a long breath slowly, she pressed her hands to the console and wound her memory back several days, replaying each step in her initial investigation.

"You assigned me to watch Yetti because he was flagged on the suspected tech smuggler list. I followed him to Battenhold from Ketal Seven to confirm a delivery. At the time, Yetti wasn't considered dangerous. Not to the wider population at any rate." She paused and added, "The telnaks believed Yetti had stolen from them. Kept a crate of Joy. They didn't find it, but figured Yetti was storing something important and were negotiating with several buyers for the contents. Did they have prior knowledge of what the carry case contained? Did they even know it was empty, and was it empty when they took it? They didn't fetch it until after Yetti was reported dead, so what did they do with the spikes?"

"But—" Charley started.

Mich continued as though she'd not been interrupted. "We know Yetti was storing six Enferrie spikes. So back to that question. Six spikes means six potential victims. No, five. The telnak's death is pretty conclusive. So, five spikes. Possibly four if Yetti was killed with one of the spikes too. Did Yetti intend to sell them or was he smuggling them in for someone as yet unidentified? He left the carry case behind when he got on that transport ship to Battenhold, so were the telnaks stealing the carry case or was it meant for them and they were just collecting their order?" She tilted her head to the side, remembering the lead telnak's anger when confronting Charley. With the telnaks and Jarrick dead, they couldn't ask. "Stealing it. They killed the guard for information. They expected to find their missing crate of explosives in that storage bay. They suspected Yetti delivered only five to 'the old man' and substituted the sixth with an inferior product.

"The telnaks are connected to this case by supplying the explosives. One was killed by the same weapon that killed Yetti. The telnaks had nothing to do with the poison. So the real case here is who shot Yetti *and* the telnaks with the Enferrie poison. And why?"

The two men spoke at once. "His injuries—"

She ignored them. "Yetti was hit by a spike before he left Ketal Seven. The killer is here." She remembered Yetti had seemed so calm, he hadn't exhibited the behavior of a man worried for his life—no nervous glances, hadn't used a pseudonym or attempted to change his travel routes at the last minute. "Why was Yetti killed? To hide his connection to someone." *Yetti's body was destroyed after the reports were filed.* Done to confuse the matter, or was there something someone was trying to hide? Something worse than the way Yetti died.

Mich spoke, her eyes closed, her voice cold. "Carma said the women who sleep with Yetti always disappear a few days later. Dead? Silenced because of who they knew or what they knew? What happened to them? All but the last two. So what changed? Yetti left the planet. Healer Bicet said a sholan and a shizernet destroyed Yetti's body ... Carma said one of the three men searching for Yetti had scarred and scaly skin. The same shizernet? She said he was sitting with a sholan. We need to find these men. Carma also described a yellow-eyed man, so that's three potentials killers.

"According to the file you gave me, Yetti worked with a number of factions, played the middleman and the supplier for the Enforcers, TRK and The Spiral Guardians. All use explosives as their weapon of choice. The Spiral Guardians in particular specialize in attacking big companies they feel are taking advantage of outer spiral planets. Yetti smuggled the Enferrie poison in for someone. Maybe for the terrorist who bombed all those labs. Yetti died the same day the bombs exploded. Coincidence? We all know how we feel about coincidences. The Spiral Guardians or TRK? Yetti was killed to stop him from talking. The laboratories were destroyed, Yetti's body was destroyed. There was nothing in the carry case." Mich snapped her eyes open as the pieces fell into place inside her mind. "The carry case was a decoy. The telnaks are a distraction. Yetti was a pawn. Sir, what aren't you telling us?"

Daeh blinked.

Mich glanced over her shoulder at Wen and Charley. They seemed stunned. Why? Because of her, or because Daeh had blinked?

Daeh blinked again. After a moment, he spoke. "Yetti was a suspect since before the bombings. The laboratories hit were all the primary developers of a pain medication derived from an outer spiral flora used by midwives as a natural sedative. Calcryon, the company in question, has been accused of harvesting too much of the flower, leaving none behind for the local population to use."

"Fits with The Spiral Guardians. They protect outer spiral planet economies," Wen pointed out.

"Threatening letters were sent to Calcryon's senior management, demanding they dispose of the drug and halt all investigations into its use."

"Doesn't sound like The Spiral Guardians. They don't threaten or warn. They just blow dresh up," Charley said.

"It's financial. They make it too much of a financial risk to stay in business on the outer spiral," Wen added.

"Repeated over and over in the letters is a warning not to trust Calcryon," Daeh said.

Wen tapped his lips. "So what's the bomber's motive?"

Before Daeh could answer, Mich asked, "The drug trial. Did anyone die?"

"Ten."

"Out of?" she clarified.

"A thousand."

"So Calcryon are covering up something. Perhaps the trial didn't succeed. It exposed or caused a fatal reaction in the participants. Ten in a thousand. Could be a motive?" she suggested.

"We're losing track here. The bombings are the focus," Charley insisted.

"No, the drug is. This *is* something. The flower is a poison. That's our motive. Perhaps Calcryon are just in the way? Taking all of the supply means the flower becomes rare. And, as a result, more expensive," she said.

"If a terrorist group is using it as a weapon, losing access is going to piss them off," Wen mused.

Charley scratched his nose. "So the company *is* the target?"

"Calcryon came to me for assistance," Daeh told them. "A number of their delivery ships have been damaged in a series of *accidents*. Tapping into Calcryon's communications, we established several persons of interest. One was a sholan named Yetti. I believed Yetti was attempting to smuggle out a sample of the test drug. I assigned you to follow Yetti to learn the name of the faction behind the attacks on Calcryon. Janelle, if I'd known ..."

Mich shook her head. "So you believe the group behind the bombings killed Yetti because he snuck the drug out? We know the target now—Calcryon. Is there a Calcryon office or warehouse based on Ketal Seven?"

"No," Daeh confirmed.

Charley leaned forward. "Is the test drug the same compound as the one used inside the spike? The Enferrie poison?"

"It's an assumption," Wen said.

Mich countered. "A decent one. Look at how he died." She didn't like this. All of her triggers were going off at once. Tripness—*kill them all*—was a courier company. Her initial failed investigation had been over the shipping of tainted drugs. Calcryon was a drug company. Everything centered around drugs or tainted drugs? It was an angle she hadn't thought to investigate before. She'd been so focused on the shipping company that she hadn't thought to look at the drug company. Her old files would have the pharmaceutical name attached to those tainted drugs. What if she had been looking in the wrong place?

Could the drug company have been at fault, not Tripness? This might be the break she'd been searching for.

I need to look into this further.

"Still, we need confirmation," Charley said, drawing her attention back to the conversation at hand. "If the painkiller drug is significantly different from the poisonous form of the flower, then who wants the poisonous form? Poetic revenge?

Destroying the company with the poison distilled from the same plant that they're harvesting to extinction is rather karmic."

Wen barely twitched. "We need Healer Bicet to examine the telnak. The poison symptoms are different in different species. If he finds evidence confirming the telnak's death was caused by an Enferrie-infused spike then we confirm the link between them and Yetti. Someone sent the shizernet, the sholan and the yellow-eyed man to kill Yetti. We have an eyewitness statement confirming they were following him."

"And I saw proof on The Dive's CCTV. The shizernet hit Yetti with a spike," Charley said. "They killed Yetti on orders. We find one of 'em, they'll lead us ta their boss."

Mich sat up. "Healer Bicet spoke directly to the men who destroyed Yetti's body. He may be able to provide us with further information."

Daeh cleared his throat. "I want a report as soon as the body has been examined." The screen deactivated.

Mich pinched the bridge of her nose to relieve the pressure building behind her eyes. Beside her, Wen initiated the warm-up sequence. "Go lie down," he threw over his shoulder.

Charley scowled at his partner, but did wave Mich out of her chair. She stood so Charley could move into the forward seat to help Wen prep the ship for take-off. Neither man commented further, so she did as suggested.

Their reactions surprised her. Why hadn't they asked what was wrong with her? It was clear Charley had figured out something was up, but he'd kept silent on the issue. Confused, she entered the outer room.

Carma glanced up from her tablet. *Are you well?*

"Fine." Mich slumped in the doorway. "Can you get in touch with the women from the bar? The ones who attended Yetti that last time?"

Terri and Sophie? Yes. Why?

"I want to speak to them. We're flying back to the city. Can you set up a meeting?"

The woman nodded.

Mich pushed herself to her feet. "I'm going to sleep for a while. Tell the boys to wake me when we arrive."

*

"What the res was that?" Rel asked when the ship's engines roared to life beneath them. His neck itched, and that only happened when something was wrong. He raked his nails over his tough raised ridge skin.

"The trance thing she did? It's a memory trick. You know, a way to remember little details."

"Not that, man. Daeh asked about her health. He was worried." Rel thought of how Daeh's face had changed as he watched her. It raised the hairs on his arms. The cold feeling was back with a vengeance. Were the rumors about Janelle true?

"Yeah, I heard. I dunno what to tell you."

"He treats her different, that's for sure. How'd he know about the headache? She didn't say a thing." She'd looked fine to Rel. Perhaps a little tired. The shadows under her eyes were noticeable but res it, Zeth had them too.

Zeth hummed. "She was assigned a Watch and Report mission, not an Investigate and Act."

"Yeah."

Zeth's pause was lengthier as he leaned back in his chair. "Rel, when we were in the storage bay, she didn't give her clearance code to the local guys. I didn't ask when we met, but does she even have one?"

Rel's mouth dropped open. "How is she running a case if she's not fully active? What the resing hell is going on here?"

"I don't know. Why would Daeh assign her case lead without a code?" Zeth lowered his voice. "Do you think the stories are true?"

"That she murdered a witness?" Rel ran back through the many stories he'd heard about the ex-Hunter. If any one of them was true, she'd be in prison. There was something wrong, though, something dark she was hiding. Oh, she'd slipped into the undercover role without hesitation when conning the tel-naks and she was a resing good shot. He'd been worried she'd flinch, but in that firefight her aim had been deadly. He'd been impressed, and Rel wasn't easily impressed. If the same secretive behavior had come from Zeth, Rel would have just waited him out, knowing that eventually he'd own up to it. He trusted Zeth to tell him the truth. Did he trust Janelle? In some ways, she reminded him of Melita. Which was nuts—they were a hundred percent different, like fire and ice—but something in Janelle's eyes called to him. But unlike Carma, who'd inspired his instant trust, Janelle was what he'd call a work in progress.

He knew Janelle was hurting. He just didn't think it was up to them to help her.

"You gonna ask?" Zeth queried.

"Res no. Ya?" The glare Zeth sent his way should have set fire to his shirt at the very least. He ignored it. "Ya wanna go with her?"

*

Several hours later, Mich and Wen strode into the entrance hall of the rundown motel Yetti had rented while on Ketal Seven, The Skein City Gem. She was annoyed Wen had accompanied her. It was only a hotel. She could've handled it on her own.

"Nice place," he commented.

"Yetti was short on cash," she replied. "Budget planet cruisers, budget hotels." As they walked in, a hand-sized rodent darted past and dove into a large hole in the wall.

"Not the safest part of town."

Mich eyed the shadowy doorways. She'd counted three missing overhead bulbs so far. "He was a smuggler. I don't think safe was part of his job description."

"You didn't get a chance to go inside when you were here before?"

In a way she was kind of glad she hadn't come inside by herself. Even the creepy vibes had an extra nasty feel. There was a moldy smell coming from somewhere nearby, but it was hard to make out over the scent of too much aftershave. "My mission was to follow Yetti, so that's what I did." Walking through the enclosed courtyard, Mich pointed out Yetti's room. "No outside windows."

"You think he knew someone was out to get him?"

"Just pointing it out." They headed up the flight of cracked flash-crete steps. Around them, the smell of urine grew stronger.

She flipped the keycard for room three oh eight over in her hand. The manager had given it to her without a word. She shook her head. He'd not even asked to see their holos. "If Yetti was hoping for protection from the staff here, he'd have been sorely disappointed," she said, holding up the card.

Wen's shoulders twitched in the barest hint of a shrug.

"The room is still booked under his name, and paid up until the end of the month. He wasn't running," she said. They exited onto the fifth floor and yanked on a wire door hanging by the top hinge. The door clanged shut behind them. The once yellow walls had faded to a mustard cream color. Paint peeled everywhere. It looked like someone had attempted to fill in the cracks, and several patch jobs seemed freshly painted, covering what she suspected were laser burns. The carpet beneath her feet was stained and rank. Blood was hard to get out of a lot of surfaces even with good products, and she doubted a place like this could afford good products.

"You know, for a motel called the Gem, it sure isn't too shiny."

Wen wasn't wrong. Yetti's reason for staying here had to be for the anonymity it provided, and because it was cheap. It certainly wasn't because it was safe.

Stopping outside the closed door to Yetti's room, she rested her hand on her weapon. Beside her, Wen pulled his from his holster. With his nod of confirmation, she keyed open the door.

Chapter 23

Rel and Carma traveled the full length of the Yoopl Bridge, heading toward a completely different hotel across town. Staring through the hovercar window at the swirling water below, Rel was reminded of the time he'd chased a suspect over a similar bridge on Telten Five. It had been a long run—and he hadn't caught the guy. He hoped it wasn't an omen.

Wet footprints showed their path from the Skein Heliskon's glass entrance all the way to the reception desk. His eyes raked the ceiling. Glass, mirrors and golden finger-width drop lights made the roof dance and shimmer. Every surface shone with reflected light. Half a dozen mini robotic cleaners were doing everything they could to ensure there was not a speck of dirt to be seen. It made Rel hesitant to touch anything for fear of leaving fingerprints behind. How had the telnaks afforded a place like this? They had more means than he'd given them credit for—or at least highly excessive tastes.

Rel smiled apologetically at the manager for their wet path and requested the room numbers for the three telnak brothers. The woman glared at them over a pair of tiny spectacles. At the sight of Rel's hologram, she sniffed sharply and passed him a gleaming gold key with two fingers. She pulled her hand back as soon as he touched her. Anger at such blatant racism curled in his stomach.

Shooting a quick look around the lobby, the manager said in a hushed whisper, "Please don't make a scene."

Dresh! He stalked away from the desk. Carma took Rel's hand and held it for the entire walk to the elevators. Her fury at the manager on Rel's behalf reminded him of Melita. He squeezed her hand in thanks. As the shiny doors closed, her pad appeared long enough for him to read her question before she tucked it back into her little bag. *Are you okay?*

"I'm good—a little hair-trigger, I guess." Rel stared at his reflection in the mirrored doors. His hair was plastered to his face, and the little patch of hair on his chin was growing little hairs of its own. Beside him, Carma's damp tresses clung to her throat. No wonder the perfectly dressed woman at the counter suspected they were trouble. His neck ridge stood out with his hair lying so flat against his skull. He scratched a hand through the damp locks and sniffed under his arm. Carma grinned. She glanced at her comm-to-text unit again, her eyes narrowing.

"Any response?" he asked.

She shrugged and shook her head.

The doors slid apart with a soft swoosh and Rel's mouth dropped open at the sight that lay beyond. The hall appeared to be made of mirrors. Their shocked reflections stared back at them from every surface. As they walked down the hall, the thick pile muffled their footsteps.

A brush of cool air against his shoulder snapped Rel around. He fought his instinct to draw his weapon on the man who appeared right in front of him, stepping out of a room briskly, without checking the corridor.

"Oh, pardon me, sir!" The young, neatly uniformed man stumbled forward as he was bumped from behind by a large trolley piled high with empty trays. The trolley was silent as it rolled back. Rel couldn't hear an engine, but the trolley rocked forward, as if it wanted to keep moving. The scent of hot meat and gravy danced in his nostrils, making his mouth water. His stomach growled hungrily. Rel felt his face heat as he caught Carma's amused gaze.

The floor assistant, whose nametag designated him Marc, bowed his head and gestured for them to precede him down the hallway.

Rel showed his hologram. "A couple of questions?" Before the man could answer, Rel continued, "How long have ya worked here?"

Marc barely glanced at the projection hovering above Rel's wrist. He ran his hands down his jacket and stood straighter. "Five years."

"D'ya often work this floor?"

"Of course, sir, I bring all meal requests to floors nine, ten, and eleven." He gestured to the trolley behind him. It rolled forward at the movement of his hand. He raised his fingers and the trolley stopped. "I am First Assistant to these floors. I've not had a single complaint in all of my five years of service."

"D'ya remember who stays here? Specifically, over the past three weeks?"

"I pride myself on doing so, sir." The young man held Rel's gaze solidly.

Rel held up the key. "Room ninety-eight eleven?"

Marc's eyes flicked away. "Three telnaks, sir. They're hard to forget. So rude. I haven't had any requests from them in the last day or so, though. I'm not sure they're in at the moment."

Rel knew they wouldn't be. He pointed down the hall. "Take us to their room."

*

"Well, this is not a good sign." Wen lowered his weapon and held it pointed at the floor as he stared around.

Mich surveyed the disaster zone that was Yetti's room. Two tables and a battered red sofa had been upended, and several chairs were slashed open, the stuffing scattered. Dirty green cupboard doors in the eating area hung open from twisted hinges.

"Clear the room," Mich told him.

He went left. She headed toward the back, where a bench counter hid the floor of the kitchen from view. Wen reappeared from the back room. "Bedroom's clear." Mich nodded and walked around the bench. A swathe of black and wide eyes was all she saw before she was hit in the chest.

She fired her gun instinctively, falling backward at the blow. The breath was knocked out of her as she landed hard, cracking her tailbone. She tried to fire again, but the figure landed on top of her, pinning her gun hand to her belly. She heard Wen shout over the snarling of the man on top of her. Mich froze—her mind went blank. Fire burned along her arms.

Get off, get off! Music filled her mind. Lashing out with every limb, she bucked and kicked, pushing up with everything she had. The weight lifted off her and she rose with it. Her vision narrowed as blackness encroached the edges. She punched and slapped at her attacker. She saw teeth and white eyes, heard a shout behind constant hissing, but didn't stop. Her hands were sticky, flashing red as she dug her fingers in. The growl became a shout.

Another voice yelled over the top of the noise in her head. "Get down! Get out of the way!"

When the words became clear, she twisted sideways and fell back. An ear-splitting whine ripped through her eardrums. She snapped her head away, gasping and slapping her hands over her head. She hit the floor, unable to see. There were thumps, scuffling sounds and more shouting, but she couldn't make out the words.

Blinking, she rolled onto her front and pushed up on her hands and knees. *Get up! Where is he? Gun! Where's my gun!* Slapping at the ground beside her, she searched for the familiar shape. Noise in front of her sent her sliding backward until she was pressed against a solid flat surface. She held her hands in front of her face, palms out, panting hard. Time lost all meaning. Microseconds, minutes, hours could have passed. All she knew was that her attacker could return at any moment. She started humming.

"Janelle!"

What? Who? How many times had he said her name? She could hear. At least her ears weren't permanently damaged. Through tear-blurred eyes, she saw a man kneeling in front of her, his face scrunched in worry.

"It's me, Zeth. It's Zeth Wen."

Wen? Wiping a sticky hand over her face, she scrubbed her tears away. Her vision, while still blurry, focused on his face.

"Hey, are you with me now?" His hands were splayed out at his sides. *Not touching—he isn't even close.* She let out a small sound and nodded, still blinking as her vision cleared. Her heart thumped painfully in her chest.

"Breathe," he told her.

She looked at him blankly. "Come on. Breathe," he said again. She heard the words, but his meaning escaped her until he put his hands over his own chest and breathed in loudly. He blew air out slowly, his eyes not leaving her face. His stale breath washed over her lips, her hair moved with the force of it. She watched his movements and found herself echoing the rise and fall of his chest. With oxygen reaching her lungs at last, her awareness returned with a snap.

"Wh-what happened?" she asked, lifting her hands to find her fingers and nails red with drying blood.

Wen didn't look away. "We surprised the bad guy. A shiz-ernet."

Oh gods. He must have been hiding behind the kitchen counter. She'd walked right into him. "I shot him?"

"Yep. Not fatal. Bastard still had life in him. Fought hard."

"Where?" she gasped, searching the room with panicked eyes.

"Gone." Wen looked pale, and he was breathing heavily.

"What? Where? Go after him!" she insisted, pushing to her feet.

"I had to check—"

"Go!" she choked out.

Wen gave her one last long look before he nodded sharply. He rose from his crouch and ran out through the door.

The room fell silent. All Mich could hear was her own breathing. *I made such a fool out of myself.* If there was any doubt before, there was none now—she was done. She'd let a suspect escape, even panicked when he attacked her. She tugged on her hair, a soft whine fighting loose from her throat. Her hands were shaking. Stumbling to the bathroom, she reared back at the bloodied, wide-eyed creature that stared back at her.

Slamming her eyes shut, she turned the hot tap on at full strength and thrust her trembling hands under the scalding spray. Red-tinged liquid poured down the drain before her eyes. She kept scrubbing, even after the water turned clear. Clawed fingers grabbed her arms. She jerked back, staring wildly around the room. No one was there.

Hands seized her neck and arms, holding her shoulders still. Healer Travnell stood in front of her. All she could see was his blue-covered chest. He forced her head back and poured tablets into her mouth, tipping water in from another cup. She choked, swallowing quickly so she could suck air back into her deprived lungs.

"Good girl," he said, patting her on the head. The hands disappeared and she was left alone, gasping into the silence around her. Patients nearby ate and danced, moaned and cried. Shadows climbed the walls. She looked around, her eyes hot and wet. Tears slid down her cheeks while inside, she screamed.

Mich snapped her eyes open. *Idiot! Don't close them.* Darkness was not her friend.

Keeping her gaze low to avoid staring into her own face, she examined her arms. Long scratches marred her skin, cutting through her jacket and shirt. *Hell's demons!* She'd have to get her jacket repaired. Again. This time there was no Tesi to do it for her. She examined the edges of the leather, ignoring the blood welling up from the slices in her skin. The leather was cut cleanly, her shirt destroyed. Claws, not a knife this time. The scarred face snarled at her, sharp teeth looming closer. She gasped for lost air as the image exploded in her mind. Shizernet! That's who her attacker had been. And her freak-out had let him escape. "Hell's spawn!"

The room was closing in on her again. Her chest tightened. She clutched at the doorway and pulled herself out of the bathroom. *Breathe.* Stumbling to a halt in the middle of the trashed room, she waited for Wen to return.

He didn't.

The door was open. There was no sign of him. No footsteps sounded in the hall. No smell of trees or ship ozone. Lifting her gaze to the ceiling, she sucked in a deep breath and held it. After a count of four, she released it slowly, letting air hiss out from between her teeth. When it was gone, she counted again and inhaled over the space of four beats. Over and over she repeated the simple meditation steps. When her body calmed and her breathing was steady, she lowered her gaze to the floor. Humming softly, she turned in a circle and studied the room.

Get back to work. Worry about explaining it all to Wen later. He'd report it to Daeh. He'd tell Charley.

She slammed her mind shut. *Stop! Focus on now. There is only now.*

The floor and the kitchen counter were streaked with red. She turned away from the evidence of her failure and stared at the living room. She picked her way through the mess. An up-ended table had been pushed against the wall and the papers it once held littered the floor. She dropped to her haunches to finger through them. The folder held an official report with a Calcryon logo. On her rapid read, it looked like an investors report. The other papers were letters, actual handwritten letters. Six of them. She flipped one over with a chipped fingernail.

Yetti,

I cannot thank you enough. You saved me. I still feel his cold hands on my skin and dread to think of what would have happened had you not appeared when you did. For that reason alone, I would have loved you. For you to give me the coin to leave that place is a dream beyond my imaginings.

You are a wonderful man. I truly thank you from the bottom of my heart.

Beshe

Mich stared at the words. "Are you kidding me?" She pulled the next letter clear.

My darling Yetti,

My love, I thank you dearly. You helped me leave Sima and I will be forever in your debt. As I hoped, I made it home in time for my mother's passing. Do not be sad for me, my love, for with your help, I was able to tell my mother I loved her one last time.

You have all my love.

Forever.

Demankika

A quick glance through the rest of the papers confirmed each letter was the same. The disappearance of the women who'd spent the night with Yetti was not suspicious at all; he'd paid for them to leave Sima's House. All of them.

The women might no longer be a concern, but Yetti's room had still been destroyed. That shizernet had been searching for something.

Footsteps sounded in the hallway outside. Mich drew her gun and moved behind the door, waiting, breathless and still. A shadow fell across the floor. "It's Wen," the man called before he stepped in through the doorway. Mich released a shaky breath and stepped out from behind the door. He eyed the gun in her hand before his gaze darted over the rest of her body.

He opened his mouth to speak but she got in first. "The shizernet?"

"Gone."

"Hell's spawn! Well, I've found something interesting." She dashed to the table for the letters. *Don't give him time to speak.* If she kept him distracted, he couldn't say she was off the team.

"Are you kidding?" he exclaimed, reading the letters. "Well, that's good news."

Her stomach dropped. "What are you talking about?"

Wen shot her a smile. "It means the missing women are fine. No more bodies to stumble across. Rel's friend will be happy."

How could Wen care about Carma's feelings at a time like this? Mich gestured to the rest of the room. "I haven't gone through everything yet."

His gaze examined the mess with a practiced eye. "I think the shizernet went through everything pretty thoroughly. We'll take the papers." They collected everything up off the floor. His gaze softened as it fell to her arms. "You're bleeding. We need to get you to a medic center."

"I'm fine," she said, not looking down. Now that he'd drawn her attention to the wounds, she noticed sharp little pains shooting along her forearms, electrical sparks that twitched and jerked her injured muscles.

"You're not." He took the papers out of her hands.

Her head rose and she narrowed her eyes at him. *Will he say it now?* He waited for her silently beside the door. She blinked, breathing in through her nose to keep her heart rate down, but to no avail.

"You're dripping," he said at last, pointing to the floor.

She glanced down as blood splattered against the floor. The disk-sized puddle grew wider as she watched.

"Fine!" she huffed. He held out his empty hand. The other clasped the papers. She eyed it, thought about it then shook her head, angry at her own weakness. With disdain soaking her voice, she said, "I can get there on my own."

*

Rel stared at the pristine room. Carma's breath tickled the back of his neck as she pushed closer to see over his shoulder.

"May I ask what you're searching for?" Marc asked from the hallway.

"Nope," Rel told him.

The uniformed man dithered, his fingers knotting at his waist. "Sir, the room is clean. My team come through daily."

"D'they remove anything?"

"Only the waste baskets, sir, and to replace items taken from the bar fridge."

"Where's trash taken?" Rel asked.

"To the incinerator, sir. Any obvious personal items are left alone, but trash is disposed of immediately."

"They been through today?"

"I would have to check for you, sir."

Rel nodded, slow and deliberate. The young man flushed. "I ... I'll go check for you now, sir." He reversed his trolley down the corridor. Rel watched him go then stepped fully into the room.

Carma shook her head.

"Dunno what ta expect, but it's worth checking."

She tapped on the wall and pointed back to the entry door.

"Yeah, maybe the neighbors will remember something."

The woman moved past Rel into the kitchenette and searched through the cabinets. Beneath Rel's feet, the suite's carpet held several footprints and drag lines in the thick pile.

He followed the marks into a bedroom and opened the bags stacked beside the bed. Rolled-up clothing, nothing more. He leaned on one hand to peer under the bed—nothing. From there, he made his way into the adjoining bathroom. The mirror and tiles gleamed brightly beneath the down lights. He was impressed with the hotel's dedication to hygiene and was devising a plan to book his next holiday with the chain when a loud knock drew his attention back to the kitchenette. As soon as Carma saw him, she pointed to the open window.

Across the road was another hotel. Shadows moved behind closed drapes, but as far as Rel could see, there was no un-usual behavior. He glanced at the street below. People walked or drove past; again, nothing seemed out of the ordinary. "I don't see—"

She pulled the window frame down, closing the window. Stretching up onto her toes, she touched the glass.

Above his eyeline was an imperfection, a hole the size of his finger cut into the glass. Rel counted at least ten windows in the building opposite with a clean shot to where he stood.

He spun and examined the floor and the walls. Beside the rear wall, between the bar refrigerator and the shelving unit, he found a finger-width silver canister. It was open at one end and there were traces of white powder inside.

He rifled through the drawers in the kitchen. *Bag? Plastic?* There had to be something here he could use. Gently, he nudged Carma to back away. She waved to get his attention, lifted her shoulder and tilted her head, signing something with quick moving fingers. "I don't understand." She scowled and raised her hands palms up. "I'm looking for—oh, there."

Rel tugged the clean trash lining out of the bin inside the sink cupboard and used it to pick up the canister, making sure not to spill any of the powder. Tying off the bag, he held the canister up to the window.

It fit the hole perfectly.

Chapter 24

As he stepped up to the medic center's back entrance, Zeth winced. Even slight movements pulled at the protective strips covering the slices on his chest. A day after running through the crop from hell, and the skin beneath the strips itched like crazy. The cuts on Mich's arms must burn in comparison. *I should stop whining.*

He was still in awe over what he'd just seen.

When that shizernet jumped out at her, she'd kept her head and shot him before he landed on her. Then she'd gone wild— every punch landing with brutal efficiency as she'd aimed for the shizernet's neck and kidney region repeatedly. She'd also targeted her attacker's ears—a known sensitive spot for the shizernet race. Zeth had felt completely powerless watching her fight, unable to shoot the attacker given his close proximity to her.

When she asked what happened, he'd tried to explain, but ever focused on the mission, she'd snapped at him to go after the suspect. Feeling completely schooled, he'd taken off after the fleeing man, reaching the street in moments. Following the blood trail, he'd tracked the injured man two blocks before the path disappeared.

Frustrated at having lost him, Zeth returned to the hotel to find Mich waiting. She'd cleaned up a lot of the blood, and her wounds didn't look as bad as he'd first feared. His relief then turned to embarrassment. He'd failed to apprehend the shizernet and Mich had been hurt on his watch. The feeling was made worse when she showed him what she'd discovered. Even injured, she'd managed to do a better job than he had.

Determined to make it up to her, he'd insisted on the trip to the medic center.

Steam had practically poured from her ears, and her glare could have melted glass as she'd made her displeasure clear. Vowing to do better in looking after his new partner, he held the door open and gestured for her to precede him into the waiting room. She shot him another fire-filled glare and pushed hard at his shoulder. He stumbled forward before he could catch his balance. "Easy there."

"Just go," she ordered, prodding him again. He gave up trying to be a gentleman and led the way, striding straight to the counter to flash his hologram identification. "Wen and Janelle. We need a healer immediately."

The young man at the desk gaped. His short blond hair was spiked high in the latest fashion. Clean-shaven, the young man's misty rose-colored eyes captured Zeth's attention. *Well, hello there.* He was talking into an earpiece, but ended the call quickly and grinned up at Zeth, showing plenty of teeth. He stood so abruptly his chair flew back and bounced against the wall as he brushed his hands down his extremely well-fitted suit jacket. *Come on, Zeth, head in the game.*

Mich snorted softly at his side and spun away. Zeth snagged her arm, releasing her quickly when she hissed in pain. "Sorry," he whispered. Her return glare was full of ice. Zeth turned back to the receptionist. "She's hurt. We need a medic."

The young man leaned over the desk, peering at Mich. "Of course. Give me a minute. All the medics here are rather busy at the moment." He sat down and tapped at his screen, his demeanor all business now. Mich disappeared into the empty waiting room. Zeth opened his mouth to suggest they didn't look all that busy, only to find the cute receptionist staring at his screen, his face twisted in confusion. "Is there a problem?"

"Healer Bicet already wants to see you."

"What?"

The young man flushed, his eyes darting everywhere but at Zeth. "There's a note here to call you, sir. I ... I hadn't got around to it yet."

"Right, well get him—"

"Sir, he arrived early this morning and went straight into autopsy. I don't think he'll be long, if you can wait?"

"I'm good," Mich snapped from the desolate waiting room.

Zeth nodded to the receptionist and followed Mich, stopping several feet away from his injured partner. Her eyes were glassy and she wavered a little on her feet. He wanted to insist she sit down, but said nothing, moving a few inches closer, prepared to catch her if she fell.

She noticed. "You should take the papers back to the ship. Brief Charley."

He hesitated. "Rel and Carma headed to the home of the women who last saw Yetti. Remember, he called on our way over here?"

"There's no need for him to waste his time going there, we found the letters. We need to focus on Calcryon."

"Rel says Carma needs to see for herself that they're okay. They didn't answer any of her messages." Zeth could understand why the woman wanted to check on her friends. If they were his friends, he'd be desperate to find them.

Mich huffed out a breath. "They've not responded because they're already gone—left town, or even the planet."

"It won't take long to check."

Mich snorted again. After a moment of silence, Zeth shuffled closer, debating whether to risk her ire and suggest she sit down. Her skin had a pallor any ghost would find healthy.

She twisted her head to pin him with a sharp look. "What are you going to put in your report?"

Report? The change in subject was such a surprise, he froze. "I haven't thought about it." That was certainly true. What would he write? He'd let the suspect get away and that she'd been injured? He figured he'd do what he usually did and put off writing it until he had something to actually put in a report. Like after they solved the case.

"It won't be in your report at all, will it?"

"What won't—losing the suspect? We'll find him." Why was she asking this? *Does she want an apology?* She deserved one. He found it hard to get the words out, preferring to stew on things in private. Rel often called him on it—Zeth had a problem owning up to his faults. One mistake tended to snowball into another, and the next thing he knew, a terrorist had blown up a cruiser full of school children.

It was time to man up. She was his superior in this mission and in skill—he owed her an apology. His skin itched. He opened his mouth, but she beat him to it.

"I've read your reports. They're a little thin on the detail, aren't they?"

A flare of embarrassment burned through him. He grabbed her arm. "How'd you get our reports?"

She gasped, shrugging off his hand. Her posture told him that he wouldn't like the answer. She continued aggressively, her narrow stare stabbing into him. "And your reports are always time- and date-stamped, images attached and thought processes recorded, right?" She shook her head. "How does he let you get away with it?" She pinched the top of her nose as the lines between her eyes deepened.

"We're not Hunters, Janelle," he retorted. "Things are a lot looser in the private sector. What's your problem?"

"I want to know what you're going to tell Daeh ... about me."

"Well, what are you going to write?" he demanded. Two could play at this game, and she was starting to piss him off. His shoulders straightened. So much for apologizing. It sounded like she was going to report everything—including his failure.

"What are you going to tell him?" she hissed again.

Stepping into her space forced her to look up at him. "What do you want me to tell him?" He knew it was the wrong thing to say as soon as he gave voice to the words. The look she gave him spoke volumes. She thought he was an idiot—an easily influenced one. He backed up a few steps. It was time. He could say the words. "Fine. Look, I'm sorry—"

"What?" Her face scrunched in confusion.

"What?" he snapped back. She was giving him shit for apologizing? His stomach twisted, sharp and hot. "Look, I'm trying to tell you I'm sorry for not spotting the shizernet." The heat in his face was more from anger than any lingering embarrassment.

"Why?" She swayed on her feet, her face suddenly losing all color.

"Whoa, are you okay?" He dove forward as she stumbled.

The receptionist appeared in the doorway. "Healer Bicet just messaged. You can enter now." Zeth released Mich and hovered until she proved she could stand on her own. Her skin felt clammy. Heat radiated from her body, and her face was still far too pale.

Picking up on the tension between the two, the receptionist stepped back. "Uh, when you're ready."

Zeth thanked him and looked Mich in the eye. She straightened her back and gritted her teeth. *By the One, she's incredible.*

"Let's get this done." She stormed past the receptionist through the door he indicated. Zeth mumbled an apology and quickly followed.

*

"Healer Bicet," Mich greeted, reaching out with two fingers to touch the bendalian's thin wrist in the traditional greeting. He pulled away before she could touch him. She glanced quickly at her fingers, searching for blood, but they appeared clean.

"Healer, Janelle requires medical assistance immediately." Wen's voice was insistent, stepping forward when the medic backed away. Yellowed gums grimaced behind the transparent mask covering his face.

"Thank you for giving me this opportunity. I've put calls into Calcryon and I'm awaiting a response from their study lead." He shook his head. "Forget that, this is more important. I need a sample of your blood, Mich Janelle. You too, Zeth Wen." Bicet gestured toward the small set of pulse-syringes on the desk. His tone was clear; it was not a request. "Mich Janelle, I will tend to your wounds in a moment, I promise."

"What's wrong?" she asked, not liking his tone or how fast he'd pulled away from her. She had a problem with people getting too close, but he hadn't struck her as having a similar issue.

When the Healer didn't respond, she fell into the closest chair. Bicet's actions chilled her from the inside out. What did he need their blood for, unless ... "Healer Bicet, what do you need our blood for? Your report or ..." She examined his tense face. "Something else?"

"Healer?" Wen's voice was softer.

Bicet didn't answer. He took Mich's blood with practiced efficiency. After he had Wen's sample in hand, he buzzed for a nurse. He did not remove his mask. Folding his gloved fingers together, he considered them both before he unclenched his hands and raised the holoscreen on the desk, clicking open a file.

"I have examined the body of the deceased telnak. The results are concerning."

"Healer," Wen interrupted. "She needs medical attention."

"Of course." Bicet didn't ask Wen to leave the room as he pulled out a second pair of surgical gloves and tugged them on over the ones he already wore. A fully covered nurse entered to take their blood samples away. The nurse's gaze skittered over them. The behavior sent a shiver down Mich's spine. Before the nurse left, Bicet requested a suture kit. The nurse returned to pass the healer a hand-sized case. Bicet stood, assisting Mich to remove her jacket. He carefully peeled the torn sides of her shirtsleeves apart, asking pointedly if she had any other injuries.

"No, nothing else." A sharp throat clearing from Wen made her add the bump to the back of her head and her pounding migraine.

"I can't give you anything for that until I check you over."

The normally chatty man said nothing more. Confused by the healer's silence, Mich leaned sideways to meet Wen's stare. His hands were clasped together and hung between his knees. Though the room was chilly, Mich felt sweat bead on her skin. Her eyes darted back to Bicet, flinching at the pinch of pain in her forearm. *Why isn't he telling us anything?* Bicet held a skin knitter to one of the gashes in her arm. The handheld device buzzed softly before it pulsed, and the sensation of pins and needles increased until her arm began twitching. She sucked in a deep breath and bit her bottom lip to stop from crying out. Bicet tightened his grip on her wrist.

"Hey!" Wen hissed. Her eyes snapped to his.

"What?"

"Think about something else."

She rolled her eyes—the only part of her not aching. "Like what?"

"Perhaps, if I tell you what I have discovered from the tel-nak's examination, it will provide the distraction you need?" Bicet said at last, moving the handheld device to the next gash. Mich groaned low into her throat as the pins and needles began again. She clenched a fist to stop from twitching. "Go ahead." She tasted blood.

"First, the telnak's injuries were substantial. It was difficult to discover the initial cause of death."

"It wasn't from an Enferrie spike?" Mich glanced at Wen in surprise.

"I did not say that," Bicet said. "There are … discrepancies. Given many of the telnak's organs have, to put it delicately, disintegrated, the spike's impact point could not be readily ascertained."

Without moving the hand holding the device, Bicet released her wrist and stretched his free hand back to tilt the screen on the desk. The remaining parts of the telnak's body were displayed. With a harsh swallow, Mich focused on the wall behind the healer's head. She'd dealt with plenty of dead bodies over the course of her career, but this was something infinitely worse.

Wen's gaze remained glued to the screen, his face pale. The pinprick-like feeling in her arm became a wave of fire. She jerked hard. Bicet's hand clamped down on her wrist. "Sorry," she grunted.

"Zeth Wen, if you would scroll down for me?"

The man leaned forward and did as asked. Mich glanced back to the display. "And enlarge," Bicet asked. "Yes, that one."

Wen tapped on the image and enlarged it until what was left of the telnak's internal organs were displayed. Bicet continued. "I discovered traces of the Enferrie powder in the telnak's throat and nasal passages. It is my determination he likely inhaled the poison."

"What? Your last report said the poison needed to be injected, hence the use of the spike." Mich lost her breath on the final word. *Dear gods, let him finish soon.* She refused to acknowledge Bicet hadn't even started on her other arm yet.

His six fingers gripped her wrist like a vice—she'd have bruises tomorrow.

"I believed it was impossible to infect a subject with Enferrie poison in this manner. You are correct; it is a liquid poison. When reduced to its powdered form it should become inert—completely harmless."

"How did the telnak breathe it in, and why did it kill him?" Wen asked.

Bicet leaned back in his chair, cracking his spine. Mich ground her teeth together. One arm down. "The Enferrie plant produces a liquid as the flowers are crushed. The liquid is then injected into the victim to kill them. To create a powder, I can only conclude that the poison has been chemically altered. The Enferrie powder in the telnak's lungs is a manufactured strain. It no longer needs to be injected to be lethal. Simply inhaling the powder will do the trick."

Mich's thoughts darted to Calcryon and the testing they were doing. "Calcryon are experimenting on the drug."

"That is why I am awaiting a call back from the study lead," Bicet said.

"They won't admit it if they did this." If the drug was designed for pain relief, how could it kill anyone? Why would Calcryon create a weapon that could be dispersed in a powdered form? The company's sales and its very reputation would be destroyed if this was true and the information got out.

Her mind examined the problem. If people grew sick—or died—and word got out that it was connected to Calcryon's experiments, it *would* destroy the company. That had to be the terrorist's plan. Take their drug and change it somehow. Use it to kill people then blame Calcryon.

She had to warn the Calcryon Executive Board and have them find a way to protect their employees. Any one of them could be the next target. Four remaining spikes meant four potential victims. She thought of the investors report. The company's stock would tank on even a hint of illness caused by their trial. But wait. If the powder could now be inhaled ... then the number of victims could be increased. *Hell's spawn.* All of Calcryon could be a target.

Bicet began work on her other arm.

"We have to warn them," she gasped.

"Who? Mich, what are you—"

"Calcryon. This is the plan. Use the company's own drug to destroy them."

Wen swore. Looking up at the Healer, he asked, "The telnak's brothers? Were they poisoned with the same powder?"

"I have examined all of the bodies from the orange stone fruit plantation crime scene. The other two men were poisoned, but were killed before the poison could finish the job."

"Healer Bicet, do you still believe the incubation period is two days?" Mich asked.

Bicet shook his head. "I am running tests now. To all appearances, the Enferrie powder requires direct inhalation. The canister Rel Charley recovered contained traces of the Enferrie poison. Luckily for Rel Charley and his friend, it appears that once exposed to air, the powder quickly loses effectiveness. I would suggest the poison must be inhaled within seconds of exposure."

"So rather than use an individual spike, the terrorist could fire a powder-filled canister like a dirty bomb, exploding it into a populated area and infecting hundreds if not thousands of people all at once?" Wen jumped to his feet.

Mich would have joined him had she been able to move. Instead, she dug her nails into her hand and tried not to flinch, gritting her teeth against the pain.

"I'm afraid that is not the worst of it. This powdered poison, once introduced to the body, has mutated, becoming what we are calling Enferrecalicus. The viral form is transmissible, and the symptoms of the infection are dependent on the race of the individual, making it impossible to track in the early stages."

"What?" *It's a contagious virus?* As the implications of Bicet's tests sank in, Mich's blood turned to ice. *Oh gods. He thinks we're infected.* Her stomach clenched.

"Coughing, sneezing, spitting, even kissing can spread the viral form of the infection. Only one telnak was exposed to the powdered Enferrie poison. It was the telnak himself who infected his brothers. Only those two telnaks and the human male found with them display any evidence of the second mutation."

"Hell's spawn!" Mich's whole body was covered in a cold sweat. She shot a glance at Wen, finding him staring wide-eyed at the Healer.

"In your handover report, you said the telnaks were discovered in an empty warehouse? We must quarantine the entire location and test any on site workers and the rest of your team immediately. Call in Rel Charley and his friend for testing. And the hotel staff where Rel Charley found the canister, to be safe. Also anyone you have since come into contact with."

"You think we've been infected?" Wen gave voice to Mich's fears. Already cold, she now felt even colder. Was this an unintentional consequence of manipulating the drug? It couldn't be intentional. Could it? She stared at Wen. It didn't look like he was even breathing. She recalled touching the manager at the Skein City Gem to take possession of the room key. Charley and Carma had been in the telnaks' hotel room and were currently at the home of the two women who'd been intimate with Yetti. Mich could understand now the precautions Bicet had taken, but if they were all infected, it might already be too late to contain the spread.

"We can only pray the incubation period is still two days. Any later and an infected person could spread this disease long before symptoms manifest," Bicet admitted.

"Can you tell if the second mutation occurred accidentally or if it was designed to act that way?" Mich asked. How far were these terrorists willing to go with their mission? If it was designed to spread, hell's spawn, everyone was a target. It changed the motivation of the terrorists. They would need to reexamine all of the evidence.

Bicet removed the skin-knit device from her arm and she clenched both fists tight, dropping them into her lap. The renewed skin on her forearms tingled.

The healer's lack of facial expression told her this was not the first time the question had been raised. He placed the device down on the desk but didn't rise. "There is a possibility the poison's effect on the telnaks is what created this mutation. Perhaps our results will conclude the strain has contained itself with the death of all three telnaks."

"And if the poison was designed to mutate, no matter who has been poisoned?"

"Then we are already too late, Mich Janelle. We have commenced your blood tests. Please remain here and call in the rest of your team." Wen had his comm unit in his hand as the door opened to admit a gloved and masked nurse. In the nurse's hands was a small bag. He removed two masks and passed them to Healer Bicet, who handed the first to Mich. The mask contained a small insert. "Please place the insert into your mouth so we can test your lungs. This should not take long."

Mich shuddered when the rubber touched her face. Memories overwhelmed her instantly.

Pale green walls surrounded her. There was no window or door. Her pulse thudded loudly in her ears while the cold bite of steel prevented any movement. A scream rose up in the back of her throat, but she couldn't release it. The mask sealed over her face with a sucking sound that echoed inside her head.

"Now, Miss Janelle, let's not undo all our hard work. Be a good girl." Healer Travnell *stood before her, holding a small injector device. She tried to pull away, but there was no escape. He pressed the device to her arm. The mask did not give her enough air. She gasped, trying to find oxygen.*

Blinking rapidly and fighting the images and sensations that came with them, Mich stared up into Healer Bicet's kind eyes and willed him to stop the memories from taking her away.

Bicet held a large gloved hand over her fingers. *"Focus on the sound of my voice."* The words floated into her mind.

Mich found herself transfixed by Bicet's lips; they hadn't moved.

Chapter 25

Rain misted over them in the dull afternoon sunlight. It was resing cold and a bitter breeze tugged at their clothing. Rel watched Carma pull her cardigan tighter around her body before knocking on the doorframe.

No answer.

She shrugged at Rel. Her eyes were glassy, her hair plastered to her head.

"Where could they be?" he asked. The three-story building arched high overhead but provided no shelter against the attacking weather.

She shook her head, frowning.

He rapped his knuckles against the doorframe and grumbled. They should have remained in *Lazydragon* and tried calling again.

He held up one hand to block the rain from falling into his eyes. *Now, that looks promising.* "Window," he said.

Carma squinted, then her eyes widened. She grabbed his arm and mouthed, *"Crazy."*

He didn't respond.

The building façade stuck out at odd angles, like giant waves, and it was only a couple of floors to the open window at the top. He eyed the balustrade around the porch. It looked sturdy enough to take his weight. From the railing, he made out several usable hand-holds in the fancy doorframe and lower floor window panes.

Carma hit his arm, hard. Glaring at him, she pointed to her watch.

"Won't take long to check. We can at least get out of the rain." Holding onto the top of the doorframe for support, he swung his right leg up to rest against the windowsill. Pushing up again, he pressed his knee into the top of the frame, catching his weight before launching up to grab hold of the window one floor above.

From there, the reach of his arms was just long enough to grip the next frame. At last, his fingers caught the open window at the top. A few contortions, one slip, and some bruised knuckles later, he fell through the window to land in a crouch inside.

He still had it. All those years of climbing in and out of Melita's bedroom before they married had taught him skills he could use for the rest of his life.

The room he fell into was empty. Neatly dressed and pretty, the bedroom might have starred in one of those altranet magazines his old school buddy used to leave open on his student screen.

Rel tugged open the door as his comm unit buzzed. "Hang on," he whispered and pushed the door shut again. He pulled a small earpiece from his pocket, jammed it tightly into his ear and pressed it on. "Yeah-lo?" His partner's voice came through clearly.

"Rel, you and Carma have to return to the medic center."

"Why?" Rel inched the door open and stepped into the empty hallway. A skylight lit his way to the stairs, which took him down into the main living area.

"Healer Bicet thinks it's a transmissible virus now."

"A virus?" Rel froze. Something in his chest clenched hard as Melita's drawn and tired face popped into his mind. *Not again.*

"I don't know," Zeth said. "Our tests are being run now, but you gotta get back here. The healer has to test you and Carma. If the virus spreads ..."

Rel imagined the chaos that would ensue from public knowledge of an uncontained deadly virus. "Yeah, I hear ya. Heading back now. We need a mask or a suit or something?"

"Just don't cough on anyone."

Rel signed off and considered his hands. He glanced at the door. Should he wipe down everything he'd touched? Given the dust-free room he'd left and the wet trail following him through the house, he figured he'd have to return to clean away his intrusion anyway. The kitchen would have some sort of disinfectant he could use; the women appeared to keep a pretty clean house.

When he stepped into the kitchen, he understood why the women hadn't answered Carma's messages.

Despro!

He covered his mouth with a hand and tried not to breathe. Sweat broke out over his body as he lifted his boot gently from the pool of blood and fumbled for his comm unit.

Moving briskly, he closed the kitchen door and headed for the front door, pulling it shut behind him with a solid thunk. While he'd been inside, the misty rain had become a downpour. Carma raised a sopping brow and gestured that they should move inside. Horrified, he shook his head, and grabbed her arm when she tried to push past.

"No!"

She pulled back, her eyes wide. Rel called Zeth back, growling into the comm loud enough to be heard above the rain. "No, we're not on the way. We're outside the house belonging ta Yetti's women. Found both of 'em dead. The yellow-eyed man, too."

As he spoke, Carma raised a hand to her face, her eyes filling with tears. He turned away from her pale face, and the blood-drenched room immediately returned to his mind. He swallowed the urge to hurl.

"I'm coming with a team. As soon as we get there—"

"Go back for testing, yeah," Rel agreed. *Do we have it?*

Carma pulled him down with her to sit on the top step. Closing the comm, he stared at his hands and prayed.

Chapter 26

Zeth struggled with his thick, black protection suit as he stepped from the vehicle. He heard a dull call behind him and turned to see Rel. He could barely hear his partner through the damned helmet he wore, his breathing sounding impossibly loud as it echoed in his ears. He hated these resing suits. The recycled air inside the helmet was too dry, and he was sweating copiously beneath the stretch-plastic.

"Hey," he said to Rel as he drew close. The rain outside had lightened to a drizzle and fell over them gently, the ever-present gray cloud cover adding to the gloomy mood. Zeth passed Rel the two carry bags containing their protection suits.

"Get dressed. The car's waiting. It'll take you back for the blood test."

"Ya good?" Rel asked. He handed one bag to Carma and pulled a set of too-big protection trousers from the other, dragging them on over his own.

"Mich's still waiting for her results. There was a delay of some sort. She's back at the center, waiting for you and the bodies." He hadn't liked leaving her there alone, but the healer had insisted she needed rest. Her body was still in shock from the injuries she'd sustained. Zeth had concurred, and Mich's furious stare had traveled with him toward the housing estate.

He gestured with his head toward the door. "What will I find inside?"

Four fully enclosed officers passed them on the stairs. One halted at the front door to press *Do Not Enter, Hazardous Materials* smart tape across the frame. The words flashed along the length of the tape.

Carma shuffled past, clasping the enormous suit to her tiny frame. The driver climbed from the dark blue vehicle to help her inside.

Rel said to Zeth, "Ya need to go in, see for yaself. The layout of the bodies, I can't make it clear in my mind. I need to know if ya see it too."

"See what?"

"I don't want to cloud ya assessment. Take a look and let me know."

Zeth nodded. "Fine."

Rel clambered into the hovercar and Zeth watched until they zoomed off into the distance before he turned and jogged up the short flight of stairs.

Rel's tests would come back clear. Zeth refused to believe anything else.

Ducking under the flashing warning tape, he followed the pointed finger of one of the suited officers into the hideous crime scene.

Two young ketallian women sat at either end of a long table, their hands bound behind them. Bruises covered their arms and faces. Their eyes were swollen shut. The woman closest to him looked badly beaten, her arm hanging loose in her bindings—broken. Both of their chins were drenched from the blood they'd vomited, enough to create a pool of red beneath each body. The puddle located close to the door contained a footprint they'd already established was Rel's.

He found the third body when he moved further into the room. A man was spread out on the floor beside the marbled kitchen bench. He lay face up, arms and legs stretched out from his body as though he'd been standing and had fallen backward as he died. Blood stained his eyes, nose and mouth. His head lay wreathed in blood.

Zeth swallowed and moved closer. The body's eyes were wide open. Yellow, just as Rel reported.

They'd found one of Yetti's killers.

Zeth examined the dead man from a distance while four suited figures—two medics and two security officers—documented the room. As soon as the closest officer indicated he had enough pictures, one of the medics bent to examine the dead man's arms. The woman scanned each wrist and shook her head. "No identification chip." She searched his pockets and removed a comm unit. It was locked; Zeth would need a tech expert to examine it.

He watched the officers catalog the rest of the scene. Even with their efficient movements, he could tell they were going to be here for a while.

Chapter 27

"Madam, may I ask where you are going with this patient?" The guard's voice was deep and scratchy, and Mich fought her desire to clear her throat in sympathy.

"To the garden, my dear."

The guard straightened. His eyes drifted over Mich again, one eyebrow raised in question. She wondered what the question was. The door swung wide with a creak that pierced the back of her skull and crawled all the way down her spine.

Her wheelchair was pushed across the threshold onto a wide porch, where she was hit with a blast of icy air that cut deep into her chest. She moaned at the pain, wanting to clasp her arms across her chest, but they were strapped to the chair.

"Bracing, isn't it, my dear?"

She was wheeled along the porch, past the stairs to a ramp she didn't realize hugged the outside of the building. In moments, they traveled over the stone path that bordered the building. The wheels of her chair trembled and rocked wildly. Without the nurse's steady grip, Mich feared she'd tip over. Humming filled the air behind her, a strange tune that danced at her periphery. She wanted to demand the nurse stop the infernal racket, but the music was in reality soft, and the hum didn't have a terrible tune. It was okay, she supposed.

Mich lowered her head to her chest. A tired yawn cracked her jaw. Her eyes felt heavy and she drifted, listening to the rise and fall of the sound, losing track of how long they traveled. The nurse continued her haunting humming. Mich's head bobbed against her chest, her thoughts slow and fuzzy. She didn't become aware of the garden until a tantalizing fragrance surrounded her.

"Wha?" she slurred, looking up. She wasn't sure when the humming had stopped.

Gray-green grass beneath her wheels was trimmed short, cut recently, if the smell of fresh clippings was anything to go by. Three bushes, about as high as her shoulders had she been standing, were right in front of her, covered in hand-sized violet flowers. The perfume emanating from the flowers was familiar, but she couldn't place it. On either side of the three bushes were large trees. In fact, everywhere she looked, she found trees with trunks wider than her waist rising up into the air. She'd never seen anything like it before. Pale blue moss grew on the tree trunks, creating great swirls of color right in front of her eyes, curling and spinning as she stared.

Initially, her stomach rebelled but slowly, the smell seeped inside her body. Cinnamon-like. Her stomach rumbled, reminding her that she hadn't eaten since early morning. This trip would mean missing the evening meal too. Not a great loss.

"This is my special place. A place I come to when I need to get away from the hospital. Beautiful, isn't it?"

Mich couldn't help but nod. It was peaceful here.

The thickness in her head increased. Blue was such a nice color. She spent a while trying to name the different tones. There was violet, navy and shades of cerulean and ocean blue. She drifted. The breeze, so cutting before, seemed unable to penetrate this silent place, leaving her surprisingly warm in her thin, hospital-issued pajamas.

"There now, isn't that better?" The nurse's voice floated to Mich's ears and into her skin. "Breathe deeply, my dear."

Mich did as asked and could almost taste the heady scent in the back of her throat. She closed her eyes as the humming *began again. Music filled her thoughts and for the first time in a very long time, her mind fell blissfully blank.*

Gentle fingers touched Mich's hand. She woke, startled, and scooted back on the bed in a rush to escape the figure leaning over her body.

The Skein City medic center's nurse widened her pink eyes over the mask that covered the lower half of her face. "I'm sorry to have surprised you, miss. You were asleep. I wouldn't have bothered you, but Healer Bicet said your results are clear. You are not infected. He asked to speak with you and Rel Charley. You have a little time to refresh before you attend him." The woman left the room.

Mich could still hear music. Sitting on the bed, she shook her head to clear the dream and stared off into the distance, wishing she had a window to peer out.

What had her dream been trying to tell her? It was so clear, clearer than it had ever been before. That woman—the green-eyed nurse in her dream—what had she been doing? Mich remembered her voice whispering, but didn't recall the words. *What did she want?*

Mich remembered little of her time at The Clinic. Healer Travnell, the nurses, the awful orderlies and even the other patients. She didn't recall being allowed outside. So why had she dreamed of a garden?

She blinked as the dream faded, and moved to the small bathroom, intending to have the fastest shower manageable. Freezing water woke her body and shocked her mind blank. Hopefully Healer Bicet would have better news for her now that she was awake.

Chapter 28

Once he was given the okay to remove the constricting suit, Rel went in search of Carma. Instead, he found a tired-looking Janelle, her pale face filled with shadows.

As soon as she saw him, she spun on one foot. "Follow me," she ordered.

"Bicet wants me," Rel told her as she leapt up the stairs in front of him two at a time.

She nodded over her shoulder. "That's where we're headed."

Exhaustion dragged at Rel. His hair was plastered to his head, still sweaty from the helmet he'd worn. He knew that if he dared to close his eyes, it wouldn't matter where he was, he'd just crash.

In front of him, Janelle opened an office door and entered. A bendalian man stood beside the window. He stared forlornly out of the frosted glass. When he didn't turn, Rel cleared his throat. "Healer Bicet?"

The long-limbed healer jolted at the sound. "Ah, Mich Janelle, Rel Charley. Come in, please. I have some news. I've spoken to the Calcryon pain study's director and when I mentioned your boss's name, they became a little more forthcoming. They are sending through a report of the study's participants and their reactions to the trial."

Rel was sure they hadn't authorized the good doctor to namedrop like that. He fell into the high-backed chair and sprawled low, trying to get comfortable. *Dresh! It's cold in here.*

He knew bendalians were used to a cooler climate than he was comfortable with, but did the healer have to bring it with him to Ketal Seven?

He clenched his fingers and contemplated stuffing them under his knees. His gaze drifted to Janelle. Worry lines dug deep between her eyes. She scratched her forearms as her eyes focused on the healer. Rel was concerned with how tired she seemed.

Bicet seated himself on the other side of the desk. "The three bodies Rel Charley found were indeed infected with Enferricalicus."

Rel closed his eyes and lowered his head. "Their names were Sophie and Terri."

"Excuse me?" Bicet looked blankly at Rel.

He shook his head. "The women. Sophie and Terri."

Bicet blinked. "Of course, Inspector. My apologies. Sophie and Terri were infected seven days ago, and the strain is a positive match to the strain Yetti exhibited."

"Died a week ago?" Rel questioned.

"Yetti infected them? Then the virus had already mutated." Janelle sighed loudly and leaned back, resting her head on the high back of the chair.

There was a long period of silence before Bicet uttered, "They died yesterday."

That was troubling.

"The incubation period is different?" Janelle confirmed, catching Rel's eye.

"Correct. I have notified my medical colleagues here, and the authorities."

Rel snarled. "They'll take over."

"Please allow me a moment to explain. This is larger than your detective agency can handle, Rel Charley. I had no choice. I can confirm the unknown male is a human from a secluded planetary sector in the spiral. The yellow eyes are created by a pigmented tattoo."

Rel winced at the thought.

"His infection strain is remarkably different. Our tests confirm he was infected prior to the women. Of pressing concern is the fluid build-up in his lungs. The same fluid was found in the respiratory systems of both women, though not to the same degree. The poison has certainly become a virus now, and a highly transmissible one."

Rel was horrified. This was no longer about destroying Calcryon. If the virus was not race dependent and was highly contagious, everyone was in trouble.

"The three bodies were found in the same room, I believe?"

Rel confirmed the healer's question with a nod.

"I can conclude the young ladies' lungs were affected after they were imprisoned."

"So that's why ya did the lung biopsy." Rel scratched at his chest. "Which was incredibly uncomfortable, ya know?"

Bicet nodded. "Indeed it is. The lung biopsy was necessary and confirmed that neither you, nor Miss Carma, is infected."

Relief immediately settled the ache in Rel's chest.

"The virus becomes dormant moments after leaving the body. Unfortunately for the two young ladies, they were already in the final stages of the Enferricalicus infection when he infected them again."

"They were infected *twice*?" Janelle looked horrified. Rel shared the sentiment.

"Yes," Bicet said. "Infection does not appear to stop the virus from multiplying or transmitting. We are in the process of analyzing the DNA. It is slow going, but we have already managed to identify several markers."

"Is there anything that can be done to speed up the process?" Janelle asked.

"A colleague here suggested we contact a scientist who works at the local university, analyzing seized merchandise for law enforcement. I've been told recreational drugs are quite pervasive at the Ketallen Third University and there are several ongoing investigations. The local office apparently has enlisted this man to help decode the drug DNA signatures in order to connect them with their creators. It is time-consuming work, and I understand he has an excellent history of correctly classifying the individual markers in the chemical compounds— particularly those of synthetic compounds. Has made it his life's work, in fact. If anyone can identify the markers of this virus quickly, I'm told, it is this man. Once we have that information, we can work on creating an antidote to the poison, or a vaccine to prevent the spread."

"What did he say when ya spoke to him?" Rel asked.

"I have been unable to get in contact."

"Let's head there now," Janelle said. "We'll bring him in to speak with you."

"The local authorities will meet you there, I believe. I've been told a man named Mason will be liaising with you to assist."

"Great," Rel muttered.

Healer Bicet held up a hand. "Rel Charley. I must have a private word with you before you go."

Rel's neck grew taut. It was never a good sign when a healer wanted to speak to you in private. He caught Janelle's eye. "Meet ya there," he told her, dropping back into the uncomfortable chair.

Bicet waited for the door to close. "I have noticed some irregularities in your blood sample."

Rel felt a stone of ice settle into his stomach. Leaning forward, he asked, "Irregularities?"

"You are part draal?"

"On my father's side." He stood, unable to remain seated, and paced the length of the room. "What does that have ta do with anything?" It always came out. Who he was, what he was. Dresh it, why couldn't they just let it go?

"I do not wish to cause distress and I apologize for asking you this, but as I have said, we have found irregularities."

Rel sat down, suddenly curious. "What d'ya mean?"

Chapter 29

Mich paced the stairs outside the Medic Center with growing impatience. The Center's organized car should have arrived already. The door burst open behind her and she swung around to find Carma running toward her, gesturing wildly.

"I take it you've been cleared?"

Carma's gestures grew wilder.

Mich shook her head. "Charley's with Healer Bicet. I'm sure you can catch him when he's finished."

The woman thrust her data pad into Mich's hands. Before she could even glance at it, the hovercar she'd been waiting for arrived, its horn blaring loudly. Mich held up the pad. "I have to go."

Carma pointed.

"I'll read it on the way."

The agitated woman grabbed Mich hard at the wrist. The driver below blew the horn again, his impatience clear. Mich tugged her arm free. "I have to *go*."

Carma gestured to the pad. Mich glanced down at the scrawled words.

Terri and Sophie were infected after staying with Yetti. If he infected them there ... and they returned to Sima's? I have to warn Sima.

"I can't allow you to do that. Go back inside and wait for Charley. When he's cleared, he'll take you. You can check on your friends then." Frustration radiated from the woman's body. Mich took hold of Carma's trembling hands and pressed the pad back into her fingers.

Carma pushed her away.

Mich gestured for the driver to wait and turned back. Her chest tightened at the blank look in Carma's eyes and the tremble in her lips. "If they were infectious, it's too dangerous to go on your own. A protection-suited security team should go. Tell Charley." It was probably too late for Carma's friends. Mich could see in Carma's eyes she didn't want to hear that truth. "I'm sorry." It was all Mich could say. She jogged down the stairs to the waiting hovercar, leaving Carma behind.

*

Wen's body snapped ramrod straight when he realized Mich had arrived alone.

"Charley's results are clean, don't worry." She held up her hands. "Bicet kept him back to talk about something else. Charley said he'd meet us here." She didn't mention Carma's request, though he clearly saw something in her face. She spoke before he could ask. "If the telnaks infected anyone between their hotel and the plantations, people are going to start displaying symptoms soon," she said. She swallowed hard and forced herself to add, "Carma's worried about Sima's House. Hell's spawn, if anyone else is infected, it's already too late to stop the spread. I told her to find Charley. We need to focus on this scientist. Bicet is hoping his tracking program can be altered to track the potential spread of the virus."

The incessant rain had at last stopped and the clearing cloud cover allowed weak green-gray winter sunlight to shine down upon them. The cold light reminded Mich of her dream. What had she been doing in the garden? Her nose twitched. She rubbed at the skin beneath her nostrils. *Is there something wrong with me?*

"Wen, the ketallian authorities are getting involved. I've been told an Officer Mason is our go-between. Bicet has already put the medical centers on alert."

The tension tightening Wen's body grew tighter. "Well, let's get on with it before this Mason and his goons get here," he said.

"Do you think the spread of this virus can be controlled at this point?"

"By the One, I hope so."

They made their way to the Admissions Hall. After a threat or two, a few glares, and a hand strategically placed upon a weapon, they were given access to the university's computer systems.

Mich briefed Wen on the scientist as she searched for his file. "There. Symod Gajob. Lives in unit eighteen, works in Lab Seventeen in the science hall of the DeMarco Building." They leaned forward to examine the man's image. Closely cropped gray touched blond hair, watery pale pink eyes and a thin face.

She sent the image to their comms. A quick glance at the timepiece on the wall had her groaning loudly. Lunchtime. "This guy could be anywhere—lab, home, meal hall, and anywhere in between." She pointed to a flashing e-flyer stuck to the wall above the terminal; it was bright orange with a date circled. "Looks like tomorrow is the latest graduating ceremony. If we don't find Gajob today, there'll be thousands of people walking around here tomorrow. We'll never find him in the crush."

"So where am I headed?" Charley's voice from the doorway surprised them both.

"Hey," Wen grunted. Charley's lip twitched and he grunted in return.

After a moment, Mich held up her hand between them. "What happened with Carma?"

Charley's eyes widened. "What happened with her?"

"She was looking for you. Worried about her friends at Sima's. I told her to find you."

"She didn't." He snatched up his comm. They all waited, tense, for a reply. "Nothing," he grumbled.

"You think she went on her own?" Mich asked.

Wen tapped Charley on the shoulder. "You want to go after her?"

Charley scowled at the comm then shook his head. "Ya need me here." He texted another message to the woman and put his comm back in his pocket. "She'll message."

Mich raised her eyebrows at him. He was fighting his instinct to go. Why?

Charley stepped forward to look at the image on the screen. He linked to the university map, which rose up in a holographic three-dimensional image above the desk. "I'll take the meal hall."

"I'll take the lab."

Mich caught the look of concern Wen sent her way and stiffened, waiting for his comment for her to be careful. He twitched his head. "Guess that leaves me the unit," he said at last.

"If we all get zero, I say we hit the bars. It is a university after all," Charley suggested, a manic expression lighting his face. Probably attempting to distract himself from worrying about Carma. Mich caught him peek at the silent comm, tugging it partway out of his pocket. She wished she could ease his mind, but feared they all knew what Carma would find at Sima's House. In her head, Mich heard the flutter of music.

She stared at Charley a moment longer and then shrugged. They had a job to do. "Get going." She pushed past the two men and led the way out of the building. They had no time to waste.

*

Carma had still not replied by the time Rel stepped inside the cafeteria. He dreaded what that meant. She hadn't waited for him at the medic center. She didn't need or want his help. It hurt, and he was angry over how hurt he felt. Carma had come to mean so much to him in such a short space of time. Perhaps she didn't feel the same way about him.

He shook the thought from his mind and stared around the noisy cafeteria, hoping to get his head back in the game.

Like every meal room he had ever been in, the hall was large and packed full of people talking, laughing, and generally getting in each other's way. The room was shaped like a large octagon with dull sunlight seeping in through the skylights above. Every wall was covered in art and numerous electronic signboards. Voices talked over each other, excitedly discussing outfits, shoes and dance moves. Hovering vendor carts filled every available space.

Healer Bicet's question warred with Rel's worry for Carma. It wasn't right that the healer had asked him to volunteer. Why should Rel help? What had they ever done for him? The *they* in his mind didn't have a face, though, unsurprisingly, the body shape was a little like Mich Janelle. He thought of all the bullies he'd ever fought and of the people who'd treated him as though he was a monster. He owed them *nothing*.

Rel had only ever been treated badly because of who he was. And now, it was that very difference that made him the only person who could potentially help them. But as Bicet had said, it was his body, his blood. Ultimately it was his choice to make.

Hopefully Zeth would give him some much-needed advice. He wished he'd had a chance to talk to his pal about it all. He wondered what Carma would think of the request. Rel knew what Melita would have thought. She'd want him to do it. He forced the dilemma to the back of his mind and refocused on the hall around him. Down the center was a counter displaying a range of hot and cold food. Robotic servers darted between tables, delivering orders. Along the furthest of the octagonal walls was a long ice-cream bar. That was the difference between military mess halls and university ones, Rel figured— the desserts.

He made his way through the hall, tempted to hit the ice-cream bar in a big way. The bar would give him a good view of the room, he reasoned as his stomach growled loudly.

He ordered a large scoop and waited, leaning back against the counter to stare around the hall. He didn't see the scientist anywhere.

Bicet's information was like a virus of its own, infecting his thoughts. Rel didn't know what to make of it. Of course he'd given the man a sample of his blood for further testing, but it made his skin crawl to do so. He should have said no—a definitive no. A no to all of it. He pulled his silent comm from his pocket again and glanced at the screen. *Where is she?*

A sudden touch on his shoulder had him spinning around, his hand dropped to his belt instinctively, ready to lash out at the offender.

"Um, whoa! Sorry!" The girl who'd touched him stepped back quickly, her hands darting up in surrender when she saw the weapon at his belt.

"What?"

The young woman kept her hands raised. Rel activated his hologram. She nodded slowly and lowered her hands. "I thought you were a little old to be a student. Are you lost? Or just early for tomorrow?" She gestured to the orange graduation ceremony smart posters flashing across the message boards. "I could show you around, maybe?"

Rel settled his stance and worked to keep his face calm. He spied a gaggle of girls over the young woman's shoulder, giggling, and bit back a sigh. *Still a carnival attraction.*

The server handed him a giant cone. "I'm all good, sweetheart," he told her, taking a large bite of the cold treat. He turned his back on her and looked toward the entrance doors. They swung open to admit more students. Rel's eyes dropped to his cone before flying back to the door. "Oh, hell."

He looked sadly at his ice cream, took a quick bite and thrust the cone into the nearest trash bin. Fumbling with his comm unit, he shouted his partner's name and ran for the door.

"You found him?" Zeth's voice floated up from the device as Rel pushed his way through the crowd of hungry young people.

"No, but I've got the shizernet." Rel raised his gun even as he caught the eye of the large, scarred man. The shizernet took off back out through the door.

Dresh!

"He made me!" Rel yelled into the comm before shoving it into his pocket. He pushed students out of his path in his desperation to reach the doors before the criminal got away. There were several shouts and a scream, which was picked up and cascaded across the room as more and more students realized Rel was brandishing a weapon.

"Inspector, this way!" the girl who'd spoken to him earlier shouted. "It's quicker this way." She stood beside a fire escape door. Rel pushed toward the girl.

He burst outside. The wind had picked up while he was inside and it was now blowing a gale. Pouring rain thundered to the ground; he was soaked in moments. In the distance, blurred beneath the torrential rain, he spotted the shizernet's black jacket and sprinted after him. They ran down a long pathway between towering buildings and onto a pebbled footpath that skirted a large gymnasium, racing toward the underpass of a flash-crete bridge. The bridge spanned the length of the ball courts, and Rel noticed large chunks of flash-crete had fallen to the ground below and slowed so that he didn't lose his footing on the uneven surface. He swiped rain out of his eyes with his free hand. His chest heaved and his legs burned as he forced himself to leap over the bridge's debris. Orange posters flashed into his mind. *Is the virus here?* Is that what the shizernet was doing? Was the university the next terrorist target? He accelerated at that thought.

The shizernet ran underneath the length of the bridge. The howling wind caused the man to lose his footing on the unstable path. Rel nearly went down too. He heard a crack. He didn't recognize the sound—not a weapon or a bone snapping—so he shoved it out of his mind.

A familiar figure jumped off the bridge right in front of Rel, flattening the shizernet to the path. Rel caught up with them as Zeth cold-cocked the man.

Rel doubled over, panting hard. He rubbed a fist against his sternum as he straightened. "Took ya long enough."

"Hey, I ran from the other side of the campus!" Zeth complained, sucking in air. He brushed flash-crete dust and pebbles off his trousers. The dust left streaks where Zeth's trousers were wet. *Flash-crete dust?* Rel's gaze darted up to the underspan of the bridge. Standing this close, the fissures looked rather large. The wind gusted mightily, forcing Rel to brace his stance.

"You good?" Zeth asked.

"Yeah." Rel straightened but clasped his sides, still breathing hard. He couldn't help glancing up at the underspan of the bridge again. "Lost an ice cream over this guy."

"Raspberry?"

"Chocolate and orange. Seriously, like, this big," he answered, gesturing with his hands. "Search him?"

Zeth pulled the shizernet to his feet as his comm unit squealed. Busy holding onto the thrashing man, he ignored it. The criminal twisted violently, hissing and jerking, trying to create enough leverage to pull away. The bandage across the shizernet's shoulder slipped and his previous wound bled sluggishly. Another crack echoed nearby, almost hidden by the wails of the wind. Rel slapped the shizernet hard over one ear. The shizernet froze, a red forked tongue poking out between the lips of his elongated mouth as Rel patted him down. "No vials."

Zeth nodded and pulled his comm from his pocket.

"You get him?" Janelle's voice sprang up from the device. Rel pulled the shizernet straight so he could pin the man's arms behind him with the plastic flash-cuffs Zeth handed over. The cuffs looked like a simple plastic string. He wrapped it around the shizernet's wrists and activated it with the button on the end. The string immediately hardened into unbreakable steel, fitted exactly to the shizernet's wrists.

"Yes," Zeth told her.

"Good," she said. "I'm gonna keep looking for Gajob. Heading into the lab now. There are restrictions here, so I'm turning my comm off."

Rel forced the bound shizernet to step forward. "Ya check the unit yet?" he asked his partner.

"Yeah, yeah. I'm going back." Pocketing his comm, Zeth jogged up the path away from Rel, following a sign pointing to the university's residential buildings.

Rel shook the struggling shizernet. "Hey, hey, settle down," he ordered, and dragged the bound man toward the university's entrance. "Who's your boss? The one behind the bombings. Huh? The poison attacks?"

Hissing angrily, the shizernet didn't answer.

"Why turn the poison into a virus?" Rel demanded. The bound man twisted, slipped Rel's hold and flipped. Impressive, since his clawed hands were still pinned together and given the bleeding wound in his shoulder. Rel tackled him. As they rolled across the ground, Rel's unbound wrists gave him the upper hand and he punched the shizernet in the wound on his shoulder. The violent man shrugged off the blow and twisted his arms, pulling them apart with a guttural roar. The metal bands fell to the ground.

The shizernet turned and clawed his nails across Rel's chest. With a pained gasp, Rel pulled away. The shizernet kicked out in an attempt to keep Rel down. Something shiny dropped from the criminal's jacket before he took off running up the path. Rel rolled, coming up on his knee beside the device. It was a black metal ring.

A finger laser! Damn it to Dresh. That was how he'd gotten the cuffs off.

Cursing loudly, Rel staggered to his feet. In the distance, the shizernet sprinted away. Rel took off after him.

A metallic screech and a thud low enough to feel in his feet snapped Rel's gaze upward.

Another thud gave way to a pop ... and then another.

Dragging his gaze back down, Rel's feet stuttered to a stop. A few women walked beneath the bridge between Rel and the shizernet, and it seemed they hadn't yet noticed the drama occurring above them. A loud screech and a crack froze Rel's heart mid-thump.

The peppering of sharp pings and the twang of something tense snapping reached him. Looking up, he swore violently as the fissure in the underspan flash-crete of the pedestrian bridge tore wider. One pop became another, and then another. Then the pops became a tearing crackle.

The fissure in the flash-crete ripped along the full length of the bridge. Rel launched forward, pushing at the women hard, screaming for them to move.

He recognized one of the faces. Ice-cream girl. He shoved her and her friend away from the bridge. Around him, students screamed and fled in panic as realization dawned. A spray of insta-asphalt and recycled super-plastic rained down over them like heavy snow.

"Go go go!" Rel urged. The two women turned to run. Rel tugged ice-cream girl back and pushed her and her friend in the opposite direction. "Run!" The bridge came down behind them with a thunderous roar. They were thrown forward. Rel landed hard and rolled, tucking ice-cream girl under him.

A thick silence fell, as though the world turned off its speakers. Rel could only make out the sobbing of the girl beneath him by the jerking of her body. A wall of gray dust smashed over them. Rel covered his mouth, tucking the woman tighter to his chest as it became impossible to breathe. Coughing hard, he waited, his heart beating frantically in time with hers.

The world became dark. Time was immeasurable.

Rel raised his head. A mountain of flash-crete, re-bar and rubble was piled where the pedestrian bridge once stood. Pelting rain turned everything shiny. One by one, shocked students began to approach the disaster area. Ice-cream girl's friend lay a short distance away. She moaned and rolled onto her back. Two brave souls climbed the wet pile, searching for anyone who was trapped, throwing rocks to the side as they answered a desperate cry for help.

Flash-crete dust covered everything, painting the area a ghostly gray that was becoming paste under the downpour. Ice-cream girl assured Rel she was fine. He helped her to her feet and left her and her friend in the capable hands of another student.

He searched the rubble for the shizernet. He found a leathery hand sticking up out of the chunks of flash-crete and swore loudly. Another clue dead. He grabbed his comm. "Zeth?"

"What the resing hell just happened?"

"Pedestrian bridge collapse. I'm fine. The shizernet, not so much."

"Can you handle university security?"

"Yeah. I've got it." While Rel waited, he checked his comm for further messages. Still nothing from Carma. He typed quickly, his fingers leaving dusty streaks on his comms's touchpad. *Carma, where are you?*

*

Carma made her way to the hidden streetside rear door leading to Sima's House, ignoring the repeated alerts from her comm. She wore the protection suit she'd dumped in a pile on her medic center room floor, holding the excess material of her suit around her waist.

As Carma made her way inside, the bad feeling in her stomach grew stronger. It was the same feeling she'd had at Sophie's, right before Rel had found the bodies of her friends.

Rel's caring face filled her mind. He truly saw her. For all of her life she'd hidden herself, forced all emotion from her face, and had smiled and laughed at the customers, pretending she wanted to be there when nothing was further from the truth. She'd pretended that she didn't care about the pinches or the innuendo or the lecherous looks. What else could she do? No family other than Sima, who'd pulled her out of the cells with her poisonous offer: stay and die or join the House.

But Rel was different. He'd truly seen her, believed in her. She wanted to help him and hoped, prayed, he'd help her in return. And he hadn't sent her away. She couldn't let him go. To truly be free, she had to find out why Sima had stopped messaging.

Since leaving Sima's House, Carma had received daily messages from Sima. The messages, alternatively begging and demanding she come back, had continued unrelentingly—until yesterday.

It was quiet inside Sima's House, and the darkness put her on edge. Sima's House was *never* closed. Taking several small steps, Carma felt for the wall with all the light switches. She had the sudden irrational fear that as long as she didn't switch on the lights, everything would be fine. Berating herself, she flicked the lights on. The room was empty. Now she was even more worried. Where was Sima? Where were all the girls and boys? Where were the customers?

On soft feet, Carma stepped through the room. She glanced at the sofas and armchairs. The cushions were clean and there were streaks in the floor pile; even the surfaces of the tables were free of dust. She knew the main room was cleaned every third day and that would have been yesterday. The room had remained undisturbed since then.

Ducking her head into the kitchen, Carma took note of the clean floors and the cleared bench tops. She made her way toward the large dressing room out the back where the girls and boys refreshed their clothing and makeup between customers.

Her comm dinged. Carma didn't hear it. Her mouth dropped open at the sight that greeted her beyond the dressing room doorway; there were bodies everywhere. Sima was slumped over a chair at the end of the room, dried blood streaking her face like tears. A girl or boy lay sprawled before each mirror. Dried blood surrounded every body.

They were all dead.

Carma stepped back. She had to call Rel. The whole House would have to be sealed, and the bar above evacuated. At the doorway, Carma stopped. She glanced back at the bodies of her friends. If she had been here, she would be dead, too. Without knowing it, Rel had saved her life.

Only days ago, Carma had helped Trinny with her new dress, and fought with Sammy over the caff machine. And Timina, poor Timina, Sima's long-legged shadowkeeper. He'd always been so sweet to her. Timina's table was the closest to the door. Carma moved to his side. So beautiful and full of life, Timina now lay silent and still, his head rested against the table top as though he'd just fallen asleep. Beneath the blood on his face, he was covered in a red rash. Carma swallowed down her nausea at the sight of the pus-filled bubbles. Why had no one run? They had to have known they were sick, that something was wrong. Carma scowled at the large woman splayed out in her favorite chair. Carma knew why none of them had left; Sima had ordered them not to, as she had every time one of them so much as caught a sniffle.

Heart beating loudly in her ears, echoing in that strange way every sound inside her suit did, she leaned closer to Timina's face. There was something stuck in the blood next to his mouth. She picked up a pair of long-nosed tweezers and with a shaking hand tugged the hair free from the blood. A long gray hair. Carma's head snapped up; she spun toward the empty dressers belonging to Sophie and Terri. Terri's diary sat exactly where she'd left it beside her eyeshadow spray. Terri wrote every minute of her life into that book. If she had written of Yetti's booking, it would be in there. Carma picked up the diary and pressed it to her chest. She could no longer help any of her friends but she might be able to help Rel. Her breath caught as her throat closed. She fumbled for her comm-to-text unit and wrote out a message to Rel.

What am I going to do? She stared around the horrific nightmare that had once been her home. Looking back, she let out a silent scream and her tears fell at last.

She was finally free. But at what cost? And what was she going to do now?

Chapter 30

Before turning her comm unit off Mich logged onto *Lazy-dragon*'s secure altranet connection to check her snifferbot's progress through Tripness's servers—*kill them all.*

Three messages pinged into her message bank. The first contained a number of shipping routes. The second was a list of dates with corresponding ship names, but no locations. The last message was an image file. The remote signal was weak and it was taking too long to download. She closed her comm —she'd have to load it later.

Pausing in the doorway of Lab Seventeen, she read the sign attached to the wall next to the sealed door. It warned that the next room was a level-three contamination lab for the examination of bio-hazardous materials. The master of the university must have pulled a lot of government strings to qualify for a level-three lab. They were meant for containing toxic substances and were required to be housed inside layers of security and located deep underground.

What kind of sponsors does this place have to get approval for this?

The red emergency light beside the door was unlit, so it was safe to enter. A sign beside the door read:

To Enter, You Must:
- Wear a university static suit.
- Remove all jewelry.
- Tie loose hair back.

She hesitated before reaching for the white static body-suit hanging beside the door. The onesie had inbuilt stretchy booties. She found no helmet or hood in the cabinet below, only a handful of hairnets. Scowling, she rolled up her braid and tucked her hair inside. The net sealed over her head like a hat; a very tight one. Scratching her instantly itchy scalp, she unlocked the door with the university-assigned master keycard and pushed it open. The entire lab was bright and shiny and exuded danger.

Three rows of metal bench tops sparkled beneath bright overhead fluorescent lights. A metal sink with a high-pressure hose attached was spaced alongside each bench. Every wall was covered in holographic screens displaying long strings of formulas. Signs indicated each bench would be separated in the event of an emergency, with force shields and the reverse air pressure activated. Oxygen masks were located beneath each metal desktop.

At the far end of the lab, there was a line of machines and a large refrigeration unit. Through the fridge's glass doors, Mich made out numerous holographically labeled containers and vials. A retinal scanner on the side locked the fridge.

Glancing up, she realized the high ceiling had to make space for four large industrial exhaust fans, one located in each corner of the room. Next to each fan was a secondary box that must have housed the air-filtration units. Warning signs posted around the room detailed long safety procedures and evacuation steps. Signs stuck to the walls below the unlit red bulbs warned that if the lights were on, it was too late to leave.

Movement flashed in the corner of her eye. Mich spun around to face the rear wall as a vacuum-sealed door popped, giving off a sucking sound as it was pushed open. The labs were supposed to have only one entrance, given the level of security. That door shouldn't be there.

A white-suited man stepped into the room. His ashy gray hair was squashed flat under the hair net. His eyes widened at the sight of her.

Mich breathed out softly as she recognized him. This was the man they were searching for: Symod Gajob.

"Can I help you?" he asked, closing the door without taking his eyes off her. He walked forward, clearly trying to behave as if he had no concern with finding a strange woman standing in the middle of a secure lab. The tension in his body and the twitch of his hand belied that façade.

Placing a small bottle onto the bench, he turned to face her. There were several tablets, glass vials and injection pods around his workstation. Mich noted the vials were sorted according to length.

"Professor Gajob? My name is Michele Janelle. I'm a private investigator and I need your help."

"What with?" He moved to block her view of his desk. The muscles in his neck bunched tight with tension. One hand flexed at his side as the other thrust a notebook into a nearby drawer.

"A virus, actually. I've been given your name as a—"

The scientist bolted.

Why is he running? Unless ... hell's spawn. He must be part of it!

She launched herself at him over the central lab bench, grabbing his wrist, and used her body to push him hard against the wall. He twisted to slip her hold, his foot sliding back to tangle between hers. She lost her balance and hit the bench hard, her wrist slamming against the cold metal as she caught herself. Pain flared along the bone, leaving her gasping.

Gajob flung several stools and trays in her direction, forcing her to duck. She growled, reaching out to snatch his arm. "Stop!" she ordered. "I just want to talk."

Dodging her hand, he ran toward the refrigeration unit.

"There's nowhere for you to go," Mich said, advancing slowly.

The scientist's hands trembled as he fumbled with the clasp of his suit.

"Keep your hands where I can see them," she ordered. Her own fingers worked her suit's zipper, anxious to get to her weapon before he did.

Gajob pulled the stopper from a vial that appeared in his hand and threw it in her direction. She dove away. The vial shattered on impact ... empty. One piece of glass remained stuck together with a label. A Calcryon label.

Heart racing, she stared at the shards of glass before jumping back to her feet and running after him.

The scientist shouted into his comm unit and ran for the rear door. It swung open before he reached it. A large gray-haired sholan filled the doorway, the pistol in one meaty hand pointed directly at her. As soon as he saw Mich, he fired.

She dove again, her knees scraping the floor as she slid under the nearest bench. Tiles next to her hand exploded. The last piece of Yetti's puzzle stalked toward her.

Mich peeked over the counter and fired back.

Where's Gajob?

A floor tile inches from her hand exploded in dangerous shards. She crawled beneath the benches in parallel with the limping sholan. What was it Healer Bicet once said? He suspected the sholan previously dislocated his knee. Heart in her throat, she darted up to fire ... only to see the giant man slam his hand onto the large emergency button on the wall. All the lab's lights went out. An ear-piercing alarm rang out and her world turned to flashing red. Desks moved as the security systems took full effect. A spray of something strangely chemical showered the room.

Behind her, the airlock entrance door sealed shut with a loud sucking sound. *Hell's demons!* Under the flicker of the red lights, every shot she fired at the sholan missed.

The drawer next to her head exploded. Flinching away from it, she dove under the sholan's laser fire and slid under another bench. To her delight, the back panel was missing. Holding her breath, she rolled through the gap and out between the sholan's legs, kicking hard at his knee. He howled in pain and stumbled.

She twisted, spun again and pointed her pistol straight into his face. Without hesitation, she shot him directly between the eyes. The heavy body collapsed forward. Mich threw herself aside as he landed hard enough to rattle the bench tops above her head.

Gasping loudly, ears aching from the still-blaring alarm, Mich lay still for a moment just breathing, her mind blank. A soft tune played in her head. *That tune.* It was the one from her dream. The dream she didn't think was real. *Maybe it is?* Her skin turned to ice at the thought. If the dream was real ...

She stumbled to her feet and backed away from nothing, unable to stop moving until she hit the wall. If the dream was real, then so was the nurse. And if the nurse was real—the voice in her head was ...

Oh hell.

Mich could no longer trust her own mind.

Chapter 31

Standing before the door to room E16, Zeth suspected no one was home. The hall was filled with young people—students of all nationalities and ages gathered in open doorways chatting to one another or playing with their comms. Music thumped from somewhere down the hall, but from Gajob's apartment, there was only silence.

Swiping the door lock with the master keycard, Zeth cracked open the door and peered inside. "Symod Gajob—identify yourself."

There was no response. A few heads poked out of the room next door. The door behind him also swung open. Zeth glanced back to see two disheveled heads pop out. Pale pink eyes blinked at him in surprise. The woman on the left looked like she'd just come home from a party. Gold glitter dusted her eyes and her hair looked spray-painted purple. "He's not there."

"Symod Gajob?" Zeth clarified, his shoe holding the door open.

"Yeah. He's never home—practically lives at the lab."

"Is he there now?"

"He's always there."

Zeth pushed the door open. He still had to confirm Gajob was not at home. In the meantime, he pulled his comm out to warn Mich.

*

Janelle hadn't checked in by the time Rel dealt with the campus security and the medics. He was ordered to wait for Officer Mason. He nodded, acting compliant until they turned their backs, then he slipped away and called Zeth. Zeth hadn't been in touch with Janelle either. He was on the other side of the university, but already on the move. Rel was closer.

There was no movement to be seen through the glass viewing circle when Rel arrived at the lab. With the alarm screaming, he tried the door. It was sealed from the inside. Rel peered into the lab.

Lying face down on the floor was a big, gray-haired sholan.

Rel grabbed his comm to buzz Zeth. He found a text from Carma: *They're all dead.*

Rel's eyes slammed shut. Dresh! He buzzed Zeth's comm.

"Yeah?"

He didn't know where to start. "Janelle found trouble," Rel told him.

"I'm on my way."

"No. I'm at a level-three lab, staring at a dead sholan."

There was a pause before Zeth asked, "Where's Mich?"

Rel peered through the display window again. "Don't know. Not here. The door's sealed from the inside. Can't see her."

"She's not there?" Zeth sounded out of breath.

"Resing door's locked. She can't have left." Rel read the warning sign stuck to the wall and eyed the static suits in the cabinet. He couldn't see any helmets.

"You said the sholan's dead?" Zeth asked.

"Sure looks dead. There's a lot of blood."

"The virus?"

Rel glanced at the door. "Can't tell from out here."

"We need to get in."

"Level three, pal."

"Then you can't open the door without a hazmat team. Call Bicet. Gajob's apartment is empty. I'm on my way back to you."

"Carma found her friends."

Zeth was silent for several heartbeats before he sighed mightily. "Not good?"

"Not good," Rel confirmed. He peered through the porthole in the lab door again. They had too many bodies. But a body in a secure level-three lab required a high protocol response, and given the sholan's connection to the case, Rel knew he would have to contain the lab before he went anywhere else. He'd call in Carma's location and ask for her to stay until security and the medics got there. He should never have involved her. Should have just done what Janelle told him to do and kept Carma out of it. If he'd done that, though, she'd be dead, just like her friends. She had no one left. No one but him.

He closed his eyes, breathed deep and refocused. Through the porthole window he examined what he could of the scene before him. The sholan's head wound looked like a pistol shot but there was no way to know if the sholan had been exposed to the Enferricalicus virus before his death.

Taking another deep breath, Rel stepped away from the lab and activated his comm unit. "Healer Bicet, I have bad news ... Healer Bicet?" he repeated when the line opened but the man didn't respond.

"Rel Charley, have you decided?" The healer sounded distracted.

"Found a body in a secure level-three laboratory at the Ketallen Third University. And Carma found an entire brothel house dead. They'd had contact with Terri and Sophie, the two women you examined who died from the virus."

The healer sighed. "Give me a minute."

*

Mich exited the corridor into a small basement. When she pushed the wall panel closed, she discovered a holographic projection snapped into place over it looking like a row of shelves. The three-dimensional image was impressively realistic, even up close. She yanked off the constricting hairnet and static suit, leaving them pooled on the ancient-looking mud tiles, and glanced around. The remaining walls were packed with real shelves of tins, crates and trays of medical tools. A wooden staircase rose up out of the darkness. It appeared Mich had stumbled into the science hall's basement storage room. Clearly the builders of this concealed passageway had been determined to keep their comings and goings confidential. It was hard to imagine such a thing remaining secret for long, but looking at the chipped and dented corridor walls and the age of the paint cans and bottles, she wondered if perhaps it had been a wartime secret passageway. It was clean. No dust. Clearly it was used regularly.

She made her way up the stairs, her weapon drawn and listening for any sound, and emerged onto a small landing. There were two doors in front of her. She waved her hand over the sensor on the left. It led to another staircase. The door on the right slid open to reveal a dark room. Linked stadium seating rose up into the black, and there was a lectern and behind it a large board that covered the entire length of the wall. A classroom. Dark shadows hid the upper level, where Mich assumed the lecture theater exited out into the main university grounds; she could just make out the little fluorescent icons pinpointing the doors' positions.

There was no way to know whether her quarry had escaped through either door. She'd have to guess. She chose the theater. For an ex-student it would be the more familiar escape. And no doubt he would know all the exits from the room.

Holding her weapon tight in one hand, cupped by the other, she pointed it straight ahead and prowled into the theater searching for the escaped man. Her heartbeat sounded a rapid drum solo, and she had to stop and force her breathing to slow, willing her heart to calm before she moved on. Gajob could be here, hiding anywhere, and she wouldn't know until she fell over him. Then again, the large hall could be completely empty.

She crept forward. Dim floor lights cast shadows that stretched and climbed the walls, causing her to flinch at the slightest movement. The shadows were all her own.

Halfway up the stairs, there was a retching sound and a breathless gasp. At her next step, a shadowy form shot to his feet two rows ahead of her.

"Stop!" she cried, pointing her weapon at the shape. "Raise your hands!"

The scientist didn't move. He seemed to be frozen in place, possibly staring at his hands. His behavior was setting off all her internal alarms. She halted, keeping her weapon steady. "Symod Gajob? Raise your hands."

He was muttering, but she couldn't make out what it was. She inched closer.

"—the final stage." His voice was clogged, his every breath sounded wet. The retching sound came again as he doubled over.

Mich paused, her foot halfway up the next step, before she backed away quickly.

He's infected!

She backed up further. "Symod. Is there a cure?"

He wasn't listening. The shadow didn't move. "Why would he do this? I did what he wanted."

Transmissible. The word echoed inside her mind. *I have to get out of here.*

She bolted back down the stairs, her lungs frozen lumps inside her chest. She pressed against the wood of the door. *Get out, get out!* But what about Gajob? *Forget him.* If she got out now, she'd be able to call for medical help.

She fumbled with her comm to call Wen and Charley, while she passed her weapon to her other hand. Sweat soaked her skin, slicking her palms. She tightened her grip on her gun. Gajob was not leaving this room alive.

There was the sound of shoes on carpet. From this distance, she couldn't see exactly where Gajob was. He was on the move, but which way was he going?

Dammit, she'd have to be closer to be sure of a shot. "Don't move!" she screamed. There was no answer. She couldn't let him escape the theater. If he got out and into the school ...

Another sound. Had he hit a seat? Damn it, she couldn't see a thing. Reluctantly, she moved toward the stairs. "Gajob!"

The door opened at the top of the lecture theater, letting in a rush of cold air.

No!

"Mich?" A figure stood in the doorway, silhouetted by the outside sunlight.

She darted forward at the shout. "Don't come any closer!" she shouted. "And don't let Gajob leave—he's infected."

"What?" Wen called back, drawing his weapon. "Where is he?"

"Find a light."

An instant later, giant panels retracted from windows high up on the theater walls and the hall flooded with dull, murky light. The dying scientist stood in the center of the theater. His gaze darted from Mich to Wen and back to his hands. Red stained his mouth, chin and down his shirt. Vomiting blood. *The ketallian symptoms.*

"Call Charley. Get a quarantine organized. We have to lock him in," she shouted.

Gajob jolted at the sound of her voice. His head swung back and forth between the two exits. No, there were four exits. Across the room from where she stood, Mich could see another door. She assumed there was another at the top of the theater too.

She readied her weapon. The charge sounded loud in a room filled only with the sounds of their breathing. "Don't try it!" she ordered.

"Gajob, where's the antidote?" Wen demanded, moving forward.

"Don't come closer!" Mich shouted. Fear flooded through her. "You'll be exposed."

"Can't leave."

It was true. If they each barricaded a door, there were still two exits the infected man could escape through.

"Charley?"

"No answer!" Wen growled.

Mich tried her comm. Blood pounded in her ears. It felt as though her heart was going to explode inside her chest. Gajob seemed to realize his time was running out and bolted for the stairs, taking them faster than she thought possible. She shoved her comm in her hip pocket and fired. So did Wen.

They both missed.

For less than one beat of her heart, she thought about running in the opposite direction. But she couldn't trust her mind. Didn't know what was right.

Her leg twitched. Wen fired.

Gajob jumped multiple stairs at a time.

Wen's shot missed.

Mich went with her body over her mind as instinct took over. She ran after the fleeing man. Her weapon fired twice more. She hit Gajob in the shoulder. He barely flinched. She had to stop him.

"No!" Wen shouted.

Mich leapt, knocking Gajob into the theater seating. Her wrist slammed against something hard and pain shuddered up her body. Her knee connected with bone and she wrapped her arms around Gajob to pin his hands. His wiry body was freakishly flexible and he kicked out, catching her hard in the hip.

She twisted, but he wriggled the other way, kneeing the same hip again. Pain exploded through her body, her nerve endings on fire, but she didn't let go.

Gajob fishtailed from side to side, fighting to escape her grasp. He got a hand free and hit her across the face.

Dodging the scientist's next punch, Mich lost sight of his other hand. Her head snapped back and cracked against a chair from the force of the unseen blow. For a second, all she saw were sparks.

Gajob slammed her in the side again. She let go, clutching at her hip. The scientist jerked, launched up and headbutted her. They both fell back with a gasp.

The sparks behind Mich's eyelids grew brighter.

Gajob growled and spat at her. She got her hand up, pistol gripped tightly, and rammed the weapon into the back of his head.

He fell limp in her arms.

She pushed his body off and sat up, inhaling raggedly. Her back burned with pain on every breath. She wiped at the moisture on her cheek and scrubbed her temples. Reaching under her suit, she pulled out her comm; it fell to pieces in her hand. That was why her hip hurt so badly!

Body trembling, she climbed to her feet and stepped away from Gajob's body. "Wen, you need to get out of here. Set up a quarantine. We have to follow contamination procedures." He didn't move from the stairs. His weapon pointed directly at Mich's chest. Slowly, it lowered to point at the floor. As he opened his mouth, she ordered, "Go! I'll get answers from Gajob. Call Bicet. Clear the building. Oh hell, clear the whole university."

Wen stepped back. "I'll handle it. Don't panic." He looked at her hands and his face fell. He took the theater steps three at a time and disappeared through the door at the top.

Mich's stomach clenched painfully. Falling to her knees, she pulled her jacket sleeves up over her hands despite knowing it was already too late, and shook the man hard. "Wake up!" she screamed, slapping a hand across his face.

The scientist stirred. His eyes blinked open, bloody red, then slid shut again.

Mich shook him harder.

"Wha?" he slurred, squinting up at her.

"You're dying."

The scientist moaned, a low, gut-wrenching sound.

Mich swallowed. "He's killed you, it's too late. Who's your boss? Who made you do this?"

"His wife died. They killed her. He wanted proof."

"He? Who is he? Who is behind this?"

"I don't know his name, but he's an old man. His wife was a part of Calcryon's drug trial."

Mich swore. "She died during the trial, didn't she? Listen, we can stop him from killing anyone else. You can help us. Where is he?"

He gulped as he pointed to her face. "You're dead too." Gajob laughed. The sound grated against her ears.

"Is there an antidote?" she yelled. He flinched. "Where are you storing it?" Her hands were shaking as she clenched his shirt, jerking him upward.

"You can't stop it. No one can stop it. We're dead." Gajob slammed his head against the floor. "Dead!"

A spike of pure fear went through her chest. He wouldn't react like this if he had his hands on an antidote. Had the poison already brought madness to his brain? *He's deteriorating too fast.*

She slapped Gajob again, feeling the wet sticky liquid on his face coat her palm. "Tell me what his plan is!" The scientist's breathing was too irregular, his eyes dilated and unfocused.

Mich took his head in both hands and forced him to meet her stare. "Hey—look at me. Hey." She remembered Wen's help during her panic attack at Yetti's apartment. "Breathe when I do." Maintaining eye contact, she breathed in slowly. Gajob stared at her. She inhaled again and exhaled slow and steady. He started to echo her.

"Here. He's *here*. Has an apartment here. University Housing. Eight hundred and eighty-three." A drop of bloody saliva hit his hand where it clung to her shirt. As it absorbed into the material, he cried out, "Why? Why did he do this to me?"

Mich let Gajob go. "What's his plan?"

"He's going to kill everyone." The scientist rolled over and clutched at his stomach, tears streaming down his face. Mich held back a gasp at their red color.

"Why?"

"He's crazy! He keeps talking to people who aren't there. He says she told him to do this and that he promised her. He said not to tell anyone. You can't trust anyone. He says he has to kill them all."

Mich pushed at the dying man. "Why? Why did you help him?"

"He lied. He told me that I was helping, that the science could show that Calcryon were wrong and that the Enferrie drug was dangerous. He said if I could prove it, I could help so many people. I believed him."

"Is there an antidote? Did you create one?" she demanded.

"I made one, but it's untested. He took it away."

"He has a cure?"

Gajob stared at his hands. "The only one."

Chapter 32

Officers encased in dark protection suits streamed into the lecture hall. A large plastic dome had been sealed over the double doors at each entrance and suited guards were stationed, preventing any access.

Zeth watched Rel pace the perimeter of the quarantine circle they were locked into, unable to leave the scene until their blood tests returned clear. He kept glancing at his comm. Zeth knew he was worried about Carma.

All Zeth could do was sit on the ground, feeling like he had a gaping hole in his chest. If Mich hadn't stopped him he would have been exposed to the poison too. She'd saved his life at the cost of her own. Why? Zeth only ever seemed to fail. He'd failed the children at the travel hub, failed to protect Mich at the Skein City Gem and now he'd failed to protect her from Gajob's self destruction. There had to be a way to save her. The sight of Mich's determined face haunted him every time he closed his eyes. "She ran straight at him."

"Ya said it several times."

"She knew, Rel. She knew what would happen. She knew, and she did it anyway."

Rel sniffed. "Yeah, well, maybe she ain't all that bad."

He grabbed Rel's arm. "She stopped me. Didn't let me get any closer."

Rel stared. "Owe her one, I guess." He stopped to stare at the doorway to the theater. The hand gripping his comm tight trembled. "What's taking so long?"

Healer Bicet arrived just as university security had locked down the area. He was already sealed into his suit. The nurse he assigned Rel and Zeth took their blood and, after a few words, followed the healer inside. The rest of the medical team trickled in behind them.

Then there was only silence.

With the medical personnel in the hall and the guards standing eerily still outside, the quiet university ground exuded foreboding. Even the air was still. Cloud cover progressively darkened the sky, adding to their sense of dread.

Rel continued to pace back and forth, staying just inside the barrier.

Zeth eyed him with concern. "Hey, are you good?"

"Yeah—memories, ya know?"

"It's not the same."

He nodded. "I know that. Dresh, I don't even like her. She gets on my nerves."

"It's not just Janelle. It's Carma too. You're worried about Carma."

"Yeah. No. Yeah."

"She reminds you of Melita, huh?"

Rel stared at his friend. Zeth stared back. Rel snorted. "It's the bravery. And the fear. She does it anyway. Cares. No matter the cost." His comm buzzed softly in his hand. He checked the screen.

"What does she say?"

"The medics and the security team have just arrived. They're quarantining The Dive and Sima's House."

"Good."

Rel shook his head, eyes cast down, reading another message. "She wants ta know why her friends died."

"Wrong place, wrong time," Zeth offered.

Rel shook his head again. "She needs ta help."

"Rel?"

"I know, I know. She's not Melita. But I do like her."

Zeth's gaze swung to the silent university double doorway. "Her friends," he muttered.

"What?"

Zeth's head tilted as he thought about it. "You said Carma wants to help? You found nothing at Sophie and Terri's house. They have belongings at Sima's, right?"

"Right." Rel texted quickly. A few moments later it beeped. "She's got Terri's journal."

"And?"

"Yetti told her about his clients."

"Which ones?"

"The man's wife was sick." Rel froze, staring at the comm.

"Rel? It's not Melita."

Rel's hands trembled.

"Rel?"

He swallowed as several notifications came through, one after the other. "She was sick and in some sort of drug trial. Yetti was helping the man. Shipped a drug to prove that the clinical trial killed his wife. Yetti figured he wouldn't notice getting cheated on one of his deliveries. Terri speculated he was telling her the story to get her sympathy, but she liked him anyway and convinced Sophie to go with her."

Zeth waved his hand around. "Go back to the drug trial. He's talking about Calcryon's drug trial?"

Rel typed quickly and got a response almost instantaneously. "They're taking Carma to the medic center," he read out.

"Did Yetti say the client's name?"

"Di."

Rel and Zeth locked eyes. "Charlmehn Di. Dresh. We ruled him out," Zeth said.

"'The old man' the telnaks said. They meant old. The OLD man. It was Di all along."

Movement had Zeth on his feet in an instant. He recognized the healer as he stepped outside, the bendalian towering above the other medics gathered around the theater's entrance. Zeth's throat tightened. He grunted to clear it, but it seemed to clog further. Clenching his hands into fists, he watched the action at the door. The medics were moving too slowly. Bicet walked toward the waiting emergency vehicles leading a sealed medical pod. A single pod.

He spoke to the security officers and made his way toward Zeth and Rel, directing the hovering pod to continue down the road without him.

Rel pushed Zeth aside to stand at the very edge of the energy barrier. Zeth stepped forward, leaning so close to the barrier his nose hairs quivered from the electrical discharge. Bicet held up a long-fingered hand when both men went to speak. "Symod Gajob died four minutes ago. Mich Janelle was most insistent that I give you this." He pressed a small notebook covered in the same plastic as the suit he wore against the barrier. It passed through the quarantine barrier without damage.

Zeth read over the words written in Mich's sloppy script.

Suspect's wife died in Calcryon trial. Gajob was working for him. There's an antidote—one vial. University housing. Unit 883.

Di's got a cure? "We need to go after it," Rel said.

"Not until your tests are back and clear."

Zeth growled and thrust the book back at the healer. It bounced off the invisible wall in front of him. "Despro!"

He felt rather than saw Rel's head swing his way, betraying his shock at Zeth's curse. Zeth figured he knew what Rel was thinking: they could still save her.

"Get us the security contact. We'll brief him from here."

"Very well." The healer returned to the hall.

Zeth waited, his body tense, ready to move at a moment's notice.

One of the suited officers standing at the theater's entrance moved in their direction.

"I'm Chief Mason. You wanted to speak to me?"

Zeth could only hope the chief would listen to what they had to say. Past experience told him it would be a battle. Local authorities rarely accepted help from off world investigators. Mason's eyes, the only part of him visible through the black-armored protection suit, widened as they briefed him on what little they knew of the poison-turned-virus, Di's motivation and now the location of a potential cure. They insisted the chief prepare for a raid on the location they'd been given. Zeth was pleasantly surprised when Mason acknowledged his order with a nod. "I'll need time to prepare an insertion team."

"Be as quick as you can. With any luck, our results will be back soon," Zeth said with a feral grin. "And Rel and I will join you."

*

She could see light.

Then there was darkness and then light again.

The regular pulses were consistent and annoying. Her eyes burned. Heat poured off her skin and as she breathed in, her chest ached. A thick pressure band tightened over her forehead, stabbing into her temples at random intervals.

Her clothing was heavy and damp, as though she'd been soaked in a rain shower; it stuck to her like another layer of skin. Sweat beaded her upper lip and eyelids and ran down her nose. She felt blocked up, all stuffy like she had a cold. When she sneezed, her head bounced off the wall above her face.

Not a wall—a moving barrier.

She struck at the white plastic surrounding her with her fists. *Out, get out! They're not taking me back!* She twisted to see her prison.

Stale air blew over her face from above. Her vision blurred, but she thought she could see small vents in the plastic. A transparent panel above her eyes was where the light was coming from; the rhythmic flashing gave her the sensation of movement.

She pushed at the plastic again. When the light above her face disappeared, she lashed out with every part of her that could move, desperate to break free of her plastic tomb. *They're taking me back. I won't go back.* She panted, finding little air. *I'm suffocating!* It would be better to die than be sent back there. Tears or sweat coated her cheeks. Music, faded but unforgettable, played back in her mind. *No!* She forced the music away. *I won't go back.*

A faraway voice repeated something over and over. It caught her attention, silencing the music. Pale eyes appeared in her line of sight. She stared up at them as the words grew louder ... her name. Someone was saying her name.

Latching onto the familiar sounds, her racing heart began to slow. The world snapped into focus and she stopped moving long enough to recognize the eyes belonged to Healer Bicet.

"Michele Janelle. Michele Janelle, please stop struggling. You will injure yourself."

She gulped frantically at the air brushing her face. "Help me, please, help me!" she begged, her voice soft. She could barely hear herself over the buzzing in her ears.

"We are," the healer replied. His eyes disappeared.

Her body shook. "Please, don't go."

The eyes reappeared. "You are ill, Mich Janelle. Your partners are on their way to capture the one who has done this. You are in the medic center. Please try to remain calm."

"I don't like it in here," she whispered. Then his words registered. "Partners? I don't have partners."

The eyes grew closer. "Can you tell me where you are?"

"No."

Tears streamed down her cheeks. The eyes pulled back and a long-fingered hand tapped the plastic above her head. She stared up at the fingers, her mouth dropping open. They were really long.

"We will arrive soon. Please inhale slowly and deeply, Michele."

"Where are we going?"

"To an isolated ward."

"Not The Clinic?" she whispered.

"Michele Janelle, listen to my voice. Stay with me." The eyes blinked. "We are in the medical center in Skein City."

She was not going to The Clinic? The reality was so much worse, she realized as her memory cleared at last. *I've been exposed. I'm going to die.* Her breathing sped up again.

He repeated her location again and again. She expanded her lungs when he ordered and her eyes grew heavy. The throbbing in her head faded.

Chapter 33

Zeth flipped the visor of his helmet down and shook his head from side to side until the screen began to analyze the data coming from outside. When a green light appeared above his left eye, he gestured to the suited men around him. "We go in ten," he ordered.

With Rel at his back, Zeth followed the security force fanning out to surround the Ketallen Third Housing 800 building. Their only action now was to find Charlmehn Di. The man had a cure. Zeth was damned if he was going to let another terrorist win.

Chief Mason's voice filtered in through his helmet comm, steadily counting down their breach of the building. On "one" the entire force moved, weapons primed and held high.

He hit the side entrance at a run, side by side with Mason. Rel was only a step behind. Mason yelled and gestured with an open hand to the left.

Zeth shouted his acknowledgment, hearing Rel's response echo a second later.

Mason fired the door open. Zeth pushed past the broken frame and into the billowing smoke. Mason turned right, with the majority of his team running with him.

Zeth and Rel raced up the evacuation stairwell to the left of the entrance, the sound of their footsteps echoing loudly in the flash-crete chamber. Zeth was desperate to reach the top as quickly as possible, conscious of the clock they were on.

Mich had forty-eight hours at most. The sooner they found Di, the better her chances.

Rel shadowed Zeth's every move, his breathing steady—only slightly raspy—in Zeth's ear.

They slowed as they reached the last step, and crept together down the corridor to apartment 883. At the door, Rel stopped and eyed Zeth. The run up the stairs had left both men breathing hard, but as soon as Rel received the nod to go, he didn't hesitate to kick open the door.

"Charlmehn Di, identify yourself!" Zeth shouted and raced inside. His senses were heightened by the potential danger they faced entering the terrorist's apartment, taking in every shadow in a glance. "Clear!"

A moment later, Rel echoed the call. Zeth's heart sank, his chest left a hollow void. Large panel shelving divided the room into three sections, but there was no sign of Di anywhere. "Where is he?"

"Look around. There must be something here."

The two men searched each section of the room thoroughly. Cupboards were empty, there were no clothes in the bedroom or bedside drawers. No bedding or bath products were left anywhere. Di had cleared out, taking everything with him.

If Gajob was no longer useful, Di must have immediate plans for the virus. The short lifespan of the drug exposure necessitated a large number of victims in an enclosed location, but where? There must be a clue to his intended target here somewhere. Zeth's mind darted to the university's flashing e-signs. The graduation ceremony was tomorrow. His breath caught at the thought.

Between the couch cushions, he found a receipt for a travel ticket. There was no destination printed, but the date showed it had been purchased only a few days earlier.

"Anything?" he called to Rel, who was searching through a kitchen smaller than that on *Lazydragon*.

Rel slammed shut the drawer he was searching. "Nothing. The place is clean."

Zeth held up the ticket.

"D'ya think he's running?" Rel asked.

"It's all we've got to go on."

"Hub's a big place."

Zeth's blood ran cold. *Not this time.*

He contacted Mason. "Di purchased a travel ticket, but there's no cruiser name." His heart thudded loudly. "We have to search the travel hub for him." He hoped he was wrong, but the feeling in his gut told him to prepare for the worst.

Mason confirmed Zeth's request and added that his teams would be right behind them. Zeth acknowledged and signed off. He eyed Rel. "We have to stop Di from leaving."

"She said there was one resing vial—what if he's injected it into himself already?"

"Then we drag his ass to Bicet and have it cut out of him."

Chapter 34

The door opened and Mich raised her hands. Three white-suited men entered her cell holding weapons pointed directly at her chest. What had she done?

One stepped forward. All she could see of his face were his eyes. "Miss Janelle, we need you to lie back down."

She tried to speak, but her lips felt sandpapery and her tongue stuck to the roof of her mouth. When she tried to speak, the words came out jumbled.

The three men stepped closer. The one who addressed her was heavy-set with squinty eyes. He lowered his weapon as the two behind him raised theirs higher. They did not look friendly. She stumbled back.

"Stand against the wall."

They crept closer. Mich had nowhere to run.

When they reached for her, she lashed out, hitting the front one in the stomach. She put her whole shoulder behind it, knowing she had to get away as quickly as possible. She kicked out and flailed her arms as the other two approached. One held a large needle.

"No, no," she begged, but was quickly overcome by the hard bodies pressing her against the wall. She felt the needle's sting and lost all strength to stand.

The men threw her onto the bed. She blinked lazily up at the squinty-eyed man. He leaned his face close to hers. "Isolation for you, bitch." She smelt cinnamon on his breath. He looked familiar, but in her haze, she couldn't connect the lines.

She turned her head, searching for aid. Someone stood at the door. Watching. Ensuring her orders were carried out. But Mich couldn't be sure there was even a person there. A flash of nurse's colors ushered the orderlies away. Mich's eyes grew heavy. She struggled to keep them open.

No help would come. No help ever came.

She was on her own.

Chapter 35

Charlmehn Di walked quickly toward Level B. The bag he carried brushed his leg as he walked. He stroked the small switch in his pocket. His breathing was steady, his mind calm. He smiled and nodded to the many passing travelers, humming softly.

Not long now.

Taking a deep breath, he moved toward the travel scanners built into the walls of the corridor and continued past, confident his package would not activate the alarm. She had promised he would get through, and she had never let him down.

The docking point door opened on his approach. He stepped onto the platform beyond and there it was, *The Sky Traveler*. The crew scurried like riled ants beneath the ship's hull, preparing for launch. The large white cruiser waited at the docking point like a pregnant sea mammal. A low buzz from idling engines vibrated the grated walkway beneath his feet.

The bag he carried was a heavy weight in his hand.

Di smiled and began to hum.

*

Zeth glanced one last time at the image Rel had found of Di with his hack of the failed legal proceedings against Calcryon—an older smallish man with graying brown hair and gold-rimmed glasses—and pushed through the crowd at the hub's check-in point, his eyes darting everywhere as he searched for that one man in all the chaos. "We need someone in the security office. This place is too big to search without a specific location."

As Zeth led the way into the hub, Rel was right on his heels. Inside the main thoroughfare, he glanced up at the giant spire, searching for the office's location.

For a moment, he just stared. The hub entrance opened into an eighteen-story open space. A glass-topped ceiling allowed weak sunlight to pour in. Every open space was filled with booths and carts, stores and racks. His gaze darted between the long, spiraling staircases leading passengers to multiple levels of the shopping precinct and along corridors that branched off in every direction, taking travelers to the hundred and three boarding stations. In the center of the giant spire rose a floating glass prism made of thousands of tiny glass shards; a lightshow was projected onto it hourly, causing light to sparkle and spray out, filling the hub with its glow.

Zeth sucked in a breath. How were they going to find one man in all of this?

"He might not even be here," Rel said, traveling back when he realized Zeth had stopped running.

Zeth conceded the point. "Then we get Mason to scatter his men throughout the terminal. Di will have to come through here if he intends to get off planet."

Rel wasn't listening; he pointed to an electronic news story rotating through a window-sized display screen. "I know where he's going."

Zeth read through the displayed article quickly. "They're here? All of them?"

In other financial news, the Executive Board of Calcryon is to gather for their annual retreat on Trax 8 at the end of this week. As is the case each year, we expect an announcement on the direction of the research and development division's long-term strategy. Years past have seen projects put forward such as the Tren insulin push and the development of the inoculation for Yaliki.

As reported previously, Calcryon's focus this year has been on a little-known natural remedy colloquially referred to as an enfer-salve—extracted from the Enferrie flower, a rare and expensive plant that can only be grown on the outer spiral. Their experiments have concentrated on its potential use as a pain modifier. At the time of this announcement, reaction from shareholders has ranged from disbelief to antipathy regarding the company's current strategy plan.

The resulting widespread condemnation from the scientific community at large was immediately felt in the company's share price.

Stock agents are cautiously optimistic, but this optimism seems dependent on a positive outcome from this retreat.

The Executive Board is gathering on Ketal Seven and will travel from this central hub to the moon of Trax 8 via company cruiser. Final reports are to be released at the conclusion of this strategic getaway and are awaited with great interest.

The article went into further detail on the company's current financial viability, but Zeth had seen all he needed. "Di's not leaving. The target is Calcryon's Executive Board."

"We need a team on that cruiser to secure the board," Rel said.

Zeth was already patching into Mason's communication network to interrupt the man's coordination of the hub's evacuation.

"Chief Mason, Zeth Wen. We know the target's objective. The Calcryon company cruiser."

Mason reacted quickly. Zeth could hear him ordering his team to locate the name and berth of the cruiser.

They had to keep the search for Di quiet. If they set off the usual alarms, the terrorist would be alerted to their presence. No one knew how Di would react to a show of force.

Zeth looked at the hub, bustling with happy travelers, filled with noise, movement and bright colors. There were people everywhere. Beings of every shape and size carried or led large bags around the bustling concourses where children ran amok.

And if Di's plan succeeded, they were all going to die in the most horrid way imaginable.

Chapter 36

She was in the garden again, and had no idea how she'd got out here. Her pulse was slow and steady, as was her breathing. A glance around the clearing showed she was alone.

Why am I here?

The bush in front of her was covered in fresh blooms. The heady scent floated in the air around her. She could almost see it, it was so thick. The fragrance filled her nose and throat until she was soaked in it.

"You were telling me about the water?" The voice was soft and seemed to come from the very air itself. Or was it all in her head? She couldn't tell. She knew she should be scared, but she felt so peaceful out here. Her eyes drifted closed. She blinked them open, finding Nurse standing right in front of her.

"Where—?"

"Oh dear, are you losing time again?"

"Wha—?" Was she? She didn't think so but then, she didn't know how she'd gotten out here in the first place. "I don't ...?"

"It's all right, my dear. It's time for you to go in now. I promise we can come out here again tomorrow." Nurse's face was down-turned, the lines around her lips more pronounced, but when Mich peered into her green eyes, she found they were sharp and focused. Was she disappointed?

Mich hurried to reassure her. "Sorry, yes, yes." She didn't want Nurse to think she didn't like the visits outside. She did. It was suffocating inside, so heavy and dark.

"Come along, my dear."

Her footing was unsteady and she was forced to grip Nurse's arm to find her balance. As she wavered her way back toward The Clinic's glass doors, she wondered if she'd been talking. Her throat was dry like she'd been speaking for an age, but she didn't recall saying anything. The not knowing ate at her sense of peace until she was breathing hard.

It's too familiar. I've done this before.

"Are you well?"

Am I?

She tried breathing slowly. "I'm okay, I'm sorry, Nurse. I don't know what happened."

Mich needed to know if this was real. It had to be the drugs. They made her stupid and tired. She thought that maybe, with a little less in her system, she might be able to concentrate more. But she didn't want anger Nurse again, so she stayed silent, biting back her request.

Right now, Nurse was humming. A smile flitted across her face and her green eyes sparkled. "I think it would be easier if you called me Madam rather than Nurse. Don't you agree?" Mich nodded, hoping Madam would return to her sweet humming.

How long had she been outside? It felt like it should be morning.

Mich lifted her head, taking in the waning sunlight. She shook her head and pressed her hand tiredly against her temples. Oh, how her head ached.

This isn't right. I'm not supposed to be here. I got out, didn't I? I'm supposed to be somewhere else.

Two men appear in my memory. They're important. But who are they?

I blink again and my vision blurs. What's happening to me?

None of this is right. I don't remember any of this.

None of this is real.

Chapter 37

Panting, his chest aching, Zeth ran through the hub, swerving around the milling families and intently focused businessmen. It was happening again.

This time Rel was a steady presence at his side. Neither man spoke, their focus fixed on only one goal: to reach the Calcryon ship before Di enacted his terrible plan.

A child darted in front of Zeth. He gave a shout and slowed enough to avoid the startled youngster, leaping over a pile of luggage to get away. A dark face topped with curly black hair was all he saw before he took off again.

The waiting area was empty when the two men skidded to a halt. The light above the gateway leading to *The Sky Traveler* flashed slowly. "They've boarded," Zeth whispered, sucking air into his exhausted lungs. He drew his weapon and confirmed its full charge. Beside him, Rel did the same.

Zeth triggered the sensor doors. They swung open and the two men crept down the jetway toward the berthed ship. As one, they swung around the doorway connecting the hub to the ship. Seeing no one in the vicinity, Zeth whispered, "Head to the engine bay, stop the ship from taking off. The board members must be seated. I'll head there."

Rel acknowledged and they separated with a nod.

Zeth slowed on his approach to the passenger area as he heard a single voice ahead. Heart thudding, he raised his weapon and stole forward on silent feet.

The compartment ahead contained twenty large reclining chairs. Only six were occupied by the executive board members, already strapped into their chairs with the cruiser's belt system. On closer inspection, Zeth realized the straps were reinforced with thin chains.

By the One—where did he get those?

A strip of tape covered the closest passenger's mouth. Zeth had to assume each passenger was bound in the same way, though he couldn't see them all. The man Zeth heard talking stood at the far end. Well past middle age, his sandy brown hair was peppered with gray and his stomach hung low over his belt. Something glinted between his fingers. *A trigger switch?*

"Not one step further, if you please." The man's voice rose sharply.

Dresh! Zeth stopped and raised his hands so his weapon could be clearly seen. "Charlmehn Di?"

"You know who I am. Do not ask questions you already know the answer to," Di sneered, shaking his head as though Zeth had disappointed him.

He wasn't sure how that could be. Children's giggles played in Zeth's mind as he inched forward. He had to get the man talking and stall for as long as possible to buy Chief Mason time to get the hub evacuated. "Charlmehn, can I call you that?"

"I prefer Di."

His voice was calm, and that disturbed Zeth more than if he had been ranting. Zeth continued just as calmly. "Can we go somewhere to talk, Di?"

Di raised his eyebrows and let out a chuckle. "Talk? Why would I want to talk? You shouldn't be here. You need to leave." He cocked his head to the side, as if listening to something or someone. Zeth wondered if he was wearing an earpiece.

Zeth snuck another step, trying to gauge Di's mood. "Why do I need to leave, Di? There are a lot of people on this ship, and many more outside. What are you planning to do to these people if I leave?"

"Stop moving," Di ordered, his face flushing red. "I see the weapon in your hand. Put it down, or I will press the switch."

"All right." With slow movements, Zeth crouched, making sure to keep his hands in Di's sight the entire time. Breathing slowly, he placed his weapon on the floor and straightened. "I've done what you asked. Now can we talk, Di? Sit down, perhaps?" He threw a chummy tone into his voice, hoping to get the man to relax, even a little.

Di's laugh was unpleasant—high-pitched, verging on hysterical. "Sit down? *Talk* with you? What will that accomplish other than to delay me? I don't even know who you are."

Zeth didn't like the man's rapid, shallow breathing. "You don't have to do this, Di. Let's talk about a different plan to get your issue resolved."

"Issue? They need to learn. They didn't listen. They're listening now." Di rubbed at his eyes with the hand holding the switch; his fingers trembled. Several of the seated figures flinched. The closest imprisoned man shook with fear, eyes wide, face contorted with guilt.

"Listen to what?"

"I have no choice. She gave me no choice." Di stumbled but recovered his footing quickly and glared at Zeth with wide eyes.

Zeth inched forward, but froze again when Di held up the hand with the switch. "Who did? Is your wife telling you to do this?"

"Emma?" Di laughed. His hand started to shake. "Emma is dead, you fool, and it's all their fault."

"What did they do?"

"They *killed* her."

Zeth fought to keep his instinctive head shake from exposing his disbelief. "Your wife was ill. They were only trying to help manage her pain. She was terminal, wasn't she?"

Di hissed, his eyes narrowed. "She was. They said they could help her."

"Wasn't it already too late, Di? There is no cure for what she had. Isn't there a chance—"

The man scratched his face with his empty hand, his eyebrows knitting together in confusion as he turned his head away. His voice faded. "She told me to make them listen."

"Who told you?"

Di looked at him sharply. "You don't know?"

"Is there someone else? Someone telling you what to do here?" At the man's flinch, Zeth raised his hand, palm outstretched in entreaty, the rest of his body held still. "Who is it, Di? Who wants you to do this?"

The man laughed. The sound set Zeth's teeth grinding.

Zeth pointed to the ceiling. "All of the people on this ship will die. Perhaps they deserve it, perhaps they don't, but it won't stay here. It will get into the hub. All those families. The families in the hub, the travelers outside, all those innocent people, innocent children. Would Emma want that? Would she want those deaths on your hands?"

Di spun. "You don't know her! Don't you *dare* speak for her! You don't know."

Zeth stepped back, alarmed at the fury exploding in the man's eyes. He lowered his voice. "Then tell me."

"They're not innocent," Di hissed. He gestured to the rest of the compartment with his free hand. Zeth watched him with a blank expression. He hoped Mason had cleared the hub.

Di opened his hand and considered the switch. Zeth's breathing stuttered. His palms dampened as he suppressed his need to wipe them. He couldn't let Di see any fear in his demeanor.

"They were in the initial stages of breaking down the drug; the scientists and the researchers fixed their results to show proof of effectiveness. They lied! For profit. They made promises they couldn't keep. Promises to help Emma. Promises they knew they couldn't fulfill. All to get market share," he spat. "They can't be trusted. She told me to punish them. To kill them all."

She?

The expression on Di's face and his tone shifted completely on that last diatribe, becoming slack, his voice almost robotic. Who was *She?* It clearly wasn't Emma. Emma was dead. So who was it? Had Di's mental breakdown conjured his wife to beg her husband to take retribution? Zeth needed to work it out so he didn't say the wrong thing and trigger the man into acting.

"They can't be trusted!" Di's voice cracked, his fingers tightened around the little switch. "And you cannot stop me."

*

Rel moved silently toward the engine bay and found the crew tied back-to-back in the middle of the hall. Running over, he discovered they were bound by a thin chain. His knife wouldn't cut through this.

"Bomb! There's a bomb!" the first man shouted as the tape was torn from his mustache.

"Where?" Rel glanced around the room, searching for anything obvious or out of place.

"He took it with him." The man wriggled. "First panel inside. Bel sheers. Should cut us free." In a matter of moments, Rel had the crew loose. The man with the mustache jumped to his feet. He was short, standing only to Rel's shoulder. "We have to send out an evacuation alarm. That nutter said it was biological."

"My partner's looking for him now."

The man shook his head. "We're still connected to the hub's air transfer. You have to clear the hub and get everybody out!"

A bomb. I should be in there, not Zeth. "Where's Di?"

"Passenger compartment." The man darted from one corner of the engine bay to the other, his hands in constant motion as he checked readout after readout. "I have to disconnect everything."

"What's ya name?"

"Leeh Tricks. I'm the lead engineer."

"Are ya talking about disconnecting the air transfer?"

"Yes, it's a part of the take-off protocols but it will take time to reach it. I can't disconnect the systems in isolation. It's the safety protocols that prevent us from accessing and turning off individual systems."

Oh the irony. "Get it done," Rel ordered. "Was Di wearing the bomb? What can ya tell me about it?"

Leeh buried his head beneath the control panel. One of his assistants spoke up for him. "He was holding it. Small—about the size of his head."

Well, that could be anything. "The trigger?"

"I don't know."

Rel's jaw ached from how tightly he ground his teeth. How could he disarm the bomb if he didn't know how the man intended to trigger it?

He contacted Zeth. When his partner didn't answer, he buzzed Chief Mason and reported their status.

"Can they disconnect the air?"

Rel glanced at the men racing around the bay. "Doing it now, but it's going to take some time."

"We're about to activate the full evac."

"Wait." Rel tapped Leeh on the shoulder. "Can ya disconnect the alarms ta stop them from sounding when we trigger the hub's evacuation? We don't want ta alert the target."

"Do it," Mason ordered.

The engineer nodded. He and his two assistants climbed under the closest terminal.

"Hardwire disconnected," a voice called moments later.

"Okay ta call evac, chief," Rel told Mason. The tinny sound of the travel hub's alarms pierced the open comm unit.

"Is the engine room secure?"

The men around him moved from terminal to terminal, inputting data with quick fingers and shouted numbers. They ignored Rel completely.

"We're good." The engineer glanced up and gestured to his team. "Working on separating the systems. Go and help your partner."

"When it's done, get outta here," Rel ordered.

Chapter 38

My vision swims again. My head is pounding and it's hard to breathe.

When I can focus, I recognize where I am. I'm watching my memories roll on like an altranet movie.

From outside, but I'm inside it too.

Waves of green were painted in broad splashes across the gray walls. Mich's right eye twitched. Her personal data port implant light was off. Then she remembered that they'd disconnected her eyeport when she was admitted.

She shifted but couldn't sit up. Turning her head, she made out wide straps fastening her arms to a bed. Her head pulsed. Her eyes burned, but as bad as she felt, she could also think clearly for the first time in a long time.

She'd been investigating the Tripness Company for shipping tainted medical supplies to Yeshele. Her contact, a man named Taskly, was killed and she'd been set up for his murder. Proof she was close to discovering who was behind the tainted drugs.

She had a fading image of a man dressed in black and the smell of cinnamon. Her attacker? She'd glimpsed him for only a moment before the drug had taken her down.

The memories were growing distant. Her thoughts traveled back, desperate to remember as much of what happened as she could. Perhaps, by replaying the details over and over again, she could cement the memories into her mind.

"Raven." A tall man dressed in a gray suit strode forward through the open door. Mich stared at him.

"Do you know who I am, Raven?" His voice was soft and without inflection.

The vision jerks, blurs and crystalizes again. This is wrong. I've done this before. I'm reliving the past. Why?
My movements continue and the words play again. Everything that happened before is happening again. I hold up my hand and focus on the skin and bone between, trying to find reality in my sense of touch. It wavers and blurs. No! The memory's sucking me back in. How can I fight a memory?

"Do you know who I am, Raven?" His voice was soft and without inflection.

He was her boss, Temok Marke. A Hunter. She was a Hunter too. Why was this happening? Mich opened her mouth, but no sound emerged.

"Raven, you are to be held here until the trial." Marke moved toward her chair and hovered, glancing around her tiny cell.

Who is Raven? She held his gaze; his intense gray eyes burrowed into hers as if trying to find the answers in her mind. Oh, yes, that was her Hunter code name. Raven; she was the Raven.

"Can you tell me about the man you killed?" Marke's sharp stare cut a swathe right through her body.

In my mind, I dig my fingernails into my palms. Fire floods my thoughts as I try to concentrate on what is real. The pain is real. I'm inside my own head reliving what happened years before.

The vision jerks and jumps, becoming static, and then freezes. Yes. it's a memory. I'm stuck in a memory.

Two men flash into my mind. Important men. They're not hunters.

I used to be a hunter. I was the raven. I'm not a hunter anymore.

I control my memories, they don't control me.

I look up as the static fades away. I find myself in a black space. There's no sound, no taste, no smell. Not a single sensation I can latch onto. I have to wind it back. What's the last thing I remember? The black around me flickers like an altranet connection. It becomes a theater. There's a dead man on the floor at my feet. His eyes and nose are stained with blood. My memories return with a snap. Gajob. Poison. I've been poisoned.

No, infected. I've been infected.

I'm dying.

The image fades and I find myself in the endless black. It surrounds my senses and fills my body when I breathe. I'm becoming one with the black. Why am I reliving the clinic? Why am I reliving the past I've tried so hard to forget?

"Fight, Janelle!" a voice whispers.

I barely hear it.

It doesn't matter.

It won't matter.

I have to let go. Let it all go.

Relaxing my body, I fling my arms wide and let myself fall.

Chapter 39

It was hot inside the ship and growing hotter. Rel must have reached the engine room and disconnected the cruiser from the hub's support systems. At least the rest of the hub would be safe if Di detonated his bomb.

Zeth's comm unit earpiece vibrated softly. He couldn't answer it; Di watched him too closely. Zeth kept his hands high above the seat backs and stepped forward again. With each step, he moved past another terrified passenger. Sweat poured down the face of the overweight man on his right, the horror in his eyes digging into Zeth's chest. Tape at his mouth peeled slightly against his damp skin, but the man made no sound. Zeth refocused on Di. "I want you to listen to me."

"No, *you* listen to *me*. You need to leave. You shouldn't die for them." Spittle sprayed from Di's mouth as he spat the words. His face shone with sweat. He swiped it away with a shaking hand, streaking grit into long dark lines down his cheeks.

"But I am here." Zeth shot a quick look at the elderly man on his left. The board member rocked forward and grunted, gesturing to the pocket of the seat in front of him with his nose. The chair on the other side of the aisle was empty.

"You want to stay here? Fine, yes. You can stay." Di pointed with the hand holding the switch. "Take a seat." With no other choice, Zeth sat down. Di was on him in an instant, locking

274

Zeth into the ship's restraints. The hopeful eyes of the man across the aisle dropped as his body sagged back into his seat.

Rel would kill him if he got out of this.

Zeth took the opportunity to examine the crazed man up close. The virus had to be in a container of some kind, but other than a shirt soaked with sweat under the brown suit jacket, there was nothing on the man. Where had Di hidden it? The switch gripped tight between his fingers must link to an explosive hidden on the ship somewhere and it had to be close. The switch was too small to carry much of a charge.

He pulled against his bindings but there was no give in the straps. Di had access to the security tablet and had locked the chair's safety restraints, pinning Zeth's arms, but Di hadn't chained him like the rest of the passengers. If Zeth could stand the temporary pain he might be able to wriggle free from his bonds, given time, but time was the one thing he wasn't so sure he had.

At the sound of his struggles, Di knelt back down. "Don't move," he yelled into Zeth's ear, spittle from his mouth flying over Zeth's face.

Zeth forced his body to relax. At least he had not been gagged. "Why are you doing this in this way? The poison. Do you know it's mutated? It's infectious now. A virus. It's spreading and it kills anyone it touches. You'll have all of those deaths on your conscience."

Di's face became a mask. "You want to know why I'm doing this?" He stood and tapped Zeth hard on the head, before leaning down into the face of the man seated beside him. "Jon Trendal, CEO of Calcryon Industries. This man signed off on the research projects." The man Di was talking to rocked sideways, his chains rattling loudly. "He signed all the lies."

Straightening, Di pointed to a woman seated two rows from Zeth. "Charline Krenshaw, Strategy Manager. It was all her idea." There was a flatness in the man's voice again and his eyes were blank.

This was not right. He sounded ... programmed?

"Tell me about the woman who told you to do this. If not Emma, then who? What's her motive?" Zeth prodded.

"What?" Di looked at him, blinking slowly. "Motive? To destroy Calcryon. To get closure. To stop the pain. Why do you think we're here?"

Zeth arched against his bindings. "Are you in pain?"

"Constant pain. It's everywhere. All over me like a stink. *She* can heal me. Make it all better. All I have to do is kill them all."

Di spun away, his voice soft. He began to hum.

Zeth's gaze flew up. That tune. He racked his brain for the memory, but couldn't grasp it.

As soon as Di turned away, Zeth worked his wrists, twisting them back and forth beneath the straps holding him in place. If he got enough space, he could twist the chair's arm to pop one of the holding screws loose.

The man beside him, Jon Trendal the CEO, gestured to his seat pocket. Now that Zeth was closer, he could see what Trendal was pointing at. A small case was tucked behind the netting. Zeth saw a flash of light reflect off its shiny cover.

Glancing at Di, Zeth tilted his head and peered up at the roof; nothing there could have caused the reflection. He checked over his shoulder. The storage space above his head was cracked open and there was something hanging out of it. A silver tip caught the light from above as it swung slowly back and forth. Zeth met Trendal's eye and he nodded.

In a voice barely loud enough to be a whisper, he asked, "Bomb?"

Trendal nodded again.

Zeth tugged harder on his hands. He had to get out of this chair.

Chapter 40

Rel was a rung away from the top of the ladder when his comm unit buzzed. Dresh! He'd forgotten to switch it to silent. At least he'd remembered to put his earphones in. He answered the voice call, hoping it was Zeth.

It was Healer Bicet. "Rel Charley, I need you to return to the medic center immediately." The man sounded out of breath.

Rel shook his head, though he knew the healer could not see him. "In the middle of something, healer."

"Mich Janelle's condition is worsening. Her vitals are spiking and I am unsure as to the cause. I need you to—"

"Healer, we've found Di. We'll get the antidote ta ya soon. Ya just have ta keep her alive a little longer," Rel said urgently. "Gotta go. We'll call ya as soon as we have it."

He closed the call before the healer could say anything more. Why did Bicet need Rel specifically to return? It had to be the question Bicet had asked him earlier—something to do with Rel's blood.

No matter. They'd get the cure back to Bicet in time to save Janelle's life, and Rel could deal with Bicet's question later. Right now, he had to get to Zeth.

Pocketing his comm, Rel threw himself up the ladder.

*

Di stared blankly at the wall, rocking back and forth on his feet. His face flushed red and his skin shone from the sweat coating it. He was still humming that tune Zeth couldn't quite place. *What is he waiting for? He has all of the board here. Why are they still alive?* The only reason had to be that he was waiting for a bigger score. But what? Without knowing, he couldn't begin to know how to stop him.

Something small and hard hit Zeth's arm. He glanced over his shoulder and hope flickered at the sight of his partner, crouched just outside the compartment's entrance. When he turned his eyes forward, Di was still humming at the wall. He glanced back again. Rel held up a hand and wiggled it around like a snake. Zeth nodded, moving just his fingers to communicate back.

Zeth kept an eye on Di while Rel crawled along the aisle, mentally shouting at the crazed man not to turn around. Closing his fingers around the cold press of Rel's knife hilt, Zeth felt a burst of adrenalin but forced his body to still. After Rel wriggled back out of sight, Zeth slowly glided the knife's blade over the thick straps trapping his arms. "Not yet, she said," Di muttered softly over and over to himself like a mantra. Zeth eyed him warily but he didn't turn. Zeth felt the straps give just as Di spun in his direction.

Zeth relaxed his hands. "This woman. The one who told you killing Calcryon's Executive Board would make everything better. Who is she?" No response, so he tried again. "She's taken advantage of your Emma's death and twisted it to enflame your anger. You don't have to do what she's told you to do. We can get you help."

Zeth hoped to get a reaction.

He got one.

Di was on him so fast, Zeth jolted back in his seat. "I have to do what she says. I can't make her angry," he shouted, raising the hand without the switch and hitting Zeth hard across the jaw. Zeth's head snapped to the side at the force of the blow. He tasted blood. Di raised his hand again.

Zeth moved. He captured Di's wrist and yanked him off balance. With his other hand, he clamped down on Di's thumb and twisted so the man couldn't press the switch.

Rel rose up behind Di and punched him so hard and fast Zeth didn't see the move but heard the smack echo through the compartment. Di slumped over Zeth, bleeding heavily.

With Rel's help, Zeth crawled out from beneath the unconscious man, holding the precious trigger switch cupped in his hand. The CEO, Jon Trendal, strapped in beside Zeth, slumped back in his seat, pale and sweaty.

"Up." Zeth pointed to the storage compartment and the erroneous strap. "Slowly."

They lifted the bag compartment hatch half an inch. Rel pushed his face against the wall and peered up at the underside. "Clear," he whispered.

Zeth nodded. They raised the hatch higher. It didn't catch or pull on the way up. The strap belonged to an open bag. Nestled inside the bag was a container and a full charger. The two men considered each other carefully and, without another word, closed the lid.

Rel gestured to the trapped board members. "Get 'em out of here."

Zeth freed his comm unit and called Chief Mason, briskly explaining the situation. Mason ordered Zeth to evacuate the cruiser immediately.

"Rel's a disposal expert," Zeth reminded him.

"Order stands," Mason said crisply.

Rel eyed Zeth. "That includes ya, Zeth. Get everyone out."

"I'm not leaving you here."

Chapter 41

Before I hit the ground, I spring upright.

No.

This will not be how I end. By giving up. By refusing to fight.

It will not be how I die.

To dresh with that. Too much is unresolved. Too much is hidden from me.

I can control this. The black is all-encompassing, but I slam my eyes shut on it, refusing to give it power over me.

Poison.

Gajob.

The man who hired him.

What was it Gajob said about the man? He said something. Triggered something. But what?

I replay the reel. An empty theater appears in front of me. A dead man at my feet. Go back further. I kneel down. With a shuddering gasp the scientist's bloody eyes open, staring at me in horror.

"What did he do to me?"

I feel my response, the same one I felt then. I open my mouth and freeze. Pain explodes through my mind. I clasp bloody hands over my head.

The dead man blurs and fades. Don't lose him now. I focus on my hands, on the pulse in my wrist and follow it all the way up my arm to my chest. I feel the jolt and listen and count each thump of my heart turning to the non-existent being in my arms. He solidifies before my eyes.

"What did you say about the man?" I whisper. Gajob in my arms flinches as though I've shouted right into his ear.

"He isn't the only one she's taken."

This didn't happen.

This is new.

"You should know. you were there. You should remember." Gajob takes my hands. I feel his heart beat beneath my fingertips. Strong and vibrant. He stares up at me and opens his blood-stained mouth.

"Who—"

"Go back to then. She was working on him, just as she's working on you."

"Who?" I know the answer. I see it in Gajob's face. I see the truth in his eyes.

"I—"

I don't want to go. But if it will wake me up, then I have to. I have to go back.

I close my eyes on Gajob's face and let myself fall.

*

Rel's eyes narrowed. Zeth remained unmoved.

Rel shrugged. "Ya funeral."

Zeth cut the chains and pulled the last of the six Calcryon Board members from her seat. Rel ordered them out of the cruiser. As soon as they were gone, he opened the storage compartment again to examine the bomb and its positioning.

"Di was holding a trigger switch," Zeth told him, appearing at his side. Rel nodded and examined the bomb in the bag carefully. It appeared there was a corresponding plate for a wireless trigger on one side of the device, but from the way it was positioned, he couldn't see how it was connected to the actual device itself without moving it. "Let me see the switch?"

Zeth placed it into his palm. "What are you looking for?"

"I can't confirm a secondary connection from here." Rel debated trying to isolate the bomb, but he didn't want to risk moving it if there was a secondary trigger. If he activated a signal jammer, he might auto trigger the device.

Still tied to the chair below, Di was regaining consciousness, shifting and moving softly.

Rel opened the trigger switch with care and snipped the lead wire. "Search him for another device," he ordered as soon as Di stirred.

Zeth patted the man down thoroughly. "Nothing."

Di peered around, confused. Zeth stepped back as the man rocked against his bonds. Laughter bubbled from his throat. His mad amusement grew in volume until it echoed around the compartment.

Rel eyed him warily but didn't move from his position near the bomb. His heart was racing but his hands were steady. He sucked in a long breath and released it just as slowly before reaching in to rotate the device.

Beneath him, Zeth grabbed Di's shirt and rattled him hard. "The cure! Where is it? Innocent people are dying. You can still save them."

"Why should I save them?" Di's laugh broke off as he began to cough. Rel blinked as Di's words rattled around inside his head, the same demand Rel had issued to Bicet.

With the gentlest of touches, Rel tilted the device. His eyes widened at the timer pressed into the base of the device.

20.

19.

18.

"Zeth. Get the ship's ejection spacesuits!" he said, his voice loud and frantic but his hands remained gentle as he lowered the bomb back to its original position and stepped away.

"What?"

Rel shoved his partner toward the labeled compartments that held the passenger zero-gravity suits. He threw one at Zeth, who was fighting to untie a feral Di. "Get ya suit on now!"

Rel dragged his suit on, yanking his helmet into place.

Di smiled. "Too late." His face was red, his wide eyes filled with madness. "*Too late.*"

Rel grabbed Di. "Get—"

"Yep," Zeth agreed, diving for his suit.

It was all Rel could do to pin Di's hands to his sides as he thrashed about.

Zeth fumbled for his helmet and slammed his hand over the seal.

Rel's internal timer went off ... above their heads, the bomb exploded.

He hit the ground hard at the force of the blast. White powder flew out, coating the compartment in an instant.

Rel caught Zeth's wide-eyed look of horror from where he'd landed, blown back along the aisle. Ice filled Rel's veins as the powder settled over Di's exposed face and hands like the first snowfall.

Di threw his head back and cackled. "Too late."

Chapter 42

The Sky Traveler was quickly secured, with only the contamination officers permitted inside.

Zeth and Rel were forced into a mobile decontamination unit while Di was carried from the cruiser in a sealed medical pod.

Part of Zeth was relieved he and Rel had avoided another hub disaster. Another part was filled with despair. They hadn't found the cure on Di, and he had given no indication he even had one. Zeth could only hope Di hadn't taken the antidote before his exposure. His manic behavior was possibly an indication that he had. There was no fear of death in his eyes. His smirk was one of knowing something Zeth and Rel didn't. In which case they had to get Di to Bicet as soon as possible, to analyze the man's blood.

"Ya don't think Di acted alone?" Rel questioned on their way to the contamination showers.

Telling his partner about Di's references to the unidentified woman, Zeth was interrupted by a suited officer. "Sirs, I've been told to escort you to the medic center the instant you clear the showers."

"What?" Rel questioned, at the same time Zeth asked, "Why?"

"I wasn't told, sir. Only to get Rel Charley back to the center ASAP."

The two men stared at each other, their gazes troubled. "Mich Janelle's condition?" Rel asked.

The officer shrugged. "I can't say, sir."

The two men rushed into the Decontam Unit.

For the fourth time this week, Zeth's body was pummeled with green foam. He stripped off the wet plastic suit and washed again, first with more foam, then a spray, and finally a cream that sealed his pores and left his skin sticky to the touch.

Blood was drawn again. *Do I have enough left to even get infected?*

Both men returned to the medic center, each encased in yet another contamination suit. Rel seemed unable to sit still. Zeth was not surprised, but something was eating at his friend. "I'm sure it's not as bad as we're thinking. She's still got a day. We'll figure something out."

Rel didn't answer.

They were separated as soon as they entered the busy emergency bay. Zeth spent fruitless minutes asking after Mich but no one would tell him anything.

With no way to find out why Rel was so desperately needed, Zeth made his way to the quarantine facility, determined to question Charlmehn Di. The man had taken the antidote, or he knew where it was hidden. Either way, Zeth was determined to discover its location.

Two guards were stationed outside Di's room, but Zeth didn't want to go in yet. Peering through the observation window, he could see Di strapped to a bed and surrounded by medical staff encased in protection suits.

The door opened, expelling a nurse, holding up a bag containing Di's clothing. "The cure?" Zeth asked.

"There was nothing on him," the nurse answered.

Now Zeth wanted to go in, but the nurse held out a hand to stop him moving past. "We have to get the patient cleaned up before anyone can enter. Healer Bicet is concerned this man's direct exposure and saturated respiratory system will mean he will be affected more rapidly. You cannot enter."

"He can tell us where the cure is."

"Not yet." With brisk steps, the nurse disappeared, leaving Zeth dithering in the corridor.

By the One, if Di dies before I get answers, Mich has no hope.

He approached the guards, hoping to appeal to their humanity. "That man has knowledge that could save a woman's life." His words didn't even crack the guards' stoic expressions.

"We've been ordered not to let anyone in," the woman told him. The name badge on her chest called her *Mary*. The look on her face said he wasn't going to get past. Zeth moved to the opposite wall and crossed his arms. He shook his head when the giant blond-headed man, nametag identifying him as Romin, offered to fetch him a drink. Zeth wasn't leaving. He leaned back and closed his eyes.

What might have been minutes or hours later, a hand prodded him awake. Zeth's arm snapped out before he was fully conscious, and he opened his eyes on the shocked face of another nurse. He blinked, confused, before realizing one of his hands was fisted in the fabric of her shirt, while the other was wrapped around her throat.

"Sorry, sorry," he gasped, dropping his hands straight away, horrified by his unconscious actions.

Mary was at his side in an instant, pushing him back against the wall. "Sorry," Zeth said again and cleared his throat. "Sorry." He hadn't come up fighting out of sleep for years. The stress of this case was clearly taking a heavy toll if he was reliving his past nightmares so violently. He could feel his hands shaking beneath Mary's unrelenting grip.

"It's okay," the nurse said, her voice hoarse. Zeth wasn't sure if she was talking to him or to Mary, but her tone remained soft as she asked the guard to release him. "You can go in now," she said to Zeth. "The patient is awake, but I'm afraid you may not get much out of him."

Mary glanced from the nurse's neck to Zeth's hands and back again. Zeth dropped his eyes and silently entered Di's room.

*

Rel knew what Bicet was going to ask, and his answer was weighing on his mind. On the one hand, how could he say no? On the other, he didn't owe Mich Janelle a thing. He didn't know her, not really. Working together on one case didn't make them friends. She was secretive, distrustful and probably unstable. It was too personal. Could he really do it? *Do I want to?* On the other hand, the madness in Di's eyes when he'd screamed, *"Why should I save them?"* had turned Rel's blood cold. Was that what he could become if he let his bitterness and anger stain his soul?

His partner had known something was up, but when Zeth asked, Rel hadn't been able to explain what was going on in his head. Zeth would expect him to do it. He wouldn't understand Rel's hesitation. Zeth would never forgive himself if he failed to save someone when he had the chance. It was why he was so eaten up with guilt and self-recrimination.

Rel thought of Melita, once in such a similar position to Janelle. Of course, Rel hadn't had a chance with Melita. The opportunity to save her had never arisen. If it had, he wouldn't have thought twice about it. So why was this decision so hard?

Because Mich Janelle wasn't Melita.

He was escorted from Zeth's side as soon as they stepped into the medic center. *Too soon, I'm not ready.* Bicet, dressed in a medical gown, met him outside the double electric doors that led to an operating theater. Rel's heart clenched. His hands were shaking. Bicet took one look at his face and directed him to a little room located off to the side. There was a set of bunk beds inside and not much else.

Rel slumped down onto the lower bunk, the weight of his thoughts pressing him further into the thin mattress. Bicet sat on a low chair opposite, practically bent double given his height, his knees nearly reaching his chin. "Rel Charley. I apologize for putting you in such a position. When we had our earlier conversation, I had not realized you would be required to make your decision so soon."

"Ya want me ta be her donor?" Rel didn't mince words. Now was not the time. He clenched his hands together and dangled them between his knees. He stared at his feet.

"There is more."

Rel looked up. "What d'ya mean?"

"I originally wanted you to consider donating your blood to help us in the analysis of a cure. We had time then, with no known infected, provided you and Zeth Wen stopped the terrorist before he could act."

Rel breathed out hard. *We were too late.*

"Before you speak, I must inform you there has been a change in my request. We have very little time left to save Mich Janelle's life. We cannot decrypt your unique blood markers in time to devise an antidote."

"So, what d'ya want?"

"I would like to try something—to give her a chance we must begin immediately. A direct transfusion."

Rel's jaw dropped. "Mix my blood with hers?"

"She is not in a position to refuse."

"I ... I need time ta think about it."

"Time is the one thing I cannot give you, Rel."

The healer addressing him by just his first name was shocking enough to raise his head. Bicet sat immobile, his gaze locked on Rel's face.

Zeth would tell him to do it. Rel wished he had time to talk it out with his pal over a drink, or ten.

He pictured Melita again, then Carma. Would they forgive him if he said no?

Would he forgive himself?

She was their partner now, and as Zeth had taught him all those years ago, you don't leave your partner behind. She'd saved Zeth's life. Rel owed her for that. Saving her life now would make them even. His chest warred with his head. All his life he'd fought to be seen. To be seen as the man he was, not the creature that gave him life. Melita had seen him, so had Zeth. Carma saw the truth of him, he could see it in her eyes.

Mich Janelle didn't let anyone in. He related to that. He could help her, him and Zeth. If she let them. He had seen the cracks in her growing smaller. If she died ... well, he wasn't going to let that happen. He needed her to see that she could be seen too. She didn't have to hide anymore.

"Okay. I'll do it."

Before he could blink, Rel found himself on a bed about to be wheeled into an operating theater. Rapid movement drew his gaze to a nurse dressed in scrubs racing toward him. His eyes widened when he realized the nurse was Carma.

She gripped his fingers tightly in her cold gloved hand. "I'm okay," he told her. She tilted her head and lightly shook his arm. "I have ta do this," he told her. "She's ... Res it. She's one of our team. She saved Zeth's life and I ... I owe her."

Carma's brows drew together. She leaned down to brush his forehead with her lips. Her flowery scent filled his nose. "I'll be okay," he promised. "When this is over," he said as a real nurse approached and Carma released his hand, "remind me to tell you about a woman called Melita."

Rel's bed was pushed away from Carma and into the operating theater.

He couldn't see Janelle from where he lay on the other side of the room, he could only watch the rapid movement around her bed. Cold air pumped into the room. He could hear it being sucked out above his head with an industrial unit that vibrated the metal of his bed.

Nurses' voices rose suddenly, sharp and urgent, their movements immediately faster. Healer Bicet's voice had not changed, but Rel could have sworn he could see fear in the other man's tightened posture. Rel desperately wanted to cough the cloying stench of antiseptic and iron from his lungs.

All at once, alarms went off. The frantic work paused and then exploded in a flurry of activity. *Oh Dresh!* Wasn't there an incubation period? They should have had days. Why was she reacting differently?

Again, Rel's mind flashed to Melita. Their time together had been so short. He remembered her smile and her laugh, the light in her eyes when he'd given her that stupid flower she'd ended up being allergic to. The look on her face when they'd realized she couldn't fight off the parasite and survive.

Screaming alarms brought him back into the present with a bang, then all he could hear was the steady flatline of Janelle's heart monitor.

Rel's breath caught beneath his mask. The machine tied to his own heartbeat danced wildly.

He had to remain still so the lines running between his bed and hers were not tangled, but that didn't stop him from crying out. "Come on, Janelle, ya have ta fight this. Don't give in. Fight, damn it!"

The alarms stopped as suddenly as they'd started. Still, the pace of the nurses' work did not change.

Healer Bicet called over to Rel. "Keep talking."

"Janelle ... Michele. Don't ya resing give up!"

*

Di was wrapped in gauze from his waist to his neck. Tubes poked out from beneath multiple layers of bandages and a strange hood covered his face, exposing the tubes attached to his mouth. Even his eyes were covered. Blood had seeped through, staining the fabric. He obviously hadn't taken the cure, which meant it was still out there, somewhere.

Zeth had to get answers. If they could get the antidote in time, Mich might still have a chance.

Di's head twitched as Zeth entered the room. Computer screens next to the bed indicated he was awake. Zeth hadn't been sure until he'd seen the man move.

Zeth thumbed on his protection suit's microphone. "Charlmehn Di." His words boomed out to fill the small room. Di's head snapped in Zeth's direction and he mumbled around the tube, but the words were unintelligible. He began to cough, harsh wet sounds that pulled him inside out as his body jerked.

Zeth moved until he stood beside the dying man. "The cure. Where is it?" Di groaned and shook his head. "Where is it, Di? Grunt once for yes. In the travel hub? Your apartment? In the lab?"

The dying man thrashed about on the bed. He coughed and moaned weakly.

"No," Zeth spat. "I know you have a cure! Tell me where it is."

Di grunted again and flopped back, writhing against his pillows. He made a pitiful sight. The screen above his head showed the usually rhythmic waves oscillating wildly as the man grew more and more agitated. Zeth didn't have time for this. He leaned down and tore the tube from Di's mouth.

The monitor screamed along with Di, who at last gasped out, "It's gone. Madam has it. They have to die. I must kill them all. It is her wish."

Zeth's chest felt hollow. He was too late. Di sounded resigned to his fate, but Zeth refused to accept that Mich Janelle would die too. "Where is Madam? Is she here?"

The door behind Zeth slammed open and medics rushed in. One pushed Zeth into the wall while the rest surrounded the bed, working to reattach the tubes to Di's mouth and silence the howling machines.

"No!" he shouted, struggling against the arms pushing him back. "He knows where it is. He has to tell me!"

Di convulsed. Red stains appeared at his ears and nose, shining wet through the hood.

"Stay back," the nurse ordered. It was the pretty nurse from earlier—Zeth recognized her eyes through the helmet. She pushed him back when he tried to slip around her, deceptively strong for such a small woman. "Zeth Wen, he is infected. If he had a cure, he would have told us. Healer Bicet is working on your partner and the draal. You have to give him more time."

Over the nurse's shoulder, Di's eyes widened. His back bowed as he snarled.

The nurse pushed Zeth from the isolation room and pointed to the guards, ordering them to keep him outside. Mary's strong arms shoved Zeth face-first into the corridor wall. Zeth was growing attached to the medic center's walls. He was spending a lot of time in close proximity to them.

Di's loud scream filled the corridor. It rose in pitch, impossibly high, and then stopped abruptly.

Zeth's stomach hit the floor at the sound, and his skin broke out in a cold sweat. He'd failed.

Closing his eyes, he slumped against the wall's hard surface. *No, One, no!*

A moment passed, then the door opened. Zeth's eyes snapped to Di's medics as they trailed out. Zeth's head swam at their slow movements and dejected expressions. He dropped his gaze. *By the One.*

The nurse touched his shoulder with gentle fingers. "He's alive. For now. He will die soon without an antidote."

Zeth stared at the nurse. She nodded her head. "He's still alive," she repeated. He looked at her but didn't see her. Hope brought warmth flooding back to his body. He straightened in Mary's grip. The nurse continued. "We've sedated him heavily;

you won't get anything from him now. Perhaps he will wake later." She didn't sound at all confident.

Zeth clutched onto the miniscule hope with both hands, and prayed.

Chapter 43

Mich's eyes were shielded behind a pair of thick sunshades, protected as she peered up into the bright indigo sky. Over her shoulder, still within the oppressive atmosphere of The Clinic's reception area, Temok Marke signed the forms to finalize her release. Her boss—ex-boss—maybe still boss—had got her out. She didn't know why or what he had done to ensure her liberation, but whatever it was, it must have been big.

She stared at the transport waiting for them at the end of the road. It didn't look real, its lines too crisp under the cold clear light.

The hovercar blurs and I blink. I'm in another memory.

Circling her feet brought her eyes to the window above The Clinic's entrance. There was a man, a patient, in the window squashing his face against the glass. He stared down at Mich. One hand waved in farewell.

She'd never learned his name.

Pulling the shades from her face so she could stare up at him without the filter, she wished she knew who he was and why he'd helped her. With a wave, he disappeared back into The Clinic's depths. She had the feeling she would never see him again and her heart ached for the loss.

Marke appeared at her side. Following her gaze, all he saw was an empty window. "Are you ready?"

"Yes," she answered.

There's something I'm supposed to be doing. What is it? I'm dreaming again, aren't I?

She let Marke help her into the waiting car, biting back her demand to know why he left her there to rot for so long.

That was what the past Mich had wanted to know. Now, I have a different mission.

Pain spikes through my head, splitting my face almost in half as I fight against the memory's demands for me to repeat my actions. I have to move. I'm here for a reason, I have to find out why.

Flinging open the door, I spring out and run from Marke's protective custody. My chest tightens. This didn't happen before. Am I actually able to change my past or is this only happening in my imagination? What if none of this is real?

It doesn't matter. All that matters is that I believe it is happening. I run back into the clinic and all sound stops. I can no longer hear myself panting, or the crunch of my shoes on the pebbled path. I hear no shout of alarm from behind me, cursing my escape. My footfalls in the hall make no sound. The rooms I run past are empty.

Broken.

Silent.

The back door is unguarded. I don't hesitate, exploding through the security door like it's made out of water. My pounding feet find a path I don't remember. In seconds, I burst into a clearing and jam my feet into the mossy soil to halt my headlong plunge. A man stands before a bush covered in blue petals. An older man with an unkempt salt and pepper beard and scraggly hair that makes him look wild, staring at me through gold-rimmed spectacles. He is looking at me as though I am crazy.

Wait, he's looking at me. Right at me.

This is not a dream.

Madam appears behind him. Her face is an expressionless mask. She's angry. I can feel it all the way down to my toes. Ice hits my body like a wall. Cold air catches in my throat, making me gasp and double over.

In my head, I hear a voice—a male voice. "Janelle ... Michele. Don't ya resing give up!"

I can't breathe.

Mich Janelle woke up screaming.

Chapter 44

An elastic band was wrapped tight around her chest; the pressure compressing her lungs prevented air from expanding them. In her mind, she flashed to a green room and a bald healer. A woman told her to close her eyes and stop struggling. There was a thumping sound in her ears, echoed by an electronic beeping from somewhere to her left.

She raised her hands higher and wiggled them around. See, she could move. The band tightened. Flapping a hand across her chest, she reached with tingling fingers to loosen it. They closed around her gown. No band, no rope. There was nothing there. She found a tube with her fingers and followed it to her nose. It was wet. She raised her hand to her eyes. Red. She could smell it: iron and cinnamon. Her queasiness ratcheted higher and she swallowed around a moan.

While holding her fingers up, she felt a tug against her elbow. Staring down her arm, she followed the tube from her elbow to a machine on the table. The tube came out the other side and ran all the way to the other bed. There was a body lying on it. She couldn't raise her eyes high enough to see the bedhead, so she examined the feet instead. Big, male, slightly hairy with a claw above the ankle. She glanced at the end of her own bed. Her feet were covered by a pale cream-colored blanket. She wiggled her toes and the blanket moved. It didn't feel like she had a claw, but the clawed feet on the other bed were familiar ...

The feet moved and the body grunted loudly.

"Charley?" Her voice sounded weird, too loud in the quiet room. She lowered it and whispered, "What are you doing?"

"Saving ya life," he answered, sounding groggy. "And it's Rel. My name is Rel."

Mich sucked in a deep breath. It caught in her throat and the resulting cough jerked her body hard. It hurt. Rel made noises next to her, but she couldn't understand what he was saying. She coughed again, gasping for air she couldn't find, and closed her eyes to concentrate on breathing.

*

Pain flooded his awareness until it was all Charlmehn Di could think about. Nerve endings fired haphazardly, spikes of molten metal stabbed his internal organs and sent sparks of electricity racing along his limbs. His body jerked at random intervals, drawing air from his wet lungs, bringing tears to his eyes. He choked around the tube in his mouth. His hands were trapped at his sides, so he couldn't pull the tube out. He gagged against the intrusion, breathing iron-scented air in through his nose.

Why is this happening? Why did she let this happen?

Music reached his ears, growing louder as his breathing slowed.

Pain shot across his face as he forced his head to turn. Familiar green eyes stared at him. The rest of her face was covered in a mask, but he would have recognized her anywhere. He gargled, "You're here."

She heard him, understanding him completely and nodded. Her humming stopped.

He waited, breathless. *She's here.* She'd come for him. She'd take the pain away.

With a bare finger, she stroked his face. "You haven't failed me, child, but you still have work to do."

Yes, yes, he did. He still had work to do. Wen's friend— the woman—was getting better. The other nurse had said that earlier. None could survive. Madam would not want that. She'd be angry.

Di tried to tell her but his words were a mess of sounds.

"Hush, child. I will release your arms. I know this will be hard for you, but I need for you to attack me. Nod if you understand."

Attack you? I can't. Yet looking into Madam's solemn gaze, he knew he could never disappoint her. All he wanted was for her to be happy. With fresh tears, he nodded.

"Good, my dear. I knew I could rely on you. There is a security card attached to my chest, can you see it?"

He nodded again.

"Take it after you attack me. Find a crowded room, as many people as you can. They all must die. Kill them all. Promise me?"

He nodded. The woman—Wen's friend—he had to find the woman and kill her first.

No one must survive. He had to kill them all.

A soft touch caressed his arm as sure fingers loosened the strap around his wrist. "For me," Madam whispered.

Anything. Everything.

*

Zeth's head hung low between his knees as he panted, swallowing back his nausea. He sat in Bicet's temporary office. A cold, long-fingered hand stroked the back of his neck. He had no idea how he'd gotten here and everything hurt. He hadn't found the cure. Mich Janelle was going to die because he'd failed.

"Zeth Wen, I need you to listen to me. Mich Janelle is alive."

His head snapped up, dislodging the healer's hand, unable to comprehend what he was saying. "Cured?" It was impossible to believe, and when Bicet hesitated, the cold flooded straight back into Zeth's chest. "What's wrong with her?"

"Not cured precisely. We could not synthesize a cure from Rel Charley's blood—not in the time we had before she was lost to us."

"Rel?"

"Is immune."

Zeth was stunned. "What?"

"There is an element in draal blood that appears to prevent the virus from taking hold."

"Di?" Zeth's voice sounded weak, strained to his own ears, like he'd recently been screaming.

"Rel Charley does not have enough blood to save both Mich Janelle's life and that of Charlmehn Di and remain unharmed himself. We have begun the transfusion with Mich Janelle. Are you suggesting—?"

"No!" Zeth held up a hand. "I apologize, healer. Charlmehn Di intended to die when that bomb exploded. If he had a cure, it's gone now." Zeth remembered the look in the man's eye as he'd talked about his "Madam." He was sure Di had been brainwashed. It was "Madam's" motivations that Zeth didn't understand. "You have to save Mich Janelle."

"I agree with your assessment, however, as a medical healer it is my—"

"I understand," Zeth cut in. "You have to do what you can."

A comm unit beside Bicet buzzed.

Zeth stood, intent on giving the healer privacy. The tall man held up a hand to stop him and shook his head. Zeth hovered while Bicet listened to the comm. The healer's eyes widened.

"Charlmehn Di has escaped."

*

Corridors rang loudly with the booted treads of Mason's security officers. As soon as the alarm was raised, the medic center went into lockdown. Healer Bicet ordered all non-essential personnel to evacuate and patient rooms sealed to prevent entry.

Zeth ran to the security office and demanded the feeds. Images from outside did not show Di exiting the building, so the current belief was that the highly infectious man was somewhere still inside.

Zeth had been unable to determine Di's whereabouts from the security footage. Rolling camera failures hid the man's path through the hospital. "What is wrong with these feeds?" he snapped. He received only blank looks from the men around him. "Find out."

The infectious man had escaped his room by violently subduing a nurse with his own tubes and killing the guard on duty. No one thought Di would have the strength to sit up, let alone fight his way from his deathbed.

Zeth watched the footage back. The nurse's face was obscured by the mask she wore. "Check on the nurse," he ordered, watching as she pushed and clawed at Di's body with her bare hands as he suffocated her. *Where are her gloves?*

"Di's intention was to infect as many people as possible in the shortest amount of time," he told the security men over their comms. "We have to assume that is still his plan. Focus your search on areas with the highest concentration of patients. Any area of connection—kitchens and eating halls, public entry points, day surgery and examination rooms—include the maternity and the children's ward. Check the air-conditioning towers, as well." He paused and then added, "Plumbing and heating, too; anything with internal duct access."

He sighed. The list was too long. "Why is there no security footage that shows which direction Di headed in?" It was too convenient. A cold feeling crept up Zeth's spine. Di must have had help, was still acting on Madam's orders.

He was highly contagious, dying and completely insane. Zeth had to stop him at all costs.

Chapter 45

Pressing his bandaged hands to the room's window, Di stared at the sleeping woman. She was attached to the man on the bed next to her via a huge number of tubes and wires. Many were stained red, but the one at her nose ran clear. The man, also asleep, had the heavy neck ridge of a draal. It was not as pronounced as Di had thought it would be. The man was only half-draal then.

The woman was not bandaged and there was a flush to her skin that made her glow. She *was* getting better.

The handle of the isolation room door wouldn't turn. He threw his whole body against the door with a scream. At the realization that they'd sealed the room, his fury became an inferno. He threw himself against the door again and again, staining the surface with red hand and fist prints.

Then he remembered the pass card Madam had given him. Music filled his mind. He hummed along to it happily.

The door unsealed with a hiss of pressure and Di was through in an instant. Alarms exploded. He had moments at best.

The blast of sound woke the draal. Groggily, he climbed off the bed. Di ignored him and jumped straight on the bedridden woman, wrapping his hands tightly around her throat.

*

Mich awoke with a start, eyes widening as she realized she couldn't breathe. She stared up into the face of the man from her dream. Frantically, she pushed at his arms, but his hands only tightened around her throat, cutting off her air supply. Spots danced before her eyes.

She arched her body to throw him off, but he hung on with a grim determination she couldn't fight.

Rel appeared from somewhere, grabbing the man around the waist and yanking hard, but the crazed man was determined and refused to let go.

He stared into Mich's face, rearing back in shock as if he recognized her. "You!" he screamed. "*You!* You were there. This is all your fault." Spittle flecked with red flew from his mouth. "You left too soon, she wasn't finished with you. You weren't supposed to leave!"

Mich bucked frantically, not comprehending the wild man's words. Her limbs were growing heavy as the lack of oxygen took its toll. Everything started to shut down, and her body fell heavily to the bed.

The old man shrieked in triumph. "She will be pleased I found you. You were supposed to be hers. She wasn't finished with you." His grip loosened.

Darkness had closed in, shrinking Mich's vision. She saw but didn't see the tubes and wires tangling around Rel's arms as he changed direction. Instead of pulling at the man, he shoved, putting his entire weight behind the thrust, and dislodged him at last. Both men fell off the side of the bed. Fire ripped Mich's arm apart as her tubes were torn free. Blood sprayed across the room.

She gasped, dragging much-needed air into her lungs. Her body was so weak. She rolled half off the bed to watch Rel struggle with the man, afraid he would return to attack her if Rel was defeated.

The two skidded across the floor. Rel climbed on top, hitting the battered and bleeding face repeatedly. The man's head bounced off the laminate. Rel twisted sharply and flung his assailant across the room. The old man hit the side of Mich's bed and lay there, stunned. With the last of her strength, Mich dragged herself up and pushed at the transfusion machine. It fell from the trolley and landed on the man's face with a wet squelch.

The room fell silent. The only sounds were Mich's gasping and Rel's panting as they both fought for air. Screaming alarms cut off with a squeal and the door slammed open. Too many protection suit-covered figures flooded the room, shouting for everyone to freeze.

Mich's heart shot into her throat. Her gasps were ragged as she whined with fear. *No! Not again!*

Wen, barely recognizable behind his mask, stood in the doorway, his pistol aimed at the dead man on the floor. "Rel?"

Rel raised his hand. It flopped back against the floor. "I'm good."

Mich pressed back against her pillow and concentrated on breathing. *Not the same. It's not the same. I'm safe now. I'm safe.*

Chapter 46

The machine hissed and vibrated on the table where it sat between the two figures, rhythmically pumping blood out of Mich, into Rel, and back again. Damage to its casing was clear in its buckled and stained frame. Their new room had been set up identical to the old one, the move made with the brutal efficiency of staff still familiar with wartime evacuation drills.

Zeth was pleased to see Rel's wave. With a tired twitch of his lips, Rel held his thumbs up and pointed to Mich. A rush of warmth filled him at the sight.

Mich Janelle looked younger when she was asleep. Her color was restored, but the bruises flaring purple and red around her neck still looked painful. The damage Di caused meant she still required the tube to help her breathe, but at least it ran clear where it stuck out of her nostrils. A sense of peace filled the hollow ache Zeth had felt since the explosion at the hub. They'd stopped Di's plans and no one else was infected. *We won.*

Carma stood beside Zeth, watching through the observation window. Her clothing was wrinkled and her hair had wilted, but still she gave him a wide smile and pressed her hand to the window. Rel gave her a little wave in return.

Zeth touched her arm. The woman's tense form slumped as she allowed him to pull her away from the glass. She walked beside him down the quiet hall, her eyes downcast, and plopped onto the bench at the hall's end. Zeth tilted his head. "You should go and rest. I'll keep watch."

She shook her head and pointed back to Zeth.

"Nah, I'll stay with you," he replied.

They stared down the corridor at the door still sealed under the center's strict quarantine protocols. Carma pulled her legs up onto the hard plastic of the bench and leaned her head against Zeth's shoulder.

"They're fine," he told her.

The words seemed to give her little comfort. She took Zeth's hand in both of hers and held on tightly.

*

Mich blinked slowly and the darkened room came into focus. Her eyes were hot, sore and scratchy. It would be so easy to close them and drift away again ... instead, she forced them back open. She needed to know where she was. Fire tore at her throat with every swallow. She glanced around, searching for water.

The itch at her nose refused to go away. Rubbing her face, she found a tube and pulled it from her nostrils, the tape holding it in place tugging at her skin as she dislodged it.

The small window in the middle of the door provided just enough light to look around. The sharp tang of disinfectant filled her nose, not quite masking the scent of copper and vomit. Machines on either side of her bed cast long shadows across the floor. At least one of the machines was monitoring her heart, its steady beep keeping time with the thud in her chest, slowing as she calmed.

No one came running at the minor increase in her heart rate. *That's probably a good sign.*

There was a bed beside her and a man lay on it, too still, too much like Taskly, the man she'd been accused of murdering ... then the man's chest moved and she let out a sigh of relief. She stretched up, pulling at sore chest muscles, until she could see the man's face. She didn't know why Rel was in the room, but he was snoring softly and she had no intention of waking him up just to ask.

Jigsaw pieces of memory rose, and when she put them together, they didn't make a whole lot of sense. She remembered a carriage filled with sholan, a purple room full of pillows and a small kitchen with soup bowls. There was a medic, tall and thin with pale eyes, slits for his nose and no teeth. Other images came in flashes—a green room, a bald healer, a dark-haired man with nice eyes. Cold hands holding her down, forcing dry tablets into her mouth. The memories made her gasp and her heart thudded so loudly, she feared it would burst right out through her nightshirt. The machine beside her began to wail.

Rel stirred drowsily. "Hey, what's going on?"

A moment later, he was gathering the tubes up around her to sit down on her bed. He stared into her face, examining her —seeing her. His expression softened. She tried to pull away when his arms came around her, but he refused to let her go. He rubbed a warm hand over her back. "Hey, now, breathe with me, okay? In an' out, nice an' slow."

She tried. Eventually, her heart stopped hammering.

"There, now," he said, holding her tighter. She didn't know why he was being so nice to her, but she needed it. Needed him. She let herself fall and buried her face into his shoulder. Tears welled behind her eyelids and she swallowed hard, trying to force them back. One escaped, sliding down her nose to drip onto the shirt beneath her cheek.

"What has ya so scared?"

She didn't know. She wanted to tell him about the memories, but it would make her sound weak and stupid. She had to be brave. She was supposed to be brave.

"Not weak. Never that," he said against the top of her head.

Did I say that out loud? Mich had the feeling he was smiling. "I said that out loud too, didn't I?" she mumbled. He chuckled, the sound vibrating inside his chest where she pressed her cheek against it.

They sat together in silence for a while. Her shoulders dropped and her hands finally unclenched from his shirt to press softly against the wall of his chest. "I keep seeing The Clinic," she whispered, hearing the tremble in her voice, ashamed by her weakness.

"The Clinic?"

She was quiet for a long time, breathing softly against his chest. Rel smelled warm. She didn't want to let him go.

"I found Taskly, a contact I was working, dead in his apartment. They said I killed him. I didn't, Rel. I swear I didn't. The killer drugged me, paralyzed me. I couldn't have done it. They said I'd become catatonic after committing the murder. It didn't matter what I argued when the drugs wore off. They said I did it and sent me away." She swallowed back a moan and waited for him to cast her aside. He didn't say a word, just held her gently. After a moment she found herself talking again. "The Clinic was supposed to be my salvation. There was a healer. He was the worst, I think. He forced drugs on me to keep me quiet. The drugs stole my voice. If I couldn't speak, I couldn't tell them what really happened, right? That healer, I think he was doing it under orders. I don't know why—or who told him to do it."

She wanted to stop, but knew she had to get it all out. If she stopped talking, she'd never start again. "There was a nurse there too. She scared me. I hear her sometimes, whispering to me in the dark, telling me things, making me afraid. But ... Rel, she was nice too. Sometimes. She talked to me, took me outside to breathe when I couldn't take the dark anymore." Mich's voice died as she ran out of air. She breathed deeply, taking time to imagine the air filling her body, making her chest expand with it.

"Was there no one ya could trust?"

"There was a man. I don't know his name. Another patient, I think, I don't know. He was nice." She remembered dark eyes and white teeth. A warm feeling filled her belly thinking of his smile. She felt Rel's chin shift against the top of her head.

"Good guy, huh?"

"Rel." Mich smiled into his chest. She wished she'd learned the patient's name. *Our secret, my dear.* The nurse's voice sounded so loud, Mich's eyes flew open, expecting to see the green-eyed woman standing in the room.

After a moment, she pleaded. "You won't tell anyone, will you?"

"I won't."

She was quiet for a long time before asking, "Am I sick?"

He didn't speak. She felt him open his mouth against her head, as if he was trying to find the right words, before he closed it again. She stopped him before he could lie to her. "It's okay," she said, her voice barely a whisper.

"It's not okay." Rel moved them both around until his back was against her pillow and Mich rested against his chest. "Ya *were* sick—poisoned. But ya getting better."

"Am I?" she whispered. "I don't think I am getting better. I feel ... wrong."

"Wrong?" He wrapped one arm tighter around her and pulled the blanket up to cover them both.

"I think The Clinic put me back together wrong." The warmth of Rel's body was soaking into her skin, making her sleepy. She relaxed further. It had been so long, too long, since she'd felt safe. Here, in Rel's arms, she did. For the first time since The Clinic, since Taskly. "Everything is too close to the surface. I can't hide anymore."

"I think we all feel that way. About life."

"Why did you do it?" she asked, her voice soft.

"Do what?"

"Save me. It was your blood, wasn't it? I should have died, Rel. Maybe ... maybe it would have been better if I had."

"It was my blood. And I had to. I wasn't going ta let you die like that. No one deserves that."

She pulled herself up, peering into his face. "You didn't have to. You barely know me."

He couldn't hold her gaze. She watched him for a moment longer before laying her head back down and closing her eyes. His reply was nothing more than a sigh against her hair.

She drifted, breathing into his shirt, warm and safe at last.

When he spoke again, she wondered if he thought she was asleep. She didn't dare move as he told her about his wife. She listened to the story of how they met. The depth of his love filled his voice and made her smile.

"I couldn't save Melita, but I could save ya." She was almost asleep when she heard him add, "And ya don't leave ya partner behind."

*

Zeth spoke to Daeh via his comm as he walked back to Rel's room. "He's fine. Healer Bicet gave me the report this morning. He's still required to stay in close proximity, but she's stable and showing signs of recovery." He thought of Rel's fidgeting the last time he checked in on them and grinned at the memory.

Rel hadn't been able to sit still, pacing the small room, sitting and standing at random intervals. His irritation was clearly getting on Mich's nerves. Those two were like siblings, needling each other to get the biggest reaction. Last night, though, Zeth had snuck into their room only to find them sitting quietly on Mich's bed. Their hushed whispering stopped the moment Zeth appeared. Rel was still tight-lipped on what they'd been chatting about.

Zeth hoped Mich would be well enough to leave soon. He had the feeling the nursing staff would be glad to see the back of them all. "I don't know the technical terms, but Bicet is pleased. He says her response looks promising."

Carma sat just outside the recovery room, wearing a different outfit from the day before. Zeth had bribed her last night with sweets just to get her to leave her vigil long enough to eat, change into fresh clothes and sleep. Dark shadows below her eyes looked like bruises under the harsh medic center lights. He doubted she'd caught any shuteye. Neither had he. "Rel is alert enough to complain, so there's that."

"And Janelle?"

Zeth thought about her for a moment. Her swollen red-rimmed eyes, her tangled lines and mussed bed clothing indicated her rest had been anything but peaceful. "Rel says she's been having nightmares." Daeh would get Bicet's report soon, so Zeth might as well tell him. "She's been talking about a place called The Clinic."

The force of Daeh's exhale over the comm surprised Zeth. "Understood. Keep a close eye on her. I want another report later today."

"Is there something I should know?" Zeth was concerned at the level of worry he could hear in the chief's voice. Rel had told Zeth that Di shouted that he knew Mich. And there was that song that they both hummed. Zeth's back crawled with the knowledge that there was a connection here he didn't understand, a connection Daeh already seemed to know about.

"No, just keep me informed, particularly if the dreams get worse."

Zeth confirmed and signed off. He'd keep an eye on Mich, and not just because of Daeh's order. There was something else going on here and he was determined to get to the bottom of it. But first, he had to get Rel to let him in on the secrets they'd been sharing.

His stomach rumbled. Spinning on his heel, he headed back toward the medic center's kitchens. Carma was probably as hungry as he was. Fetching dinner for them both gave him a mission he could focus on—for now. And as soon as Mich fell asleep, he and his partner were going to have a conversation.

It was going to be a long night.

Chapter 47

Mich was going crazy. For ten long days, she'd been stuck in this little hospital bed, in this little hospital room, on this stupid little planet and she was *bored*.

Days one and two—she'd been told—had consisted of sleeping, hallucinating, and vomiting. She'd been stuck in the quarantine room with Rel, hooked up to several large machines and surrounded by a lot of red. Three days on and she was more lucid, but still stuck in bed. She'd slept a lot. Rel told her she'd been having flashbacks of her time at The Clinic.

Great. He knew everything, every secret she'd tried to hide had spilled out into the open for all to see.

It wasn't until day six that she'd attempted to climb out of bed, making it to the bathroom and back. It was as far as she could convince her trembling limbs to travel but it felt like taking her first steps into freedom. It reminded her of the day she'd been released from The Clinic. Thinking about that place sent a shiver down her spine and filled her dreams with nightmarish images of dark cold buildings, looming shadows and a colorful garden.

As the crazy old man knelt over her, squeezing her throat, she'd seen recognition in his eyes. In her sleep, she'd seen his face—with her at The Clinic. And with the nurse who starred in Mich's nightmares. Rel had told her his name. Mich wanted to know why Charlmehn Di had been at The Clinic, and why they'd let him go. But she had no way of knowing if the hallucinations she'd witnessed in her fever-induced night-mares were real or not. What she remembered of them didn't make sense.

Her memory told her she'd gotten into the car when Marke finally sprung her. She hadn't run back in. There was no way she would have voluntarily stepped back into that place, let alone run out to the garden. So why had she hallucinated that? Or had it been real and it was her memory that was faulty? She shook the disconcerting thoughts away. She couldn't know.

On the eighth day of her recuperation, Mich had her first shower and it felt truly amazing. Day nine, she was allowed out of her room and at last, on the tenth day—today—Healer Bicet returned to review her progress. He stood at the foot of her bed, flipping through her charts humming softly to himself. She didn't recognize the song, but the sound made the hairs on the back of her neck rise. *Not the same. It's not the same.* She played with her communication unit, absentmindedly flipping it from one hand to the other while she waited. Nibbling on her bottom lip, she feared hearing her results.

He'll let me go. Of course he will. Unless I'm still sick?

She sat on top of the bed covers with her boots off, but otherwise dressed and more than ready to leave.

When Rel pressed her old jacket into her hands, she'd felt the last bit of tension in her neck slip away. She'd actually missed the stupid thing. Someone had sewn up the slices in the sleeves. It was a hatchet job of needlework, but the effort brought a smile to her lips and a tear to her eye.

"Still belongs in a scrap pile," Rel told her. The truth was, he'd kept it safe for her and that said more than words. She didn't acknowledge it or thank him, but held his gaze steadily and made a joke about his hair. She was calling him Rel now. She had no idea when that had happened, but it felt right, so she didn't question it further.

Healer Bicet continued to hum while Wen and Rel updated her on the latest happenings of the investigation.

Wen—no, Zeth, she should call him Zeth—sat in the chair beside Mich's bed. Shockingly clean shaven, his hair was now shorn close to his scalp. He said it made cleaning easier, given the number of times he'd needed to be decontaminated. His eyes were bright and clear as he spoke, though he sat sprawled in his chair, taking up far more room than he needed.

Rel sat at the end of Mich's bed, still hairy, still scruffy and little pale but she'd grown used to his appearance and was surprisingly comfortable in his presence. She barely noticed he sat well within her comfort zone, resting his hand gently on her ankle. She was sure, given the amount of blood they'd shared, he was a part of her now and she was almost okay with that. As his partner talked, Rel's fingers flexed randomly against her leg. She flicked at his arm. He smirked when she caught his eye.

Healer Bicet entered a few notes into his data pad. Mich was amused by the healer's casual attire now that the emergency was over. Pink robes swamped his thin frame, the wide strips of material brushing the floor every time he raised his arms.

He tapped on his pad and announced, "You are still infected."

The smile fell from her lips. A glance at Zeth and Rel's emotionless expressions said this was not news to them. "But I'm getting better. I *feel* better." The spaciness inside her head flowed back over her body at the news, making her dizzy and a little nauseous.

Bicet's gray eyes locked with hers. "You are better," he confirmed. "But you are not cured."

The feeling in Mich's stomach increased, swirling uncomfortably. Her stomach cramped and she pressed her hand into the muscle to alleviate some of the pressure. "Then why—"

"Rel Charley's blood cannot be infected. There is an element in it that acts as a barrier that the virus cannot pass. We tested the element against all of the infected samples and returned the same result. We thought that if we could replicate the element and infuse it with healthy blood, we could attempt an immunization. Draal blood appears to fuse well with any blood type. When you were infected, the limited time frame gave us only one option, a direct transfer. I had hoped to prevent the virus from attacking your system further. Unfortunately, the virus does not break down in the body as the replicated draal blood does. As long as we maintain the balance, the virus stays dormant. Without it, you will become sick again."

"Without it? You mean ... I have to have more of Rel's blood?"

Bicet nodded.

Rel tapped on her leg and shrugged. The skin around his eyes tightened and his shoulders were tense. He didn't say anything; he didn't need to. She was nothing more than a burden. His burden. They were stuck together now. Her nausea worsened.

Hundreds of questions burst to life inside her. Only one made it to her mouth. "How often?" she asked.

Rel met her stare with his own, his face expressionless. *Hell's spawn.* Did he blame her for this? Of course he did.

She shifted her body away, uncomfortable in her own skin at the sudden reliance on him to stay alive.

"At this stage, we are not certain. We will continue to test you and monitor the results carefully. You will be required to undergo blood tests regularly. At this stage, we will transfuse you once a week. You are responding well to the enzymes and with luck, we'll have a vaccine soon. For the time being, you need to see me next week. We'll go from there."

A gaping maw of silence opened in her chest. "What about Rel? He and Zeth could be assigned halfway across the spiral. What happens to me if I relapse?"

Zeth cleared his throat. "Rel and I have been taken off the active case list. Daeh decided we need to remain close to you for the time being. Speaking of which, you've been reassigned. Welcome to Team Five officially."

Rel raised his hands in a false cheer. "Yay."

"What?" she said. "*Your* team?" Her gaze darted from one man to the other, searching for their true feelings in the unconscious language of their bodies, but she couldn't read them and their faces were masks of indifference.

Worse than babysitters, they were being forced to keep her. How they must resent her.

Zeth threw a tissue dispenser at Rel's head. Rel twisted so it flew past his nose and landed next to Mich's thigh. She watched the eye interplay between them and knew something was up, but didn't have the strength to give voice to the question.

Rel turned and shot Mich a grin. Zeth chuckled. Mich looked from one to the other in shock. "You're messing with me? You're really okay with this?" There didn't appear to be any anger coming off them. She didn't understand it. She couldn't taste despair or resentment in the air. They seemed ... fine?

Mich slumped against her pillows as the two men threw the box back and forth, and closed her eyes. Still stuck on light duty and now even more restricted. She had dragged their team into the mire with her.

"It could be worse. We were lucky to have contained the infection to Di and yourself," Zeth continued.

"So, no outbreak at the university?" she asked, opening her eyes. A thread of cotton had poked up from the blanket she sat on. She picked at it with a fingernail.

"No," he answered. "And no further outbreak stemming from Sima's House. We were lucky."

"Lucky." Mich snorted. It was a lot of dead people. "So, the sholan, the shizernet and the yellow-eyed man worked for Di? And Yetti was killed because he knew too much?"

"More likely because he had a big mouth. He told Terri and Sophie all about Di."

"And the telnaks?"

"They were in the way," Rel said.

Mich stared directly into Rel's eyes. "And Carma?"

Rel's cheeks bloomed with a pink tint. Mich grinned at Zeth's snort. "We ... I have ... I said we'd help her disappear if that's what she wanted. Start a new life away from here. Away from all of this." *And him.* He didn't say the words but she read them clearly in his eyes. "Then I mentioned, well, Daeh needs a new assistant. The last one didn't work out. Apparently. She interviews for the role next week. She's excited about the opportunity."

Mich let out a soft laugh. Rel's grin told her he was happy Carma wanted to stay close by.

Leaving the thread on the bed alone, she picked up her comm and flipped it over and over again on the mattress. She glanced at the screen and saw her message bank had a red bar across it. A message waited to be accessed. She swiped to begin the download.

"While the two of you were stuck in here, Mason's men quarantined Lab Seventeen, Sima's House and the orange stone fruit plantation. Each location was destroyed to ensure every trace of the virus was eradicated."

The way Zeth reported it, it sounded so easy. He couldn't be telling her everything. "So, Di didn't infect the Executive Board at all?"

Zeth shrugged lightly but his gaze was dark. "The Executive Board of Calcryon, while appreciative of our rescue, have agreed to increase their safety protocols and slow the human trials around the Enferrie flower, though they refuse to acknowledge Emma Di's death was in any way connected."

"A little too pointedly," Rel cut in.

Glaring at Rel, Zeth said, "I think this case had little to do with Calcryon's research. I think Di was sent to attack Calcryon, like a dog given an order. Di was convinced to act by someone else."

Madam? Mich's realization appeared and disappeared so quickly, she wasn't sure she'd even thought it. Her mind drifted back to her fever dream ... or had it been a memory? Had anything been real?

Rel tapped her ankle. "We should talk about it."

She glared at him and dropped her comm to the bed. "I know."

"Di recognized ya. He said ya were there," Rel added. "He was very insistent about it, if ya recall. He was talking about The Clinic."

Bicet spoke up from the foot of the bed. "I requested Di's medical records from his healer on Senth Prime. They arrived yesterday."

The three investigators looked up, their expressions a mix of wide eyes and open mouths. "What did they say?" Mich asked.

"Charlmehn Di was indeed a patient at a facility on Janing known as The Clinic. His records indicate he suffered quite a history of mental illness and was under an involuntary psychiatric hold at the request of his wife. A series of prescribed medications apparently had a positive effect and he was released into her care without further monitoring. The chemical results of Di's autopsy indicate the specific drugs he'd been given were absent from his system at the time of his death. It is my view that his wife's death caused a relapse and, without his medication, he suffered a psychotic break."

"That's not it. Someone was directing him, a woman he called Madam," Zeth insisted.

Mich started as a memory hit her quickly. Green eyes stared into her, so close they were all she could see. Whispered words filled her mind. *Our secret.* Mich closed her eyes as her skin tingled. Di was in her dream. What had Nurse been telling him? Why couldn't she remember?

The question that circled around and around inside her head couldn't be settled. Was her mad dream state a product of the fever, or was it a part of her mind trying to escape? Di was insane at the end.

Am I?

Healer Bicet excused himself and left the room.

"Mich?" The concern in Rel's voice made her realize she'd zoned out of the continued conversation.

She stared into Rel's eyes. "The nurse I told you about ... the voice?"

"I remember."

"What nurse?" Zeth asked, moving closer. He shot Rel a glance. Rel nodded back.

When Mich pictured Nurse—*Madam*—a spike of pain stabbed her behind her eyes. She fought past it to try again —green eyes were all she could manage. She couldn't tell them about her dreams. It would make her sound crazy. She suspected she'd rewritten her dreams in order to see Di with Madam. But how had Mich known what he looked like?

"I ... I don't really remember. Just vague feelings and a voice."

"Di escaped from his hospital bed here because he was assisted by a masked nurse."

Mich's eyes flew to Zeth. "What?"

"Di was locked into his isolation room. He couldn't have gotten out on his own. And the nurse assigned to his room is missing."

She's here? Oh gods, she's here.

Mich's hands shook, and she clenched them tightly into fists.

The two men spoke to each other through their silent eyeball game of tag, and after a moment Rel shrugged. Zeth leaned forward. He interlocked his hands and dangled them between his knees. "There's clearly something else going on here. We want to look into it further."

Mich stiffened, her neck twinged from how tight her muscles had become. "You want to look into The Clinic?" *You want to look into me?* She concentrated on lowering her shoulders from her ears to release the tension in her frame and reached for her comm to fiddle with the plastic case again. Rel had saved her life—was still saving it. She was a part of their team now officially. And he'd told her, you don't leave your partner behind.

She had to tell them. They had to know.

Perhaps she didn't need to investigate her own history alone anymore. Her partners were already suspicious about The Clinic. They could help her. But did she trust them?

Looking from one man to the other, she realized that yes, she did. Warmth spread through her body at the thought, finally clearing away the sick feeling in her belly.

"Di was humming on the cruiser. The same song you hum," Zeth stated suddenly.

"The woman Di was talking about, I think it's the same woman I remember from The Clinic. I think she did something to him." She caught Rel's eye. "I ... I maybe .... I think she might have done something to me too." Their expressions didn't change.

"Go on," Rel urged.

It was time they knew the whole truth. She took a deep breath. "It started with my investigation into the Tripness Company. The stories you've probably heard about me? None of them are true. I was looking into the tainted supplies of medication sent to Yeshele. My contact, a man named Taskly, was murdered and left for me to find."

"You were set up." Zeth's comment was a statement, not a question. He believed her. *They believe me.* The last of her skepticism shriveled and faded away. The safety she felt with Rel extended out to embrace Zeth.

"I was arrested, drugged, and sent to The Clinic. Temok Marke—my old Hunter boss—got me out, but the damage was done. I had no home, no job, no life. I told Marke someone at the Agency betrayed me. He told me I was wrong. That was the last time I saw him."

"Who betrayed ya?"

"I don't know. Someone who knew I was investigating Trip-ness—someone who knew I was meeting with Taskly."

"Who knew?" Rel asked.

She shrugged. "I made regular reports. My contact officer, the office, Marke."

"So, anyone at the Hunters' agency," Zeth confirmed with a nod.

Mich shrugged. "I'd planned to look into who had access to my files but—"

"No access. They booted ya out," Rel said.

Zeth rubbed his hands together. "So you came to Daeh looking for a job."

"Used our computers, huh? Well played." Rel nodded in respect.

"You need to get back to Janing," Zeth said.

"That's where we start looking," Rel said. "We go to Janing and visit this clinic, right?"

Zeth grinned. "Sounds like a plan." He looked to Mich. "Well?"

She nodded. "We go back to Janing." She didn't know what they were going to find when they got there, but she now had two partners to watch her back. She smiled.

Her comm pinged, signaling the completion of the download. It was from her snifferbot. Her determination to search into Tripness felt like it came from a lifetime ago. Could it all be connected? "As you figured out, I was working, unofficially, on hacking Tripness's server. Before I was infected, I inserted a sniffer into their files." She flipped her comm and pressed the button to open the message. It was an image file. The photo was of the Tripness Company headquarters on Planet Five.

Two men stood in the center of the frame shaking hands. One was a nondescript man wearing a black suit; the other was Temok Marke.

Mich dropped her comm, her mind reeling. It wasn't true. Her old boss? Temok Marke, the head of the Hunters' agency ... he'd done this to her?

"What is it?" Rel asked, reaching for her comm.

She put her hand on top of his to stop him from turning the device over. "If you really want to do this, we can't tell anyone."

The two men nodded. Sucking in a deep breath, she handed the device to Rel. "Temok Marke. My old boss."

Rel examined the image quietly. His face didn't change. He handed the device to Zeth.

Zeth's jaw tightened, his eyes widened briefly and a tic appeared in his right eye. "Well, that's unexpected."

"Looks like we ain't the only ones keeping secrets," Rel muttered. He locked eyes with Mich as Zeth handed the device back. "Well, ya weren't paranoid, thinking someone was working against ya."

"You still want to do this?" she asked. "The nurse ... I'm worried she did something to me."

"Ya don't leave your partner behind," Rel reminded her.

Beside him, Zeth nodded. His hand was pressed to the mattress near her leg. She rested her hand on top of his and clenched his fingers. The look in his eyes drove the last of her fear away. She was no longer alone.

"We're going to help you, Mich. We'll get to the bottom of The Clinic and the nurse, and Marke if we need to. You're stuck with us."

For the first time in a long time, Mich smiled.

Epilogue

The heavy-set man shifted uncomfortably in his seat, unable to find a position that didn't increase the ache in his lower back. The cruiser had left the hub hours ago, but the fasten security belts sign was still lit, meaning he couldn't stand to relieve the tension cramping his muscles.

Covering his mouth, he stifled another cough. *Damn it, I'm too busy to get sick.* He shifted the data pad on his lap awkwardly. This presentation was proving to be such a pain in his ass, and the bastards probably wouldn't even read it. He coughed again. A speckle of red flecks appeared on the seat-back in front of him. He stared at them open-mouthed. One trembling finger swiped at the blood.

"We will be arriving at Battenhold shortly. Passengers for the outer spiral, please change cruisers at Battenhold. Passengers for Janing, also change at Battenhold. This cruiser will then run express to Telkeck. On behalf of TS Cruisers, I would like to take this opportunity to thank you for traveling with us and hope you have a safe and pleasant journey."

ACKNOWLEDGMENTS

I'd like to thank the following people who helped *Blood Fever* become what it is.

Linh, Margo and Carolyn for reading it over and over, and for your CP & Beta-ery goodness! Every time I received an email from you my writing became better. You are just fabulous. Keep on keeping on. I can't wait to read your words soon.

Mum and Dad, who read it time and again, and didn't sigh too much when I said I had another version.

To Hayley. I'm sorry I'm making you read another science fiction!

Marissa Fuller, Kate Foster & Rebecca Carpenter, Kit Carstairs & Stuart MacDonald, Libby Turner & Vanessa Lanaway—you make my words sing! Thank you for everything. Your guidance and assistance with this one was soooooo needed. I appreciate you all.

Gerry for loving me and for listening to my doubts, changes, thoughts and edits. I love you. Yes, another one for you to read. Sorry.

To the #Auswrites crew. You keep me inspired. You keep me motivated. You keep me writing. #readmoreaussiebooks

To the Australian Book Lovers!! Thank you for your support and for your incredible website and podcast. Veronica and Darren you are amazing. Thank you for everything that you do. Readers, if you don't know about this website—I forgive you, but get onto it immediately! www.australianbooklovers.com. Aussie authors are the best!

To my amazing cover art designer, Pat Naoum. You are incredible. Thank you, Red Tally Studios.

Thank you to Mark Furness and Liquorice Light Publishing for your amazing work putting *Blood Fever* together with me.

James Gatherum-Goss and the team at Dymocks Knox City in Victoria, Australia. Thank you for all your support. To see my books on your shelves is a dream come true. Thank you for supporting local authors. Readers ... get out there and support your local bookshops and booksellers! They are truly awesome people.

I love you all so much. Thank you!

And for all the friends and family who are not big sci-fi fans but who have promised to read it anyway. I love you all.

Please consider leaving a review on your favorite bookish website.

Learn more at my website: www.solothefirst.wordpress.com

OTHER BOOKS BY LAURIE BELL:

WHITE FIRE

Everybody lies. Watch your back.

Sure, Agent Toni Delle has trust issues. Mate, her canine robot partner and Zach, her attitude-enabled shipboard Computer Intelligence Interface constantly tell her that—but as she told them, that was because of The Smuggler.

She would have refused her new mission altogether if it wasn't for the insane amount of money ... Oh, who was she kidding—danger, betrayal, secrets, lies—these were all the things she loved about her job. She just didn't expect The Smuggler would be involved. If she'd known that she would have told her boss to jump out of an airlock, in space, without a suit.

So she takes the mission: find and stop a new weapon being manufactured and smuggled into the hands of criminal elements all over the galaxy. And hey, while she's at it, can she also find the missing weapons designer linked to these shipments?

The only problem is she has to rely on information provided by The Smuggler himself. And he may not be the only one capable of betrayal.

THE GOOD, THE BAD AND THE UNDECIDED

Everyone - the good, the bad and the undecided - has a story.

While Toni Delle is crisscrossing the sector, investigating a criminal empire intent on war, other members of the White Fire world are busy with their own endeavors. The business-man closing a treasonous deal that will bring conflict to the galaxy. The politician giving the biggest speech of her career in the shadow of an assassin. The smuggler who can't be trusted, desperate for redemption. The Good, the Bad and the Undecided is a collection of twelve short stories set during the thrilling events of *White Fire*—A Toni Delle Adventure. A cast of guns-for-hire, undercover agents, revolutionaries and rogues reveal their part in Toni's adventures. Because everyone—the good, the bad and the undecided—has a story.

BOSS FROM HELL

Starting a new job can be murder ...

Mig Solder's new place of work is a little ... odd. Sure, there's unlimited free coffee, but there's also personal messages that seem to have no sender, colleagues that don't seem quite, well, human, and random emails warning her to run. Now.

When she discovers her predecessors didn't quit, they just disappeared, Mig decides to put her obsessive attention to detail to good use and investigate. With the help of her mysterious new neighbor, her spirit-contacting best friend, and her wild grandmothers, Mig uncovers a plot way above her pay grade. And once she starts dabbling in the supernatural, the consequences won't just appear on her performance review, they may just take her life—and her soul.

THE BUTTERFLY STONE
The Stones of Power Book One

"Don't let the shadow touch you."

Beware! Something is after Tracey Masters, a Mage-kind teen in a mostly non-magical world—a world where people like Tracey are often feared, and oppressed. Add to this stress a crazy family life, the schizo pressures of school, friends, and bullies, and working a boring job as an assistant at her uncle's detective agency for magical types, and life isn't just hard, it's chaos! That is, until a mysterious woman walks through the door with a case about a missing necklace known as the Butterfly Stone.

The case seems to be the big break Tracey is looking for to prove herself and her abilities as a Mage-kind. But she un-expectedly finds herself dangerously connected to it when the evidence takes a turn that reveals secrets from Tracey's past, and places her friends and family in mortal danger.

She also discovers that she's being hunted by a shadow that senses her magic is the key to unlocking the power it's after.

The magic within the Butterfly Stone is too powerful to be contained, but if Tracey doesn't learn how to control it, and escape the threat of the shadow that surrounds it, she could lose everything and everyone she cares about ... beginning with her younger sister, Sarah.

VIA WYVERN'S PEAK PUBLISHING

THE TIGER'S EYE
The Stones of Power Book Two

"Remember the lost ..."

Tracey Masters is ready to train harder, dig deeper, and get more in touch with the magic that is pulsing inside of her. She has faced the threat of the shadow, and it nearly consumed her. With the help of her family and close friends, Tracey overcame the darkness and now realizes just how hard being a Mage-kind teenager really is. She won't be caught off-guard again.

Clawing at the edges of her mind—of her memories—she senses a new evil encroaching. As Tracey sets off in search of the other Stones of Power, she continues to wrestle with questions about her past. Racing to discover who she really is, Tracey must decide how far she is willing to go to protect her family and friends.

What cost—what sacrifice—is she willing to pay in order to find herself, locate the other stones, and break an ancient curse that is destroying generations of family history?

Painful betrayal, a threat that's too close to home, mind-altering visions, dangerous magic, and a new heartthrob at school all scream for Tracey's attention. But can she trust her own choices, or her memories? What is real, what is fake? Tracey must decide if she can believe in her own magic, and her friends, before everyone she loves is erased from existence.

VIA WYVERN'S PEAK PUBLISHING

THE CROW'S HEART
The Stones of Power Book Three

"I see how it ends ... I will be alone ..."

The Tiger's Eye is secure, and Timothy is trapped inside the Serpent's Kiss. The shadows of the past finally seem to be behind Tracey Masters.

Hot off the heels of victory, Tracey and her friends waste no time in pursuing a lead on the fourth Stone of Power. However, that lead, her uncle's client, takes them across land and sea, to a mansion from an older age ... the very same that the Sect of Six lived in. When they arrive, the client mysteriously cannot be reached.

Working under the guise of actors on the newest Prince Henry film, Tracey has a limited amount of time on this so-called getaway to find the fourth stone, find out what happened to Uncle Donny's client, and to save her crush's sister, all while avoiding the ire of their at-odds chaperones. No pressure!

If that wasn't worrying enough, the group of Mage-kind and Norm teens are attacked by a monstrous entity on their way to England. With Timothy silently locked away in his own Stone of Power, suspicions turn inward, with clues pointing toward the very council that oversees Mage-kind.

Shadows may be in the past, but there is a devil in their midst.

VIA WYVERN'S PEAK PUBLISHING

www.ingramcontent.com/pod-product-compliance
Lightning Source LLC
Chambersburg PA
CBHW020326120726
47904CB00002B/298